The bailiff offered up a quick prayer, his eyes closed, then peered all around again. His teeth clenched, Simon drew his sword and, steeling himself, slowly crept forward until he was at the edge of the trees. As soon as he reached the clearing, he rushed on, running to crouch in the middle of the open space, whirling and glaring around, his sword grasped in both hands and the hot blood hammering in his ears.

But there was nothing. The clearing was only some twenty yards across and there was nowhere for anyone to hide apart from in among the trees. There was no sign that anyone had ever been here apart from the blackened embers of the fire, which lay over at the other side of the clearing, a darker stain among the shadows. He wandered over toward it, but as he drew near, his feet started to falter.

He had only covered half the distance when he stopped. Eyes wide in horror, he gagged and dropped to his knees, staring at the patch of burned grass and the tree in front of him. With a high scream, he turned and ran, rushing away from the sight in a mad, panicked flight back to the road.

The smell of cooked meat came from the man who had been roasted, like a convicted witch, over the flames.

Books by Michael Jecks

The Last Templar

The First Knights Templar Mystery

MICHAEL JECKS

AVON BOOKS

An Imprint of HarperCollinsPublishers

This is a work of fiction. Names, characters, places, and incidents are products of the author's imagination or are used fictitiously and are not to be construed as real. Any resemblance to actual events, locales, organizations, or persons, living or dead, is entirely coincidental.

AVON BOOKS
An Imprint of HarperCollins*Publishers*
10 East 53rd Street
New York, New York 10022-5299

Copyright © 1995 by Michael Jecks
ISBN: 0-06-076344-2
www.avonmystery.com

First Avon Books paperback printing: January 2005

Avon Trademark Reg. U.S. Pat. Off. and in Other Countries, Marca Registrada, Hecho en U.S.A.
HarperCollins ® is a trademark of HarperCollins Publishers Inc.

Printed in the U.S.A.

10 9 8 7 6

*For my parents
and for Jane, my wife,
for their patience and support*

—

The Last Templar

There was a subdued feeling in the crowd in front of the great cathedral of Notre Dame that morning, an air of tense expectancy, as if the people knew that this was not just another public humiliation of a criminal. It was more important even than an execution, and it seemed as if the people of Paris knew that the occasion would be remembered for centuries as they turned out in their thousands to come and see; standing and waiting with the restless expectation of a crowd waiting at the bear pits for the baiting to begin.

If these had been ordinary men, if they had been thieves or robbers, the throng would not have been so heavy. The Parisians, like most inhabitants of northern cities, liked to flock to see the punishments meted out to wrongdoers, enjoying the carnival atmosphere and the cheerful, busy trade in the market. But today was different and it seemed as if the whole city was there to see the end to the Order that they had all revered for centuries.

The sun occasionally flared out from behind the clouds and gave brief flashes of warmth to the people in the square, but mostly the crowd waited beneath a gray and leaden sky filled with thick, heavy clouds. The intermittent gleams of brightness merely served to add to the air of gloom and dreariness in the square, as if the sudden bursts of sunshine were teasing the men and women milling slowly by, highlighting the somberness all around. But then, when the sun did flash from behind its cover and brighten the area, catching the people waiting for the arrival of the convicted men, catching the colors of the clothes and the flags, it offset for a moment the cool of the March day and gave the whole area an aura of almost summery gaiety, as if the men and women were there for a fair and not for the destruction of thousands of lives. It was as if the sun was trying to detract from the grave reason for the gathering and attempting to lighten the spirits of the crowd with its life-giving warmth.

But then, almost as though it too was nervous and fearful of the outcome of the day, it would take cover again, like a man peering out from a secure hiding place to look for danger before quickly scurrying back behind his shelter, as it dodged back to the security of the clouds. To the tall, dark man standing alone, leaning against the wall of the cathedral, the dark clouds and sudden flashes of daylight simply added to his sense of unreality and dejection.

He was a lean and rangy man, with an arrogant air that seemed curiously muted among the common people all around, as if he was not used to the company of such men and women. He was quite broad under his cloak, looking to many like one of the itinerant knights who were so common then, who, having lost his lord, was now without either income or reason for existence. He was not dressed for battle, not arrayed in his master's uniform with proud insignia on display, but clad in a worn tunic and dirty, gray woollen cloak, looking as if he had spent too many days and nights in the saddle or sleeping out of doors. But his hand was never far from the hilt of his sword, always ready to reach for it, as if he expected a threat at any time and was constantly on alert for it, although his eyes were rarely upon any of the people close by. It was almost as if he knew that no man near could present any danger to him, that he was safe enough from humans. No, his eyes were mainly fixed on the makeshift stage beside the cathedral wall, as if it was the wooden construction itself that symbolized his jeopardy.

It had begun so long ago now, and yet he could still recall the day when the unimaginable had happened: Friday the thirteenth of October in the year thirteen hundred and seven. It was a date he knew he could never forget, a date created by the devil himself. Oh, he had been lucky, he had been out of the Temple with three companions, visiting the ship at the coast, and had missed the arrests that had caught so many of the other members of his Order. He had not even heard about the events until he had been travelling back to Paris, when, just outside a small hamlet, he had been warned not to continue, that if he went back he would be arrested as well and questioned by the Inquisition.

It had been a woman who had warned him about the crime being committed against his Order. He, his friends and their esquires, had stopped by the side of the road to eat when the woman had seen them. She had been walking past, one of a group ranged about an ox cart, a small, ashen-faced woman, who seemed to be well-born in her rich clothes, for all that they were gray and travel-stained now. As she and her companions passed by the quiet group of knights, she had appeared to be despairing and in deep misery, walking with her head cast down and stumbling in her pain and sorrow, but when she glanced up and caught a glimpse of them through her tears, she had started at the sight of the bearded knights with their helmets off as they sat on the verge. Initially she had seemed struck senseless with hope, her eyes quickly passing from one to the other of the men quietly eating as her mouth gaped, before she had rushed over, her optimism giving way to grief, weeping loudly and ignoring the cries from her companions.

She had begun calling to them before she had approached more than a few paces, her voice broken and her speech faltering, making the knights stop their meal in their astonishment and wonder whether she was mad as they heard her wailing tirade, but then her words hit them with the force of a hammer-blow. Her son was a Templar too, she told them, and she wanted to help them, to protect them. They must avoid Paris and get away to safety, to Germany or England—anywhere but Paris. They were not safe in Paris, maybe not anywhere in France. The knights sat, astonished, while she spoke, her thin body wracked with sobs for the son whom she knew was being tortured, for the son she knew she could never see again unless it was at the stake.

At first the knights could not believe it. All the brothers of the Temple arrested? But why? She could not explain: she did not know; all she knew was that the Order had been arrested and that the knights were being questioned by the Inquisition. Aghast, the knights watched as she was dragged back to rejoin the travellers around the cart, still calling out her warning to them, begging them to save themselves, while the patient oxen hauled at the wagon and the people followed as quietly and slowly as a cortège. Deeply troubled, heeding her menacing counsel, the men slowly continued on their way, but not now to Paris. Now they headed west, to the duchy of Guyenne. It was there, at the camp they made with another small group of Templar knights they had met on the road, that they started to hear the reports.

It still seemed inconceivable that Pope Clement could have believed the tales spread against them, but he seemed to be supporting the French king, Philip, in his campaign and did nothing to save the Order that had existed solely to serve him and Christianity. The stories had spread like a tidal wave, smothering all argument and giving no opportunity for defense; for to deny the charges would have brought down the weight of the Inquisition on the defender, and that could only mean destruction. Against the Inquisition there could be no defense.

At first it had seemed ludicrous. The knights were accused of being heretics, but how could *they* be heretics, they who had given so many lives in the defense of the Christian states? Their whole reason for existence was to defend the crusader state of Outremer in Palestine and they had fought and died for centuries in that cause, many of them choosing death in preference to life—even when they were caught by the Saracens and offered the chance to live in exchange for renouncing Christ, they chose death. How could anyone have believed that they could be heretics?

There was a rumor that even the common people found it hard to believe. For two centuries they had been taught that the Order was unsurpassed in its godliness, ever since Saint Bernard had given it his support during the crusades. How could they have fallen so low? When the orders for the arrest and imprisonment of the knights were sent out, the king had been forced to explain why he was having to take this action. He obviously felt that otherwise his orders might not be carried out. After all, the accusations were so shocking as to be almost unbelievable. The king had given a written statement to each of the officers in charge of the arrests accusing the knights and their Order of inhuman and evil crimes, and ordering that their goods should all be taken and the knights and their servants arrested for questioning by the Inquisition. By the end of that Friday, all the men in the temples were in chains, and the Dominican monks of the Inquisition began their questioning.

Could they be guilty of such crimes? Surely it was not possible? How could the most holy of all the Orders have become so amoral, so wicked? The people could hardly believe it. But disbelief transformed itself to horror when the confessions began to filter through. After the unimaginable tortures inflicted on them by the Inquisition, after hundreds had suffered the agonies of weeks of unremitting pain and many had even died, the admissions began to seep out to the ears of the populace like ordure leaching from a moat to pollute a clean well, and like all such filth, the rumors contaminated all who were touched by them. Their guilt was confirmed.

But who could doubt that after seeing comrades lose feet and hands in the continual anguish of the torture chambers they would confess to anything to stop the pain and horror?

The torture lasted for days and weeks on end, the pain ceaseless, in cells created inside their own buildings because there were not enough prisons to hold so many.

They confessed to whatever the Dominicans put to them. They admitted renouncing Christ. They admitted worshipping the Devil. They admitted spitting on the cross, homosexuality, *anything* that could save them from the pain. But it was not enough, it only meant that the monks went on to the next series of questions. They had so many accusations to confirm that the torture continued for weeks on end. Many individuals confessed to the unbelievable sins they had committed, but still it was not enough. It would only permit the king to punish individuals, and he wanted the whole Order to die. The torture continued.

Gradually, slowly, under the continual, patient questioning of the Dominican monks, the admissions began to change and the statements started to implicate the Order itself. The Knights were given satanic initiation rites, had been told to worship idols, had been forced to renounce Christ. Now, at last, Philip had his evidence: the entire Order was guilty and must be dissolved.

In the square, the man's eyes were hot and prickly now as he remembered them, his friends, the men he had trained and fought with—strong, brave men whose only crime, he knew, was to have been too loyal to the cause. So many had died, so many had been destroyed by the pain that was so much worse than anything their Saracen enemies had ever inflicted on them.

They had all joined taking the three vows: poverty, chastity and obedience, like any other order of monks. For they were monks; they were the warrior monks, dedicated to the protection of pilgrims in the Holy Land. But since the loss of Acre and the fall of the kingdom of Outremer in Palestine over twenty years before, people had forgotten that. They had forgotten the selfless dedication and sacrifice, the huge losses and the dangers that the knights had suffered in their struggles against the Saracen hordes. Now they only remembered the stories of the guilt of the greatest Order of them all, the stories spread by an avaricious king who wanted their wealth for his own. So now this crowd was here to witness the filial humiliation, the last indignity. They were here to see the last Grand Master of the Order admit his guilt and confess his, and his Order's, crimes.

A tear, like the first drop that warns of the storm to come, slowly ran down the man's cheek, and he brushed it away with a quick, angry gesture. This was no time for tears. He was not here to bewail the loss of the Order, that could come later. He was here to see for himself and his friends, to witness the Grand Master's confession and find out whether they *had* all been betrayed.

They had discussed it at length when they had met three days before, when they had all heard for themselves that this public show was to be made. All seven of them, the men from the different countries, the few who remained, the few who had not gone into the monasteries or joined one of the other orders, had been confused, sunk in despair at this Hell on earth. Had there truly been such crimes, such obscenities? If the Grand Master did confess, did it mean that all that they stood for was wrong? Could the Order have been corrupted without their knowing? It seemed impossible, but it would be equally incredible that it was not true, because that would imply that the king and the pope were conniving at the destruction of the Order. Was it possible that the Order could be betrayed so badly by its two leading patrons? Their only hope was that there could be a retraction, an admission of error, and that the Order could be found innocent and fully reinstated to its position of honorable service to the pope.

The seven had discussed their options and they had all agreed with the tall German from Metz that they should send one of their number to witness the event and report back. They could not rely on reports from others, they must have somebody there, someone who could listen to the statements and tell them what had been said, so that they could decide for themselves whether the accusations were true. The man by the cathedral wall had drawn the short straw.

But he was still mystified, unable to comprehend what was happening, and was not certain that he could give the affair the concentration it needed. He was distraught; it seemed so unbelievable, so impossible, that the Order he had served could have been so badly perverted. How could the dedicated group of knights that he had known, and remembered still, have been so warped, so debased? All of them had joined the Order because they could better serve God as soldiers than as monks. Even if a Templar decided to leave the Order, it could only be to go to a stricter one, to the Benedictines, the Franciscans or another group of monks living in the same enforced poverty and hidden from the world. How could the Order have been so badly betrayed?

He brushed aside another tear and walked listlessly through the crowds, his face set and glowering in his fear and worry. He peered at the stalls of the market for some minutes without really taking in the wares, until he found that his aimless strolling had brought him back to the platform, and he turned to stand more squarely in front of it, standing as if challenging it to allow the charade to go ahead, challenging it to permit the Order to be destroyed.

It loomed like a gallows in front of him, a great wooden construction with fresh timbers that shone as the sun caught it. At one side a series of steps led up to the flooring above. As he gazed at it he suddenly shivered. He could feel the evil almost as a force—not the evil of his Order, it was the evil of this ugly stage upon which he and his friends would be denounced. Somehow he could feel now that it would be pointless even to hope. There could be no reconciliation, no resumption of past glories. The sensation washed over him, as if before he had not truly been aware of the depths to which the Order had fallen, as if he had kept a small glimmer of hope alive through the last hard years that the Order could be saved but now, here, at last even this tiny flickering flame had died, and he could feel the despair like the pain of a sword wound in his belly.

The platform held his horrified attention. It seemed to symbolize the absolute failure of the Temple as it stood stolid and unwavering in front of him, as if it mocked the transient nature of the Order's honor when compared with its own strength to destroy it. This was no place of confession, it was a place of execution; it was the place where his Order would die. All that he and the thousands of other knights had stood for would die at last—here, today. As the realization sank in, it seemed physically to hit him, making him suddenly shudder as if from a blow. There was no protection, no defense against the implacable tide of accusations that would destroy them all. It was inevitable; the Temple's absolute destruction could be the only result.

But even as he realized it, even as he felt the finality of it, the certainty, he felt the hope struggling again within his breast, trying to break free of the shackles of despair that bound him so rigidly.

He was so engrossed in his own misery that he did not notice at first when the noise of the crowd changed. There was shouting, then jeers, from the mob as the convicted men were led forward, but it soon died down to a subdued murmuring, as if the people all around recognized the awesome implications of the occasion. The hush grew until the square was almost silent, the crowds standing and waiting for the men as they were led forward, the leading actors in this sad drama. The men were not in full view of the witness yet, they had not arrived at the stage, but he could tell that they were coming by the way that the people in the crush in front of the platform started to jostle, pushing and shoving to get a clearer view. Meanwhile, more people came into the square and tried to force their way forward, attracted by the sudden quiet and increased movement. He found himself having to control his fury, smothering his anger that these common men and women should push against *him,* a knight, but soon the sight in front made him forget all about the people around him.

Over the heads of the crowds he could just make out the four figures as they were pushed and manhandled up the small gantry to the floor of the platform. Then, at a sudden almost tangible heightening of tension in the crowd, he stared, feeling a rush of optimism buoy his spirits. They were all wearing their robes! It was the first time in the long years since the thirteenth of October in thirteen hundred and seven that he had seen men wearing their Templar uniforms; could this mean that they were to be reinstated? He leaned forward with a surge of renewed hope, his mouth open as he strained to see their faces, the desperate wish for the Order's recovery tightening his features, the desire an almost exquisite pain.

But then even that last dream was dashed, leaving him feeling empty and broken in his dejection. The quick lifting of his spirits fell away as soon as he peered over the heads of the people in front, and he had to struggle to control the cry that fought to break from his throat. It was obvious that the four were only wearing their robes so that they could be identified more easily; as they were pushed to the front of the platform and made to stand there, gazing dully at the people all around, he could see the heavy manacles and chains that smothered them. There would be no reprieve.

He felt himself shrinking back, sinking behind the people in front as if he wanted to melt away, wiping at his eyes with the heel of his hand to prevent the hot tears from springing back with his anguish and desolation, bowing his head as if in prayer as he hid from the stares of the men on the platform, not wanting to catch their gaze in case he could be associated with them and thereby broken as they had been. He did not want to see the despair in their eyes, the fear and the self-loathing. He could remember them—he wanted to remember them—as the strong men he had respected, as warriors; he did not want to remember them as they were now.

For they were wrecks; they stood shaking in their fear and dread as they surveyed the crush of people that had come to witness their downfall. Gone was the glory of their past. Jacques de Molay, the Grand Master, stood a little in front, looking small and insignificant somehow in the great white robe which hung from his shoulders formlessly, making him look as if he was wearing a shroud. He was over seventy years old and his age showed as he stood, ashen-faced, bent and swaying under the weight of the chains, mutely watching the people in the square, looking both nervous and frail.

The man in the crowds stared at him, horrified by the difference. When he had last met de Molay, seven years before, he had been a strong and vibrant man, secure in his power and his authority as the leader of one of the strongest armies in Christendom, responsible to no man but the pope. He had spent months producing a report for the pope and was convinced that with another crusade it would be possible to take back the Holy Land. His report showed how it would be possible to reconquer it and then keep it permanently safe. He had been confident of his ability to persuade the pontiff to begin planning for it and was already making his soldiers prepare, organizing and training them all, reinforcing the strict Rule of the Order and making them all comply with the original codes of conduct. Now he was completely broken.

He looked like a tired old man, shrunken and withered by the pain of seeing his Order ruined, by his inability to defend it, as if he could feel the failure of all that he had tried to achieve. In thirteen hundred and seven he had been the supreme ruler of the oldest and greatest military order, able to command thousands of knights and foot soldiers and answering to no lord or king, only the pope. Now, stripped of his rank and his authority, he looked merely old and tired, as if he had seen too much and was ready for death. He had given up; there was nothing left for him to live for.

In the crowds, the silent observer pulled the cowl of

his hood over his head, blinking and frowning to stop the tears that threatened to streak the dirt on his face. Now he knew it was all over. If they could do that to Jacques de Molay, the Order was ended. He retreated into the seclusion of his cloak as the depression took him over, blocking out all sound of the announcements and hiding from the final humiliation of his Order—and his life.

Unaware, not heeding the ritual going on at the platform, he turned slowly and started to push his way through the crowds. He had seen enough. He could bear no more. He just wanted to get away, to leave this scene of horror, as if he could leave his despair and sadness behind in this accursed square.

It was difficult to move. The crowds were too thick, with people struggling to get in and move forward to see the men on the stage. It was like pushing against the tide, and it took an age to go only a matter of yards. Shoving desperately, he tried to move around the people to escape, barging into men and women as they tried to hold him back until, at last, he found himself in front of a broad, swarthy man who would not move aside to let him pass but stood rooted to the spot and glared at him. Then, as he tried to move around the man, he heard de Molay's voice. With a shock he suddenly realized that it was not weak and quaking, as he had expected, but powerful and strong, as if the Grand Master had found a hidden reserve of strength. Startled, he stopped and whirled back to the platform to listen.

". . . Before God in Heaven, before Jesus his son, and all the earth, I confess that I am guilty. I am guilty of the greatest deception, and that deception has failed the honor and the trust of my knights and my Order. I have confessed to crimes that I know never happened—and all for myself. I confessed to save myself, from fear of torture. My crime is my weakness and it has led to the betrayal of my people. I declare the crimes attributed to the Order to be false. I avow the honesty, the purity and the holy sanctity of the men of the Temple. I deny wholly the crimes ascribed to the Order.

"I will die for this. I will die for confirming the innocence of the men already dead, the men murdered by the inquisitors. But now at least I can die with honor, with . . ."

Jacques de Molay seemed to have grown. He stood, solid and strong, up at the front of the platform by the railing, his head high as he proudly reviled his accusers and declared both his and the Order's innocence in a firm voice that carried over the crowd standing in shocked silence. But soon the man in the crowd became aware, as if it was from a great distance, of an angry muttering all around him. This was not what the mob had expected; they had been told that the Templars were here to confess, to admit to the crimes they had been convicted of. If this man denied them all, why had they been so brutally punished? A soldier pushed de Molay away and to the back of the dais and another Templar stepped forward, and to the obvious confusion of the soldiers and monks around him, stated his own denunciation, rejecting the accusations against the Order in proud and ringing tones.

In the crowds, the man stood and listened to the angry roar of the people around, his eyes gleaming in pride at his leaders' retractions. Even after the years of suffering, his honor, the Order's honor, was confirmed. The wicked rumors were false, he knew that now. So who could have levelled the accusations? Slowly his feelings gave way to anger, rough and raw, as he thought about the men who could have caused this, who had caused so much pain and anguish, and he squared his shoulders under his cloak with a new resolve.

The crowds were furious—they had been told that the Templars were evil, wicked men who had committed great sins against Christendom, and yet here were the two greatest Templars denying their guilt. These were the statements of men who would die for their evidence, they *must* be believed. But if what they said was true, then the crimes committed against them were of an unimaginable scale. The people pushed and shoved forward in their anger, shouting and swearing at the soldiers and monks who hurriedly pulled the four men from the stage and led them away, leaving the man on his own like a rock on the beach after the tide has ebbed.

He stood, eyes prickling with unshed tears, feeling the sadness and pain, but also pride and rage. He had no doubts now. No matter what would be said of the Order, he knew that the accusations were false. And if they were false, someone was responsible. His life had a new purpose: to find the men who had caused this injustice and have his revenge. The Order was innocent, there could be no doubting the conviction in those two voices. Slowly, he turned away and walked back to the inn where he had left his horse.

~ 1 ~

Simon Puttock felt elated, but not without a certain trepidation, as he meandered along the road that led from Tiverton to Crediton, letting his horse take him at a slow walk as he thought about his new position.

He had worked for the de Courtenays for many years now, as had his father before him, and he supposed that he should have expected a promotion—but he had not. It had been completely unexpected, a sudden shock; if they had told him he was to be imprisoned for robbery, it could not have surprised him more. Naturally he hoped that his lords were satisfied with his work over the years, but he had never dreamed of being given his own castle to command, especially one so important as Lydford, and every now and again a quick smile cracked the serious expression on his face as his glee momentarily flared, quenching his nervous contemplation.

The de Courtenays, the lords of Devon and Cornwall, had been able to rely on Simon's family for decades. Peter, his father, had been the seneschal of their castle at Oakhampton for twenty years before his death two years ago, carefully looking after their estates and keeping the peace during the long, regular absences when the de Courtenay family went to visit their lands farther north. Before that, Peter's father had been the family's chamberlain and had fought loyally with his lord in the troubled times before King Edward came to the throne. Simon was immensely proud of his forebears' association with, and honorable service to, this ancient family.

But even after so long in the de Courtenay family's service, the honor of being given the castle of Lydford to look after was still an unexpected delight—and a fearsome opportunity. If his tenure was successful and the land was profitable, he could expect to become wealthy, a man of power and influence in his own right. Of course, as the bailiff of the castle, he was also held responsible for any failures: for lower tax revenues, for reduced productivity from the demesne lands—for anything. Now, on his way home to his wife, he was gathering his thoughts, framing the best way of putting to her the possibilities and options that the role presented. Being a realist, he not only felt pride at the recognition he had been offered; he was also aware of the awesome immensity of the job that he had been given.

Ever since the Scots had defeated the English army at Bannockburn two years before, matters had got progressively worse, he knew. It was not just the continual attacks on the northern shires by the Scots or their invasion of Ireland, it sometimes appeared that God himself was angry with the whole of Europe and was punishing it. For two years now the whole country had been blighted, suffering under the worst rainstorms ever known. Last year, thirteen hundred and fifteen, had not been so bad down here in the far west; his people had hardly noticed any lack of essentials. Now, though, in the late autumn of thirteen sixteen, the rain had again been constant, and it had ruined the harvest for a second year. In other counties the people had been reduced to eating their horses and dogs in the vain search for sustenance, although it was not quite so bad yet here in Devon. It did mean that there would be a lot to plan for, though, and in his new job as the bailiff of Lydford castle, Simon intended to do all he could to help the people he was responsible for.

Lost in his thoughts, he had a deep frown on his face as he rode. He was a tall and muscular man with a body honed from riding and hunting, in his prime at nearly thirty years old. His hair was thick and a uniform dark brown, with no gray or white hairs to mar the youthful looks that hid his age so well. His complexion was ruddy from the days regularly spent in the open air and the saddle. Fortunately his daily exercise had so far prevented the build-up of fat that he remembered so well hanging under his father's chin as heavy jowls, making him look so much like one of his mastiffs, but he could still feel the early onset of thickening around his waist from the heavy beer that his household was so proud of.

From his sun- and wind-burned face his dark gray eyes looked out with a calm confidence. He was fortunate to have grown up near Crediton, and to have been taught how to read and write by his father's friends in the church—a fact that would surely make him unique among the other bailiffs in the district—and he was confident that he was fully capable of the responsibilities that had been given to him.

Looking up at the sky he could see it was already starting to darken as the sun slowly sank over to the west, and he threw a glance back at his servant, who plodded along behind on his old carthorse. "Hugh," he called, resting his hand on the rump of his horse as he twisted in his saddle to face backward, "I think we'll stop off at Bickleigh for the night, if they'll let us. It'll be dark long before we get home to Sandford."

His servant, a lean, morose, dark-haired man with the narrow, sharp features of a ferret, glared back. His demeanor was that of a prisoner being taken to the gallows who had been asked about the weather—angry at the interruption of his thoughts and suspicious of the reasons for the comment.

Satisfied that the remark was made with no malicious intent, he grunted his assent as he lolled in his saddle. He had no desire to ride any farther tonight, and Bickleigh was known to have a good stock of wine and beer—it would be a fine place to rest as far as he was concerned.

The bailiff smiled to himself. Although Hugh had travelled a great deal with his master in the five years since he had taken up his position, he had never fully mastered riding. His family were farmers near Drewsteignton where they kept a small herd of sheep, and until he started to work for Simon he had never ridden a horse. Even now, after a great deal of individual tuition, he still sat too loosely, radiating discomfort as he allowed the horse to plod along with him on its back.

Simon had once asked him why he seemed so ill at ease with horses, partly out of concern, but also from a degree of frustration because his servant's slowness held him up when he had far to travel.

Glaring aggressively at the ground, Hugh had taken some time to respond, and when he did at last answer it was with a low and mumbling voice. "It's the distance. That's what I don't like."

"What do you mean, the distance?" Simon had asked, confused at the taciturn response. "If that's all you're worried about you ought to go faster so that we can get there more quickly."

"That's not the distance I mean. I mean the distance down," Hugh had said, glowering truculently at his shoes, and Simon had stared at him for a few moments before roaring with laughter.

Remembering, Simon grinned to himself as he turned back to face the road ahead. It led along the River Exe here, meandering with the turbulent water at the edge of the forest, and he found himself watching the darkness between the trees on his right with wary interest.

Since the beginning of the rains the previous year, the shortage of food had led to a number of the poorer people taking up a life of robbery and thieving. He was not really very worried with this area, but he was all too aware of the problems. As always, when food became scarce the prices rose, and people who would normally have been law-abiding were forced to resort to rougher methods of obtaining what they needed. Now that the crops had failed for a second year several bands of outlaws had grouped themselves together to be safer from the forces of the law. These people, known as "trail bastons," were trying to eke out a living by taking what they could from unwary travellers. Simon had not heard that any had come to his own area, but he had been warned that one group had apparently started operating a little farther north, in the king's forest up near North Petherton. There had been no news of them coming this far south, but just in case he kept an eye open for an ambush.

It was with some surprise that he recognized the feeling of relief as they came up to the hill that led to Bickleigh, as if he had been under a high level of tension for hours. He had not realized that he had been so on edge, and so it was with a small smile of rueful disgust that he should allow himself to be so worried about outlaws when there was no need to be, that he turned into the track that led to the little castle.

The little keep was one of many built over the years to help defend the shire from the men of Cornwall, held by the de Courtenay family. It was a small fortified building, a square stone tower, with a simple wall surrounding it for protection. Like so many castles built in its time, the entrance to the building was through a door on the first floor, reached by a small external staircase. Bickleigh was used more now as a hunting lodge than a defensive post, and was visited only infrequently, once or twice each year, by Lord de Courtenay. It had its own bailiff who was responsible for tax collecting and the maintenance of the farms on the land all around, but beyond that it was a quiet place, nestling deep in the woods at the side of the hill over a mile from the main road to Tiverton. It had originally been used as a small fort and had been permanently garrisoned against attack, but now it was left alone, a small rural backwater, ignored even by its lord in favor of other larger and more imposing castles with strategic importance—and better hunting.

For Bickleigh was not important now. Oh, Simon knew it had been, back in the days after the invasion when it was essential for the Normans to have their outposts well positioned all over the country they had won. Then it had been crucial as a staging post between Exeter and Tiverton, one of the hundreds built by the invaders to pacify the population that was always ready to revolt against their new king—especially the Wessexmen of Devon. But now? Now it was superseded by the others.

Simon rode up to the front of the old wall and dismounted at the gate, leading his horse through into the courtyard beyond. Warned by the loud clatter of the hoofs on the cobbled yard, a smiling groom arrived and took the bridle from him, pointing to the great oak doors at the top of the stairs that led inside to the living quarters. Smiling back, Simon nodded before mounting the stairs and walking in through the main door where he met John, the de Courtenay's bailiff of Bickleigh.

"Simon, old friend," he said, holding out his hand as his eyes wrinkled in a smile of welcome. "Come in, come in. Would you like some refreshment? It's good to see you again."

Smiling and squeezing John's hand, Simon nodded. "Thank you. Yes, some beer and food and a place to rest for the night, if I may. I'm on my way back home and I can't stay in the saddle any longer today. Do you mind?"

"Mind?" John put his arm around Simon's shoulders and laughed as he led him along the screened passage to the hall. "Come on, let's get you fed!"

The little castle echoed in its emptiness as John led the way to the hall. It always surprised Simon that a castle, one he had known to ring to the sounds of cooks, servants and guests, could seem so deserted when the lord was away. It was almost as if the whole building was in hibernation, waiting for the master to return. As they walked, the sound of their booted steps seemed to ring throughout the tower as they trudged along the flagstones of the passage, until they came to the hall where John had been sitting before a roaring fire. Soon servants arrived carrying cold meats and wine, which they placed on a table near Simon, and he sat and helped himself. Hugh arrived after a few minutes—he had been helping to see to the horses—and sat with his master to eat, losing his customary moroseness as he surveyed the array of food before setting to with gusto.

Later, after John had watched them eat their fill, he had them draw their seats up beside the fire and, leaning over, refilled their cups with wine. "So what's happening out in the world, then?"

Simon grinned at his older friend, who sat in front of him on his settle, his face warmed where it was lit by the orange glow of the flames, but then he turned his gaze away to peer around the hall.

It was like a tall cavern, almost square at the base, and lighted by the fire and the candles, sitting in their brackets on the walls, that guttered in the draft that fed their flames, the tapestries that covered the windows giving no protection from the gales outside. The floor was covered in old rushes and the smell of the place was a pervasive mixture of bitterness and sweetness— from the dogs' urine and from the putrefying remains of ancient meals and bones that lay hidden among the stems on the floor, the normal smell of an old hall. Simon would have been happier if the rushes had been replaced more often, but he knew that John held to the old view that it was better not to change them too regularly—that was the way to bring in infection.

When he looked back at John, there was a slight concern in his eyes; his friend had aged since they last met. He was only ten years older than Simon himself, but his body was skinny and seemed ancient, prematurely hunched under his tunic from lack of exercise and from too often sitting in the cold and reading by candlelight. The thin face looked strangely pale and waxy from spending too much time indoors, and the lines on his forehead and either side of his mouth made deep grooves on his features, casting their own dark shadows in the firelight. When they had last met John had borne a head of thick graying hair, but now it was almost a pure white, as if he had been given a sudden shock. Simon had not expected to see him so greatly changed in only seven months, and as he looked at his friend he suddenly realized how much pressure he would be under with his own new position at Lydford.

"Apart from my new position, you mean? The only thing people were talking about in Taunton was the price of food." They talked for a time about the effects of the rains on their crops, and the sudden increase in prices after the last failed harvest, until the door opened and both fell silent, watching a servant enter and stride quickly across the hall to speak to John. After a moment he rose with an apology.

"Pardon me, Simon. A traveller has arrived and asked to speak to me," said John as he stood and walked to the door.

Simon raised his eyebrows in surprise and looked over at Hugh. "A traveller? At this time of night? It must be more than three hours after dark!" Hugh shrugged with indifference and poured himself more wine.

After only a few minutes, John came back with a tall and strong-looking man, obviously a knight, wearing a heavy cloak over a mail hauberk that looked old and appeared to have seen several battles, from the scars and scratches that were visible. Behind him was a servant, a lean and wiry man of Simon's own age, with eyes that seemed to flit over the whole room as he entered as if he was looking for any signs of danger. As he came in he moved to the side of the knight so that he could see directly into the room, then followed along behind.

"Simon," John said with a smile, "This is Sir Baldwin Furnshill, the new master of Furnshill Manor."

Rising, Simon took the stranger's hand. He seemed calm, but Simon noticed a subtle wariness in his eyes, a slight hesitation as he shook hands, and as soon as Simon released his grip, the knight took a step back and shot an enquiring glance at John, who swiftly introduced them while Simon's eyes flitted inquisitively over the two strangers.

The knight was tall, probably a little taller than Simon himself, and carried himself like a lord. Broad and thickset under his mail, he stood proud and haughty, like a man who had fought successfully in several battles. Simon had to peer to see his face in the dark room; it was scarred on one side—not too deeply, merely as if he had been scratched by a knife, a normal mark for a warrior. But that was not what Simon first noticed. No, it was the deep weals, the lines of pain that stood out, the furrows of anguish that travelled from underneath his eyes, past his mouth, to finish in the hair at his jawline. They pointed to great suffering, as if he had known a level of pain so deep as to be almost unbearable, although he did not seem very old.

Simon placed him at around thirty-five; his dark hair and the neat, almost black, beard (an uncommon feature with modern knights) that just followed the line of his jaw seemed to hint at no more than that. When the knight turned back and smiled, his dark brown eyes creasing in welcome after John's eulogistic description of his younger friend, Simon could see the hurt there as well. It was a shock to see it, as if it was a blemish that should have been polished away long ago. But it was there, a melancholy that seemed as though it would never be able to leave, a depression that appeared to have taken such deep root that to exorcise it would remove the knight's very soul, and Simon could feel the sympathy stirring in his breast at the sight.

"Please, come and sit. You were travelling very late, sir. Please sit and rest," he said, shoving Hugh to make more space on the bench.

The knight bowed slightly and his mouth twitched in a half smile as Hugh sulkily moved farther up the bench away from the flames.

"Thank you. But there is space for me here," he said, indicating John's trestle and slowly easing himself down onto it, sighing as his muscles relaxed. He gratefully accepted a cup of wine from John and took a long, contented draft. "Ah, that's good." His servant stood behind him, as if waiting to be given an order—or was it that he was standing ready to defend his master? "Edgar, you can sit as well."

Simon glanced up at the servant as he moved round to sit, and was vaguely disturbed by the expression of wary distrust he could see in the dark features, as if he was being weighed up, measured and assessed in comparison with other potential dangers. Then, to Simon's vague annoyance, this arrogant servant seemed to decide that the bailiff was no risk, as if he was not of enough significance to merit being classified as a threat. Edgar glanced down and seated himself, staring around the room, his eyes occasionally lighting briefly on the other people present. He seemed a distrustful man, Simon felt—even when seated he seemed to be glowering, as if doubting his, and his master's, safety.

The bailiff shrugged and looked over at the knight, who was happily accepting more wine from John. "Why are you travelling so late at night, sir?" he asked, watching as the knight stretched his legs slowly and started to rub at them, pulling his mail aside—Baldwin raised his eyebrows as he stared back, a hint of sardonic humor showing in his dark eyes. He seemed to be close to laughing at himself ironically.

"It's been a long time since I travelled these roads. I am the new master of Furnshill Manor, as John said, and I'm on my way there, but I was held up today, in my pride and foolishness. I had a wish to see some of the old views, but it has been many years since I came along these roads and I forgot my way too often and . . . well, I got lost. It took me a lot longer than I expected to find the right roads." His head rose and he gazed straight into Simon's eyes as he gave a sudden smile. "Have I broken the law in being out so late, bailiff?"

Laughing, Simon happily took another cup of wine from John. "No. No, I'm just naturally inquisitive. So are you on your way to Furnshill now?"

"Yes. I understand my brother died some time ago, so the manor becomes mine. I came as soon as I heard he was dead. I was going to continue tonight, but if I can get lost so easily during daylight, what hope is there that I can find my way in the dark? No, if John could allow me . . . ?" He finished with an interrogatively raised eyebrow as he peered over at the older man beside him.

"Of course, of course, Sir Baldwin. You must rest here the night."

Simon studied the knight carefully. Now he could see the man's features more clearly as the firelight and candles caught his face, and he could see the family resemblance. Sir Reynald had been known to be a kindly master, and Simon found himself hoping that his brother Baldwin would be too. A cruel man in an important manor could be disruptive to an area. "Your brother was a good man, always ready to help another in need and was known to be good to his people," he said speculatively.

"Thank you. Yes, he was a kind man, although I've not seen him for many years. It's sad I didn't have a chance to give him my farewell. Oh, yes, thank you, John." He held out his cup again for John to refill, and his eyes caught Simon's for an instant and held his gaze. There was an arrogance there, Simon noticed, the arrogance that came from experience, from battle and testing his prowess, but there was also a humility, a kindness, and an almost tangible yearning for peace and rest, as if he had travelled far and seen almost too much and only wanted to find somewhere where he could at last settle.

The young bailiff was intrigued. "So how long is it since you were here last, if you got lost on your return?"

"I was last here in my seventeenth year, that was in twelve hundred and ninety," he said blandly, and then smiled at Simon's obvious calculation. "Yes, I am forty-three, bailiff."

Simon stared at him. It seemed almost incredible that he could be so old, especially now, as he smiled in amusement with the firelight twinkling in his eyes. He seemed too vigorous somehow, too quick and sharp to be that age, and it was only with a mental effort that Simon managed to stop his jaw dropping.

"You honor me with your surprise, anyway," said the knight with a small smile. "Yes, I left in twelve ninety, over six-and-twenty years ago. My brother was the elder, so he was the heir. I decided to go and seek my fortune elsewhere." He stretched. "But it's time for me to come back. I need to be able to ride the hills again and see the moors." Suddenly his smile broadened and he quickly looked over at the bailiff with his eyebrows raised in an expression of humorous lechery. "And it's time I started breeding. I intend to take a wife and begin a family."

"Well, I wish you well in your search for peace and marriage," said Simon, smiling back at him.

There was a glint in the knight's eyes, not of anger, but more of quizzical interest as he gazed over at him. "Why do you say 'peace'?"

Simon was aware of, and annoyed by, a slight stiffening in the servant beside the knight. "You say you have been away for many years and want to settle down at your home." He drained his cup and set it on the bench top beside him. "I hope that means you want to find peace and not battle."

"Hmm. Yes, I have seen enough of war. I feel the need for rest and, as you say, peace." For an instant Simon saw the pain again, reflected by the flames as the knight stared into the fire, seemingly lost in his past, but then the moment was gone and Baldwin smiled again as if he was silently reminding himself of the others around and putting the pain away for the present.

"Well, if you wish, you may travel with us tomorrow. We will be passing close by Furnshill Manor on our way home."

With evident gratitude, Baldwin inclined his head. "Thank you, I would be happy for your company."

*   *   *

The next morning was bright and clear, the sun shining down from a perfect blue sky, and after a breakfast of cold meats and bread Simon and the new owner of Furnshill left the little castle with their servants and made their way back up to the lane toward Cadbury where the knight's manor lay.

Simon found himself covertly watching the man and his servant. They seemed to move in accord with one another, a complete unit in themselves. There was never any sign between them that the bailiff could see, but whenever Baldwin wanted to move slightly, whether to look at a view or at a flower by the side of the road, it seemed that his servant was already moving, as if he had anticipated the knight's wish. Wherever they went, the knight was always in front, but the servant was never far from him, leading the small packhorse on its long halter just behind and to the knight's right. Simon found himself thinking how the two were perfect complements, and for an instant wondered whether he would ever be able to train Hugh to ride properly so that his own servant could behave in the same faultless manner. He threw a glance over his shoulder to where Hugh was sulkily jolting along behind, and with a sardonic grimace gave up on the thought.

Sir Baldwin rode into the lead shortly after they began the climb up the steep hill from Bickleigh and seemed surprised at the slow pace of Hugh.

"Hugh has only been riding for a short time," said Simon with an ironic grin, in answer to the enquiring gaze. "He's always nervous that the horse will canter off and leave him behind. I don't like to worry him too much by going too fast for him."

The knight peered ahead contemplatively while his servant stared back at Hugh with a sneer of disgust on his face. "I can remember this lane," Baldwin said, "I can remember riding here when I was very young. It seems so long ago, in a way . . ." His voice trailed off.

Simon looked at him. He seemed to be reflecting, his forehead puckered in thought as he studied the road ahead, until they came over the crest of a hill and could see the view. Pausing, they waited for Hugh. From here, up on top of the rise, they could see far over to the south and west, all over the moors and forests of Devon, even as far as Dartmoor.

In the mid-morning haze it seemed, at first, as if they were alone in the world as they sat in their saddles at the top of the hill and waited for Hugh to catch up with them. Then the signs of life became evident. Some four miles away they could see smoke from a chimney rising between trees. Just beyond was a hamlet, nestling on the side of a hill above a series of fields that sprawled down into a valley. Farther on, the scene colored blue with the distance, were more houses and fields with, here and there, the inevitable columns of smoke to show where fires were alight for cooking. Simon smiled as he looked over the area with a feeling of proprietorial pride at the sight of this, his county. When he looked over at the knight beside him, he was surprised to see him leaning forward and resting on his horse's neck, a small smile on his face as he contemplated the view.

"It's good country, isn't it?" said Simon softly.

"The finest," Baldwin murmured, still staring at the view. Then, shaking himself out of his reverie, he swiftly turned and flashed a smile at the bailiff. "I cannot wait for your man any longer. This road needs a quick horse to let the memories flow. My friend, I will look forward to seeing you at the manor. As a friend and companion of the road I will be pleased to offer you some refreshment before you continue on your way home."

Before the words had sunk in, he had dug his heels into his horse's flanks and was away and rushing down the hill, his cloak streaming out behind him and billowing in the wind, his servant still maintaining his position slightly behind and to the knight's right. Eyebrows raised, Simon watched them race down the hill until Hugh arrived at his side.

"He's in a hurry to get to the manor," he said somberly. His master nodded.

"Yes. It's been many years since he last looked forward to anything so much, I think. He looks as though he feels young again." Slowly they started off down the hill toward the manor, some two miles away.

"Strange man, though," said Hugh pensively after a few minutes of jolting along.

"In what way?"

"He looks all lost sometimes, like a lamb that's lost his ewe, then it's like he's remembered who he is again and his smile comes back."

Simon thought about his comment for the rest of the way. It certainly agreed with his own observations from the previous night. It was almost as if the knight was coming back to forget something in his past, as if in returning to his old home he would be able to forget the years spent away. But when Simon had asked him what he had been doing since he left so many years before, he had simply said, "Fighting," with a terse curtness that seemed strangely out of character, and would not explain further.

It was odd, he knew. Most knights were pleased to discuss their exploits, they were always happy to boast and tell of their valor and courage in the field. It was only natural for warriors to be proud and arrogant, describing their battles in detail and telling of their bravery. To meet a man who did not want to talk about his past at all seemed curious, but then again, as Simon knew well, if a knight lost his lord he could well lose all his wealth and property. He would have to survive as best he could—by whatever means—trying to gain a new lord to keep him in armor and food. Perhaps this knight had fallen on bad times and had been forced to struggle to maintain himself and now wanted to forget. He shrugged. Whatever the reason, if Baldwin wanted to keep his past to himself, he would respect his wish.

Even at Hugh's shambling pace they were not long in getting to the road to the manor. For once Simon was quite pleased to meander along slowly—it gave his mind more time to wander over his new responsibilities and he found himself planning for the inevitable visits he would soon have to make. First there were the other bailiffs—he would have to go and see them all, his new peers, and see what the state of the lands around Lydford was. He wanted to visit the constables in each of the hundreds, the subdivisions of the shire, as well and make sure that they were ready with their allocation of men in case of war. It did not seem very likely, but a bailiff should be ready at all times in case his lord needed him and his men. He was not too concerned with the other responsibilities of the constables—if there was a hue and cry, the constables should be able to cope, calling up the men and forming a posse to catch the offenders.

In a society where most men were living in a state of

poverty, it was inevitable that there were often robberies. Burglars, draw latches, thieves, cut-purses and poachers were a constant problem, but all men living within the law were expected to be ready to fight for their lord at a moment's notice and could be called up by the constables quickly to chase criminals. After all, the king himself wanted the folk ready for the defense of the realm, and everyone was expected to be able to arm themselves quickly to defend their homes. The people living within Simon's new area were all hardened countryfolk and were well used to using their weapons for hunting. God help any man who tried to commit a crime. He would be chased like a wolf by some of the best hunters in the kingdom until he was caught. It would not be difficult; few people needed to travel, so any stranger in a district would always be questioned by the locals, and news of travellers would always filter back to Simon's friend Peter Clifford, the priest at Crediton. If there was a hue and cry shortly after a newcomer had arrived it would be obvious who would be the main suspect.

He was just thinking this when he was surprised to see, a little beyond the lane to Furnshill manor and travelling from Cadbury on the road to Crediton, a small group of monks. Wondering who they were and where they were going, he coaxed his horse into a trot and left Hugh behind to catch up with them. Since his schooling with the priests at Crediton, where he had met many monks as they travelled on their way to Buckland Abbey and beyond down into Cornwall, Simon had enjoyed meeting these godly men who had exchanged worldly sins for lives of poverty, helping the people and dedicating their years to God.

There were five men in the group, four walking

slowly, one of them leading a pack-mule, another on horseback. From their habits they must be Cistercians, the same as the monks of Buckland.

As he came closer, he slowed his pace to a walk and greeted them. "Good morning, brothers, where are you travelling to?" At the sound of his voice, the man on the horse whirled suddenly and Simon was shocked to see the fear on his face.

He was a large man, running to fat, with flabbiness around his heavy features and showing in his jowls and chin, but for all that he looked muscular and rode like a knight, sure and steady, if a little hunched. He looked as though he had been a strong and sturdy man in his past, but had now developed too keen an interest in good food and drink.

"Who are you, sir?" he asked, in an almost petulant voice with a heavy accent in which Simon recognized the tones of France—but that was normal with many monks now that the pope lived in Avignon.

"Simon Puttock, sir. I am the bailiff of Lydford," he answered, smiling to put the man at his ease. It did not seem to help. The man was plainly terrified of strangers, and his eyes flitted over Simon as he rode alongside. Unconcernedly, Simon looked at the other men in the group. The eldest, a jovial-looking man with almost white hair and a cheeky smile, grinned at him as if in mute apology for the rude introduction, then turned his eyes to stare fixedly at the road ahead, the remains of the smile showing as a slight grin that played around his lips. The others simply walked on quietly and ignored him, to his faint surprise, because usually monks, like other travellers, would be happy for any diversion on the road.

"You are a long way from Lydford, bailiff."

Simon laughed briefly. "I've only just become bailiff, sir. I'm on my way back to my home in Sandford to collect my wife and tell her, then I will be going to Lydford to take up my new responsibilities. So where are you going? To Buckland?"

"Yes." The man seemed to pause. "Yes. we are going there. I am to become the new abbot of our monastery." His eyes quickly darted from Simon to the road behind.

Catching the glance, Simon smiled again. "That is my servant, abbot. You need not worry on your journey in these parts. I've not heard of trail bastons this far south, they all seem to be near Taunton and Bristol. Your journey should be safe."

"Good, good," the abbot said absently, his brow furrowed, then glanced over to the bailiff with a calculating stare. "Tell me, my friend, which is the best way to Buckland from Crediton, do you think?"

Simon drew his mouth down as he thought. "There are two main ways, either west to Oakhampton, then south through Lydford. I know that way—the roads are good and there are places for you to rest overnight. The other would be to go to the east of the moors and down that way. I've never been that far, although I did go to Exeter once. The Oakhampton route would be my choice."

"Good. Then we shall take that road." He seemed to think a moment, staring at the road ahead, then turned back to Simon. "Would you travel with us? I would be grateful for the protection of the bailiff on the road."

Looking at him, faint surprise on his face, Simon said, "But, as I say, there's no need to fear robbers. The country is quiet here."

"Maybe, maybe, but your company would be added

protection and desirable, sir." When Simon looked over at him, he was shocked to see the expression on the man's face—he seemed to be trying to smile, but he could not hide the anxiety on his face. His eyes were wide and staring, almost as if he was pleading with the young bailiff, and Simon found himself wondering what could have created such fear. He almost asked, but decided not to—he might cause offense.

"I'm afraid that I'm going to visit a friend not far from here, Sir Baldwin Furnshill at Furnshill Manor. Why don't you join me? We can go on later," he said, and, although he could not be sure, he felt that the older monk nearby shot him a sharp glance on hearing the name "Furnshill."

"No, no. We must get to Buckland as soon as we can. You must come with us now."

Simon found himself repelled by this man, who was so obviously scared for no reason. It seemed almost obscene to be so fearful in such a quiet part of the country. Of course travel was dangerous, no matter where the destination, but to be so terror-stricken here in Devon . . . He thought a moment. "No, I must go to the manor, I gave my word. But I will not stay there for long, so perhaps I shall overtake you on the road later. At least I can go with you as far as Crediton."

"But why can't you come with us to Buckland?"

"I must go to my wife first and take her with me to Lydford."

"Could you not collect her after coming with us to Buckland?" His voice was whining, like a child begging for a sweet.

Simon almost laughed, but then he saw that the abbot was serious and checked himself. "That would mean I would be delayed for seven or eight days, abbot. No, I can't do that. I must get to Lydford with my wife."

"Oh, very well," said the monk petulantly.

They rode along in silence for a few minutes, until Simon said mildly, "So you are sure you will not join me and visit the manor? It will at least break your journey a little, and I'm sure your companions would like some refreshment." Out of the corner of his eye he saw the oldest monk nod his head in approval at the suggestion and then wink, as if he knew Simon could see him but the abbot could not.

"No, we are all well. There is no need."

"In that case, I will wish you a good and safe journey," Simon sighed. "I must go back to the manor. I hope I shall see you soon, abbot. For now, goodbye."

The abbot grunted and, annoyed at his demeanor, Simon wheeled his horse to gallop back to the lane to the manor. As he turned he caught a brief smile on the face of the older monk, as if in gratitude for his offer. The bailiff nodded to him and urged his horse into a gallop.

At the lane, he found Hugh moodily sitting on his horse and waiting.

"I thought you must've forgotten me, riding off like that."

"Oh, shut up," said Simon, having had more than enough sulkiness for one day, and led the way down the lane to the manor.

2

I t was getting close to noon when they finally clattered their way up to the front of the old manor.

The house had been built by the Furnshill family over a hundred years before when they had first arrived in Devon to serve their lords, the de Courtenays. It stood high on the side of a hill, almost hidden from the sides by the thick woodland all around. It was a long, whitewashed cob building, with black timber to reinforce the single-story walls. It looked much like the farmhouses of the area, and sat as if peering over the lane that led to its door. Small windows were set into the walls just below the thatch and the door was almost in the middle of the building, giving it a cheerful and pleasant aspect. This was not a fortified manor built in fear, a place constructed for defense. It was a family home, a strong and welcoming house.

Behind and to the right were the stables. They were a group of large buildings, similar to the main house, surrounding the trodden dirt of the yard. Here, as Simon knew, were areas for the horses and the oxen. There was even one large shed for the farm implements. Simon and Hugh ignored the entrance to the yard and rode up to the front of the house before dismounting, whereupon a pair of stablemen appeared from nowhere, making the bailiff smile to himself. Obviously the whole household was trying to put on a good show for the new master.

After Simon had got off his horse and handed it to the waiting hostler, he stood and took in the view. From here he could see for miles, over the tops of the tree-covered hills to the moors, lowering in blue-gray malevolence in the far distance. Tugging off his gloves, he turned to the door as Baldwin came out to welcome them.

"I think I was right to come on ahead," he said, smiling as he shook the bailiff's hand. "You have taken an age to get here, Simon. Can you not teach your servant to ride a little faster?"

Simon felt Hugh stiffen behind him, but smiled in return. "It was my fault, sir, I stopped to talk to the monks."

"What monks?" asked the knight absently as he led them in through the thick wooden door.

"Didn't you see them? We came upon them at the end of your lane here. Four monks and an abbot; they're on their way to the monastery at Buckland."

Baldwin frowned slightly. "No, I didn't see them," he said with disinterest, and shrugged, seeming to put them out of his mind as he smiled again. "Wine? Or would you prefer some beer?"

The manor did not seem to have suffered the privations of so many other parts of the county during the rains. Simon and Hugh were given a hearty meal of mutton stew with fresh bread, all the while having to answer a stream of questions from their inquisitive host, who seemed to want to know everything about his new estates, how they had changed in his absence and how the people had fared while he had been away. At last, as they all pushed themselves away from the table and sat closer to the fire, he smiled and apologized.

"I'm sorry if you had to pay for your food so dearly, but I want to be a good master to the people here. I have seen too many lords who treated their people badly and taxed them heavily. I want to be known to be fair to them, and to do that I must know all I can."

"I think you have a good and strong estate, sir—" Simon began, but the knight interrupted him.

"As bailiff to knight, I think we can talk to each other as equals."

Recognizing the honor, Simon smiled and inclined his head. It was not his imagination—he could feel that already there was some kind of bond between him and this grave knight. The man seemed to be seeking his friendship and Simon found it flattering, even though he knew that it was likely to be only the interest of a lonely newcomer seeking the acquaintance of an important neighbor. He continued, "Thank you. So, Baldwin, your estate has not been so badly affected as some others. The rains have been very bad this year, but Furnshill is high enough to have missed the worst of the damage. The lower-lying areas were badly flooded, but your crops were not too badly affected, not as badly as some. In other shires the people are starving, but I think your people haven't suffered much."

"Certainly all I have seen and heard shows that the people of Guyenne and France are without food. And I saw that the people in Kent were suffering when I passed through." He seemed to be thinking, drawing in on himself with a frown of concentration.

"When was that?"

"What?"

"When did you pass through Kent? Was it recently? I just wondered whether things are still that bad or whether they're getting better."

"Oh. Well, it would have been about nine months ago, I suppose. But I have spoken to many travellers since then and things do not seem to have improved." He sighed. "It sometimes seems unfair that so many people have to suffer so much to survive, does it not?"

"Yes," agreed Simon, staring reflectively into his mug. "But it is the natural way. We all have to serve, whether it is our master or our God, and the people must work to serve us, although some are more harshly treated than is needed."

"In what way?"

"As you say, it can seem unfair sometimes. When you see men being taxed too heavily, or the sheriffs taking money from the taxes to put in their own purses, or when you see robbers taking all the profit from a farmer who will have to try some other way to feed his children. It's not only the weather that causes problems when you are a farmer."

"No. No, of course not," said the knight reflectively. "But, tell me, why do you mention the sheriffs? Is there a problem with the man in Exeter?"

"No, we're lucky here. He seems a good and honest man. No, he's alright, but you must know about the others, surely? Only a couple of years ago almost all of them throughout the country were changed because of their corruption."

"I hadn't heard that, no. But I was out of the country at the time, so . . ."

"Well, as I say, most were changed. There were

many cases of false indictments, and you can guess who benefited. I think it's beginning again. And, as usual, it's the poor that are hit hardest."

"You seem to feel strongly about it, Simon."

"I do, I do. I want to be known to be fair to the people in my area and known to be their protector. I don't want to be thought of as a heavy and unfair taxer, as being interested in lining my own purse at the expense of others. And I want to make sure that the people here can travel safely. Thank God we are not yet plagued with outlaws here!"

"Yes. We seem to be lucky in that."

"We are, none have come this far west yet, although they are moving closer. Apparently there are some outside Bristol, and another group at North Petherton. We can only hope that they fade away before coming down here."

Baldwin stared musingly at the flames for a moment. "I wonder why people join the trail bastons? They must know that they'll never be able to find peace. On our way here we heard of a number of farmers and merchants attacked—even one knight, I believe, but he managed to save himself. I think the outlaws are getting more desperate."

"Why?"

"Even if they manage to steal, it can hardly ever be enough to support the large gangs we have now." His voice drifted, his face pensive as he seemed to consider his words. Catching a glimpse of his frowning concentration, Simon nodded.

"Good! There's no excuse for them. The sooner they're all arrested or killed the better."

Baldwin stared into the flames with a sad grin lifting the corner of his mouth, twisting his moustache. "I know. We can't have the peace of the shire ruined by a few, and the highways have to be kept clear. But what else can the villeins do? There's no food for them, and what there is costs too much. If they wanted to, they wouldn't be able to get work—some lords have even thrown out their retainers. There's a rumor that some *knights* are resorting to banditry because they can't afford food. How can villeins survive?"

"Not by robbery. Life may be harsh, but outlawry is no way out. No, we must make an example of the ones we *do* catch," said Simon decisively. "We have to show them they cannot expect to escape punishment—no matter where they go, they'll be found and made to pay. It's not just the hurt they cause to travellers, there's some who live out in the king's forests and break the forest law. They must be taught that they cannot rob and murder without expecting to be punished. Where would we be if these men were allowed to escape? Being *poor* is no excuse—if it was, we'd soon have all villeins going over to the trail bastons. No, we must catch them and punish them. If a man has been an outlaw, he must be caught and made an example of. There's no other way to prevent others from following in his steps."

"But what if the actual crime was not significant? What if the guilty man could still be useful to his lord?"

"Ha!" Simon gave a short harsh bark of a laugh. "If he could be useful to his lord he would be unlikely to be charged!" To his surprise, although Baldwin nodded, it was not with conviction—his head moved only slowly, as if in automatic response. The bailiff knew that it was only right that the law should be upheld—if he didn't believe that, he would never have been able to accept the position at Lydford—but Baldwin's contemplative silence made him consider. Being a fair man, he began to wonder how he himself would react if he found it impossible to live, if his livelihood was taken away and he still had to find a way of getting food for his wife and daughter. If Margaret and Edith were hungry and he could not provide for them, what would he *not* do? If they did not have the small farm and its food, what would he do to survive? He had the uncomfortable suspicion that he too could be tempted to join a band of outlaws and try to survive that way.

Shaking himself, he tried to force the idea out of his mind, but the awareness of the fear and despair that such poverty could cause would not leave him, and lowered his previously high spirits.

The movement seemed to wake Baldwin from his reverie. Looking up, he appeared to notice his guest again, and with a start he rose, his voice decisive. "My people will not be harshly or unfairly treated. I will be fair to them all. I have travelled far and I have seen how many injustices there are in the world. I want to be seen and known to be a good master."

Simon finished his drink and stood. "I think you will be," he said seriously. "And now, I think we must leave and finish our journey. By your leave." He bowed and led the way to the door.

The two shook hands briefly outside while Hugh went off to the stables to fetch their horses.

"Thank you for the meal, Baldwin. I hope to see you again soon."

"It was my pleasure. There will always be wine and beer for the bailiff of Lydford at my house while I am here. Goodbye, and safe journey, my friend." Just then Hugh returned and Baldwin stayed there, watching

them mount and make their way down the track to the
lane that led back to Cadbury and on to Sandford.
When Simon turned at the bottom of the lane, the
knight was still there, staring after them with that
thoughtful frown still darkening his face.

After their lunch Simon changed his mind and decided
to go across country rather than follow the main road.
It was more direct, and now, it being the middle of the
afternoon, he was keen to get back to his own house
and see his wife. Although Hugh was silent as he rode
along beside him, he knew that his servant would be as
keen as him to get back home again.

He was also happy to be able to miss the monks. He
had found the abbot's fear deeply unsettling. It was
normal, he knew, for a traveller to be wary, but the
abbot almost seemed to be in mortal fear of his life. It
was much more deep than the usual nervousness that a
wanderer through a new land would feel, it was an almost tangible terror as if the abbot knew that he *would*
soon be attacked, and the company of a man so obviously scared was not relaxing. He would be bound to
demand Simon's company for the rest of his journey
again, too. No, it was easier to avoid the monks.

As they left East Village and made their way down
to their home in Sandford, following the tortuously
winding lanes that led south and west, carrying them
up and down the low and rolling green hills of the
shire, Simon put the man out of his mind. For the most
part he rode contentedly, with a smile of satisfaction on
his face. Here, close to home, he knew all the lanes
around, and it was with a thrill of pleasure that he recognized trees and fields, as if he was seeing old friends
again for the first time after a long absence. The wind

was chill but not strong, cooling them as they rode and preventing them from becoming too hot, and the bailiff took delight in standing occasionally at the top of the small hills and staring at the views.

It was always the same for him with this country. Even from the lower summits the views were good, showing the gently rolling land and the hamlets nestling under the hills. From the higher rounded and soft hills he could see for miles. To the southwest was Dartmoor, to the north Exmoor, and he peered in both directions, contrasting the blue-gray ruggedness of the southern hills ahead with the softer, more gentle contours of the sweeping moors behind. At last, though, they were riding down the track to their home, and here Simon forgot the views in his anticipation of his wife's pleasure at the news of their new position.

It was with relief that he climbed down from his horse and stretched his shoulders. Rubbing his rump, he walked over to help Hugh with the packs. Then the door burst open and his daughter Edith erupted, running out to greet him, laughing and screaming her delight. Grinning, he swiftly dropped his bags as she came close, snatched her up and kissed her, feeling the pride and joy of fatherhood at her exuberant welcome. He had just set the six-year-old on his shoulders when Margaret, his wife, appeared at the door.

She stood quietly smiling as he walked over to her, a tall and handsome woman with a slim but strong body, and as he kissed her, holding her close, he smiled with the feeling of warmth and comfort she always gave him.

Margaret was almost five years younger than him. He had first met her when he was visiting her father eight years before and he had known immediately that she would be his wife, although he had no idea why the thought had come into his head. At first he had been attracted to her serious smile, her slim, fair face and her long golden hair, so rare in the country around Crediton. Now, as he held her and she wrapped her arms around him, he marvelled again that she had agreed to marry him. When she tried to break the embrace, he held her, squeezing gently to hold her close, and smiling down into her blue eyes.

"Welcome home, Simon," she said, smiling softly up at him.

"Hello, my love. How are you?"

"Fine now that you're home again. So how was the journey?"

He laughed. "The journey was fine, but not as good as the meeting! You're holding the new bailiff of Lydford." As she gazed up at him with her eyes wide in her surprise, he suddenly grabbed her to him and laughed, bellowing his joy infectiously, squeezing her in his delight as his daughter clung to his hair.

"Simon, Simon, let go," his wife said at last. Free again, she stood, hands on hips, as she frowned at him in mock exasperation. "Don't forget your daughter's on your shoulders, you fool! So you're the bailiff, are you? What does that mean? Will we have to give up the house? What will we do about the farm?"

Still smiling, he caught his daughter and carefully, as if she was a fragile and precious object, which she was to him, he put her down in front of them, where she stood staring up at them both. "We can if we want, but I think we ought to rent it out. We can afford to while we live in the castle."

"So we'll have to arrange for all our things to be moved to Lydford, then," she said, with a small frown of concentration. She turned and went into the house, Simon following, and led the way through to the hall. Here, in their living room, she walked over to the trestle by the fire and sat, chin on her fist, gazing into the flamcs. Simon slowly wandered over to the wall to pick up another bench, which he carried round to the other side of the fire, so that he could sit and watch her.

Margaret was deep in thought. She was wondering about Lydford and whether she would like the new responsibilities that were going to be imposed on her husband as inevitable adjuncts to his job. Looking up, she saw his gaze fixed on the fire, a small smirk of pride on his lips, and she sighed. She knew that she would not stand in his way—he was obviously delighted with his new position, so she would be too. But it would be difficult, she thought as she looked around the hall of their house, it would be hard to leave this place that had been their home since they married, the home where their daughter had been born, where they had known so many happy times.

As if it was the first time, as if she had never really seen it before, she peered around their hall, *her* hall.

The fire was in the center, sitting on a bed of clay in the solid, packed earth of the floor. Rushes, fresh each month, were liberally spread all over. The high windows were open to the air, letting in thin streams of daylight. At night they would be covered by the tapestries in a vain attempt to exclude the cold gusts of winds that came across all the way from the coast. Tables, long and heavy, were against the walls with their benches underneath, all except for the one that they used each day, the long one that could seat the family and their four servants. That stayed out, close to the fire.

Would she really miss the house that much? she wondered. It was only a house, after all, and a castle was surely an improvement. She thought of their solar, the little family room that lay hidden behind the tapestry at the far end of the hall, curtained off so that she and her husband could sleep away from the inquisitive gaze of the servants. Like the rest of their house, it was drafty and almost always cold. Surely the castle would be, at the very least, warmer than that!

But what about the new duties? That was the real trouble, she thought. Glancing up quickly, she saw a troubled frown on Simon's face and knew that he was thinking the same. As bailiff and wife they would have to be available to any of the local people whenever they wanted help. There would be no privacy and little opportunity for rest. How well could their little family cope with that strain? And there was the town as well. Lydford was a stannary town, crucial to the tin trade. Tin meant money, and where there was money there were arguments.

She sighed. This was more difficult than probably even her husband had realized. After her father had been killed two years ago while he was out riding with the posse, she had kept hidden her awful terror—that one day her man would die while out trying to uphold the law. It was so common—too common—for many outlaws were like small armies, like regiments on the march, taking what they could from the countryside and people. Now, as he went higher up the ladder, Simon would be more obvious as a target to any trail baston with a bow and arrow. Did she want him to take on this extra responsibility?

With another sigh she knew that it was pointless to speculate. Her father had only been a farmer, a local man called to the posse. So Simon was a bailiff, so what? Maybe it meant he would soon be promoted again, taken away from the risks of laws and control. Would he be in any more danger than her father had been? She thoughtfully glanced around the room again, already beginning to estimate costs of removal and assessing what could be left behind.

Simon watched her with a degree of trepidation as he followed her gaze around the room. He could easily sense her feelings, and he knew he would do anything to stop her being depressed—even if it meant his rejecting the position at Lydford. If she felt that she could not be happy at the castle, they would have to stay here, at their home. It could wreck his prospects, but he had decided, when he chose her for his wife, that she was the most important thing in his life. And any job could be no substitute for her happiness.

So it was with absolute delight that he saw her eyes light on him again, with a calm acceptance. He knew without asking that she had chosen, that she had accepted.

The next two days went by in a whirl as Margaret began organizing the move and arranging for a wagon to help them take their belongings. Hugh was kept busy with the constant stream of visitors who arrived to offer their congratulations. The news had spread fast from the time that he and the bailiff had returned, apparently, and there seemed to be no end to the farmers and landowners who kept coming to pass on their best wishes.

It always astonished Simon how quickly news could travel in such an empty area. The whole of Devonshire only contained a few thousand souls, and yet it seemed that no sooner had he been told than the whole of the county was aware. He even received a message from Walter Stapledon, the bishop of Exeter, expressing pleasure at his new position.

But Simon soon began to fret at being kept indoors by the continuous flow of visitors. After having to travel, and now with these guests arriving at every spare minute of the day, he felt as if his life was not his own. Three times he had promised to play with his daughter, only to have to stop to see another man come to offer his congratulations, and she had made him swear that he would spend a whole uninterrupted day with her after the last cancellation. He complied, mainly to halt the inevitable flow of tears.

He had not even been able to get time to go for a ride, and at last, on the third day after the announcement had become public knowledge, the day he was to ignore all visitors and stay at home with Edith, he saddled his horse early, before she rose, and went out for a ride to loosen his taut muscles and get a brief spell of freedom before honoring his promise.

It was still early when he left, only a little after dawn, and he started out slowly, warming up his horse and himself before taking any serious exercise. They rode quietly up the hill behind his house, following the old tracks between the fields in the early morning chill. The night had brought more rain and he had to splash through puddles and small streams as he made his way along the narrow tracks that bordered the fields and woods. At the top of the hill he turned west and followed the ridge for a couple of miles until at last he was up on the tall spine of land that pointed toward the southern moors, a straight and easy canter. He paused a minute in anticipation, he and his horse standing still, with a slight glow lighting his face from their ride so far. Then, with a grin like a naughty boy, he peered round behind him to see that no one was watching, and whipped his horse into a gallop.

They raced down the lane, the heavy horse pounding through the muddy water that lay all around, and splashing it liberally over both of them, both revelling in the sudden burst of energy and enjoying the sensation of rushing furiously, as quickly as possible over the rough track, feeling the cold wind tugging at their hair and snatching at Simon's cloak as they went. They charged down, hammering over the lane like a knight and his mount rushing into battle, with no thought for anything but the pleasure of the race.

At the far end of the road they slowed, Simon reining in gently to slow the great horse and stop the animal from over-tiring himself, and gradually eased into a comfortable walk. By the time they got to Copplestone, a small village that lay hugging the edge of the moor and forest land of Dartmoor, the only evidence of their gallop was the broad grin of sheer pleasure on the bailiff's face. They sedately clattered into the hamlet. It was an ancient vill lying some four miles out to the west of Crediton, at the fork in the road to Oakhampton where one arm led to the north and up to Barnstaple. But there were also several small lanes leading south, and he turned into one and wandered aimlessly for a few miles, his eyes fixed on the moors ahead.

The local superstitions had always implied that the moors were unfriendly to people, and from here, looking up at them, he could understand why men should feel that—they seemed to be watching him as he rode. Certainly they were impressive, looming like great beasts on the horizon ahead, but they were without the aura of focused viciousness that he could sense in wolves and other wild animals. There was a malevolence there, he could sense that, but it was the uncaring, unfeeling cruelty of a vast being that feared nothing for smaller creatures. It seemed to him as he rode that the moors noted him as a man might an ant, and, like a man, they seemed to know they could crush him without noticing.

Shuddering at the thought, he quickly turned off, away from the moors and to the east. He would go as far as Tedburn St. Mary, then north and back home.

Now, feeling more relaxed after burning off some of his frustration, and comfortable as he sat on his horse, he let his mind wander. At first his thoughts were only of the coming move and the change in his circumstances that it would bring, but then, as he swayed along from side to side on the back of his horse, he started to think about the people he had met on the road.

He was interested in Sir Baldwin. The knight seemed so worldly, so experienced, that he was fascinating to a man like Simon who had never been more than a few days' travel from Crediton. Simon longed to get him to talk about his travels, to discover where he had been, what he had seen, what battles he had fought in—because he obviously had fought in several. He had the arrogance and pride of a warrior; even though it seemed to be kept on a close rein and almost hidden, Simon had felt it. But there was a kindliness and humility about the knight as well that seemed oddly out of place in the bailiff's experience. Knights were rarely humble or pious—and if they were it was usually a calculating godliness. It had more to do with ensuring salvation in the face of previous offenses committed against God than with any desire to follow Christ's teachings.

At Tedburn St. Mary he turned off to take the road back to Crediton, and a sudden similarity between this road and the one near Furnshill made his thoughts move to the party of monks. He was still thinking about the frightened abbot when he arrived back at his house.

He was surprised to see a horse tethered at his door when he arrived. His eyebrows rose in vague interest as he took his horse into the stable before going to see who it could be—no doubt it was only another visitor passing on his good wishes—and he had just removed the saddle and taken off the blanket underneath when Hugh came in and took over.

"Man here to see you."

"Oh." Simon glanced over his shoulder toward the house and shrugged disinterestedly. "Someone else asking how I am and when I go to Lydford?"

"No, it's a man from Blackway. Someone's died over there last night."

Simon stared at him uncomprehendingly for a moment, then balled the blanket and threw it at him as he ran for the house.

Inside, a man leapt up as soon as he entered the hall. He had been sitting on a bench with his back to the door, obviously warming himself by the fire, and he knocked over a pot of ale when the bailiff strode in, letting out an audible groan in mortification—though whether at seeming clumsy or at the loss of the beer, Simon could not be sure.

His visitor was a slender, almost effeminate youth with pale and thin features under a shock of thick, mousey-colored hair. The face was almost hatchet-sharp, but without any hint of deviousness or weasel cunning—it was simply the kind of face created for a slim man who would never be a soldier; this was one who would not go away to fight, this man would spend his life in the rural safety of the priest's house, probably never going more than fifteen miles from the town in his whole life. His face seemed to redden under the fixed gaze of the bailiff, not from fear but from his embarrassment at knocking the pot over, almost as if he expected to be shouted at, and Simon grinned at him to calm his obviously frayed nerves. When he smiled back, Simon was sure he recognized him—there was something about his thin, colorless mouth as it stretched tight across his face. Where had he seen that face before? Of course! He worked for Peter Clifford, the priest at Crediton. This was one of his stablemen, wasn't it? Simon walked to the bench and indicated that the young man should be seated before sitting himself and considering the man again.

"It is Hubert, isn't it?"

"Yes, bailiff, I'm Hubert. I work for Peter Clifford and he sent me to fetch you as soon as he heard about it—"

"What is it, then? Tell me your message."

"Oh, sir, it's horrible! A man came to us in the early morning—Black, the hunter—he lives over that way himself, and it seems there was a fire there last night, well into the early hours, over at Harold Brewer's house. His place is out on the edge of Blackway, down south of Crediton. Black said that the men tried to put out the fire, but they couldn't even get close for some time because it was too hot."

"Well? Why should I be told?"

"Because Brewer—the man that lives there—his body was seen inside."

3

I t was well past noon when he arrived at the small village of Blackway, some seven miles to the south and west of Crediton. There had seemed little need to hurry on the way, there were bound to be many people all around—not just the priest but all the villagers and, no doubt, quite a few others. Whenever there was a disaster, Simon was amazed by the speed demonstrated by the people who came to gawp and stare at another man's personal misfortune, whether it was caused by an accident or by the maliciousness of a neighbor.

The signs were obvious from a long way distant. As he came up to the old Weatherby Cross, where the road from Crediton was cut by the Moretonhampstead track that led down to Exeter, it became clear he was not the first person to pass there that day. At the best of times the track was rutted and worn, being a popular route for travellers heading down to the ports on the coast. Now, in the early afternoon, it was even worse than normal.

Usually the trodden dirt, with the deep ruts caused by the wheels of the carts, was solid enough, but now, after so many months of rain, it was a morass. The mud clutched at his horse's hoofs, sucking and belching as the animal pulled his legs free of the red-brown earth, trying to carry on. Only the passage of a large number of people could have so quickly destroyed the fragile surface. Cursing under his breath, Simon steered his horse over to the verge, where the grass promised solidity and an opportunity to continue less encumbered. In this way, stepping carefully, they made their slow and painful progress to the hamlet.

Blackway was a tiny village that lay straddling the road south as if it had fallen there, dropped like a disregarded plaything by one of the ancient race of giants that was supposed to have inhabited the area before man arrived. It was a cluster of houses lying on either side of the road, not modern longhouses like Simon's with their timber reinforcement, but old cob, or clunch, hovels. The bailiff could remember the place distinctly—he had been there only recently while on his way to the coast to visit a merchant on his lord's business—and he tried, as he rode, to recall the house of Harold Brewer.

The village had some seven or eight properties, one inn and a tiny church, which relied on a chaplain appointed by Peter Clifford, who was nominally the rector. As Simon turned his thoughts back to the last time he had ridden through, he could clearly bring to mind the general layout. The hunter, John Black, had the first cottage on the right, a simple house with one large room like all the others, except that it was smaller than most. Black lived as a hunter, catching and killing his own food and receiving pay for destroying the wolves and other pests in the area. He was known for his ability to track animals for miles over the barren waste of the moors, and when the de Courtenays were in the area they would often call upon his services to help them find their quarry. With this life style he had little or no need for a large house, just a place big enough for his wife and their two children.

Beyond his house was the inn, the first of the large houses. Simon did not know who lived there, but he believed that it had been owned by Brewer in the past. Then there were the main houses of the village, with Brewer's place out at the southernmost edge, only one house lying farther, as he recalled. All of the houses surrounded the small area of common land, the road curving sharply round it like a meandering river—possibly because it followed the stream, the Blackwater, that gurgled down on its way to Dartmoor.

At the northernmost tip of the vill, where Black's house stood, the ground was thickly wooded. To the south the land opened to give views all the way to Dartmoor, and in the hamlet itself there was a cheerful balance between trees and open land. Most of the houses were to the west of the stream and the strips of fields lay to the east; an ancient clapper bridge led from one side to the other and also crossed the new sewer that led into the stream. It gave the vill a pleasant, rural aspect as Simon rode in from the north, although he was struck by the sight of the great trees that crowded in from the forest behind the houses. It appeared to him that they were almost threatening in the way that they towered over the human habitation.

From a half mile away Simon could see the tall pillar of smoke that hung over the surrounding landscape, and he also became aware of the smell of burning, the stench increasing as he came closer to the village.

It seemed outrageous that such a quiet and peaceful

little hamlet should have been so violated by fire, but it was, as Simon knew only too well, a very common occurrence. The old houses did not have chimneys to direct smoke and sparks away from the thatch of the roofs, they relied on the height of the roof itself as protection. If they all had chimneys the number of cottage fires would reduce dramatically, because the sparks would alight on the external and damp thatch. As it was, the glittering motes that rose from the flames were carried up into the eaves, where they often lodged. Every once in a while they would make the dry interior thatch catch fire. And, when that happened, all the people inside could do was get out quickly and hope that water thrown at the roof would save the main part of the house.

Riding up through the center of the village, Simon could see that it had been too late for this place at least. To arrive at the house he had to ride past the inn, then follow the road round to the left as it lazily swung down toward the moors. As he followed the road through the village and turned to face south, the house became visible and he paused, motionless, as he took in the sight that met his shocked gaze.

The old building was almost completely destroyed. The roof was gone; presumably it had fallen in when the flames got too hot, or so he supposed. The wall at the side was still visible, but the far end of the house, the end farthest from the road, had collapsed, and taken down a large section of the side wall with it. Even Simon, who knew little about building, could see that the damage was irreparable.

He kicked his horse into a slow amble and continued up to the house. All around lay a covering of soot, lying surprisingly thickly underfoot. In Simon's experience even the hottest fires produced far less than this, and he found himself pensively considering the ground as he rode forward, wondering what could have produced so heavy a layer, until he heard his voice called. Looking up, he saw his old friend Peter Clifford standing with a small group, not far from what had been the main door.

Peter was standing and talking with some of the local men, one of whom Simon recognized immediately as the hunter, Black. The others he had not met before, he thought, and assumed they must be locals to the hamlet. Judging by the number of men walking all over the area, this made them fairly unique: the tiny hamlet could not have contained even half of the people gawping and staring at the wrecked building.

To Simon's disgust, there was almost a fair-time atmosphere in the little village, as if the fire had been staged as an inaugural celebration, a cheery blaze to begin festivities. There were people of all sorts standing and staring at the destroyed house, fascinated by the sight of the remaining walls standing up like the fangs of a massive beast. He could see a family he knew from Crediton, a merchant and his wife with their young son, pointing and talking while their son giggled and played, as if this was only another place designed for him to enjoy himself and not the scene of a recent death. Snorting in disgust, Simon dismounted and strode over to the priest.

"Afternoon, Peter. What happened, then?"

The rector of Crediton church was a slim and ascetic man in his late forties. He was dressed informally in a light tunic that came down to his knees, with warm woollen leggings underneath. His dark eyes glittered with intelligence in his pale face, his skin soft and light from the hours spent indoors reading and writing. The hair that Simon remembered being a light red was a faded straw color now and the face was worn, though not by troubles—the lines that creased it were caused not by pain and fear but by too much laughter and enjoyment of life. The lines at the sides of his eyes, deep cracks of crow's feet, all came from joy. Now they wrinkled into furrows in his pleasure at seeing his friend again.

"Simon!" He held out his hand. "It's good to see you. Come, you know why you were asked here, I hope?"

The bailiff nodded. "I believe there was a man inside there when it went up?"

"Yes,"—this was John Black, the hunter—"I saw the fire when I came back from my work last night. The place was well in flames already then."

He stood firmly, a small and compact man, confident and self-assured. The wiry frame of his body looked as if it could chase an animal from one end of the kingdom to the other on foot, and the litheness of his movements reminded Simon of a wolf, as if in hunting the wild creatures a little of their ways had rubbed off and been absorbed by him. His face was square, flat and stolid, as uncompromising as a slab of granite, and his eyes gleamed darkly. Above thick eyebrows that formed a continuous line across his brow his hair was a deep black, almost raven, and hung in lank wings around his serious face.

"Why did you think Brewer was inside?" Simon asked.

"I didn't at first. I thought he could be somewhere else. But when we started to try to put the fire out, when we could see inside, we saw the body. It's still on his bed."

Involuntarily, Simon glanced over at the building, as if almost expecting to see a figure rise from it. He frowned at his superstitious fancy and concentrated again on the evidence of the hunter.

"As soon as I saw that, I told the others to carry on with putting out the flames, and I went straight over to get the rector."

Simon nodded absently and looked at the priest. "Yes, John arrived just after dawn, and when I had heard his tale I sent Hubert to fetch you. I came straight here to see if I could help. By the time we arrived the flames were out. We were waiting for the building to cool before going inside to get the poor man's body out."

"How long before we can go in, do you think?" said Simon, peering back at the wreckage.

Black turned to follow his gaze. "I reckon it'll be a little longer. One man's dead—there's no need to risk any more lives to get his corpse. We might as well leave it until we're sure it's safe."

Nodding again, Simon started walking toward the house to have a closer look. The soot and ashes under his feet seemed soft and yielding, not hard and crisp like the ashes in his fire at home. What could have produced such snowy-soft residue? There were several people standing and gawping nearer the walls, and Simon had to push some out of his way, glaring at them when they murmured angrily. Ignoring their complaints, he walked up to the front door and peered inside.

The door was a charred and broken mess, hanging haphazardly from its bottom hinge. Inside, the rubble was still very hot; he could feel the glowing embers warming his face, as hot as summer sunshine. At first it was difficult to make out anything much, the inside seemed to be a mass of gray or black, with different shades all around, but with nothing to differentiate one pile from another. The timbers of the roof must have collapsed brutally, he thought. If someone was underneath, there was no chance of surviving that huge weight when it fell in. He could see the massive beam lying where it had fallen across the center of the floor, one end still supported by the wall, the other on the ground. Suddenly, before he could avoid it, a sudden gust of wind blew air from the room into his face. Caught unawares, unprepared, so that it hardly even occurred to him to try to evade it, he inhaled the stench.

The wind was filthy, carrying the noisome odor of death almost as a solid, physical mass but that was not all. It was not just the nasal reminder of the body inside that caught at the throat and made the eyes water, it was the burned feces, the remains of the excreta of the livestock that had lived in the house with Brewer, the ordure of decades, that, now subjected to the fire, seemed to grasp at the lungs with invisible, poisoned tentacles of bitter virulence. Gagging, he turned and coughed, soon wretching miserably.

He could take no more and, turning away, he stumbled, choking, back to where the others waited.

"Foul, isn't it?" said Black conversationally, grinning, as if passing comment on the weather.

Still coughing, Simon gave him a baleful glare before hawking and spitting, trying to clear his throat of the viscous tang. It was while he was spitting with venom that Baldwin Furnshill arrived.

He appeared on a huge gray horse, Edgar as usual just behind, and dressed in a white tunic with a small emblem on his breast, which even at this distance Simon could recognize as the de Courtenay badge. The knight had soft leather boots on his feet and seemed to have left his armor and weapons off for the day, although he still wore his misericord, his long, narrow-bladed knife named for its task in battle; the "mercy" was the blade used to finish off the wounded on the battlefield.

Seeing the small knot of men, Baldwin kicked his horse and ambled over to them, his eyebrows raised a little as he saw a new coughing fit taking over the bailiff. The other men, he could see, were grim-faced and dour. Smiling at the priest and hunter, he nodded curtly, "Hallo, friends," then turned a perplexed grin to the bailiff.

"Have you come to gawp as well, Baldwin?" said Simon, squinting up at the knight bitterly. Was everyone from all around going to come and stare? It seemed depressing that even his new friend was exhibiting ghoulish tendencies.

"No, Simon. We were out riding and wanted to make sure that the people here did not need help. This *is* my manor's land." His eyes glittered darkly, as though he was ready to take offense at Simon's attitude, but then, as he peered at the scene and saw the people standing, pointing and chattering, he appeared to understand Simon's feelings and gave a small dry smile. "I told you I wanted to take an interest in my villeins, didn't I? How are the people that lived there?"

"Only the one man, thank God! But as far as we know he's still inside. It's too hot to fetch him out yet," said Peter. "A sad business, eh? Surely there's enough misery for the poor without being burned to death in their beds?"

"He wasn't that poor," said Black, a faintly ironic smile on his face, as Baldwin sprang lightly from his horse and threw his reins to Edgar.

"No?" Peter seemed surprised, a slight frown on his face as he peered at the hunter. "He always seemed to be, or at least he always said he was."

"Ah, well, yes. He was always hard up when someone wanted money or alms, or at least he always said so. People here have wondered how he always seemed to be able to buy ale, how he could afford a full team of oxen, how he managed to buy his way out of his duties as a villein when he wanted."

"What do you mean?" said Simon. "Are you saying he was a thief or something?"

The hunter gave a short laugh. "Oh, no. No, I don't think so. No, I think that the old tale's true. I think he made a lot of money when he fought in the wars five and twenty years ago and he's been able to live off it since then. Story goes that he had a metal box full of gold under the floor in there," he said, jerking a finger at the wrecked house. "You'll find it hard to keep people away until the whole of the floor's been dug up. And even then, if nothing's found, people'll start to dig up all his land."

Baldwin frowned at him. "We'll have none of that here if I can help it. Simon, would you like me to have a man or two placed here to guard it until we can find out whether there is any money here? We have to try to ensure that it's saved for this man's relatives. Do we know whether he had any relatives? I understand he was alone in the house as far as we can tell?" He looked at Peter, but the priest merely smiled and shrugged, gazing at the hunter. It seemed clear to the knight that he knew nothing about the dead man's private life.

"He was alone when *I* got here," Black said, then drew the corners of his mouth down and stuck out his lower lip with the effort of memory. Frowning at his shoes, he said, "I do seem to remember someone saying as he had a son in Exeter. I can see if anyone else's heard anything about a boy."

"Yes, do that, Black," said Simon.

The knight seemed to be staring at the hunter speculatively. "Were you the first man to see the fire?"

"Yes, sir." The hunter seemed ready to show the knight the proper level of respect, treating him as a superior where he had obviously looked upon the bailiff and the priest as equals—perhaps, Simon could not help thinking, because as a hunter he had his own rules and arcane skills. But a knight was different. A knight was no holder of secrets, no minister of hidden knowledge. A knight was the most secular creature known: what he wanted he would take. And, if asked by what authority he presumed to remove whatever he wanted, any knight, any member of the older Norman families, would draw his sword and say, "This is my right! With this sword my sires took this land. With this sword I shall take what I want. With this sword I shall keep what I desire." Simon sighed and concentrated on the conversation.

Baldwin was half-smiling at the hunter now, a slight puckering of his forehead showing that he was thinking about, but not doubting the truth of, Black's tale as he related the events of the night before. As the hunter drew near to the end of his story, Baldwin seemed to withdraw into himself. He wrapped one arm around his chest, rested his chin and mouth in the palm of his other hand and watched the hunter with a raised eyebrow, as if dubious of some part of the story. Black stumbled in his account, obviously feeling the doubt emanating from the tall, dark knight, and seemed to finish on a defensive note, almost as if daring the knight to call him a liar.

When he had finally ground to a halt, the small group stood silent for a moment, as if aware that a silent challenge had been issued, although none of them was sure who had offered it or why. It was Baldwin who broke the quiet, speaking slowly and ruminatively.

"Very well. So the fire was first seen by you at some time after midnight, would you say?"

"Yes," said the hunter slowly, obviously thinking. "Yes, I think it must have been. I'd been setting traps, down over at the edge of the moors, and I'd put out twenty. I hadn't left until dark, so it must have been after midnight before I came back."

The knight considered, staring at the ground by his feet. "So you came back . . . which direction would you have come back from?"

Pointing up the road, away from the village, Black said, "There. From the moors, like I said."

"So who did you go to first of all? To raise the alarm, I mean. Who did you go to first?"

Black jerked his chin in the same direction, toward the moors. "Roger Ulton. I came round the lane and saw the fire up here—well, there seemed no point coming all the way down to the village and then getting someone to fetch him later. His house was nearest, so I went back to it and knocked him up."

"And what then?" The calm eyes were fixed firmly on the hunter's face.

"Then? I came into the village, of course. I banged on the doors and woke up all the men, got them to help me put the fire out."

The bailiff nodded. The men would have hurried to help, keen to smother the flames before the winds could carry the sparks over to their own houses and put their properties at risk. Baldwin seemed to agree as well, turning and looking at the building that lay, still smoking, so near, with his arms crossed over his chest. As if he had been dismissed, Black looked from one to the other before slowly strolling off, walking over to chat with a little knot of villagers.

Baldwin sighed and kicked at a stone near his foot. "Sad, isn't it. A man at home and very probably asleep. To die like that! God! I hope he didn't suffer too much." He sighed, feeling strangely sorry at the death of this man, someone he had never met. Shrugging, he thought it must be because it was such an apparently senseless death. There was no honor or glory to be gained from such an end, and it was a mean and horrible finish. Thinking back, he considered the other black burned corpses he had seen and sighed again, recollecting the twisted and tortured figures, the way that they always seemed to have been fighting death, struggling to live. It was not the way he wanted to die.

"Yes, well, I'm sure he'll be happy where he's gone now, anyway," said Simon reverently. "May his soul rest in peace."

He was surprised to see a cynical twitch to the knight's eyebrow as he shot a quick glance at the bailiff, as if he wanted to express doubt, and the realization shocked the bailiff. This might be a secular man, a warrior, but that was no excuse for blasphemy! Staring back at the knight, he was astonished to see a grimace of self-deprecating embarrassment, as though he knew that his thoughts had been picked up by Simon and wanted to apologize. He seemed to give a small shrug, with a grin, as if to say, "Sorry, but I am a knight—what do you expect?"

Peter Clifford did not seem to have noticed their silent communication. "So, then, Baldwin, I suppose you'll want to take the best of the man's beasts?"

"Eh?" He turned, evidently confused.

"The beast. Your heriot. You own this land; he was your villein. You have the choice of his best beast, just as I have the choice of the next best for the mortuary. Why? Didn't you know about the death taxes?"

The knight stood, staring at the priest with absolute amazement on his face. "His cattle survived?" he said at last.

"Yes, of course they did. They're all over at the common now—the villagers rounded them up once they had seen to the fire."

Turning back to the burned remains, Baldwin said, "I will be interested to have a look around the house when it has cooled enough," and without saying more he walked away to talk to his servant.

Simon watched him go, and as he gazed after the knight he wondered what Baldwin meant by that comment. Then, drawing his eyes away, he could not help a sudden shudder, as if of quick, chill fear, and his face was troubled as he turned back to the smoking ruins. Why did he have the feeling that the knight was suspicious about this apparent accident?

4

I t was another two hours before they felt happy about entering the blackened and still warm shell. Black led the way, a small team of local men following, all with cloths tied round their mouths against the dust, and Simon, the priest and the knight waiting by the doorway, where they could watch the men inside.

The body was easy to find. It had not been hit by the heavy oaken beam that had fallen from the roof, but still lay on the remains of the palliasse that had been the man's bed, over near the far wall. At first Simon could see little—the haze from the heat distorted the view, small gray clouds of smoke rose here and there from the embers, and the beam itself with its accretions of burned waste obstructed the scene with its solid mass, seemingly unaffected by the flames that had destroyed the house around it. Amongst all this mess and desolation, Black's small group walked with confidence, along the length of the beam, to duck underneath where its end was still supported by the wall, and walk back along it until opposite the door where the simple mattress lay.

Simon could hear the muttering as they came close

to it, a curse of disgust, a call for assistance. He could not help thinking how foolish this all seemed. The walls over to his right had collapsed, were now simply a pile of rubble. The men had no need to enter by this door, by this old gap in the wall that had been constructed decades before. Why did they go in here? Was it a politeness? Was it a sign of respect for the corpse that they should only use the door that his guests would have, as if in so doing they were receiving his approval? Or was it simply force of habit that they should go in where they knew there to be an entrance, as if their minds could not quite accept the fact that the whole house had been changed?

Beside him Baldwin stood, chewing on his moustache and frowning. When he threw him a glance, Simon was surprised to see that the knight's eyes were not, like his own and Clifford's, following the men inside, but were staring fixedly at the massive doorway at the other end of the house, the doorway for the oxen.

He seemed perplexed by something, Simon thought. Noticing his look, Baldwin grinned shamefacedly. "I always seem to look for a difficulty. It must be part of my nature," he said, and turned away to watch the party inside. But Simon could not help noticing that every now and again his eyes would drift back to that large doorway, as if dragged unwillingly.

The men seemed to take an age to fetch the body out. They rolled it onto an old blanket, then with one man at each corner they hefted it and began to weave their circuitous way back to the entrance. They had to try to keep the blanket taut in order that the cloth did not touch the hot embers all around, and the force necessary was evidently great, making the men bend away from their load and each other as they struggled over the rubble and mess, stumbling and tripping as they went. They had difficulties when they had to bend under the beam, at last reaching some mutual arrangement whereby one man went through—was it Black?—then another, each man at his corner crouching individually and making his way under before standing and waiting for his companions. Then, at last, they were making their way back to the doorway, and the others stood back to give them room as they made their way out, dropping the blanket with its unwholesome contents with irreverent haste as they grasped at the cloths covering their mouths, tearing them off so that they could breathe the sweet air again, away from the stench and dust inside. The body rolled from the covering to lie on its back a foot or two from the waiting men.

"It's him," said Black before stumbling away coughing.

At the sight of the body, Simon could not help wincing in disgust and taking a short step back. Then, as he became aware of Clifford's muttered prayers, he felt ashamed and peered closer.

The blackened and ruined body was clearly that of a well-proportioned man, broad in the shoulder and fairly tall. His clothes had burned away, or so it seemed, and the body was rigid and fixed, like clay that has been in the furnace. But the bailiff recoiled and he had to turn away at the sight of the face, sucking in deep breaths in an attempt to keep his bile at bay.

Baldwin grinned as he saw Simon spin away. It was natural at the sight of victims of the flames, he knew, but this was not the first time the knight had seen bodies ruined and burned, and he stared down, noting the position of the limbs with an impersonal detachment.

But when he studied the face his interest suddenly quickened. Where he would have expected to see agonized pain in the twisted features, there seemed to be none.

Puzzled, he stared at the body for a moment, then looked up toward the house. Then, like a hound on a scent, tense and eager, he strode up to the door, leaving Clifford and Simon gazing after him in their surprise.

Marching quickly, the knight strode through the door and, holding a sleeve to his nose and mouth, moved to the middle of the ruined house, peering through slitted eyes at the beam and the rubble all around. Something was wrong, he felt sure. Other bodies he had seen after a fire had shown signs of the fight for life, of the desperate attempt for survival—Brewer's did not.

He stood and glowered at the door for the livestock, where the wood, at that end of the building almost untouched by the flames, still showed the scars from the horns and hoofs of the terrified oxen. Then he kicked at the ground a few times and crouched, apparently staring at some of the mess on the floor, before rising and leaving the room once more, coughing.

As the knight left the group, his departure made Simon turn and watch, and this sign that someone else at least was relatively unaffected made him determined to shoulder his responsibility with more dignity than he had so far exhibited. Squaring his shoulders, he forced his eyes down again. To his surprise, now, after the initial shock, he found himself less horrified, and he could look at the body with a degree of equanimity. At least, he felt, the man had no apparent signs of pain. His arms, he could see, were restfully at his side, not clawed to scrabble a way to safety, the legs were straight rather than contorted in an effort to crawl away. It looked as if the man had passed away quietly in his sleep. Simon could sense a sadness, a fleeting empathy for the lonely end of this man, but little more. Then it struck him—why had the man not recognized his danger, awoken and tried to escape? Surely he could not have slept through it? His brow wrinkled at the thought.

The huddled blackened shape seemed to have no fears for Baldwin either. He returned and stood, arms on hips, glaring at the body as if daring it to argue with him. Interested, Black wandered over to the group and glanced at the body, then at the men encircling it. He saw Baldwin catch Simon's eye.

"Looks very relaxed, doesn't he," said the knight. It was not a question, it was a flat, dry statement, requiring no response, and Black saw Simon gazing back and nodding pensively.

Clifford looked from one to the other with a frown of mild impatience. "What do you mean? Of course he was relaxed. He died in his sleep, I suppose. The smoke got to him while he slept."

Baldwin kept his eyes on him as he said, "Black?"

The hunter grunted. He too was frowning, wondering what the knight was driving at.

"Black," Baldwin continued, "how many of this man's oxen died with him?"

"None, sir. All eight got out."

"So what?" said Clifford, gazing from the knight to the bailiff. "So what if they did? I don't . . ."

"What about other animals?"

"No, they all got out."

"If they got out, they must have been scared by the flames," said Baldwin deliberately. "You must have heard the noise that scared oxen make. You wouldn't be able to sleep through it, would you?"

Simon ventured, "Well, maybe he was overcome by the fumes, maybe he—"

"Oh, come now!" the knight's teeth showed briefly in a white grin. "The beasts would have been terrified from the first sign of flames. They would not have slept until the house was almost consumed, they would have woken as soon as the fire began. If they did, the man would have been woken by them—he was sleeping with them after all."

The priest, frowning, stood shaking his head. "I still don't quite . . ."

"It's obvious—or it is to me, anyway," said Baldwin, suddenly serious. "I think he was dead before the fire was started. I think he was killed and the fire started to cover the murder." Black could see that it was Simon who seemed to take this announcement most calmly. While the others gaped, the bailiff considered, looking up at the knight, peering at the building, then scratching his head and frowning at the ground.

"So what do you suggest we should do then, Sir Baldwin?" asked Clifford, consternation raising the pitch of his voice.

Baldwin shot a glance at Simon. "That's up to the bailiff, isn't it?"

"But I don't see how we can show he was already dead!" said Simon irritably. "Not without someone having seen him when . . ." His voice trailed off. Could someone have seen something? God! He had only just been given his job—and now this knight already thought he had found a murder! Forcing his thoughts back to the problem in hand, he said musingly, "We don't even know that he *has* been murdered. Couldn't it have been an accident?"

"I don't think so," said Baldwin pensively. "As soon as the fire started the oxen would have panicked, I think that is clear. If he had been asleep that noise would have woken him quickly enough, so he would not have been found in his bed. We would have found him near an entrance, or at least on his way to one. I cannot see any reason why he would have gone back to his bed after realizing that there was a fire—that, surely, is inconceivable. So he cannot have been woken by his oxen. And if he wasn't, he must have been dead already. I refuse to believe that any man could be so heavy a sleeper that eight oxen stampeding nearby would not stir him."

"Even so, sir, we cannot simply assume this. How could we be sure?" said Clifford softly.

"There is one other thing that makes me suspicious," said the knight. "When you go to your bed, what do you do to the fire?"

Simon shrugged. "Well, bank it up. Make sure there's enough wood to keep it going quietly over the night."

"Yes. You put fresh logs on it to keep it going overnight. Brewer's fire seemed too low. It looked as if it had not been touched since the morning. That seems to show that he had not set it up for the night, but it also means that it would be unlikely that any sparks would have reached the ceiling. The fire was too low. I am certain that he was killed. The question is, who did it?"

They all went to the inn and sat on the benches at the front while they waited for food to arrive. From here they could see in both directions along the road, south and west to the burned-out shell of Brewer's house, and north and east to Black's. In front of them the road formed a red and muddy boundary to the small strips of the fields beyond, where the families of the hamlet grew their crops on those days when they had no responsibility to the fields owned by the manor.

The sun was past its zenith, sweeping slowly across a sky that was, for once, almost miraculously free from clouds. Its brightness lit up the scenery with a soft splendor. In front of them at the other side of the road was the sewer, but beyond it was the stream with the flat stone slabs of the clapper bridge crossing both, and over the ridge were the strips.

They seemed almost to have been created to assist the inn by giving it a pleasant aspect. It was as if they were radiating out with the inn building at their center, and their colors—soft red from the earth, white-yellow from the older crops, green from the grass—seemed to emphasize the rural nature of the scene. Beyond, the trees took over again. The great oaks and beeches, elms and sycamores dominated the whole area, lurking with indifferent case at the edge of the habitation. How long, Simon wondered, how long before these trees are removed and the strips expand farther into the forest? How long before new assarts are developed to push the trees back so that these poor people can have more lands for fields, so that they can have more food and not be so dependent on so little? But, looking at the ring of trunks, he wondered whether they could ever be pushed farther back. They seemed too substantial, too massive for puny humans to destroy.

Against his will, Black had agreed to join them, and he sat now in between Simon and the priest, while Baldwin had a stool, sitting in front of them. Edgar stood a short distance away as usual, his eyes flitting over the men with his master.

"It's really very simple," Baldwin was saying. "We simply speak to the people who were here yesterday and try to see who might have had a reason to kill this . . . this Brewer."

"But there are loads of people here, sir," Simon protested. "You don't mean to speak to them all, do you?"

"Yes." His voice was uncompromising. "We must. If I'm right, a man has been killed. The very least we owe him is to find out why he was killed. Black?" The hunter started at being addressed. "Black. Do you have any idea why someone should kill this man? Is there anyone in the village who hated him enough to kill him?"

"Not that I know of. No, this has always been a quiet hamlet. It seems unbelievable that Brewer should have been murdered."

Baldwin took a long swallow of his beer and carefully set his pot down on the ground beside him before leaning forward, his hands clasped and dangling between his parted legs, his eyes fixed on Black. "Tell me about the other people in the village. How many families are there?"

"Oh, seven. Seven families in seven houses. Of course, there are some adult sons in a couple of them. Thomas has two sons old enough to have their own places now, so has Ulric."

"I see. Well, tell me about this man Brewer. What was he like?"

Black shot a glance at the priest, who murmured gently, "Don't worry, my son. Just tell the truth."

"He was not liked."

"Why?" asked the knight.

"Well, he had several acres. He had eight oxen. That made the other farmers jealous. And there was always the rumor that he had more money in his chest, hidden. It seemed unfair. Everyone here works hard for their living, working their strips, borrowing whatever they need from their neighbors and working on the manor's lands when it's time, but Brewer, he seemed to be able to survive on his own. He paid the bailiff so he never had to work on the lord's land. And he kept buying more land. He kept taking more from the forest. The lord—that is your brother, Sir Baldwin—let him keep taking over new assarts. He could afford to take on the land in the woods and pay for men to go and clear it, so all the time his money was increasing. All the time he was getting more land and increasing his crops. It made people jealous." As if he suddenly realized how long a speech he had made, he subsided, glaring at his boots.

He was rescued by the innkeeper arriving with their food. On a heavy wooden tray were earthenware bowls, one for each of them. In the bottom of the bowls was a thick slab of bread, and a heavy stew had been ladled over the top.

After a few minutes, Baldwin frowned at Black again as a thought hit him. "What about the man's son? You mentioned a boy in Exeter."

The hunter sniffed, scooping another spoonful of stew into his mouth with every sign of pleasure. Wiping his mouth on the back of his hand, he belched. "My wife might know something about him. She's lived here all her life."

After their meal, Peter announced that he would have to leave them. He had his church work to attend to, he said, although Simon did wonder whether this was mainly for show and the priest was thinking that the affair was simply a wild-goose chase.

Simon was not sure how to treat the knight's allegation. It seemed too unlikely, somehow, that one of the peaceable villeins from Blackway could have committed murder. It was far more likely that, as they had first thought, the man had died in his sleep. But could Sir Baldwin be right? Could the man have been killed first and then dropped onto his palliasse, so that any others coming later would assume that he had been killed by the thick smoke of his homely pyre? It was possible, he had to agree, but was it likely? Somehow it did not seem so. But the knight was full of nervous energy at the mere thought.

He had bolted down his food, eager once more to be off, and when his companions completed their meals at a more relaxed pace, possibly, although unintentionally, indicating their doubts about his theory, he seemed almost to panic, so intense was his desire to get on with what he termed "our investigation." Simon was amazed by the difference in the man. When they had first met, so few days ago, at Bickleigh, he had seemed reserved and aloof, tolerant it was true, but aware of his station and noble birth. Now he seemed keen and eager to meet with all the villeins and cottars, the most humble of the serfs of the hamlet, purely to satisfy his curiosity about the death of a man he had never even met. And even the death itself seemed unremarkable to all save him. Was that it? Simon wondered. Was it simply that having proposed what seemed at first sight to be a preposterous concept he now wanted to try to justify it to the others? Or did he need to justify it to himself?

Baldwin Furnshill knew that he did not. He had

been ill for months, first with a physical ailment, and, more recently, with a brain fever of alarming proportions, but he knew that neither had had any effect on his thinking about the death of the old man in his house. Of course he was aware of the skepticism of the others—he would have been surprised if they had not displayed any, for it did seem very strange that there should have been such a crime in so quiet a part of the land. He could think of many places where death and murder would have been less surprising— London, Bristol, Oxford, and hundreds of towns and villages in between—but here?

And why an old, harmless man who was close to the end of his life anyway? What was the point?

He was still mulling it over when they came to Black's house at the northernmost edge of the village, over at the west of the road. Although smaller than the other houses in Blackway, it was one of the newest. It was a more solid-looking place, all of cob, but with a strong timber frame that showed around the door and the windows. Baldwin raised a half-amused, half-suspicious eyebrow at the sight of the wood, wondering whether to make a comment, but decided against it. He looked at Black with renewed interest, though. If this hunter was prepared to break the forest laws and steal the king's wood, he could be a useful man to know for the future. After all, taking the wood could result in a noose at one of the verderer's courts. Then another thought struck him. If this man was unafraid of the king's displeasure, would he care about killing a neighbor? Putting the idea to one side, he bowed to the hunter's wife as she came to the door.

Black stood between her and the others, in an obviously defensive posture, as if trying to keep the world from her—and Baldwin could see why. Jane Black was a strong and pleasant-looking fair woman in her early twenties. She wore a simple woollen shift that reached almost to the floor, with long sleeves and a carefully embroidered pattern on its front. From the noise indoors, she clearly had already given her husband a pair of young sons, but her face and her figure did not show it. She was a little under Black's height, a healthy woman, unmarked as yet by hard work. It was obvious that the hunter kept the best of his meat for his family, for there was a pleasant roundness to her youthful body. Her face was a little too narrow for Baldwin, her mouth perhaps too thin, and her breasts could have been larger for his taste, but there was no denying that she was extremely attractive.

But even as he took in her looks, noting her smile and the warmth of her gaze, he realized that this was too superficial an evaluation—this was a very intelligent woman. Her intellect was clear in her appraising eyes, in the speed of her glance as she subjected the men to a minute scrutiny, in the measuring, almost bold and defiant, stare when she caught the eyes of the others.

Her husband seemed almost shy as he explained why they were there, as if he was more afraid of worrying her than he was of upsetting the knight and bailiff, and instinctively Baldwin knew his concern was unjustified.

Jane Black was intrigued. She had never seen such important men in her village before—Blackway was too far from the normal routes for any officials to bother to stop off—and she was not sure why they were so interested in old man Brewer's boy. The visitors did not seem to want to explain, but that did not matter to her; she knew that her husband would tell her all about it later. As she listened, though, it was the knight who caught her attention. He seemed so earnest, so intent, as he watched her, and as she responded to their questions she saw that his gaze fell upon her lips, as if trying to make sense of her words before their meaning could even be imparted to his brain by his ears, as if everything she said was so crucial, of such fascination, that he had to listen with his whole soul.

"Do you remember his name?" Simon asked.

Jane Black slowly wiped her hands on the cloth that served as an apron while she lost herself in her past, in the times when she was a young girl, long before she met John Black, and when the Brewer family had been together. Slowly the pictures started to come to life, as she recalled faded visions of years long passed, of a boy with a simple rough tunic who always seemed to be close to tears from the beatings his father gave, a boy who longed for a mother, but whose mother had died during his birth, a boy who wanted love and affection from a father who seemed to blame him for his widowhood. He had always seemed cowed, like a dog that was thrashed too often, waiting for the next whipping. She had always felt a sneaking sorrow for him, as if she could have taken him up and helped him, perhaps by becoming the sister he had never had. But kindness between children was difficult. She had given in and joined in the vicious jibes and sneers of her friends. When had he left the area?

"His name was Morgan; he was named after the father of his mother," she said, her eyes seeing only the past.

"Why did he leave, Mrs. Black?" said Baldwin, a scowl of incomprehension darkening his features.

"Why? Oh to get away, I think. He managed to save some money and went to Exeter. He got his lord's agreement—that was your brother, Sir Baldwin. It's not surprising. Brewer was a hard man. I can remember seeing Morgan bruised and hurt on mornings when his father had been in his cups the night before."

"Did he often get drunk, then?"

She gave a chuckle. "Oh yes, sir. Very often indeed! It was rare for him to get home sober. Many was the night he had to be helped home from the inn or from a friend's house after too much ale or cider."

Baldwin nodded slowly. "And he became violent when he had too much to drink?"

Her eyes seemed to film over as she looked at him. "Yes," she said at last. "He would often abuse others. If he had drunk too much he tried to fight—and he was strong, sir, very strong. My father used to try to avoid him, but others would be hit by him. He even used to hit the very men that were helping him home. Oh, yes, he could be very violent."

"This son, Morgan. You think he's still in Exeter?"

"No, I doubt it. If he had any choice, I think Morgan would have gone as far away as he could. He had no need of his father's money, I think. He earned enough himself in the city and could easily afford to travel farther."

"Do you know where he can be found?"

"Oh no. No, I've no idea. And I doubt whether anyone else in Blackway will, either."

Preparing to leave, Simon and Baldwin stood and waited on the doorstep while Black took his wife back indoors to give her his farewell.

"Are you really sure that this man Brewer was murdered?" said Simon at last.

Baldwin shot a glance at him, then smiled sardonically as if mocking himself. "Oh, I don't *know*. Not really *know*. But I am sure he was dead before the fire started. And I'm equally sure that the blaze was not caused by his cooking fire."

"Why? How can you be so sure of that?"

"Because of what I said. The fire was too low. It couldn't have thrown up enough sparks to light the roof."

Simon scratched his neck and squinted at the tall, dark figure beside him with a skeptical grimace. "Baldwin, you may be right, but just what the bugger do you think we can do even if you are? We can't show that the body was injured—it was too badly burned for that. We can't prove that anyone went there to kill him—what do you want?"

"Of course we can prove it," said his friend, looking at him with an expression of patience mixed with frustration. "All we need to do is find the man who did it and get him to confess."

"Ah," said Simon sarcastically. "So that's all, is it? I may as well go home now then, if you have it all tied up so neatly already!"

hen Black came back out again, he was amused to see that the two had obviously quarrelled. It was plain from their silence, from the fixity of their stares—which were aimed anywhere but at each other—and from the grin on Edgar's face as he stood a little behind the two of them, out of their sight.

When Black looked at the servant enquiringly, Edgar merely shrugged, the indication of disinterest being totally refuted by his simultaneously expanding smile. The hunter was not aware, but Edgar was, only too painfully, of how close Baldwin had been to death in the previous year. Since then, since his suffering from the brain fever, he had been regularly morose and taciturn, rarely allowing a smile to crack his features, almost never showing petulance or selfishness of any sort, but continuing quietly and with a gentle calm, eternally grateful for the kindly ministrations of his servant. It was a delight as well as a relief for Edgar to see his master in an argumentative mood once more.

The four men slowly made their way back up the street, Black pointing out the houses and indicating the people who lived in each. They were all very much the same, built of the same materials and to the same size. Some had the small front door for the human occupants, each had a larger door, or pair of doors, at the side for the larger inhabitants—the oxen, pigs and goats that represented that family's wealth. The small, unglazed windows peered at them with apparently bovine calm, as though intrigued by these curious creatures, but not in any way scared or threatened. From the thatch, the smoke drifted aimlessly in the still air, small wisps and tendrils breaking free to climb up the pitch of the roofs before dispersing at the top, like morning mist under the sunshine.

They had almost passed the inn when Baldwin halted, spun round and rushed in through the door. Simon and the others stood and waited, and soon he came out again, the landlord drifting along behind him.

He was a huge man, the innkeeper. He was only a couple of years older than Simon, or so the bailiff thought, but he gave the impression of vast knowledge. The appearance of accumulated learning was helped by his head, which was bald. But that was due to his shaving his pate every morning. His eyes were cheerful and twinkling, deep-set under a heavy, sloping brow, and, looking oddly out of place, his jaw and upper lip were covered in a thick and bushy growth of dark hair, making him appear inside out somehow, as if there had been an accident at his birth leaving his whole body inverted. His tunic was filthy, but then that hardly mattered in the darkness of his hall, and its pale, stained front seemed to have served as a cleaning implement, apron, carrying sack for wood and meat, and towel as well as clothing. In fairness, its size made it an ideal means of transport. The man's girth was vast, and any cloth that could encompass his belly, Simon thought, would be able to carry a significant load of goods.

"Black, your wife said that Brewer was a heavy drinker, yes? Good, now, innkeeper, tell these men what you just told me," said Baldwin, motioning toward the little group.

The innkeeper leaned back against his wall, rubbing his hands on his noisome tunic, and gave a quick belch. "About old Harold Brewer, sirs. He was here last night. He came in, like normal, just after dusk and stayed until too late. I suppose it must've been gone eleven by the time he went. It must've been getting close to the middle watches."

"So he decided to go home then?" Simon asked.

"Well." The man's eyes were sly, and almost seemed about to wink. "Well, no, he didn't decide to go. I decided for him. He was getting loud again, and when he started his roaring I let him know he might be better off in his bed."

Baldwin leaned forward. "You got him outside, you put him into the lane. What then? Please tell my friends."

"Well, I got him out, and there was this other man walking up it, going his way. I called out to him, said, 'Take this one with you, we've had enough for one night,' and he seemed to be happy enough to help. He came over and took Brewer by the arm. Well, that was enough for me, I went back inside to clear up."

"But, as far as you could see, this man was taking Brewer home with him?"

"Oh, yes. Even after I shut the door, I could hear Harold shouting and cursing him. He wanted more ale, he wanted to stay here, he wasn't ready to go home yet. 'Course, he wasn't getting any more to drink from *me*.

He was ready to start a fight again—and I've had enough of him fighting in my inn over the years. I felt sorry for the man, though. It sounded like he was getting the rough end of Harold's tongue alright."

"Didn't you see who it was, this helpful stranger?" said Simon, and the twinkling, merry eyes were fixed on him. For an instant he saw through the friendly exterior, to the selfishness, the disinterest that lay behind, before the façade dropped down again like a portcullis.

"No. It was dark and I had just come out of the inn. I could only make out a figure, and I shut the door as soon as I called out to him. No, I never saw who it was, and I wasn't very interested. All I wanted by then was to get Harold out and get up to my bed."

The men left him at the door to his inn and made their way farther up the street, Black seeming deep in thought, and Simon staring at Baldwin with an expression of puzzlement. "So how can we find out who this man was?"

The knight turned and faced him with a smile. "We ask people, Simon. We ask people."

6

I t was getting late now, the air was more chill and the shadows were beginning to grow as the little band trooped after the knight. As they went he shot questions at Black, pointing at houses and asking about the occupants—how many people lived there, how long for, had their parents been there before them? Black seemed to know a fair deal about all of the villeins in the hamlet, he was often asked to fetch food for them on his travels, even though he had only been living there for some four years, since he married and agreed that he would move into the area so that his wife did not have to leave the village she had grown up in.

Baldwin cleared his throat. "This man walking back in this direction, whoever he might have been . . . I suppose it would make sense if he lived in one of the houses in this direction. Of course, he might have been out to do some chore and was going to return home later, if he came from farther down the lane, but it would make sense to me to ask whether anyone at this side of the village, this side of the inn, was out late last night. What do you think, Simon?"

The bailiff nodded, his animosity toward his companion forgotten now in his interest. "Yes, I would think that should make sense. Black, who do you know who could have been out that late at night?"

He considered, scowling at the road ahead and scratching at his belly, his mouth drawn down into a crescent of near-humorous misery in his deep contemplation. "Well, there's four that would be up at that time that I can think of. Cenred, the warrener, is often out late. He has to be, to try to get the badgers and foxes and keep his rabbits safe. Then there's Alfred, the young Carter boy. He has to look after the sheep over by the tor, so he's sometimes late back. Edward, his brother, often joins him. And there's Roger. He's often out late."

"Why?" said Simon, his eyes narrowing at the lack of explanation and peering at the hunter.

He was rewarded with a rich laugh. "Because he's wooing a woman over at Hollowbrook. Emma Boundstone. He gets back as late as he can most nights!"

They were almost back at the ruined house now. The crowd that had come to see the fire was thinner, the people, losing interest, having dispersed after the body was removed. The remaining spectators were the locals themselves, standing around in small huddles and talking in low voices, their eyes flitting suspiciously over the men with Black as they came close.

"Black," said Baldwin, "I want you to point out the four men you just mentioned. Then bring them over to us. Now, which are they?"

"That there's Alfred, his brother's beside him," the hunter said, indicating two young men. The first was slim but fit-looking, a lithe man with tallow-colored hair, a dark, ruddy complexion and quick, shifty movements, reminding Simon somehow of a rat. His brother was a little taller, but his hair was mousey, thin and wispy. His figure was more expansive, fuller, as though he liked his beer too much, and even from fifty yards away his bright, rosy cheeks seemed to hint at excessive consumption. His eyes, though, seemed as quick and sharp as his brother's, almost eagerly tripping over the bailiff and his friends with quick, snapping glances.

The hunter's finger jabbed out again. "He's Roger Ulton, him over there." He seemed to be indicating a quiet, bookish-looking man with a thin, pale face and sunken eyes. For all that he, by the look of him, was only some nineteen years old, he looked squashed and nervous. Simon looked at him with interest. The man's air was of a fearful dejection, as if he was waiting to be accused, knowing that he was bound to be assumed guilty.

"What about the other one—the warrener?" asked Baldwin quietly.

"Cenred? Can't see him here. I suppose he's out at work."

"Good. Right, go and get the two brothers first, would you, Black? We should be able to get this matter over with fairly quickly now, I think, with only five men to see."

"Five? But there's only four, surely," said Black, looking surprised.

"No, there's you as well, Black."

His face as dark as his name suggested, the hunter soon brought the two young men over. It seemed that Alfred was the younger of the two, and his sly, cunning eyes seemed to be everywhere as he stood in front of the others, whereas his older brother stood as if nervous, his eyes on the ground in a display of humility. Alfred looked as if he was only just out of his teens; he still had the boldness of youth, as if he did not understand that he was being questioned about a possible murder. He seemed fearless, unabashed in front of the bailiff and the knight as they sat on a fallen tree trunk with Black and Edgar standing behind.

Simon looked at the man with interest. His tallow hair seemed too bright, somehow, for the dull, monotonous life of a cottar, and his lively and cunning manner did not fit in with the bailiff's opinion of how a villein should appear. He wore a faded blue tunic beneath a leather jerkin. His worn and stained leggings were patched and mended, showing their great age, and around his waist was a thin leather belt, with a wooden-handled knife in a leather sheath hanging in front. He gazed back at the men with arrogance and defiance in his eyes.

Edward kept his eyes downcast. He had more the appearance of the servile country laborer that Simon expected. The bailiff was by no means a harsh or cruel man, but he did understand the differences between men, and he knew how they were expected to react. The son of a castle seneschal, Simon knew that it was impossible to constantly keep servants quiet and humble. The nature of his fellows was such that they could only take so much, but then they would snap. After all, any man needs self-respect, and that can only be achieved if respect is given by others. Simon knew this, and he gave his men an according amount of regard. But, even so, most of his own men would be humble in front of a new lord when presented for the first time—no matter what they might say afterward!

This older man was dressed simply, with thick

stockings, tightly bound with the thongs from his sandals under a light tunic and short cloak. He looked warm in his clothes, and Simon was surprised to see that all his garments seemed fairly new—there were no stains or patches as yet, unlike those of his brother.

Baldwin appeared to have noticed the same disparity, shooting little glances from one to the other as he sat. Then, "I understand that you were out late last night, both of you. Where were you?"

He waited to see which would answer, his eyes small glinting sparks under his lowered brows. At last Alfred, quickly shooting a confirmatory look at his brother from the corner of his eye, said, "I'm a shepherd for my father's flocks. We were up with the sheep."

"Aren't you a little old for that type of work?"

His face was blank. "No, I'm only twenty, and I'm the youngest in the family, so I normally go out to see to them and make sure they're alright. Edward often comes with me."

"Ah yes, Edward. What do you do for a living?"

"Me? I sell goods at markets. I collect them from the town and take them with me on my cart. Why?"

"Why do you help your brother with the sheep?"

"Just so that we can get out of the village and talk alone. And it means he's finished sooner. Why?"

The knight ignored the question for the second time. "What time did you return last night?"

"Oh, I don't know," said Alfred, seeming keen to speak again, as if nervous that his brother would say too much. "I suppose we left the hill at about half past ten o'clock. I doubt whether it would have been much later."

"How long did it take you to get back?"

"What, to get home? Oh, I suppose about a half hour, I don't know."

"Did you see anyone else on your way home?"

The young man glanced at his brother as he answered for him. "No, no one." Simon was sure that he saw something—anger, or fear maybe in his dark eyes. Why was that?

"When was that, when you got into the village?" asked Baldwin, frowning in the manner that Simon was beginning to recognize as demonstrating intense concentration.

"Yes, just as we came into the village."

"And you saw no fire as you passed Brewer's house?"

"No, there was nothing—I could stake my life on that!"

Baldwin believed him. Alfred seemed absolutely convinced that there was no sign whatever of the fire then, but that still left the question: when did it start? He glanced at the younger man again, who was staring at him with vague interest—or was it hostility? Then, looking at the older man once more, "Did you part at any time on the way back?"

To his surprise it was Alfred who answered before his brother could open his mouth. "No. We were together the whole time."

As the two were led away and Black fetched Roger Ulton, Baldwin raised the corners of his mouth in a poor mockery of a grin and faced Simon. "Well?"

"I didn't like the look of the younger one, and I didn't trust him. But whether they were capable of killing Brewer and trying to hide the fact afterward—well, I just don't know."

"No, neither do I," said Baldwin reflectively. "But it

did seem as if the younger one—Alfred—was trying to hide something. I don't know. Edward seemed honest enough, or at least he didn't say anything that I could put my finger on."

"No. Well, let's see what this Roger has to say for himself," said Simon, and they both turned to the man walking toward them with Black.

Close to, he looked less anemic than he had from a distance. He was a thin young man, surely not an uncommon sight after the last two years of famine, and his emaciated appearance was heightened by a curious pallor in his complexion. His clothes, light brown woollen shift and leggings, seemed too large for him, and Simon immediately wondered whether they were originally made for a brother—or a father? His boots were worn and flopped as he walked, adding to the general effect of decay that he seemed to project, and they looked too large for his feet. His tunic had a hood, but it was thrown back as he walked to the knight and bailiff, to show an effeminately long, thin neck. Like his features, this was very pale, and Simon found it attracted instant attention. Almost as a disability draws the eyes against the wish of the onlooker, this neck, swanlike in its elegance, seemed to exert some power over the vision, as if wanting to emphasize its own vulnerability by dragging the gaze to it, so that the observer could wonder how the red blood could pump beneath such pure alabaster flesh.

It was with an almost physical effort that the bailiff had to wrench his eyes away and lift them to the face of the witness. By the sudden twitching jerk at his right, he knew that Baldwin had been similarly affected. They both studied the face in front of them with interest.

Like Edward before him, Roger kept his eyes cast downward in humility, the perfect example of a poor serf. But his eyes flickered occasionally as he tried to glimpse the faces of the two questioners before him. His face was as thin as his neck, and as pale, creating a disturbing contrast with his hair, which was raven black, as dark as Black's own. But where the hunter gave off an aura of strong and vibrant health, this man seemed weak and sickly. His mouth was a thin streak slashed under his nose, the nose looked as though it should have a permanent dewdrop dangling, and his eyes, when he looked up, seemed watery and almost colorless, as if, like a colored book in the rain, their paint had been washed off. The whole impact of this man was unappealing—there was not even the interest, Baldwin thought, of young Alfred. At least he had a spark of individuality; he would make a good trader. This one seemed to have nothing.

The knight looked down at his own feet, wondering where to begin, and then, as he looked up, caught a fleeting glimpse of a different Roger. For a split second he caught and held the man's eyes, and, in that moment, he realized that the man was not as weak as he had thought.

"You are called Roger?" he started sternly.

"Yes, sir." He had a strangely deep voice, an unexpected bass from such a thin body, and he spoke with almost reverential respect.

"Last night you went to visit your woman, this Emma . . ."

"Emma Boundstone, sir. She lives with her parents at Hollowbrook."

"Yes. What time did you leave her?"

Perhaps it was the curtness of the question, or the

frowning glare from the knight, but whatever the reason, the young man's face colored instantly.

"Why, sir?"

"What?" Baldwin slammed his glove down onto the trunk beside him, and bellowed, making Simon jump and nervously stare at him. "I asked you when you left her! Do not presume to ask me *why* I ask. Answer the question."

"Sir, I mean no offense, I . . . it was about ten o'clock, sir. Ten o'clock. No later, I think." and he subsided, his face down once more in apparent misery.

More softly now, Baldwin said, "How far is Hollowbrook from here?"

"About three miles, sir. Not more, I should say."

"So you were back here again at . . . what, about half past ten, maybe eleven o'clock?"

"Earlier rather than later, sir. Nearer half past ten than eleven."

"And did you see anyone on your way home?"

"No, sir. I saw no one."

"Do you live alone?"

"No. My parents are still there. And my brother."

"So they would know when you got in?"

"Oh no, sir. They were all asleep by then. No, I came in quietly and went to my bed without disturbing them."

Baldwin nodded and looked over at Simon. "Do you have anything to ask?"

"Yes," said Simon, leaning forward and fixing a glowering stare on the man. "Where is Hollowbrook from here?"

"Where? It's over there, sir," said the man, pointing back down the road, to the south.

"So you wouldn't have passed Brewer's house to get

home?" When he shook his head, Simon gave a dismissive gesture. "Fine, that's all I wanted to know. You may go—for now."

They watched him leave, slouching away to the lane and up the road toward his house, then, "Well?" said Baldwin enquiringly.

"I have no idea. They all seem so damn scared. It's probably no more than the fact that we're not villeins like them. We terrify them. I wouldn't be surprised if the only way to get the truth out of most of them would be to put them on the rack!"

"Don't!" Baldwin's short, anguished cry made Simon stop in horror, shocked at his friend's pained expression. Seeing the concern and anxiety in Simon's eyes, the knight reached toward him, an arm falteringly held out as if in supplication—or was it to hold him at bay? The bailiff took the proffered hand, fleetingly feeling the agonized, convulsive strength in the knight's grip. After a moment, the knight's fingers relaxed, but Simon was shocked at the way that the misery and depression remained in the dark eyes.

To Black it seemed as if the world had stopped with that single, agonized cry. He felt, rather than saw, Edgar move forward a little, then stop as if undecided, his hand on his dagger hilt, his gaze fixed on the two men in front. Clearly he was in two minds, the hunter could see that. It was as though he wanted to leap forward to defend the knight, but was held back by the fact that he knew there was no real danger near. Black looked from the knight to the bailiff, and then quickly back to the servant, and relaxed as he saw the servant's hand drop from his hilt. Licking his now dry lips, Black let his own hand fall from his skinning knife. He liked the bailiff and was not going to see him killed without defending him.

Baldwin was breathing quickly, not from exertion but in an attempt to regain his composure, as he held Simon's hand. "My friend," he murmured, "don't think that the rack or other tortures would help. I have seen them, and the effect of them. They do not work; all they do is destroy a man. They cannot force him to tell the truth, but they can force him to tell a lie, just to stop the pain. They do not help us to find the truth, all tortures can achieve is the breaking of a man so that he is destroyed, ruined." His eyes held Simon's for a moment, as firmly as his hand had grasped the bailiff's, and the fear and disgust was there again, together with . . . what? Pleading? Was this knight begging for him to understand, or was he asking for forgiveness? Simon felt nervous, unsure of how to react, concerned that he might upset his friend even further, but certain that Baldwin needed reassurance.

"Baldwin, we'll not use any torture in this matter," he said, and that seemed to be enough.

The knight slowly took a short pace backward, as if he was unwilling to lose contact with the bailiff, his eyes fixed on Simon's face. There was no denying it, the knight knew he was still too badly affected by his experiences in France. To have erupted like that! When it was obvious that Simon was only joking, too. It was ridiculous.

Turning, he began to lead the way back to the inn, but as Simon followed, his eyes were fixed on the knight's back with a pensive glower. What had made him react like that? It was almost as if he himself was a criminal, the bailiff thought to himself.

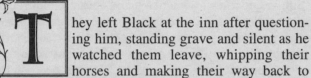They left Black at the inn after questioning him, standing grave and silent as he watched them leave, whipping their horses and making their way back to Crediton. He could not help them much beyond the statement he had already given. Returning home late he had seen the flames and raised the alarm. There had been no one around then, at least no one he had seen.

Simon was apprehensive, worrying about his new friend. He watched Baldwin covertly as they rode, aware of the unblinking gaze of Edgar, as if anxious that the bailiff might attack his master, that he might add to the damage that he had already done, however unwittingly, by mentioning the rack.

Riding stiffly, his mind obviously on other matters, with his eyes fixed on the road ahead, Baldwin seemed far away, so far that Simon felt instinctively that even if he were to call out his name he would not hear. He was back in his past, his expression fixed and hard, his hand a tight fist where he grasped the reins, and the muscles of his jaw clenching fitfully.

The bailiff let his eyes drop to the neck of his horse. No doubt when he was ready the knight would tell him about this horror, this evil memory. Until then he would have to wait and hope that the vividness of the apparent nightmare would fade. Then, glancing up, he saw that the knight had lost his haunted expression, had recovered some of his previous good humor.

The knight's eyes met and held his for a minute, and the two stared at each other, until the knight grinned, said, "Come on, we'll be all night at this rate," slapped his horse, and the three cantered off toward Crediton.

Simon had left the other two just before Crediton. The road forked as it came into Crediton from Blackway, one arm leading east, to Exeter and thence to Tiverton, passing Furnshill on the way, the other leading to Crediton and north to Sandford. It was here that the three parted, Simon going on alone to the left.

The route took him into the center of Crediton, and he had to turn off by the ancient church. Passing it in the street, he wondered whether to stop and beg a drink from Peter Clifford, but even as he passed the open doors, he heard the voices singing in praise and realized that the rector would be too involved to talk, so he carried on past. Carefully avoiding the open sewer, and wincing at the fetid stench, he went along the narrow lane that bordered the old graveyard, past the cottages where the church workers lived, and so up to the hill that led out of the town.

In daylight he always found this road slow, relaxed and pleasant. It curved gently up the hill, winding like an old stream, with a wall on one side that protected the church estates. On the other side the road gave directly on to fields, a sweep of narrow strips that led to the forests on the hill above. It was a rural scene of tranquillity, a pastoral picture, in green where the grass and crops grew, and in red where the dark earth had been plowed, that never failed to please him. When he was upset or peevish, a ride along this road would inevitably calm him. It was the sight of how man could change nature, bend it to his will and manipulate it to provide him with his food and protection. He felt the same whether he was looking at the strips of the fields or the coppices. Both seemed to him to be proof of the mastery of mankind over the anarchy of wild nature.

But now, as he crested the peak of the hill and followed the lane down into the valley on the other side, the road seemed to change. Now, as darkness came on, he was into the other part, and like the scenery, his feelings changed too. Here the wild had never been pushed out. Here the woodcutters had not wanted to go, it was too far from the town. The farmers would not clear the trees here, the fields would be too far to bring seed to. Animals would be kept nearer the town where they could be seen and protected.

No, here the land was still wild and untamed, here nature still ruled and men walked cautiously. The dark and threatening woods crowded closer at either side of the road, as if struggling to reach the humans that travelled along it so that they could squeeze the life from them. The brambles sprawled from the edge of the trees in an attempt to colonize the packed dirt of the lane, catching and ripping at the clothes of any passerby unwary enough to walk too close. In between the trees, he could sometimes hear the tick and crack of the wood settling, but to his fearful ears, raised from the cradle to be scared of the various spirits that haunted the moors and hills of Devon, they sounded like the voices of the unspeakable, ghostly horrors as they hunted for humans. In the dark, this road reminded him of the most fearsome of all: Old Nick and Old Crockern.

These two characters were well known in Devon, their fame was boundless in the countryside, and Simon found himself unwillingly considering each with a degree of trepidation he had not felt for many years. After the death of old Brewer—he still found it hard to believe that it was a murder; easier by far to consider it one of those sad but all too common accidents, a stray spark in the thatch, and, by all accounts, a man too drunk to wake—the stories and legends seemed to crowd in on him as he wound his lonely trail home.

Old Nick was the devil himself. The tales told of him riding a horse, a headless horse, all over the moors and beyond in his search for souls. At his side was a pack of hounds, evil, wild-eyed creatures whose baying showed that they had the scent of a human spirit ready for taking. The wild hunt was reputed to be a regular event, not requiring fogs or mists to cover its cruelty as the horde swept after its quarry.

The other was a more understandable spirit, if just as unpleasant to meet. Old Crockern was the ancient soul of the moors. He was everywhere, but on occasion would make himself appear to those who threatened his lands, and would destroy them. It was true that he would normally use simple methods, like bankrupting a farmer who decided to take more of the moors than he needed, by ensuring that he could grow nothing on the ground he stole, but if Old Crockern found someone intentionally affecting the life and security of the moors, it was rumored that he would come and take the perpetrator away, to a hell more evil than ever Satan could devise.

As Simon passed by, the lanes were darkening. The sunset had been a warm, orange glow on the horizon, promising another dry and clear day ahead, and he had been momentarily pleased to reflect on the fact before his mind drifted back to consider the ancient superstitions. It was not that he was overly credulous himself, but the lanes leading up to Sandford were narrow and lined with dark ranks of trees, standing silent like accusing monsters from a far-distant past. The great twisted, primeval boughs loomed gray and foreboding on either side, reaching upward into the swiftly gathering darkness as if trying to block off the light, as if trying to strangle any remaining glimmer before it could reach the road. Simon could almost fancy, as he rode along, that the branches were attempting to touch over the road, and that when they did their gnarled and tortured limbs would drop, plummet down, to smother any passer-by . . .

He shook himself vigorously. A mist swept silently, malevolently, across the road in front of him, and he shivered. "God's teeth!" he thought. "How old am I?" And he spurred his horse faster.

But he still looked over his shoulder occasionally.

By the time he arrived home the dark had settled heavily over the land like a gray velvet carpet, and his fears retreated at the sight of the orange glow from the windows of his house. Taking his horse round to the stables, he gave it a quick rubdown and settled it for the night before going in.

It had been costly, but he was pleased that he had paid, as Margaret had suggested, for the wood-panelled passageway. It cut the hall off from the kitchen area, the buttery and servants' quarters, and stopped some of the more vicious drafts from the front door that had whistled around the hall and disturbed the rushes.

At the other end of the hall was his solar, the family room, blocked off from the hall itself by the huge curtains. He had intended, when he had been able to afford it, to have that panelled off too. His lip curled into a self-mocking sneer. Too late for that now. There would be little point in spending money on the place with the move to Lydford coming up.

His wife was sitting in the hall with Edith, both on the large bench in front of the fire. His daughter seemed to be asleep, lying down in her light dress, her head resting on her mother's lap. Margaret was sitting and stabbing at a tapestry with quick, vicious thrusts, looking as if she was trying to kill the cloth.

Simon stared at her. She did not look up, but said, as if through gritted teeth, "There's stew for you in the pot," without looking up from her needlework.

He quietly stepped over to the fire in the middle of the room. The stew sat in its small cauldron, hanging from the steel tripod, and he could see that it had been ready for some time—the meat had all but collapsed in the liquid.

"Hugh!" he shouted, and when the servant rushed in, told him to fetch a bowl and spoon. When he had his earthenware bowl filled, he sat beside his wife and began shovelling the stew. "All right, so tell me what's wrong."

She threw down the cloth and glared at him, her fury mixed with despair at his lack of understanding. "What's wrong? You were supposed to be here all day and instead you've been out! You promised Edith you'd spend the day with her, how do you expect me to explain when you disappear?" Feeling Edith squirm, the prelude to waking, she broke off and gentled her daughter, picking her up and carrying her out to the solar. But soon she was back, and speaking low, her voice a sibilant hiss, she said, "Why couldn't you have sent one of the others—the constable, Tanner, or just left it to a priest? Why did you have to go there and see to a fire yourself?"

She glowered at him, feeling the injustice of it. Margaret was no shrew, no nagging vixen, but she needed him to understand. Of course, she knew full well that now, especially now he was bailiff, he had responsibilities that he must meet. But she too had important jobs to perform, not least of which was managing the household, and when their daughter was expecting her father to spend the day with her, she could be very fractious and difficult. She had been today.

Margaret had counted on being able to reorganize the buttery and prepare for their next brew of cider, but every time she had tried to have a word with Hugh she had found Edith nearby and wanting attention. Every time she had gone out into the kitchen Edith had followed and asked her to join in a game or simply kept asking questions until Margaret had lost her temper and told her to play outside and leave her alone.

It was then that her diminutive and tyrannical daughter had told her that her father would never say that to her and that she hated her.

Margaret had been shocked and deeply hurt—for all that she knew it to be untrue, that it was just a sudden flaring of temper that would soon be forgotten, and that she, the mother, would be expected to forget it too. But she could not. And it had made her resentful that Simon had been able to spend his day, yet again, out of the house and involved in uninterrupted work. Why was it considered right that the father should be free from his encumbrances when the wife, with as much work to do, was not?

So, after being able to leave her anger and annoyance to establish themselves and develop for the afternoon, she felt justified in lashing out at him on his return. But as she glowered at him, her anger undiminished by the absence of the cause of her afternoon's disturbance, he started to grin, and she soon found herself torn between fury that he could still have this effect on her and pleasure at his happiness.

"Why don't you come here and tell me what's the matter?" he said, motioning to the bench seat beside him.

So she did. She wandered over to him, sat, and told him of her day. As she knew it would, the telling made her feel better—calmer and more at peace. "But what were you doing? Why were you so long? It was only a house fire, wasn't it?"

As soon as she said it she felt him stiffen, and, sitting upright, she rested her hands in her lap and concentrated on him as she listened. "Tell me about it."

And he did. He started to tell her all about the body they had found in the house, the charred and unrecognizable figure of old Brewer, who had died so alone that no one even knew where his son was, or if he was alive. His face calm, yet distant, she watched him and listened as he told of Baldwin, the new knight, and how he had taken a different view of the fire. She frowned in concentration as he told of the men who had been there, of the Carters and Roger Ulton, who seemed to know nothing, and of Cenred, whom he hoped to question soon. At first she listened in disbelief, but then with a feeling of growing concern, as if in simply being told of Baldwin's suspicions, she could be similarly persuaded that a crime *had* been committed.

"So do you think it was murder?" she asked at last.

"I don't know what to think. It could have been, like Baldwin says, but I really don't know. It seems so unlikely. I could understand it happening in a city like Exeter, but in a quiet hamlet like Blackway? It just doesn't seem possible."

While he gazed thoughtfully into the fire, she asked, "What if Cenred says he knows nothing as well? What will you do then?"

"I don't know. I think Baldwin will want to speak to the whole village—question everyone there and try to find out that way. The trouble is, there's no proof that there has been a crime! How can we expect people to accuse someone when there's nothing to show that there's been a crime?" He stopped and frowned at the flames as if he could divine the answer there.

"So what are you going to do tomorrow?" she asked.

"Oh, I'll have to go back there and see if I can make any sense of it. I'll have to speak to Cenred, at the very least, and then maybe to the others again. Baldwin will meet me there, he said, and I suppose we'll know what to do afterward."

Jane Black cuddled closer to her husband in their bed, trying to help him calm with the warmth and promise of her body, but it did not seem to help. It was the same when he had lost his favorite dog, Ulfrith the mastiff, to a wolf two years before. Then too he had lain in bed until late, not moving, hardly breathing, but not sleeping either, as she knew all too well.

It was obvious from the rigid set of his body, from

the tautness that was as far removed from rest as she could imagine, and she was desperate to help him, but how?

"John," she said softly, "why don't you tell me about it? I might be able to help."

She could feel his chest catch, as if he was holding his breath to listen better, as she had seen him when he was out hunting. But this was different, this was more as if she had broken a chain of thought and he was concentrating on her words and assessing their worth. But then she felt his chest move again and he slowly turned toward her. She could feel the rasp of his bristly beard, and then the smell of his breath.

"They think that Brewer was murdered. They think it had to be someone who was out late last night. That means they think it could have been me."

She froze. "But you wouldn't do something like that, you had no reason to kill him. Why should they think you could—"

"I was out. They knew that, how could I hide it? I was the one that found the fire!"

"But John, John, if it was you there would be no point in telling anyone about the fire. They'll see that, you'll see. Don't worry about it."

"But I am worried. Apart from anything else, who *did* do it? It must have been late in the evening. Who could have done it? Who was it that took Brewer back from the inn?"

"Well, what about Roger Ulton?"

"Roger? What, while he was on his way back from Emma's? But he wouldn't even have gone near the inn on his way back from the Boundstone place."

She withdrew a little, peering toward him in the dark, and when she spoke her voice was low and troubled. "But he didn't. I saw him walking back up the lane, and he wasn't coming from the south, from Hollowbrook or his house, he was coming from the north, going home."

"What?" He moved suddenly, his arm gripping her shoulder tightly. "Are you sure? But . . . what time was that?"

"I don't know, just before I went to bed. I think it must have been almost eleven, but—"

"And you're sure it was Ulton?"

"Oh, yes. Of course."

"And he was going back toward his house?"

"Yes."

The hunter released her, settling back to stare up toward the ceiling. If Ulton had been coming down the lane, he must have lied about coming back from Emma's house. Why? Could it have been him that killed Brewer? He must tell the knight tomorrow. That should take the suspicion away from him.

To his wife's relief, she soon heard his breathing slow and felt the tenseness in his body relax. Only then did she settle herself and, with a smile in her husband's direction, she rested her head on her crooked arm and searched for sleep.

imon arrived at the warrener's house in the mid-morning of the next day. As the sunset had promised, it was a bright and clear day with no hint of rain in the air.

The journey, by the same roads he had taken the previous evening, made him sneer at himself. Where were the fearsome terrors he had imagined?

In the morning sunlight he rode along between the trees and looked in among their leaves with sardonic self-deprecation. Now they looked like friendly guards—sentinels standing watchfully to protect travellers from the perils of their journey. In the warm daylight they lost all sign of that menace that had seemed so clear and terrifying the night before; now they appeared friendly, a sign of security and comfort on his way, and he welcomed them as he might a companion.

The village was slumbering in the bright sunshine, the houses seeming new and cleaner somehow, the grass greener, and as he rode up the lane past the inn he could almost imagine that none of the events of the previous day had occurred.

There were few people around. He could see some women down by the stream, washing their clothes, he could see the lye and clay in the pots and the wooden paddles used for pounding the recalcitrant cloth. The women were laughing and shouting, their dresses gaily colored in the sun, and he felt a pang of jealousy that he could not be, like them, carefree and happy on this morning.

Then, as he rode farther up the lane, they became aware of him, and their laughter and chatter died, so suddenly that it seemed to him that they might all have disappeared, that they had all been whisked away by some strange magic, but when he turned to look they were all there, silent and unmoving as they stared at him, the unknown traveller through their village.

It was disconcerting, this stillness where there had been good-humored noise and bustle, and he felt a prickly sensation of trepidation, as if this was an omen, a warning that his presence was unwanted, an unnecessary intrusion. He watched them for a minute as he rode, until he passed the sharp bend in the road and they were obscured by a house. He was grateful to lose sight of them—their silent staring had been deeply unsettling.

The warrener's house was a smaller property even than Black's. It lay a short distance back from the lane, with a strip of pasture in front on which a goat was contentedly feeding. As the bailiff drew near, it stopped chewing and fixed him with its yellow, unfeeling eyes with their vertical irises. Simon found that his sensations of discomfort returned under the yellow stare of this creature, and he could not shake it off as he tethered his horse. There was no sign of Baldwin: should he wait for the knight? He turned and peered back down the lane, debating with himself whether he should await his friend, but then a picture rose in his mind of Margaret saying, "Why did you have to spend the whole day away again?" and that decided the matter for him. He turned back and walked up to the front door, feeling the goat's gaze on his back as he went.

The cottage was old, a clunch hovel with just two rooms. Unlike most of the other houses in the village, this one had no need to contain animals, and the air was clean and fresh all around. The building seemed to have suffered a collapse years before, as was so common with the older cottages when the walls could no longer support the weight of the roof. At some time it had been almost twice its present size—the outline of the old walls could be made out in the grass to the side. No doubt the end had fallen down and the hole created had been blocked up in some way to keep the remainder of the property habitable. It appeared to have been well looked after recently—the walls were freshly whitewashed, the wood painted and the thatch seemed well cared for, with little sign of moss and no holes created for birds' nests.

The warrener opened the door himself. He looked as though he had just risen from his bed, with his tousled hair and sleep-fogged eyes, which he was rubbing as he stood on his threshold, blearily staring at the stranger on his doorstep.

"Are you Cenred?" Simon asked and, when the man nodded, "My name is Simon Puttock, I'm the bailiff. I'd like to ask you some questions about the night before last."

The warrener blinked. "Why?" he said.

Simon could have wished he had asked almost any other question. "Because it's possible that the man who died that night—"

"Old man Brewer," said the warrener helpfully.

"Old man Brewer," Simon agreed, "could have been murdered, and I'm trying to find out whether he was or not." Somehow he felt a certain degree of relief that he had managed to finish his introductory speech, and he continued with more confidence. "So I want to know what you were doing that night and where you were, when you got back home and so on."

The man's face was still sleep-blurred as he stared at Simon. He had friendly, open features, a large, round head on top of a thick, square body. He was obviously faintly amused as he looked at the bailiff; a small smile played around his full, red lips, and his dark brown eyes were creased where the laughter lines lay. The hair on his head seemed thin, as if he was soon to lose the crown, but his chest made up for any loss with the thick, black, curling mass that peeped from the open top of his smock. He was bearded, and the hair here too was dark, except at the point of his chin, where it showed ginger, as if it had been dipped in paint and permanently stained when he was young. He was probably only eight and twenty years old, but his face seemed more wise than his years implied, and Simon found himself feeling nervous, as if he should apologize for interrupting the man's sleep.

Shaking off the feeling, he said, "So where were you that night? The night before last?"

Cenred appeared to find the question mildly funny—he looked almost as if he was about to laugh—but then he saw the earnest expression on Simon's face and seemed to reconsider. "Come inside and have a glass of beer, bailiff. We can talk more comfortably indoors, and I'm sure you're thirsty after your ride."

He was right, Simon knew. His throat was parched

from the journey, and it would be more pleasant to sit. He nodded and followed the man into his hall.

It was a simple room, but with signs of modernization. The first thing that Simon noticed was the chimney. This was the first small cottage he had been in where there was such an innovation—most people were happy enough to let the smoke drift out through the thatch of the roof as their forebears always had, but this man obviously wanted more comfort than a smoking fire offered. In front of the fire was a large, granite block which served as a hearthstone, and here the man had placed his mattress. He rolled it up and set it beside the fire to keep warm.

"I was up all night trying to catch a fox. You woke me," he said simply and walked out to the back to fetch the beer. Simon walked to a bench and pulled it over to the fire, setting it down on the rushes by the hearth to wait. Cenred was soon back, carrying two large earthenware pots, one of which he passed to Simon, before dragging another bench from the wall, so that he could sit facing the bailiff.

"So you want to know where I was night before last, eh?"

The bailiff nodded silently, studying this large, comfortable and, above all, confident man. It was the confidence that shone like the light of a lantern in the dark, in vast contrast to the hesitant nervousness of the three men whom he and Baldwin had seen the day before. Where they had shuffled and twitched this man seemed to be positively enjoying himself, sitting comfortably, legs outstretched, one hand on the seat beside him, the other gripping his pot of ale.

"Well, now. I left here in the late afternoon. I had to go up to my coppice to get poles for fencing to replace a section that fell. I took the poles straight over to the warren and fixed the fence, then went round the traps. At one of them there was a badger, which I killed, but near another I found the pelt of one of my coneys. Well, I spent a good half hour looking around to see if I could find the trail of the beast, but I couldn't, so I came back here, had some supper, and—"

"When would that have been?" interrupted Simon.

"When? Oh, I suppose about dusk. Say about half past seven. Anyway, I went back up to the warren then, to see if I could find the animal that did it. I stayed up late, but I couldn't see any sign, so I came back."

"What time did you arrive home?'

"I really don't know. It was long after dark, I know that, but more than that I can't say."

Thinking, Simon said musingly, "To get home you don't go through the village, do you?"

"No, the warren is down on the moor, about half a mile to the south from here, so I only pass the Ulton house and Brewer's on my way home."

"Hmm. Tell me, what do you think of the Ultons?"

"Oh, they're alright. They're jealous of me, or at least Roger is, but they seem friendly enough."

"How do you mean, jealous?"

"I am a free man. Everyone else in the village is either a cottar or a villein, but I earned my freedom. I earned it by buying it from the Furnshill estate, and it has made some people a bit difficult. It's foolish, because others—look at Brewer—are more wealthy than me, but that doesn't stop them envying me."

"What do you know about Brewer? No one has been able to tell me much about him. Did you know him well?"

The warrener's friendly smile did not leave his face,

but his eyes lost their focus, making him seem to almost go into a daydream as he thought. Now when he spoke, his voice had fallen, becoming quieter and lower.

"He was not an easy man. Everyone hereabouts was sure that he had a lot of money, but I don't know whether that's true. It didn't make him popular, anyway."

"No?"

"No, he had money but he kept it for himself. And he was a heavy drinker, and when he had drunk too much he got violent. He was a big man, Brewer, and when he decided to hit someone, he could hurt."

"Did anyone have a reason to hate him, then? Did he hurt anyone recently?"

The warrener gave a sudden laugh, a great gale of amusement, and had to wipe his eyes with the back of his hand before he could answer.

"Oh, sorry, bailiff, sorry! Yes, you could say that. He was a drunkard, often got into fights, was always sneering at others and belittling them. I don't think you really understand how people felt about him! Round here it's hard to find anyone who did like him!"

he bailiff must have shown how much this comment depressed him, because the warrener stood, walked over, and patted him on the shoulder.

"Come now, bailiff! It's quite likely he just died in his bed and it was an accident. Are you sure you're not chasing a wild goose? Come on, give me your pot. If you like my beer, you may have another pot with me." So saying, he took Simon's mug and went through to the back room.

By the time he returned, Simon had managed to recover to the extent that he was able to smile again in gratitude for the fresh ale. "Thank you. Do you mind humoring me a little further? For example, did you see anybody when you did finally get home? We have been told that someone helped Brewer home on the night he died, but no one seems to know who it could have been. Do you?"

"Well, no. I didn't see him being helped—I assume you mean he was being dragged home after he was thrown out of the inn again? I thought so. No, I didn't see him."

"Are you surprised that someone would help him? After what you said, about him being so unpopular?"

"No, people often helped him home. Oh, he was hated alright. Arrogant and rude, and he would always use his fists when he couldn't find words, but this is a small vill. We need to get on. Otherwise, if there's arguing, how can we get the harvest in, or get the plowing done? We have to get on together—it's just that he made it hard."

"How?"

The warrener's eyes crinkled again in amusement. "Do you like braggarts? No, well that's how Brewer was. The rumors about his money—well, I don't know if they're true, but he certainly helped put them about. He owned his own oxen, always had money for ale, and always seemed happy to put others down."

"I see." The bailiff peered at the fire. "And you didn't see him that night?"

"No, I didn't," he said, but then he put his head on one side and glanced at Simon with what the bailiff felt was a faintly shamefaced smile. "But I think I might have seen *someone* on my way home."

"Who?"

He gave a short giggle. "I'm not sure! It was far too dark. I'll tell you how it was, though. I'd finished trying to catch the fox, or whatever it was, and was on my way home again. I was annoyed and tired, and I had just got past the Ulton place when—"

"Have you any idea what time it was?"

Cenred gave him a pitying look. "I don't know why you keep asking me that. Look, I don't carry an hour candle with me out of doors, bailiff. How could I know what time it was? All I know is, it was dark. It could have been just eleven o'clock or well past midnight. How could I tell? No, all I can say is it cannot have been more than one, and it was past ten, but beyond that I don't know—I was too tired to think about it. Anyway, as I came past the Ulton place and down the road toward my own, I could have sworn I saw a figure at the edge of the road. It would have been down by Brewer's house, I suppose, opposite, in the trees on the other side of the road. At the time I did nothing—I . . ." He paused, embarrassed. "It seemed like a slim, dark figure. You know, what with the dark and the shadows from the moon and everything, when I saw this shape scuttling into the trees in front of me I sort of thought back to the old stories and, well, I walked past and tried to forget I'd seen it. Anyhow, it was around Brewer's house, on the other side of the lane, where the trees come and meet the roadway. You know where I mean?"

"Yes, yes, I think I do," said Simon. But he was thinking, who could it have been? What time was it, was it one of the two brothers? Was it Roger Ulton? Was it the man who had led Brewer home? Or was it someone else?

Simon stood outside the warrener's cottage for several minutes when they had finished talking. He wished that Baldwin was here, that the knight could have heard the evidence of Cenred, so that he could have the advantage of his opinion, but the knight still had not turned up. Kicking at stones and pebbles, he made his way back to his mare, untied her and walked south with her, away from the village.

The road curved away to the left almost immediately after the warrener's house, heading more directly south as it passed the ruins of Brewer's cottage. Keeping to the lane, the bailiff walked on, hardly giving the wreck a glance. It was strange, he felt, that now that

Baldwin had firmly planted the concept of a murder in his mind, the actual reality of the death seemed almost irrelevant. The house was of no importance anymore. Brewer's animals held no relevance. The only issue that could hold his attention was the man responsible.

Once past the collapsed and smoke-stained building, the road opened out a little, pointing straight to the blue-grayness of the moors. Here, it was clear, the road had moved away from ancient holdings, away from fields and pastures, away from possessions and owned land, because it suddenly gave up its meandering and ran, straight as a rule, leaving the stream behind on its left bank.

It was here, where the road continued in solitude toward the distant hills, that the Ulton house stood. It was a once-large, solitary longhouse. It must have stood here for more than a hundred years, a cob building, basically constructed of old clay, earth and dung, originally positioned for a farmer and his children, but with his master's security in mind as well. For here the sweep of the country could be seen ahead, an enemy, whether it be a Cornish horde or Vikings from the coast on a chevauchee, could be seen early and the alarm raised. Simon knew that now, since the fortunate ascent of William of Normandy, the raids and killings of the foreigners had all but ceased, but where the privations from alien armies had been halted, there was always the threat of attack from a less distant foe.

It was not many years since the last civil war, a vicious and senseless time during which alliances were made and broken with monotonous regularity, while men tried to juggle their loyalties to stay on the side that was most likely to give them power and wealth—

should they win. And if they seemed less likely to win? Change loyalty quickly!

From this house, with its massive walls and tiny windows, the occupant could not only see for miles along the track, a view unhindered by trees for most of the way, he could also put up a spirited defense. As with many of the older properties, the old farm had one large door to give access. To attack it would be fool-hardy, and probably costly, as the defenders could use the windows as bow-slits.

But the years had not been kind to the old house. When it was built, it would have given security and protection to a good-sized family and to the cattle, geese and hens of the yard. The single-story house would have enclosed all livestock as well as the hu-mans. Not now. The western wall had collapsed—pos-sibly due to too much rain on a badly thatched roof, maybe because of too many dry summers followed by the rains of the last two—for whatever reason, the cob had failed, and the resulting disaster was plain.

The wall must have fallen initially at the corner, Simon thought, and had smothered a large area, as if pushed out by the weight of the roofing behind, creat-ing a semicircular space of mud and filth. The roof had followed shortly afterward, the thick timber of the ridge showing like a stark, black spine, the rafters drooping like ribs from the wreckage of the thatch.

The damaged portion amounted to almost half the house, but the remaining part was still apparently hab-itable, and now, as he came round to the southern-facing wall, he could see that strenuous efforts had gone into protecting the rest. Balks of timber, probably rescued from the roof, had been propped against the walls to prevent further slippage. Where the roof had disappeared, granite blocks had been set on the top of the walls to give some defense from the rain and stop the cob being washed away, and a new wall was being built inside, under the thatch, to close the huge hole. It might mean that the house would be half its previous size, but it would at least be usable.

The bailiff stood pondering for a while. This family obviously had need of money—if they believed the tales of the wealth of Brewer, if they believed that he had a money box hidden under his floor, was it not possible that they might try to take it? He was such a drunk, might they not have felt that if they went to his house late at night they could take it while he slept? And if he had seen them, they might have killed him to hide their theft, then fired the place to hide their guilt.

"Bailiff!"

Simon turned slowly, still considering, to see Black walking toward him. "Ah, John. Have you seen Sir Baldwin yet today?"

"No, bailiff. I've not seen anyone but you so far. I think I may have some news for you."

He quickly explained what his wife had seen on the night of the fire—Simon still could not quite call it murder—and the time when she had seen it.

"So, young Roger was coming back from the wrong direction. He can't have been telling the truth when he said he was with Emma all evening. Why else would he lie, other than to hide his guilt?"

Simon scratched his neck thoughtfully. "I don't know, but I think we ought to go and see this Emma and find out what she has to say about it before we speak to Roger again."

* * *

There was still no sign of Baldwin, so they rode out of Blackway together to cover the four or five miles to Hollowbrook. For the most part they went in silence. Simon was brooding on the testimonies he had so far been given and trying to see where they fell down, if any of them did. He had no desire to convict anyone of murder, least of all an innocent man, so he was reconsidering all of the evidence so far in an attempt to assure himself that he was right to suspect Roger Ulton.

The house owned by Emma Boundstone's parents was large and relatively new. The whitewash gleamed in the early afternoon sunshine, and the yard in front of the big door was cleared of muck. It seemed plain that the people living here were proud of their property.

Simon stood back when they arrived. He had never met any of this family, whereas John Black was well known in the area. It would be better for John to knock and introduce himself first.

The door was opened by a short, cheery, middle-aged woman, dressed in a black shift with a gray wimple covering her braided gray hair. Her face was almost completely round, and seemed to be composed of circles—the eyes were twin dark beads, her nose was a small button, her cheeks had patches of red like two small rosy apples, and even the chin was an almost perfect sphere. As she stood in the door, Simon found it impossible not to return her smile. It would not merely have been rude, it would have been almost obscene to so reject such a happy and pleasant woman.

"Well, John, so how're you this fine day?"

"I'm well, Mrs. Boundstone, well. How's your husband?"

"He's fine, John. Fine. Is it him you're looking for?"

"Ah." He hesitated, glancing back at Simon.

"And who's this, then? Don't think I've seen you before."

Simon stepped forward. As he came closer, he could see that her head only came up to his shoulder, and so she could only be some five feet tall, and from the look of her that was probably the same as her diameter. "Good day, Mrs. Boundstone. My name is Simon Puttock. I'm the bailiff of Lydford. Could we speak to your daughter, please?"

The little woman's smile hardly flickered, but he could see the shrewd eyes glinting as she looked up at him. "Ah, you want our Emma, do you? Yes, she's inside. Wait here, I'll get her."

She had hardly left the door when Emma arrived, and Simon found her a disappointment. He had been wondering what this young woman would look like, what kind of girl could desire the young Ulton boy— and now he discovered that opposites could attract.

Emma Boundstone was as large, in her way, as her mother, but without her charm. She was a little taller, maybe five feet two or three, and well rounded, but there the similarity ended. Hers was a plain face, long and heavy-set, much like her body. She gave the impression of weight, although it was more sturdiness than fat. From a high and sloping forehead, her face dropped away, square and solid, from the flinty little eyes, past a thick nose, down to a slit of a mouth. Her braided hair looked like rope in the way it hung down either side of her cheeks. Her body was thick and heavy, and would have looked less out of place on one of her brothers. Simon found himself wishing he could forget questioning her and return to the comfortable warmth of her mother's gaze.

As the girl came forward, she stood aggressively,

one hand on her hip, as if daring them to begin. "Well? You wanted to speak to me?"

Simon nodded, wondering how to start. "Yes, you see, I would like to ask you about the night before last."

"What about it?"

"I understand that you were with Roger Ulton, from Blackway?"

"Yes." It was clear she was not going to try to help them.

"What time did he arrive here to see you?"

"I don't know."

Simon could feel his patience starting to crack. "Then give me a rough idea, Emma."

"Well," she put her head on one side in a gesture that would have been coquettish in a smaller woman. In her it appeared merely clumsy. "He got here after dark. I suppose it must have been about seven or so. Why?"

Ignoring the question, he continued, "And when did he leave you?"

"About half past eight."

"Are you sure?"

A spark of defiance glimmered in her eyes. "Yes, I'm sure. Why don't you ask him, if you don't believe me?"

The two men looked at each other, and suddenly her voice became peevish, petulant, as she said, "He's alright, isn't he? Is he hurt or something?"

"No, he's fine as far as we know. Why did he leave so early, we thought you and he were considering betrothal."

She tossed her head with a gesture of impatience. "Oh, yes. We were. But we argued, if you want to know. He refused to marry me until he had finished re-

building his father's house, and that could take him
until next year! I told him, if he wants me, he had better hurry up—I may not wait for him. We argued, and
in the end I told him to go. That's why he left me earlier than usual."

That night, sitting with Margaret in front of their fire,
Simon related the day's events. He had left Black on
the way back from Hollowbrook—it would have been
close to dark by the time they got to Blackway, and it
seemed pointless to go there when he could continue
and get home earlier for once.

His wife had been pleased to have him return so
much earlier than usual, and after their meal they
played quoits with Edith, currently her favorite game.
Now, at last, she had gone to her bed in the solar, and
they had two brief hours of peace before they too went
to their beds.

"So, this warrener, what was his name?"

"Cenred," said Simon sleepily.

"Yes, Cenred. What did he have to say?"

She was lying with her head in his lap again, while
he stroked her hair with one hand, his other resting on
her belly. Outside the rain was sheeting against the
walls, and occasional gusts made the door rattle and
the tapestries billow.

"Not much, really. He says he saw someone, someone who tried to hide when he came close. Apparently
just opposite the Brewer house. The fool was too
frightened to look, he thought it might be Old Crockern or something, and just walked on to his own place.
Anyway, it's the other one, Roger Ulton, that interests
me now."

"Wasn't he one of the men you saw yesterday?"

"Yes." Simon's eyes dropped to her face and he smiled, though she could see that he was exhausted. His face was quite gray, even in the light from the flames and the two thick candles that stood on their metal tripods nearby. In the smoky room, the big circles of tiredness under his eyes made them look deeply bruised, and she wondered whether the search was getting too much for him. Touched by a sudden whim she reached a finger up to his cheek, a sympathetic and loving gesture, and was pleased to see his smile broaden as he felt her.

Outside they could hear the rain. It had held off all day, but now, in the darkness of the night, the heavens had opened and the water was steadily dripping from two holes in the thatch. Margaret was glad that at least her husband was indoors with her. She would have been worried if he had been outside in this weather. She stroked her hand over his cheek, wondering at its roughness where the short bristles forced their way through his skin, so unlike his chest and the rest of his body, which was so smooth and soft. She stared at her fingers as they brushed his face, enjoying the tactile sensations, giving herself over to the pleasure of the feel and smell of her man, and she almost missed Simon's next comment.

"Sorry?"

"I said it's very odd." he said again, grinning down at her. "This man Roger seems to have been trying to woo a local girl, but that night he argued with her. He says he was with her all evening, but she swears he left early. Then he says he walked home straight from her house, but Black's wife saw him go past her place, at the other side of the village. All in all I'm fairly sure it was him who took Brewer home. But if it was, why didn't he tell us?"

"I'm sure you'll find out tomorrow. What else did you find out?"

They chatted for another hour or so, but Margaret soon decided that her husband needed to sleep, and led him out to the solar and their mattress. But even then, when they were in bed, she could feel his wakefulness.

He was miserable, a huddled dark figure sitting wrapped in the thick travelling cloak, the hood pulled over his head, in front of the attempted fire that still gave off a thin wisp of smoke as if trying to buoy his spirits by its promise of heat and warmth. But it was still-born. Before the heat could approach his still figure it was dissipated by the gusting wind that hurled the thick raindrops against his back.

"Only a year ago. Only a year," he muttered, his voice thrown aside by the wind that eddied around, searching out a gap in his clothing, trying to stab him with its chill. Shuddering with the cold, he grabbed a loose fold of his cloak and pulled it to him again, suspiciously glaring around the clearing.

Of course, he could have gone to one of the farms and begged for some food and the chance to sit in front of a fire, but at dusk it had seemed warm enough and hardly worth the embarrassment. After all, he was still a knight, and that kind of behavior was demeaning for a man born to a high family.

"One year!" he spat out viciously through his gritted teeth.

It was only one year ago that his lord, Hugh de Lacy, Lord Berwick, had died. Just one year. And since then he had lost everything. All he possessed was with him now—his father's sword and a small bag of belongings. Everything else had gone. His position as marshal of the castle overlooking the town had been given to that bastard, the son of his lord's brother. The rooms in the castle were kept only by right of his position, so they had gone too, and when his successor had suggested that he might prefer to find another home, as if he was to be distrusted, in his rage he had agreed.

But leaving so quickly had cost him dear. He could not wait to take advantage of any remaining credibility he possessed, he wanted simply to leave and forget the pain and despair of seeing his office being debased by that fool. He had ordered his horse to be prepared and had ridden out that very night, feeling the same pride and excitement he had felt more than fifteen years before when he had first become a knight. But that was then, and Rodney of Hungerford had travelled far since then.

He had been surprised at first how quickly his money had all been used. It seemed as though, wherever he went, prices rose before he arrived. Initially he had not worried: after all, a knight does not concern himself with money, that is only of concern to a lord. But it disappeared so fast, his little store of coins, that he began to realize that he would soon have to earn some more to replace it.

How long was it since he had last stayed in a bed, a real bed in a building? he wondered. He huddled his shoulders against the bitter wind that swept across from the moors. Two weeks? Three? No, it was two. Two weeks since he had been allowed to stay in the priory overnight. The prior was a kindly man and had offered him a bed for longer, but Rodney could not accept. It would be too much like taking alms, and that was beneath the honor of a knight born to an old family. So he had refused and mounted his horse.

The fire was dead now, and he gazed at the remains with an expression of sadness, a soft smile that seemed to show pity for the flames that were no more, as if it was a living creature that had finally given up the struggle for life and collapsed in front of him, giving itself up to the peace of fighting no longer. It could not compete against the cruel wind that tried to cut through his defenses with slow inexorability, like a rusty sword battering at him, seeming to know that he could not continue much longer.

There was not much point, he knew that. Now that his horse had died he could hardly carry on to Cornwall to his brother. It must be well over sixty miles still. Sixty miles over the moors and through the forests.

At the thought he looked up and sneered at the trees around him. Here, although deep in the woods and far from a road, the trees were too close to the moors and were thinly spread. Their stunted, shrivelled shapes stood like the tortured victims of the wind that howled past like a banshee on the way to seek out the night's prey. In the absolute dark of the cloudy and moonless night, their thick boles stood around him like an army of damned souls, their Hell being this place of misery and despair.

The thought pleased him. An ironical smile curled one corner of his thick, red mouth, making his face light up momentarily. It made his face lose some of its harshness and returned to him a little of his youth. He was thinking that there was no need for him to worry about Hell anymore. After tonight, he knew exactly what it was like.

Sighing, he slowly stood and shouldered his pack. There was no point waiting here for death to take him, he would fight his mortality as he had fought everything else in his life. The wind snatched at his hood and ripped it from his head, expanding and filling it, tugging at it as if trying to yank it from the cloak it was a part of, but he ignored it. Slowly in his exhaustion, moving like a rusty machine, he lifted a foot and dropped it a short step away. He lifted the other foot and dragged it forward to take another step and gradually continued on his way to the west.

The hood trailing out behind him, his hair was whipped into madness by the gale, dancing and leaping, each separate black strand seeming to try to break free from his scalp. His eyes were slitted as he trudged on among the trees trying to keep the driven rain from them, but they still glittered with cold rage among the maze of wrinkles at his treatment and bad fortune. The face had a harsh charm and stolid elegance above the thickly muscled neck, except for the thick nose with its heavy scar that stretched from the bridge and over the right cheek: it seemed too brutal for the other features. It sat with its pink cicatrice like a solitary mountain looming over a rugged plain, out of place and strangely threatening above the large sensual mouth, giving warning of his true nature.

The cloak was torn from his hands and he gave up trying to hold it and continued on his way, ignoring the wind's cold pinpricks stabbing at his body through his tunic and mail. His body was immense and square, like a bear's. But as he knew, even bears die. He sighed again.

Then, even as he began to entertain thoughts of relaxing, of sitting by a tree and letting the cold seep into his bones, of resting and possibly never rising again, he heard a sound, a wonderful, miraculous, heavenly sound—the whinny of a horse!

Were his ears playing him false? He turned his head, one ear jutting toward the noise like a weapon as he tried to hear above the roar and hiss of the elements. Yes, there it was again! A horse.

Somehow he found a little more energy—from where he could not tell—and strode off into the trees. Surrounded by the trunks of the wooden sentries, he could only hazard a guess at the correct path to the horse and, hopefully, security and warmth. He forced his way through branches that seemed desperate to stop him, he kicked at trailing tentacles of creepers that caught at his feet, he struggled over thick bushes, trying to get to the horse. And then he saw it. It was ahead of him, standing and shaking in its fear and horror of the elements. The knight looked around in amazement. Where was the owner? There was no sign of anyone, no fire, no shelter, just this horse. Automatically his hand grabbed at his sword hilt as he stood just inside the line of trees and stared. But there seemed nothing to be afraid of; no sudden movement from the trees at either side, no noise from men running to him, just the incessant wind.

Frowning now in his perplexity, he slowly walked to the animal, which rolled its eyes in terror. Patting the neck, he could see that it was a mare and, to his surprise, she was still saddled and bridled. The harnesses looked rich even in the darkness and he could feel the quality of the leather under his fingers. Even in the rain he could see the flecks of lather that remained on her chest and flanks. Why? Had she been running because her owner was attacked? Why had she been left here?

What had happened?

He reached for the reins and pulled, but they appeared to be caught and, when he looked, he saw that they had snagged on a thick branch. Had she been running and got them stuck, making her stop? Shrugging, he collected them and led her away, patting her head and neck and talking to her while his eyes flitted around. There was no sign of her owner anywhere. Slowly, like a man who has forgotten how to and who is instructing each muscle in novel and unfamiliar functions, he permitted a smile to crack his face, and he offered up a quick prayer of thanks. Surely this was his salvation! This horse, evidently lost by another, would allow him to cover the remaining miles to his brother.

But it was when he felt inside the saddlebags that he began to understand his real fortune.

One was filled with coins.

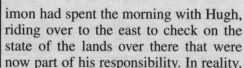

imon had spent the morning with Hugh, riding over to the east to check on the state of the lands over there that were now part of his responsibility. In reality, as far as he was concerned it was a good excuse to get away from the affairs at Blackway and to go for a good ride. Hugh, as usual, was not delighted with the thought, but when Simon mentioned the inn at Half Moon his interest suddenly developed and they were soon on their way.

They had left early, only an hour or so after dawn, and they were there before the local estate seneschal had finished his breakfast, so they had gone on without him, with the result that they were finished before ten thirty. After two swift pints of beer they started off home again.

But back at the house they found Edith standing and waiting. "It's Tanner, father. He says there's been a robbery on the road," she said, her eyes huge in her horrified fascination.

With a groan, Simon rolled his eyes heavenward in a theatrical gesture. "What now? A cockerel has been taken from a yard? Someone has mislaid his best hauberk? What now?" He smiled down briefly at his daughter, dropped down from his saddle, and passed the reins to Hugh before striding toward his door, Edith following.

Inside, he found Stephen Tanner, the constable, talking to Margaret. She came forward quickly and kissed him, then left them alone, going through to the yard behind the house with their daughter, casting an anxious glance back at him as she left. Hugh stayed in the room with Simon and Stephen.

"Stephen, how are you?" said the bailiff. "So what's all this about a robbery?"

Tanner was a large, slow block of a man, a figure of enormous bulk, tall and broad. He had a square face on top of a body that would have suited one of the moor's dwarf oak trees, solid and compact with the promise of great strength. Under his black brows his face was cragged and scarred by the weather, but his eyes were kindly and gentle. His mouth was a thin line, and always seemed fixed, rigid and straight, as if always pursed, making him look as if he had seen something that he greatly disapproved of. When he was unsure of something, his eyes held a constant look of frowning confusion that hid a careful and sensible intelligence and a shrewdness that had been the downfall of many a thief. Built as strongly as Simon's house, he was known to be a good and honest man, which was why he had so often been re-elected to his position. Now, though, his face was troubled.

"Hello, bailiff. Sorry to come round like this, but I had a message to go over to Clanton Barton this morning, that farm on the other side of Copplestone on the Oakhampton road. Seems that John Greenfield there was working this morning when he saw some men coming up over his fields. They'd been set upon and robbed on the road to Oakhampton late last afternoon. He says they were in a terrible state, what with the rain and everything. They had tried to find somewhere to stay, but there's not much down that way so they got stuck out all night. Well, he put them in front of his fire and sent his boy to get me. I'd heard you'd been made bailiff, so I thought I'd better come here and get you before I went over there. I know it's my duty to catch thieves here, but now you're a bailiff you have that job too. And if we need to get a posse together, I'd be grateful for your help. We don't have too many robberies around here. If this is a band of outlaws, you may be able to get men from Oakhampton to help us catch them."

"Yes, of course. I'd better come with you. Wait here, I'll just go and get my things," Simon said. As bailiff, he was his lord's representative in the court at Lydford, in charge of the local constables. Clearly, if by helping Tanner he could see thieves arrested, he was performing his duty. Even though Lydford did not cover Tanner's area, it was every man's responsibility to help catch felons. He walked out to the yard at the back of the house, shouting instructions to Hugh to saddle up a fresh horse, then swiftly kissed his wife and daughter before snatching up his sword and leading Tanner out to the front of the house.

There they paused, waiting for Hugh. Simon fretted at the delay and when Hugh arrived with his horse he snatched the reins from him and was quickly in the saddle. Tanner mounted his great old beast more slowly, heaving his massive frame up with slow inevitability. The sight reminded Simon of watching a tree fall: there seemed the same slow beginning, the same initial faltering, followed by a sudden acceleration, until, at last, peace. The tree lying on the ground, the constable sitting in his saddle, with a small smile of achievement on his face, as if he too had doubted his ability to mount. Then they were on their way, gently cantering off to the Clanton farm.

"So did he say anything else about these people?" Simon asked.

"No. Seems they were travellers, but that's all I know. The boy, he was tired out when he got to my house—couldn't hardly talk. I left him with my wife."

"We may have to call up a posse," said Simon reflectively. "When we get to the barton, we'll find out where they were robbed and what happened. If we need the posse we can organize it from there."

"Yes, that's what I thought. We may have to ride straight past the men's houses anyway, if they came back this way."

They rode on in tense expectation, hardly talking for the rest of the journey, Tanner sitting stolid and imperturbable on his mount and Simon warily casting around as he went. He was staggered that this should have happened—especially so soon after his position had been granted. In all his years in the area he had only heard of three robberies, and the last was months ago. It seemed an appalling forewarning of his tenure of office that this should have happened so soon—especially after Brewer's death. And for some reason he had a vague presentiment of evil, a suspicion that this affair would not be as easy or as straightforward as Tanner's message seemed to imply.

It only took them a matter of an hour to get to the Greenfield Barton, or farm, a solid building of granite blocks with the dark red mortar showing clearly between each. A fire was obviously lighted inside, the smoke was pouring out of the chimney, lending an apparently tranquil air to the surroundings.

The two men dismounted quickly and tethered their horses, then Simon strode to the solid wooden door and rapped loudly. He could hear voices inside, and stepped back a little. There was a shuffling, and then the door was opened a little and a square, whiskered face peeped out, holding a suspicious frown in the old, faded blue eyes. Seeing only Simon, the door opened wider and he could see that it was Greenfield, a farmer whose fair hair, rumored to have come from his Viking ancestors, had lost its color and was now a pastel gray. The eyes peered out cautiously at the bailiff from around the edge of the part-opened door. Normally a calm man, easy-going and casual, the extent of his caution at the knocking of a stranger was concerning. His lined and worn face only cleared when he saw Tanner standing behind.

"Ah, Stephen. Hello, so my boy got to you, then?"

"Yes, John, I left him at home warming himself in front of the fire. He was worn out by the time he got to my house."

"Ah, well. At least he made it. So, it's Mr. Puttock, isn't it?" he said, turning to him. Simon nodded.

"He's the bailiff now, John. That's why I waited before coming over. I wanted to bring him."

"Ah. Best come in, I reckon."

They followed the old farmer through the doorway and into the screens: a wide corridor, lit by a series of sconces set into the wooden walls, built at the end of the hall to partition off the parlor and animal quarters. A heavy tapestry gave into the large, dark hall beyond, where four men sat ranged around the roaring fire, watching the farmer's wife as she stirred a pot and prepared food over the flames.

"Here's the bailiff and the constable," Greenfield said as he led the other two through the door, and as he entered, Simon recognized the men with a sudden shock. They were the four monks he had seen walking with their abbot while he was on his way to Furnshill.

"Where's the abbot?" he asked as he walked over to the men. They all gazed up at him, their faces lit by the fire, and as he looked at them, waiting for an answer, he saw that they were all frightened, as if fearful of his question. He looked enquiringly at the farmer. "Well?"

Greenfield shrugged, as if he had no knowledge of an abbot, that these were the only men that had appeared. With a frown of concern on his face, Simon turned back to the monks. "Where is he?"

At last one of them dropped his eyes and looked at his lap. "We don't know," he said sadly, and then his breath caught in his throat as if he was close to sobbing. "He was taken from us. He was taken hostage."

Simon walked over to lean against the wall not far from the fire, his eyes flitting from one to another as he crossed his arms. "Tell me what happened," he said gently.

At first it was difficult to get any sense from them. It took long enough merely to persuade them to talk. It was not only the shock of their experience, it was also the miserable night they had spent in the open, with no shelter from the bitter wind and rain. The oldest of them had completely lost his smile and genial appearance. He seemed to have suffered more than the others, he looked close to collapsing from fear and shock, and could hardly keep his hands from shaking as if he had the ague, his eyes downcast as though he wanted to avoid the bailiff's gaze. Seeing this, and sensing his pain, Simon directed his questions to the youngest-looking, a man almost as old as himself, who seemed the least affected of them all.

He began fitfully, with many pauses and sidelong glances at his companions to check that he was not leaving out any points of importance. "We . . . we were going on to Oakhampton . . ."

"Why did it take so long? I left you days ago, you should have been there by now."

"We . . . the abbot wanted to rest and the . . . we stayed at the church at Crediton. We only started out again yesterday and . . . We got to Copplestone—"

"Where were you when it happened?" Simon asked quietly, his hand toying with his sword hilt as he tried to control his impatience and the urge to make the man speak faster and get to the point.

"Out beyond the village. We had left the village . . . must have been two hours before—"

"Were you still on the road?"

"Yes. Yes, we were—"

"And you were all together?"

"Yes, we were all walking, except for the abbot on his horse. Two men came up from behind us . . . they had swords. They rode through us—we had to get out of the way. They got to the abbot and . . . and . . ."

Simon stepped forward softly and crouched in front of the man, looking at him gravely. At first the monk dropped his eyes as if embarrassed, but then, gradually, his eyes came up again with a kind of defiance, and he spoke directly to the bailiff, his eyes staring straight into Simon's and his voice losing its nervousness and slowly gaining strength from the sight of the grim officer in front of him, who listened as though with his whole body and soul in silent intensity.

"We . . . we were scared. The abbot had been worried for days. He was sure that we'd be attacked. He never said why, but he was sure of it. He seemed to feel that we were always close to being attacked." Simon nodded—that certainly matched his own observations. "Then these two men came up from behind and scattered us all. They wore helms, we couldn't see their faces. Their swords were out and they went straight to the abbot . . . they knew what they wanted . . . One took the abbot's bridle, and he . . . The abbot had all of the money on his horse . . . We thought they'd go then, take the packs and go, let the abbot down and leave us alone, but, but they didn't . . . they took the abbot's reins and took him with them . . . They went off into the woods by the side of the road with him. We couldn't do anything about it . . . We . . . we started to follow, we ran after them, but then we realized that if they saw us they might kill the abbot to get away . . . They shouted at us . . . they said they'd kill the abbot if we followed . . . We . . . they said they had others in the woods . . . They said they'd kill us as well if we didn't leave . . . We had to leave them and come back . . . We tried to find somewhere to rest, but there wasn't anywhere . . . we had to sleep on the road. We tried to get back to Copplestone, but it was too far . . ."

Gently Simon touched his shoulder until the young monk subsided. "Did they have any marks on their helms?"

"No . . . no, I don't think so."

"How about their tunics? Any signs on them?"

"No, nothing."

"So there was nothing to identify them?"

"No."

"What about their horses—what color were they?"

"They were both brown. But one was a great big horse, like a knight's. The other was smaller."

"Were there any marks on their clothes? Anything to show they were knights?"

"No, no, I don't think so," said the young monk, frowning in concentration. "But it all happened so fast . . ."

"So they simply rode up and took the abbot?" said Simon musingly, his brow puckered as he peered at the young monk in incomprehension, trying to make sense of the situation. "Did the abbot say anything?"

"No, sir, he was completely silent—I think he was scared," said the monk simply.

Simon frowned at him for a moment, then, his face serious, he stood. "Stephen, we'll need to go and look for the abbot. I'll go on ahead and see what I can find. You must raise the posse and follow me when you can. We'll have to try to rescue him." He turned back to the young monk. "Would you come with me to show me where it all happened? Can you ride?"

It was only as the monk gazed back at him with the fearful eyes of a petrified rabbit that the bailiff suddenly realized the full impact of the news. The abbot was taken! The abbot of an important and wealthy Cistercian monastery, almost certainly a high-born man! He must be found, and quickly—before he could be harmed.

But who would hold an abbot hostage?

reenfield had a massive old gray horse that he used for pulling his cart, that Simon secretly felt should have been killed years before as an act of kindness, but he was grateful enough that the monk could borrow it when they left the farmhouse.

Tanner, now he knew that a man, and an abbot at that, had been taken hostage, moved swiftly to his horse and was soon riding away to rouse his men. Simon and the monk had to wait for a while for the old horse to be saddled, the bailiff fretting at the delay, but soon it too was ready and they made their way quickly down from the old farm to the road. Once there they turned their heads to the sun and set off at a quick lope.

"What's your name? I forgot to ask back there."

"It's David, bailiff."

"Fine. Keep your eyes open, then, David. I want to know as soon as we are getting close to the place where the abbot was taken yesterday. Alright?"

The monk nodded, the fear still plain on his face. Of what may have happened to the abbot, Simon wondered, or of what may happen to us? Grimly he reached down and made sure that his sword was still at his waist. The feel of the hilt comforted him a little, but he was still wary and felt nervous himself about what they might find.

They had covered more than seven miles from Copplestone when the young monk reined in his horse and slowed to a trot, falling back. Simon, noticing him out of the corner of his eye, slowed as well and let the monk ride up slowly and overtake him. He could see that the young man had a fixed frown of concentration on his face, and seemed to be glaring at the trees all round as he trotted forward. He stopped and waited for Simon to catch up.

"I remember this bit," he said, pointing up at an ash tree that had been blasted by lightning. "I noticed that just a few minutes before it happened."

Simon nodded and dropped lightly from his horse. The highway here was a wide track through the woods. Although the king's order many years before had commanded that all roads should be cleared for yards on both sides to help stop outlaws from making ambushes, many like this one had not yet had the undergrowth cut down. The tall trees on either side seemed to enhance the sense of their solitude, as if reminding them how far they were from a hamlet or even a house, and the noises of their horses' hoofs and harnesses were deadened this deep in among them, heightening their feeling of isolation.

He tossed his reins to the monk and walked forward slowly, the monk following on his horse, as he carefully examined the hard-packed earth of the road. Occasionally he paused to study the ground in more detail, but the spoor of the monks and their attackers was too mixed in with the marks of other travellers, and the rain from the previous night had been heavy enough to wash away most of the signs. He shrugged.

Maybe a hunter could follow what had happened here, but he knew he could not. He continued on, the monk trailing slowly after him, his eyes flitting from the bailiff to the trees in his apprehension.

Simon was concentrating so hard on the road that he was startled by the sudden cry from behind.

Spinning round, he ran back to the monk, part-drawing his sword from its sheath in his fright. "What is it?" he hissed.

Pointing in among the trees that lined the road, his eyes glittering, the monk turned to face him. "It was here," he said simply.

Sighing in his relief, the bailiff followed his finger. He could see that the ground was heavily disturbed at the verge on the north side of the road. Reseating his sword in its scabbard, he walked up to the fringe of the trees and peered into the darkness. Warily he subjected the woods to a minute study, his eyes going from tree to tree, until, at last content that no one was watching, he dropped to a crouch and looked at the ground. It was obvious that three horses had passed through. He could see the tracks clearly in the dirt between the trees—the rains from the night before had not washed the marks away. Simon frowned and peered into the darkness again, wondering what to do. It would be sensible to wait here for the posse to arrive, but that could be a long time. Tanner would have to visit twenty farmsteads and hamlets to call up all the men in the hundred, so by the time they arrived it would be dark. He made a decision and stood up.

"David, I want you to wait here. The posse will be along soon enough, and you'll be safe here. When they get here, tell them to follow me if I'm not back. I'm going into the woods to see if I can find where these tracks lead to."

The monk gripped his reins tightly in his fear and looked from the bailiff to the trees all round. When he spoke it was with a voice hushed by his concern and trepidation, as if the trees nearby were hiding the abbot's abductors. "But . . . but, what if they come back? I can't face them again . . . And what if they see you? They might . . ."

"I don't think so. We'll be alright, whoever took the abbot has probably gone by now anyway. Don't worry, all you have to do is wait here for the others. I should be back soon," said Simon with more confidence than he felt. He glanced into the trees and felt his brow pucker into a scowl. He felt as nervous about going in among them as the monk was about waiting here on the road, but he had a responsibility to see whether he could track the hostage and his abductors. He patted the neck of his horse absent-mindedly, smiled up at the monk, and was gone.

It seemed to him, as he stepped in among the trees, that the woods themselves were listening and watching him. There was no sound apart from his feet as they occasionally crunched small twigs and leaves. Even his breathing sounded unnaturally loud. There was a hush, a deadness, that sapped his will, and it was only after he had paused to look back and seen that he had only managed to cover forty yards that he continued. In his nervousness it seemed as if he could feel a malign presence lurking near: if he had been out of sight of the road he felt that he would have run back, but knowing that he could still see it made him impatient with himself and with his fear, so with a quick and angry gesture he forced himself to carry on.

As he went deeper into the woods, he started to hear small noises. There was a scratching nearby, then a rasping, and all around him the tick and creak of the trees, which all together made him even more tense, the muscles of his scalp tingling with the strain as he stretched his ears to pick up any human sounds. At one point a bird high above clattered off from its roost, making him jump behind a large trunk in his alarm, only to grimace to himself in disgust. He heard a sudden yapping, then a sharp screech from far away that made him stand stockstill for a moment, hand on sword-hilt, but there was nothing more. Slowly he untensed his muscles and forced his feet forward again, but now he kept his hand on the sword. He heard a quiet scraping and whirled, but it appeared to be one branch rubbing against another. He looked all around, considering whether to get back to the road, but then, glowering, he straightened his shoulders and went on. His fear was beginning to leave him now, he was moving less from a need to force himself to do his duty and more from a desire to help the abbot if he could. He could not forget the terror on the man's face as he had asked for Simon's help and company, as if— Simon suddenly stopped. As if he had known this was going to happen? He shook his head and continued. There would be time for speculation later.

Maybe if he had agreed to join the abbot this would not have happened, though? Perhaps the sight of the bailiff and his servant would have put the two robbers off? And, if that was so, he had let the man down, and let him down badly. That thought, having taken root, built a small flame of anger deep inside him. It was not just the fact that the abbot was a frightened man who obviously wanted his protection and aid, it was that he was a man of God. He should not have *been* attacked, his cloth alone should have been sufficient defense on the road. The thought that someone here, in his own

shire, could rob an abbot and take him hostage made
Simon's anger smolder.

He froze again as another bird crashed off from its
perch, upset by his sudden presence, but then his eyes
dropped to the tracks, which led forward still, and he
cautiously followed them, thinking to himself that with
all these noises there was not likely to be any other humans about. If men were present, the other creatures
would have fled.

As he walked deeper in among the trees, the dark
came crowding in, forcing him to concentrate harder as
he followed the tracks farther into the woods. He soon
found that they became a blur, a smudge on the ground
in front of him, and he had to pause more often, not to
listen for any sounds from ambushers, but simply to
make sure that he had not lost the trail. The undergrowth was thick, with shrubs and young ferns struggling to grow in the permanent semi-darkness under
the tall trees, and several times he found that he had
missed the spoor completely and had to go back over
his own footsteps to pick it up. After he had done this
for the fourth time, he began to follow the gaps in the
trees instead, where it looked as though a horse with its
rider could pass, occasionally checking down by his
feet to make sure that the horse tracks were going the
same way. Every now and again he looked all round,
making sure that he was not being watched, his nerves
feeling as though they were ready to snap, and when at
last he heard the noise it was almost a relief, as if now
his fears of being surprised could depart. The tenseness
left him, to be replaced by the watchful expectancy of
the hunter, mixed with his growing caution.

It was the sharp yap of a dog fox. Simon stiffened,
taut as he listened, then let out a long, low sigh and

glanced up at the cover of the leaves far overhead. A few last rays from the setting sun were fighting their way through the dense foliage—he must have been walking for over an hour, slowly and carefully edging his way deeper. He ducked behind a tree and leaned against the trunk. Breathing deeply, he considered what to do. Go back or carry on? Had he come far enough? Should he try to go back and get the others? But what if Tanner wasn't back yet, what if the posse hadn't arrived? If the men and the abbot were ahead, surely he should continue? After all, he might be able to overpower the robbers, whoever they may be, surprise them in the dusk and rescue the abbot. At the least he should try to get closer and see whether he could attempt it; it wasn't completely dark yet, and it should be easy to retrace his steps.

He gripped his sword-hilt tightly and slowly continued on his way, looking down every now and then to make sure that the tracks still led in the same direction, breathing shallowly as he listened for any sign, any hint, that he might be close.

There it was again! A yapping. His brow wrinkled as he considered: it came from ahead, from the direction of the trail. If there were foxes there, there were not likely to be any men around—those shy creatures would avoid men wherever possible. Why, he found himself wondering, do foxes make that noise? He felt the tension return, the prickle of excitement, as he edged on farther, slowly checking each step before he put his feet down, looking at the ground and avoiding twigs and other undergrowth that could give him away. At each pace he paused and stared ahead grimly, half expecting a crossbow bolt or arrow to strike him, almost as if he was daring someone to try to hit him as he surveyed the tree trunks in front. He tried to follow the spoor while walking in the shadows of the trees, trying to maintain some cover as he went, trying to use them as protection from the men who had captured the abbot.

It took him another half hour before he could see the clearing—half an hour of slow and careful pacing, with each step measured and checked, with each step taking all his concentration, with all his senses screaming at every sound, with his ears straining as he tried to distinguish any noises that could have been made by a human; but there was nothing. This deep in the woods it seemed as though even the animals had run away. There was nothing, no sound, not even a squeak or a rustle to betray a nearby beast apart from the occasional excited yapping. It was as if the whole forest was dead and he and the fox alone breathed the dank and thick air.

With the gloom growing, the hairs on his head began to rise, and he felt the breath straining in his throat. It was not the fear of humans, that he could cope with. No, it was as if with each minute, as the dark crept on toward night-time, his superstitions grew in strength. Here he was nearer the bleak moors, nearer the center of Crockern's power, and as if there was an affinity between the ancient trees here and the primeval stones so close, he seemed to feel his own presence as an abomination, as if he was loathed by the very earth under his feet for his trespass. It was with a physical effort that he forced himself on.

At last he could see an opening in the trees. He began to move even more slowly, inch by inch, with the infinite patience of a lizard hunting a fly, until he came into the lee of a massive oak and could stand silently watching from under its protection.

There was a sudden rustling as if two kittens were

playing on the leafy floor. Simon concentrated. He could discern nothing in the gloom ahead, too much was obscured by the boles of the trees. Gradually he relaxed his grip on his sword-hilt and flexed his hand as he listened, feeling the sweat break out cold and chilling. But there was still nothing. He wiped the sweat from his palm and gripped his sword again, then crept forward, carefully moving from tree to tree as he made a wide circle around the clearing.

As he moved forward he could catch brief, frustrating glimpses: now a great oak, now a towering elm. It was as if there was a tapestry that had been roughly cut into pieces and he was trying to put it together in his mind, arranging the various parts and trying to associate them although the threads around each section were badly frayed, making it impossible to be sure which connected with which. All he could do was attempt to build the picture.

At last, when he had almost half-circled the empty area, he felt he could not continue, and began to edge his way in toward it. The blood was pounding in his ears with the tenseness of his fear and excitement as he moved forward at a crawling pace until he was at the very edge of the trees.

In the dim light he could see the ground clearly. His eyes flitted over the space, looking for any signs of humans or animals, but there seemed to be nothing. No sign of man, no blackened remains of a fire, no parcels or packs lying on the ground, no gleam of metal where a sword lay. Suddenly he felt his fear return, concentrated and almost overpowering in its intensity. There, just a few yards in front of him, lay a small pyramid of horse's dung. For a horse to have created so perfect a shape, it must have been stationary. It must have been tethered there, surely. Had the robbers been here? And if they had been, where were they now? He paused and considered. There had been a horse in the clearing, at least one. Either it was the abbot's or it was one of the robbers'. Could the abbot have escaped? If he had, could this be from his horse? But then, what if this horse belonged to a robber? He could be close by. Simon's eyes quickly flitted all over the ground again, but even as he gazed all round, he started wondering. If it *was* the abbot's, where was he? And what if it was a robber's horse? Had they rested here last night and then ridden on? Or were they even now waiting, watching him, preparing to attack?

He studied the area again and tried to clear his mind, trying to decide what to do. It seemed impossible to make a clear choice, to know what was best. Go on or return to the road? Deferring the choice and frowning, he continued his slow progress.

It was only when he had almost managed to get all the way around it that he smelt the burned wood and cooked meat. Slowly he eased himself into a crouch, sniffing as quietly as he could. It was not the smell of a fresh fire, it seemed damp and dead. There was no acrid smoke, no sharp tang to the smell, just a dull, burned odor that was almost stale. It seemed to come from over to his right, just a little farther on.

The bailiff offered up a quick prayer, his eyes closed, then peered all around again. He felt that he had been stalking for days—the fatigue was giving him cramps in his legs—and it seemed, now he was close to the end of the trail, that the tiredness was settling on him heavily, like a leaden cloak that smothered mind and muscles alike. He could not control a swift, hopeful glance over his shoulder, as if he half-expected to see the posse coming through the trees toward him, but there was no one there. He would have to go on alone. His teeth clenched, he dropped silently to crawl on his hands and knees toward the smell.

After only a short distance he came to another small clearing, a slight opening in the trees where the trunks were not so closely crowded together, and carefully looked in. From here he could smell the old fire: someone must have made camp here, far away from the nearest houses and any risk of discovery. There it was, just by a tree some twenty yards away that had been blackened by the heat. Even if the smoke had been seen, nobody would have come this deep into the woods to investigate. He could see little apart from the dark smudge of the blackened undergrowth between the trunks that stood between him and the clearing, so he began another slow and careful progress around the camp, crawling from tree to tree, stopping and watching, then moving on again. There was no sound, no movement. It was as if the camp had been abandoned years before and had been left, undisturbed and untouched by human or creature.

Then he heard the yap again and, even as he tensed at the unexpected noise, he saw two foxes gambolling around, near the old fire, springing and jumping as gleefully as kittens.

With a brief flare of impatience, now that it seemed that his careful tracking was all in vain and there was no reason to be afraid, he stood up carefully and scrutinized the clearing. It seemed absolutely deserted apart from the two creatures. Nothing else moved. The only noises were from the trees as, high above, a breeze caught the branches. Taken with a sudden fit of anger at the thought that his exertions had been unnecessary, he bellowed out, "Is anybody there?"

His only response was the sudden explosion of noise as the two foxes bolted in their terror, both leaping for the safety of the dark trees at the edge of the clearing. Then the silence returned. There was nothing to betray a human's presence, not even the scuffle of a man woken by his shout trying to grab at a club or sword: nothing. Simon drew his sword and, steeling himself, slowly crept forward until he was at the edge of the trees. As soon as he reached the fringe, he rushed on, running to crouch in the middle of the open space, whirling and glaring around, his sword grasped in both hands and the hot blood hammering in his ears.

But there was nothing. No one sprang to attack him, no one ran away into the surrounding trees, there was not even the sound of a disturbed animal to break the all-embracing silence. Gradually, shrugging shamefacedly, he relaxed, and lowered the point of his sword, taking stock. The clearing was only some twenty yards across and there was nowhere for anyone to hide apart from in among the trees. There was no sign that anybody had ever been here apart from the fire. He turned and looked for the blackened embers to see how long the clearing had been empty. It lay over at the other side of the clearing from him, a darker stain among the shadows.

He wandered over toward it, but as he drew near, his feet started to falter, and he stumbled as he frowned at a tree. He had only covered half the distance when he stopped. Eyes wide in horror, he gagged and dropped to his knees, staring at the patch of burned grass and the tree in front of him.

With a high scream, he turned and ran, rushing away from the sight in a mad, panicked flight back to the road.

The smell of cooked meat came from the man who had been roasted, like a convicted witch, over the flames.

hen Tanner and the others arrived, the constable was surprised to find the monk and the bailiff sitting by the side of the road in front of a small fire. The monk rose immediately and ran to greet them, his nervous features cracking with an expression of desperate relief, and when Tanner caught a glimpse of the bailiff he began to understand why he was grateful for the new arrivals. Simon did not move. He sat still and quiet with his cloak wrapped tightly around him as he stared into the fire. Tanner dismounted and walked over to him.

"Thank God you've arrived! We were wondering whether you'd all wait for morning before coming and we didn't want to stay here alone all night," said the monk, breathlessly, as Tanner walked to the bailiff. The constable nodded absently and continued on, leaving the monk to welcome the others.

"Bailiff? What's wrong, bailiff?"

Simon could only slowly bring his eyes up from the fire. After the horror in the woods he felt more tired than he had ever been in his life before. The nervous energy and the anger that had kept him going through the woods had drained him, and the horror of the sight in the clearing and his mad rush back to the road had finished the job. Now as he looked up he seemed to the constable to have aged by twenty years since the afternoon; his face was gaunt and pale and his eyes glittered as if he was in a fever, and Tanner crouched quickly beside him, his face full of concern. Simon hardly seemed to notice him. Almost as if he wanted not to see the constable, he turned his gaze back to the fire and stared vacantly into the flames.

"Bailiff? What's happened?" said the constable in shocked amazement.

"We got here just before dark," Simon said quietly. "We found it easily enough. David—that's the monk—he found it quite quickly. The tracks were clear, going off into the woods over there." He pointed briefly with his chin to the opposite side of the road and returned to his solitary stare, talking softly and calmly while the constable frowned at him in anxious concern. "I told David to wait here for you and I went in alone. I must have been going for over an hour when I found a small clearing. One horse at least had been kept there, there was a fresh pile of shit where it had been tied."

Simon looked up suddenly and the constable felt the pain in the bailiff's eyes as they searched his face for a moment before returning to their introspective study of the flames. "The abbot was not far away. I carried on and found him. He had been tied up—tied to a tree. Someone had gathered up a load of twigs and branches and piled them underneath him." Tanner saw him shudder once, involuntarily, but then his voice continued calmly. "Then set light to them and burned the abbot to death."

Tanner stared at him steadily. "What? He was burned at the stake?"

"Yes," said Simon softly, almost wonderingly. "He was burned alive." Then he winced, his voice strained and harsh with the horror of it. "He must have been screaming when he died. Oh God! Stephen, you should have seen his face! It was dreadful! The flames were not hot enough to burn the top of his body, it was like he was staring at *me!* It felt like the devil himself was looking at me through his eyes, I could see his face clearly. God! It was awful!"

"But who could do a thing like that? Who would do that to a man of God?" said Tanner with a frown of consideration. Of course, outlaws were known for their brutality, exceeding even the viciousness of the pirates from Normandy, but neither French nor English bands were known here in the heart of Devon. Tanner was older than the bailiff and had served in the wars against the French, so he had witnessed the cruelty that men could show to each other, but even in war he had never heard of a monk being killed in this way, like a heretic. He was puzzled rather than horrified.

But he was worried too—if these two outlaws could do that to an abbot, nobody could be safe until they were caught. He looked up at the other men as they hobbled their horses and came forward to the fire, laughing and joking as they came. Their humor seemed almost sacrilegious after what he had just heard, and he had to bite back a shout at them.

Tanner was a calm and stable man. As a farmer he was used to the changing seasons and the steady march of the years as he watched his animals and plants grow, flourish and eventually die, but he was also used to the cruel and vicious ways of the wild, where the stronger creatures survived and the weaker died. Even so, to him this crime seemed strange in its barbarity. Animals could do that to each other, killing for food or pleasure, but for men to do this seemed curious in his quiet rural hundred. Constables in towns might be more used to cruelty of this type, he reflected. He had seen such acts at time of war when he had been a foot soldier for the king, but he did not expect them here, not during peace. Why should they do this to an abbot? He sighed and looked back at the bailiff, sitting silently absorbed beside him.

"You need to rest, sir. Lie down. I'll organize a watch and get the men sorted out."

"Yes," said Simon heedlessly, nodding slowly. He was gradually losing his feeling of horror under the stolid gaze of the constable and it was slowly being replaced by a distracted confusion, as if he had seen the whole of his world toppled. He had lived here all his life and in that time he had never seen a murdered man—or any man who had died in such an obscene manner. It seemed as though all that he had ever believed and known about the people who lived in the shire had suddenly been destroyed, and that he must reconsider all of his deepest held convictions in the light of this single, shattering event. A tear slowly dribbled from his eye and ran down his cheek, making him start, and he wiped it away angrily.

As if the gesture itself had awoken him, he looked over at Tanner, who was staring in his turn at the flames. "Right. Tomorrow we start the hunt for these killers, whoever they may be. I want them brought to justice," he said, almost snarling as he felt the disgust and hatred rising again. He was angry, not for the crime alone, not just for the hideous death of the man in the woods. It was for his own heightened sense of vulnerability, for the feeling that the men capable of this act could kill others, and would. They must be destroyed, like mad bears—hunted down and slaughtered with no compunction. "You get one of the men to ride on to Buckland and let them know what has happened here. The rest of us will follow the tracks and see if we can find them."

"Yes," said Tanner, startled by the venom in Simon's voice. "What about the sheriff? Shouldn't we send someone to Exeter?"

"No. This happened here and it's our responsibility. *We'll* get them. For now, though, I'm going to get some sleep." He stood slowly in his exhaustion, gazing at the men in faint surprise as if he had only just noticed them, and wandered over to a tree. He sat, leaning against the trunk, pulled his cloak around him and was soon asleep.

Tanner watched him for a while, but then, as a man walked by him with a jug of cider, reached up and caught him by the arm. "There's been a murder here. Tell the men that we'll be up at dawn, so they'd better get some sleep."

The man, an older, stout farmer called Cottey, with the red and rosy cheeks of the cider drinker, stared at him uncomprehendingly. "A murder? Who's dead?"

"Abbot of Buckland," said Tanner shortly as he rose. "I'm going to stay on watch. Tell the others to rest or I'll let one of them do it instead." A sudden shriek of laughter made him glare round, his voice hissing in his rage. "And tell the daft buggers we're not on a trip to the fair. The killers could be watching us now."

He walked over to a tree near Simon's sleeping body and stared out at the trees, away from the fire, as the men all began to settle, squabbling and bickering mildly as they fought for positions nearest the fire.

Soon, apart from the low murmur of conversations, the camp fell quiet and Tanner could hear the night sounds of the forest come back, as if they could bring normality with them.

But he could not lose the sensation of brooding evil. The murder had unsettled him, and he felt too disquieted to rest as he stood and maintained his vigil. All he could think of was that someone was out there, maybe even now watching him from deep in among the trees, someone who had killed the abbot. Whoever could do that was capable of anything.

As he rolled himself up in his cloak and made his first circuit around their camp, he was thinking of his home, where the fire would be roaring now, the flames leaping from the cured oak logs.

Rodney too was thinking of the heat that a fire could give him as he rode into the little town of North Tawton. Frozen and miserable, he knew that he needed to sit in front of flames and thaw himself out. At the same time, his horse needed a dry place and fresh hay, a place to rest the night.

The small hamlet was little more than a street with fifteen houses, one of which was an inn, and it was here that the knight reined in. There was a stable block at the back, reached by a low gateway, so he dismounted and led the mare in before walking through to the inn's main room.

The next morning was chill and damp. A thick mist lay all around, with no breeze to disperse it, and the men all rose stiff and cold from their sleep.

Tanner had periodically thrown more branches on the fire and kept it going through the night, so they all huddled round it and tried to absorb a little of the heat. The constable walked up and down as they sat and crouched, hunched against the cold, and only when they all seemed fully awake did he gently shake Simon by the shoulder.

"Come on, sir. Let's find these bastards!"

Simon woke slowly, and when he did he still seemed dazed, as if he was still half asleep, the shock of the previous day lying heavily on him as if the sleep had not relaxed him at all. Tanner brought him some cured meat where he sat and stood over him while he ate, like a guard protecting his lord. He would not let Simon get up until he had finished the food, which he did with a wry grin, and then led him over to the men.

"Right. The bailiff here found the body of the abbot in the woods yesterday—"

"Let me, Stephen," interrupted Simon quietly. He faced the men and continued softly, talking slowly and carefully. "The abbot was taken hostage by two men and taken into the woods. His companions thought he was being taken for money, and they raised the alarm. But the men tied him to a tree and killed him—they killed him by burning him at the stake. We *have* to find the men who did it. While they're free, all of us are in danger, because if they can do this to an abbot they can do it to anyone. Who's the best hunter here?"

"That'd be John Black," said one of the men and, following his gaze, Simon saw him, his short, wiry figure sitting close to the fire as he held his hands out to the flames. He did not even look up as Tanner continued.

"John? Do you think you can track a horse through the woods?"

"Yes," said Black calmly.

Simon looked him over. The man exuded a quiet confidence and seemed certain of his ability.

"Alright. We'll need someone to go over to Buckland as well to let the monks know what's happened. Paul, could you do that?" said Tanner. Paul, old Cottey's son, a slim youth of some sixteen years, nodded with evident relief, clearly glad not to have to follow the tracks. He had a fast horse and should be able to get to Buckland more quickly than any of the others.

They split up and caught their horses. Swiftly, now that dawn had broken, they all packed up and loaded their baggage on to their animals, then, when they were all ready, Simon motioned to Black and he led the way into the forest, pulling his horse gently by the reins. Simon went next and the others followed on behind.

Simon was surprised to find that the trees seemed to have lost their feeling of lowering malevolence in the fresh green light that filtered through the leaves. Perhaps it was the other men behind him, maybe it was the fact that he already knew what lay in the clearing, but, whatever the reason, he felt none of the trepidation of the previous evening, just the slow burning glow of his anger. The other men all seemed to be nervous, walking quietly and without speaking as they led their horses into the trees. They seemed aware that this was no ordinary murder, that until the killers were caught they would all be forced to live in fear. Perhaps they were aware that even when they were caught and had been punished, their lives could not be the same, because even when the murderers had been destroyed, their lives would still be marked permanently by the killers' actions in these woods, as if the killing of the abbot had scarred each of them by its viciousness.

There was another factor as well, which Simon was only too well aware of. The abbot was a wealthy and important man, of noble blood—for no one else would be given the position of abbot. That meant that he, as bailiff, must catch his murderers, no matter what. Brewer's death must wait, he was merely a villein and it was not even certain that he had been murdered, whereas this abbot . . . He twitched, as if he felt the responsibility as a physical burden, then sighed as he stumbled on. If he could catch the men responsible, it would enhance his position—but if he failed?

It took them over an hour to reach the first clearing. They all stood among the trees while Black scrutinized the ground all round, then studied the droppings. Shrugging, he rose from his crouch and followed Simon's pointing finger to the clearing where the body stood. As he followed Black, Simon could feel his legs become heavier. It was almost as if he was unconsciously trying to keep himself away from the sight of the body, but he forced himself on, walking steadily behind the tracker.

As he came through the line of trees, Black stopped suddenly and Simon could hear his quick intake of breath as he took in the surroundings. Then, as if he had given himself a swift rebuke for allowing himself to be distracted, he concentrated on the ground again.

He looked over his shoulder at Simon, his brow furrowed with the effort of his hunt and his dark eyes troubled, and tossed the reins of his horse over to him before slowly walking over the ground and studying it intently. He paced around the small clearing, walking all round the perimeter until he came to the opposite edge, and stood there staring at the trees for a few minutes. Then he continued pacing the circumference until he arrived back with Simon.

"Not much to tell, sir," he said, his brow still wrinkled with the effort of his search. "Three men came in the first clearing, all on horseback. One left his horse there. Other horses were tethered nearby. The dead man was dragged here and tied to the tree, you can see where his feet dragged on the ground. Then the others piled up brushwood round him and made a fire. Looks like they waited until the prisoner was dead, you can see where they sat down over there to watch." He pointed. "When he was dead, they led their horses away through the trees at the other end of the clearing, over there. The last horse ran off at some point, obviously before the others left the place. They didn't bother to chase it."

"Can you follow the trail?"

"I reckon. One was a big horse, heavy. The tracks are quite deep and they've not been washed away or anything. Just one thing—I reckon he's lost a nail on the back right hoof and it's been some time since the horse was last shod. May be useful. The other horse was smaller, lighter." He paused and glanced quickly back at the trees opposite. "We can't go too fast in these woods. We'll have to do the same as them, I reckon, and lead the horses from here. Maybe we can mount farther on. I don't know, never been in the woods this far west myself."

Simon nodded and called to Tanner: "Get two men to cut the body down and take it back to Greenfield's farm, give it to the monks there and wait for us to send a message." Tanner immediately started to organize the men while Simon looked over at the monk, brother David. "Do you want to go back with them? I don't think you can help us with the chase. It may be better for you to go back with them to the Greenfield farm and get some rest." David nodded, staring at the body of his abbot, the shock and horror plain on his face. Simon sighed and nodded at the hunter. "Come on, then. Let's get on and find these bastards.'

Then he paused as a sudden thought occurred to him, and he called out to the monk, "David! The abbot's horse, what was it like?"

"Oh, a light gray mare. Very gentle. Very good-natured."

"Was there anything that would help us recognize her?"

The young monk thought for a moment, then, "Yes. Yes, she has a scar on the left side of her withers, about three inches long. It's plain."

"Fine. We'll let you know if we find her," said Simon, then, "Black, should we go after it, do you think?"

"No. We can look for it later, the prints'll be easy enough to follow. No, we ought to keep the posse together as far as we can, so we're in strength when we find the men who did this."

When Simon nodded, Black took his horse back and led the way over the open space and back into the woods opposite. Simon followed, watching over his shoulder as the two men Tanner had asked to see to the body went up to it. They had only just got to it and begun cutting the leather thongs that held the arms round the tree when, thankfully, the trees obscured his view. With relief, he dragged his eyes away from the blackened, twisted thing that two days before had been a living man, set his jaw, and glared ahead into the trees that could even now be hiding their prey.

The trail led them up a hill, still deep in among the trees, and in the thick woods they could hardly guess at the direction they were taking. The tracks seemed to be going fairly straight, leading onward through the trunks as if the men had known the route well, and Simon found himself wondering whether this crime could have been committed by local men. It seemed unthinkable, somehow, that someone from this shire could have done it, but it was equally unlikely that anyone who did not know the area could have forged such a straight path through the forest.

On they went, crossing innumerable little streams and rivulets, occasionally stumbling and falling as they scrambled up steep banks and hills, pulling their horses after them. There was no path; the whole way they had to follow the tracks of the killers through the thick undergrowth between the trees. It was plain that they had not bothered to hide their trail—wherever the shrubs and plants on the ground thinned out, the footsteps and the horses' hoofprints showed clearly. Perhaps they had not expected to be followed so soon after the murder, Simon wondered. Or was it possible that they had so shocked themselves by the killing that they were past caring? Whatever the reason, they were very easy to follow.

At last, after stumbling on for over three miles, Simon could see a glimmer of light between the trees. They must have been travelling for over two hours by now; his back and thighs were feeling the strain of having to drag his horse up the hills, and his calves hurt from walking down the other sides. He threw a glance at Black. The hunter did not seem to have noticed the light, his eyes were still firmly fixed on the trail at his feet. Simon peered ahead again. It *was* clearing. They must be coming to the edge of the woods. With a feeling of relief, Simon realized that soon they would be able to mount their horses and at last give chase, no longer wandering slowly; now they would be able to travel fast at last. He felt a mounting excitement as they slowly covered the last few yards, and had to work to prevent a grin of anticipation from spreading over his face.

Now Black noticed the lightening too, but apparently without the same pleasure, Simon noticed. He seemed concerned as he came up to the last few trees, frowning and looking up every now and again from the tracks. Then, when they came to the edge of the wood, Simon suddenly realized why.

With a sinking feeling, he looked out from the trees and groaned as he saw the road. It was the main road up to Barnstaple; not a very busy one, but busy enough—the dirt of the track was well trodden and rutted from the number of carriages and wagons that regularly passed by, and between the wheel marks it was compacted into a solid mass. With a wince of despair, Simon realized it would be impossible to follow the trail on this. He sighed and watched silently with his feelings of despondency growing as Black slowly stretched and wandered out from the trees. His eyes swivelled, tracing the last distinguishable marks of the horse and rider on the verge as they had left the trees, but then they stopped, obliterated by the multitude of tracks in the mud of the road itself.

Close to tears in his frustration, he watched Black thoughtfully loop his horse's reins over a nearby branch. Surely they could not lose the trail after following it so far? He felt the first prickles of the tears starting to heat his eyes, ready to begin weeping in his frustration, the pain and despair of failure clutching at his heart as he watched the methodical and efficient hunter trying to find the trail.

Black was walking in a series of circles, going from one verge to the other, and each time moving the center a little farther so that he was gradually moving down the road toward Crediton in a series of sweeping loops, his eyes fixed all the time on the ground and occasionally flitting over to the verges to make sure that no one had left the road. He went slowly, and when he had covered twenty yards he came back and went off in the other direction, up toward Barnstaple. At last he stopped and strode back.

"Sorry. Nothing I can do. Trail's here, but it's been covered by all this other lot," he said shortly, waving a hand vaguely and looking up and down the road. "All I can do is guess. I just don't know." He shrugged, looking up at Simon with dejection in his eyes.

Simon stood and stared at him, feeling the waves of dread and fear wash over him. There *must* be a way of finding the killers. Whoever had done this must be mad: until they were caught there could be no peace in the area. Oblivious to the others, he stood fixed to the spot and stared into the distance. He felt Tanner walk up behind, but remained staring in his misery without acknowledging him.

"Problem?" asked Tanner quietly.

"See for yourself," said Black shortly. "There's no way I can track someone on this lot. The only way is to guess which way they could've gone and hope for the best. I've done the best I can." He almost seemed to be pleading with the taciturn constable, as if he needed confirmation that he had done the best he could.

"Bailiff?"

"I don't know. We can't just give up! We *have* to find the bastards or they'll do it again," said Simon, confused and desperately trying to see what to do. "I . . . leave me alone for a minute."

The other two watched him as he walked into the middle of the road and peered up and down, Tanner standing calmly and Black scratching his head as he gazed at the ground with an expression of morose defeat.

Right, Simon thought. The murderers took the abbot, robbed him, and killed him—but why *burn* him to death? Why not just stab him? And if that was all they were going to do, why not kill him nearer the road? Christ Jesus, help me!

He squatted, peering at the road surface, then gazed into the distance again as he thought. "I can't guess why they killed the abbot. All I know is they did and we have to get them. Otherwise they'll do it again. So we have to find them, and quickly. Where did they go? To Crediton? Or Barnstaple? They could have gone either way."

Abruptly, Simon swivelled and looked back down the road toward Crediton. But which way? Which way would *I* take? If *I* had just murdered someone, where would I go? If I was passing through I would go on to Barnstaple, but if I came from round here would I go home? Could someone local have done this? Why would they? Who could have done this?

"Bugger." He reached a decision, stood and strode back to the small posse. "Tanner, Black, come over here a minute." When they were with him, he spoke again quietly. "Look, we can't tell which way they've gone. If I'd done something like this I would have gone to the moors and hidden, but these men have obviously gone on. Tanner, where would you go if you were them?"

The constable looked blank and drew down the corners of his mouth as he considered. "If it was me and I was passing through, I'd go on to Barnstaple quickly, I suppose, then down to Cornwall."

"Black?"

"I'd go home quick. I'd get back to the house and pretend I'd not been out at all."

"Hmm. I think so too. If I was a traveller, like you think, Tanner, I'd want to get away from the area. But if I was a local, I think I'd go home and keep my head down."

"Does that help us?" said Tanner with obvious doubt.

"Yes, because it means we have no real choice. We divide into three teams. Tanner, you go on up toward Barnstaple and see if you can find any sign of strangers passing by recently. Ask at the houses you pass about one man on a large horse, could be a farm animal or a war horse, and another on a smaller one. They dressed like knights but wore no signs to show their names or their lord's. We'll go back to Crediton and check to see whether we can see any sign of them that way. The other men, the third team, will have to ask at all of the cottages in the woods near here. Tanner, you go as far as Elstone, if you can't find anything you may as well go home after that. We'll see if anybody saw anyone."

"We'll need a tracker with both teams going by road," said Black. "We'll have to keep an eye open for any signs leading off the road and into the trees."

"Yes. Tanner? Any idea who else we can use?"

"Yes, young Fasten, he's got good eyes. I'll take him with me. What about the third team?"

"So long as they know the area, two men should be enough. Make sure they do know these parts, though, and the people in it. All they have to do is ask around—has anyone seen two men recently, probably in armor, one on a big animal like a war horse? Have they seen a gray mare? She may have been found after she bolted. Did anyone see or hear anything the night before last? Someone *must* have heard the poor soul— a hunter, a coppicer—I don't know, someone *must* have heard him!''

"Alright, bailiff, I'll arrange it. Mark and Godwen know these parts well enough."

"Fine. When we get back to Crediton, we'll start asking and see if anyone was out when this happened. We may get lucky and find that somebody saw someone on the road. Well, then. I know it's hopeful, but I can't see any other way of trying to find them, can you?"

They both shook their heads. Quickly, now that they had decided what to do, they walked back to their men, divided them into two groups of six and one of two, mounted up, and were off.

Black took the lead again as soon as they took the road back to the town, his eyes constantly roving from the verge at one side of the road to the other and checking the surface in between in his search for signs of the murderers. Simon rode behind, mulling over the motive for what seemed to be such a senseless killing.

It was the manner of the murder that was such a surprise, and he carried a perplexed frown as he rode. Murder was not so rare that a killing after a robbery was unknown, even if it was rare down here. But to kill in such a vicious way, in such a strange way, seemed very odd. If they had not wanted the abbot as a hostage, they could have killed him quickly, much nearer the road, and gone on to make their escape. Why kill him in such a cruel manner? It meant having to travel farther with the hostage, so that the smoke from the fire would be hidden from the road and the man's screams deadened by the trees. Why go to all that bother, when all they had to do was leave the abbot, take the money and get away?

Simon sighed deeply and concentrated on his tracker, putting the thoughts about the murder to the back of his mind. If they caught them, they would soon have the answers. For now the main thing was simply that: catching them.

They arrived back in Crediton in the late afternoon, tired and hungry. Simon thanked all of the men, especially Black, and sent them home to get some food, but told Black to organize them to return the following day and begin asking at all of the houses to see if anyone was missing or had been out at the time of the murder. Then he turned his horse's head to home and quickly made his way back.

The house was silent when he arrived, so he unsaddled his horse himself and tended to it before going in and sitting in front of the fire. Deep in thought, he was not aware of his wife and daughter until they burst into the room, his wife standing back as she always did, with a small smile at the sight of her daughter's excitement at seeing her father again. At last, when Edith had calmed enough, she walked forward to greet him herself.

"What is it?" she asked as she pulled away from their quick hug and looked up into his eyes. "You're very tense."

"Don't worry," he said with a wry smile. "It's the robbery over at Copplestone."

"Why? What's the matter?"

Sending Edith to play outside, he took his wife's

hand and sat with her in front of the flames. "Well, it wasn't just a robbery. The thieves took a monk—an abbot—hostage and killed him, and I've no idea *why*." He broke off and gazed unseeing at the fire. When he spoke again his voice was soft and almost wondering as he considered the incident once more. "They took the abbot—two men in armor with their faces hidden. The abbot seemed to know that something was going to happen—even I guessed that when I met him on the road. The men came up with swords drawn, took the abbot away and killed him. Why? Why would they do that if all they wanted was money?"

She drew her breath in softly as she absorbed this. At no time in her life had she felt threatened in this, her shire. She was fortunate in that the raids and killings of the last centuries seemed to have reduced, and those that continued only really affected the coastal towns. But if Simon was right and there was a man, maybe two men, who were capable of this, then what would they *not* be capable of? It was not just fear for herself, it was for her family—for Simon and for Edith. If these killers were to attack here, what could they do to protect themselves? Or, worse, what if they found Simon on the road and captured him? What if he was killed as well, as her father had been so many years before when he had been robbed on the highway? She felt her chest constrict in her sudden fear, but tried to keep her voice calm as she said, "Maybe they thought they could get more money for the abbot's life? Perhaps that's why they took him."

"But why kill him, then? There seems to be no reason for it. Why kill a monk?"

"Well, maybe the abbot tried to get away."

"No, I don't think so. The tracks seemed to mean

that the monk was killed as soon as they were far enough from the road. It seemed as though he was killed immediately they had an opportunity."

"Maybe the abbot recognized them?"

"Yes. That's possible. But no, why should he? The killers could have kept their helms on if there was a risk of being recognized."

"So? What if someone came upon them and the men killed him quickly to stop him getting away?"

Simon looked at her. "No. Whoever killed the abbot didn't do it in a hurry. He was burned—burned like a heretic at the stake. Only instead of a stake they used a tree in the forest."

"What?" Her eyes were round in her horror. "He was burned alive? Why would anyone do that to a monk?"

"I wish I knew," said Simon, staring back at the fire. "I just wish I knew. God! There must have been a reason, but what?"

"Are the men looking for them now?"

"Yes. They came out of the woods on the Barnstaple road. We couldn't track them on that, so Tanner's taken some of the men west to see if they can see any traces along the way. We sent two men to search among the locals as well, and we came back to Crediton in case they came this way. No one seems to have seen them, though." He stretched his arms over his head and yawned. "Still, maybe Tanner'll have more luck."

As he lowered his arms again, Margaret said, "So, what now?"

He caught a yawn, stifled it, and then had to blink to clear away the tears of tiredness. "It depends. It depends on what the men find. If we—"

"No, Simon," she said gently. "I meant, what about

Brewer, what about our move to Lydford? Do we forget his death for now, and postpone the move?"

"Oh, yes. Yes, there's no way we can worry about them for now. The abbot's murder is going to be of more interest to everyone than Brewer's. What is the death of an old farmer compared to the murder of an abbot? And there's no way I can move to the castle until we have some idea about what happened to the abbot."

She nodded, saddened. She knew he was right, of course, but it hurt to hear her husband, the man she knew to be a thoughtful and caring person, say that the death of the farmer was irrelevant. All she said was, "And tomorrow?"

"Ah, tomorrow, my love, I think I'll go back to Clanton Barton and talk to the monks again. I don't think they've been as helpful as they could have been."

They lapsed into an uncomfortable silence, both absorbed in their thoughts of the killing as they stared at the flames dancing and dying on the packed clay of the hearth. Suddenly Margaret drew in her breath in a shocked gasp.

"What is it?" said Simon, startled.

"Oh, Simon," she said, turning a face filled with terror to him. "What if the two men who died were killed by the same men?"

"What?"

"Brewer and the abbot were both robbed, both killed and both killed in the same way. By being burned. Simon, I'm afraid!"

ext morning, Simon was up early and had soon set off with Hugh trailing along behind. Margaret had agreed to let Black know that he would not be at home, and had sent one of the farm helpers to ride over to his house. She had also arranged for a man to go to Furnshill Manor to explain that the bailiff would be absent for a while and could not help with the investigation of the farmer's death. But then she had overcome all his objections and forced him to take his servant with him.

Her concerns annoyed her. Margaret knew full well how unlikely it was that he would be attacked, but she could not forget how her father's body had looked when the men brought it back. The sight had almost destroyed her and she did not want ever to suffer that sort of devastation again. To see his corpse, hacked and violated like that . . . If she saw Simon's in a similar state, she thought, it would make her lose her mind. So now she was softly persuasive, insisting gently, "I know he'll slow you down, but I don't care. I need to know that you are travelling safely, just in case these men are still in the area."

"But we don't know that they're round here, my

love, they could be anywhere. And Hugh'll slow me down."

"No, we don't know where they are, because you couldn't follow them. So they could be here, so you'll take Hugh, just in case."

"No, but . . ."

"So you'll take Hugh, just so that I know you'll be a bit safer."

"Well, the only thing is . . ."

"Because that way I know that there's someone who can help to protect you."

So at last he had shrugged and given in. He knew Margaret should be safe enough with all the men at the farm, even if the outlaws came here, so it did make sense for him to take Hugh with him. Even so, the thought of the journey did not seem to have put Hugh in any better frame of mind than Simon himself. Hugh was loyal, and had shown himself to be capable in a fight when they had been attacked by three cut-purses many years before, during market day at Moretonhampstead. Simon had been amazed to see his surly and reserved companion suddenly explode into action and, with his bare hands and the use of a cudgel retrieved from one of the band, put the three of them to flight.

"Where did you learn to fight like that?" Simon had asked, more in astonishment than surprise.

His servant had immediately lost his look of grim pleasure at his victory and instead became shifty, as if shy of demonstrating his skill, wary of earning a new reputation as a fighter. At last, after continual prompting, he looked up again and said, "You try to look after sheep on the moors when you're small for your age. You try to keep them together when bigger boys come and try to take one or two of yours, because they want to hide the fact they've lost a couple of their own. You try it when your dad'll take the skin off of your ass if you lose even one. You'd soon learn how to fight then, too."

But that was two years ago now, and he was obviously unhappy about the thought of being waylaid and possibly having to fight with steel. He spent the journey constantly looking all around, which, if possible, seemed to make them go even slower than usual, to Simon's annoyance.

After a while Simon dropped back until he was level with his servant. "Come on, Hugh. What's the matter?"

"Hunh?" Hugh looked at him, and Simon was concerned to see the fear on his face.

"I've never seen you like this before, what're you so worried about?"

"I've never had to fight serious before. I've never known anyone burn a traveller at the stake. I'm just worried that we could get caught by them."

"But there were only two of them. We should be able to defend ourselves against two."

"Two knights? Two men in full armor? Two men who're prepared to risk eternal damnation for killing an abbot? You think we can protect ourselves against them? God!"

Simon rode forward, his face frowning at his servant's anxiety. It was understandable, certainly, but the bailiff was irritated that his own man could already be anxious. It seemed to show how other people would feel, scared and fearful of travelling until the killers were caught.

They rode the rest of the way in silence, both deep in their own thoughts. The sky was slightly overcast, with thin, watery clouds moving swiftly over the sky and keeping the main heat of the sun for themselves.

They were forced to keep up a good pace merely to keep warm, much to Simon's delight and Hugh's disgust, and they seemed to cover the distance in no time.

When they arrived at Clanton, Simon was surprised to find David, the young monk, standing quietly leaning against the gate post to a field, and apparently meditating.

"Good morning, David."

"Hello, bailiff," he said, but there was no cheeriness in the welcome, only a kind of blank confusion, bordering on despair.

"Are you alright, David?" asked Simon, feeling sympathy stirring at the sight of the obvious misery of the man.

The monk glanced up at him, with a look of loathing, as if furious at such a facile question. "Alright? Alright? After what we saw yesterday? An abbot killed like a heretic? How can I be alright?" His voice dropped to a low mutter, like a child who has been cheated of a promised toy. "We set off in good spirits, and now our leader is dead, murdered in an obscene way. Nothing can be alright again. All I want to do is go back home again, to Tychfield, and now because of this I must go on to Buckland and give my condolences to the priory. I'm sorry, bailiff," he said suddenly, looking up at him with a small frown. "I'm sorry to be so curt, but I am not used to seeing such sights, and that it should have happened to him . . ."

The bailiff and his servant dropped from their horses and walked toward the farm with the monk. "I am sorry, it was a foolish question. But this is not: do you have any idea why the abbot was killed?"

Apart from a shrug of the shoulders, he received no response. Simon grunted, head down in his shoulders as he slouched along. "Hunh! I only wish *I* had the vaguest idea. Why on earth anyone would want to try to hold a man and then make off before he could demand the ransom money . . . and then to kill the hostage like that—it just makes no sense."

The monk shrugged again. He was obviously just as confused.

Simon turned a frowning face to the young monk. "Tell me, David. How well did you know the abbot?"

"Not at all, really. I met him when he arrived at Tychfield, my abbey. He was on the way down to Buckland and I was asked to join him and take some goods and gifts with me. He wasn't very talkative on the journey, he seemed too engrossed with his own thoughts for the most part, so I never really spoke to him much."

"Oh. Oh well. So what *do* you know about him?"

"Well, not very much. He came from France, I know that. I saw his letters of introduction from the pope."

"From the pope himself?" Simon was surprised. "What was he doing going to Buckland, then? I'd have thought he would have stayed in Avignon."

David cast a quick glance at Simon, narrowing his eyes and obviously assessing him. "He may have found it better to be out of France."

"What do you mean?"

"Well, the new pope didn't like the last one, so quite a number of men who were in favor then aren't any longer. I think the abbot was unpopular with the new pope and he was given Buckland to get him out of France."

"Oh?"

"He never wanted to talk about it, but . . ." He fell silent and pensive for a moment, but then continued in a rush, as if he wanted to get the words out before he could change his mind. "Well, I think that's what happened. I think he wasn't in favor anymore. I think the new pope heard about something he had done and he was sent here to be out of the way, and the fact of it hurt him deeply—especially his pride. He was very proud."

"Why do you say that?"

The monk gave a short laugh, sounding a little bitter. "I'm a monk! I may be young and new to the order, but even so . . . We're supposed to be humble. He behaved like a knight in the way he treated others, always arrogant and often abusive. There were several times when he got drunk and insulted other people, and we had to calm them to stop him fighting them. But if you want to know more about the abbot, you'll need to speak to brother Matthew. He came over with the abbot from France. He must know something about him."

"Which is brother Matthew?"

"He's the old one, the happy one—well, usually, he's not happy now. Poor man! He seems to have taken the whole affair worse than any of us. I suppose because he came over with the abbot from France."

"Were they friends?"

"Oh, I suppose so . . . that is . . . well, yes." He seemed unsure.

They continued in silence for the rest of the journey. David seemed to almost regret having said as much as he already had and merely grunted at any attempt at further conversation, leaving Simon with the uncomfortable sensation of being a confidante without the pleasure of a secret to hold. He was relieved when they finally came up to the farmyard of Clanton Barton, and he looked forward to speaking to the others with anticipation, hoping that they would be able to shed some light on the affair.

But when he walked into the room with the great fire blazing away he was struck by a complete inability to frame his thoughts clearly, let alone ask any questions. It seemed grotesque to be asking about the abbot's past in front of these good men when he had only just died, but he could think of nothing else to do. And then again, he knew that he must try to find out as much as possible about the man. It was not a pure guess that he would find answers in the man's past, it was more a premonition that there must be a logical reason for the murder; especially the method of the killing. Why else would he have died in that way? Either it meant that the killers had taken him and murdered him for no purpose, or they knew him and wanted to kill him for some very specific reason. So the question was: would anyone want him dead? Why would they want to kill an abbot? The only way to find out was to question the monks—surely one among them must have some knowledge of the man who had led them?

"I suppose you have all heard that we found your abbot's body?" he started, as he walked in and sat down, looking around at them all. They had all started at the sound of Simon's voice when he had entered, all turning swiftly to stare, as if panicked by the mere sound of a human, looking as frightened as a flock of sheep upon hearing a dog. Now they seemed to be listening intently, sitting forward on their seats as he spoke and staring at him with the fixed, eagerly frowning concentration of men who would try their best to help. He sighed, this was not going to be easy. "He was killed by someone who tied him to a tree and burned him—probably while he was still alive. Obviously he was robbed, but that hardly explains the matter, does it? Why should he have been killed in that way? Why would someone burn him like a heretic? I have no idea why or what could have happened, and I need your help."

He stood and slowly paced the room behind the huddled monks, who turned to watch him. He kept his eyes on the ground, carefully thinking as he went, as if he was talking to himself and not to them, almost as if he was unaware of their presence. "He was taken from you, as if he was to be kept for a ransom; he was taken deep into the woods like a hostage. But robbers normally go in larger groups, they don't usually go around in pairs. They stay within a group so that they can ambush travellers more easily. So were these men part of a bigger group, or were they alone? Only the two were seen, there were no tracks of any others, so it seems that they *were* alone.

"They took the abbot into the woods. That would be normal, to avoid the roads and make an escape before the hue and cry could be raised. But normally it would mean that the robbers would be trying to escape, to go somewhere safe, somewhere to hide with their hostage and his money until they could claim the ransom. These men simply tied the abbot to a tree and set fire to him. Why? Why would they do that?" He spun around and glowered at the monks. "I can't see a reason."

He slowly tramped back to his chair by the fire, sat and stared at them again. "So I want you to tell me all you can about this abbot. What was his name, where did he come from, why was he going to Buckland? Everything. Who knew him best, out of all of you?"

He tried to ask the question as gently as possible, but the monks all stared at him in silent alarm, as if they were scared that he might accuse one of them of wanting the abbot dead. Perhaps it was the shock of the realization that this seemed to be no ordinary attack by robbers that held them so quiet, but after a few minutes Simon could feel his confusion at the lack of response turning to impatience.

He looked over at David, his voice harsher. "One of you must have known him, even if only a little. Who was he? What was he like?"

"He was a proud man." It was a statement of fact, a mild comment, as if it was an easily pardonable fault in one who ranked high in God's army. The oldest monk had spoken—no longer the cheerful monk who could wink as if sharing a joke, now he was a small, worried man who sat with his eyes cast down as if he feared the response of his brothers, but even as Simon looked at him, his gaze came up to meet Simon's questioning scowl with calm defiance. He seemed to consider for a moment, then continued. "He had been a knight in France and had served the pope well, which gave him his pride, and he was favored by Pope Clement, rest his soul, until Clement died. Afterward he was offered Buckland, and he resolved to come here to spend his last years in peace and dedication."

"Your name?"

"I'm Matthew."

"Thank you. So who was he?"

"His name was Oliver de Penne."

"Why would he have been offered Buckland? Why not an abbey nearer his home? Why was he sent so far from the pope?" asked Simon, his eyes narrowing as he tried to understand.

"Why Buckland? Maybe the pope thought it would be far enough away from any old temptations, from anything in his past that could persuade him to stray."

"How do you mean, a woman?"

The old monk smiled gently. "There are many temptations, bailiff. I do not know. Maybe, yes, a woman. Who can tell?"

"Do you have any idea why he was so worried about being attacked on the road?"

"Worried about being attacked?" The old man seemed genuinely surprised at the question.

"Yes. When I met you all on the road near Furnshill, he seemed very worried about being attacked. He kept asking me to join you on your journey and seemed annoyed when I refused."

"Perhaps," said the monk, shrugging. "I think many people are anxious when they are in new lands, when they don't know the roads and the villages. I am sure that he was simply hoping to have the company of a man who knew the area."

Simon thought for a minute. "Possibly," he admitted. Now he thought about it, could he not have been wrong? Maybe it was just the natural fear of a man of peace in a new and seemingly threatening country? No, even as he wondered, he knew that the abbot's fear was more than the normal caution of a traveller. It seemed to be a deep-rooted terror, almost as if he expected to be attacked. "But, surely, if he had been a knight and was proud he would not have been so fearful of a new land? He must have travelled before."

"Ah, yes, bailiff. Perhaps he had."

Simon sighed. "Can any of you remember anything else about him? Anything that could help me?" None of them moved. They sat staring at him in silence, apart from the older monk, Matthew, who gazed imperturbably at the ceiling.

Simon held up his hands in a gesture of disgust. "Is there nothing more you can tell me? There must be something, *something* in his past that could give us a hint why this should have happened to him. I cannot believe that he was killed for no reason—even a madman would have had to have a reason to kill an abbot." He had no answer. The monks sat still and quiet, staring in their shock and fear. "In that case I can do no more here. Good day!"

He strode out angrily and paused outside in the long, dark-panelled corridor. He knew that they were confused and worried after the attack and the death of the abbot, but surely there must be a reason for his death? It was inconceivable, surely, that it was just a random attack? And one of them must know why he had been so scared of being attacked on the road.

As he put his hand on the latch to let himself out, he heard his name called, and on turning he was surprised to find that David and Matthew had followed him out. He nodded curtly, and with a questioning eyebrow raised.

"Bailiff, we will be continuing on our journey soon. Before we go, Matthew would like to have a word with you," said David, and went back into the room.

Simon stood and waited. The monk seemed not to mind the silence, staring gravely at the bailiff.

"Shall we go outside, bailiff? It seems sad to be indoors like rats when the sun is shining, especially after the rains of the last two years."

Matthew waited while Simon opened the door and held it open for him, then led the way out into the lane and slowly strolled up it meditatively, as if unaware of Simon's presence alongside.

"There are some things, bailiff, which are better left unsaid in front of my brothers," he began quietly. "They are unused to the secular world. Even David, who has only been in the order for a matter of a few years, has not really had much dealing with the outside world. This whole affair has upset them all very deeply, as you can imagine. That is why I stopped them all running after the robbers. David wanted to give chase, but I stopped him. I thought the others could be put into danger—and I thought the robbers might kill de Penne if they knew they were being hunted. It seemed sensible to get help instead." He sighed. "I was wrong, it seems. Perhaps if we had given chase we could have saved him." He stopped suddenly and turned to the moors reflectively. "They are magnificent, aren't they?" he said as he stared at them blankly.

Glancing past him, Simon nodded, but then, wanting to keep the monk talking, he said, "So you think that his past would shock the others?" and was pleased to see the quick, suspicious frown that Matthew shot at him.

"His past? Well . . ." he paused, seeming undecided as he considered. "Yes, quite possibly, but not for the reason you think." They started to walk again. "You see, the Church is a simple place for many. They think it is dedicated to the worship of God, and to the improvement of people who want to dedicate themselves to God. My brothers know that, and that is all they wish to know. I am different, because I was called late in my life. I have been many things, seen many places and peoples." He laughed briefly, a sudden gust of laughter. "I have even been what they would call a pirate!"

"So?"

"So, my friend, I know what the world is like. They do not. I try to be humble and assume the best in people, but always I have to struggle with the cynicism that I developed in my youth. It is hard, sometimes. So, when I was called to become a monk, I felt that I could live the life of seclusion well and help others, but I cannot totally believe the reasoning behind all of the orders from the church. They do not all come straight from God. Some come from men. The other monks all accept any order as if it comes from God without any human interference."

"I don't think I quite—"

"No, my apologies for rambling. You are right. What I am trying to say is that my friends cannot comprehend what life at Avignon is like. I can, because I was born in the secular world and lived in it for many years. And then, when I was called, it was at first to become a senior monk, joining an ancient and noble order, where it was essential that honor and honesty should be upheld. It was only quite recently that I joined this order, my friend, and I spent my first years at Avignon. Bailiff, the pope is Christ's vicar on earth. He should be the leading Christian—pious, faithful and honorable. But this is not always so. You see, Holy Mother Church is organized and run by men, and they are as fallible as any other men. Control of the Holy See carries with it a great deal of power and wealth, so within it are many who wish to usurp that power. Men come and are promoted for money; men are given indulgences for gold. And sometimes, when the pope wants to allow it, a ruler can purchase a position for a friend. And that friend becomes strong and even more wealthy by his new position. But if the pope then changes, if the old pope dies and a new one takes over, then those men in power can suddenly have their wealth and authority removed, and they are left to find a new position.'

"Yes. So do you think that's what happened to de Penne?"

The monk laughed again. "I have no doubt. I think he was a favorite of King Philip of France and the last pope. He nearly told me as much one night when he had drunk too much. He was miserable, bemoaning his fate, and complaining about his misfortune. He said that he had been a member of a great order, and that he had performed a service for Pope Clement, and that this was the reason for his position of power, but that the new pope disliked him, and had him removed from the papal court. Hence his move to Buckland."

"Did he say what this service was?"

"No, my friend. Nor did I care. When you have spent some time at Avignon you tend to ignore the moaning and wailing of people who feel hard done by. There are too many who feel just that. Too many forget their vows of poverty and chastity in these harsh times."

"So you think he was sent here as a punishment? He was banished?" said Simon, frowning.

"Well yes, but you're right; it was not a very tough penalty, was it? After all, I understand Buckland to be a thriving abbey, and in beautiful country. No, I think he was simply sent away to where the pope, or another of his enemies, could forget him. He rose up—and then was caused to fall."

Simon frowned at his feet. "Could an enemy from Avignon have sent someone to kill him?"

"No. I suppose you mean the pope, but no, I'm sure that he would not do such a thing. Perhaps one of his bishops, but I doubt it. No," he said, pausing once more and staring at the moors as they lay lurking in the distance. "No, I think it is unlikely. I would dare to guess that it was simply a chance encounter, that the robbers killed him for some slight or insult. After all, he was a proud man, maybe he insulted them and they decided to punish him for it. Nothing more."

"But that *can't* be it! I just can't believe it, brother.

They must have been either mad or . . . or they knew exactly what they were doing and intended to kill him that way, to make some kind of point, perhaps."

"Then they were mad," said Matthew evenly, still gazing at the view, but with a certain tenseness, a stiffness, Simon felt.

"But why? Why take a man and kill him like that? Even if they *were* mad, surely they would have found another man to kill? Why an abbot? It makes no sense!"

"There are many reasons to kill, bailiff," said the monk, turning sharply to face him, but without rancor; more with an expression of sadness on his face. "Too many reasons for you to understand, perhaps. I have known some—fear, hatred, jealousy. Oh, yes, I have known many. And sometimes I have been mad while I have killed." His eyes seemed to mist over, as if he was moving back in time as he remembered and drawing away from Simon as he spoke. "When I was a soldier I killed many men. So the abbot's end was a bad one . . . I have seen worse—I have done worse. That was why I joined the order, to try to forget, and at the same time for atonement. Now, as I look back, none of the killings I did made much sense."

"So you really think it was madmen?"

"Yes, I do. Someone was mad when they did that to de Penne."

"Then we must catch them, to stop them doing it again."

"Must we?" the monk said, looking at him with a gentle sadness. "I do not think they will do this again, bailiff."

"Why not?" Simon asked, confused now.

"Whoever did this was mad, but they are well now and will not do it again. I feel sure of it. Your people are safe from them."

Simon stared at him. "How can you say that?" he managed at last, controlling his anger with difficulty. "How can you say that? The man was killed horribly and you imply that his killer was mad but now is alright? How can I believe that?"

The monk shrugged, and after a moment Simon calmed a little. "So you do think it was somebody who was after the abbot?"

"I think his time had come and the Lord decided to end his life. I think the Lord selected an agent to perform his task—and maybe that agent was afflicted with a madness while he did the Lord's will. But, now God's will has been carried out, the killer is probably normal again. And now"—he glanced up at the sky, "Now I think it is time you returned home before it gets too late." He turned and started back to the house.

"Brother! Wait, please. Will you not explain more? Why do you think—"

"No, my son. I think I have said all I wanted to. Don't forget what I have said."

Simon stood and watched him go back to the house. He turned at the door, as if wondering whether to say something more, but shook his head vaguely and went in. Simon was left with the distinct impression that the old monk knew more than he was letting him know. He shrugged and wandered over to the horses, where Hugh stood, whittling at a stick with a knife. As Simon drew near he looked up and hastily put his knife away.

"Are we going back now?"

"Yes. Yes, we're going back."

They mounted their horses, and with a last, frustrated glance at the farmhouse, Simon wheeled his horse and they rode off.

*   *   *

They were deep in the woods here, and Godwen caught the occasional glimpse of the cottage as they came toward it through the trees. "Thank God!" he thought, "this's the last one. After this we can go home."

Godwen and Mark had been sent by Black to visit the assarts in the woods near where the abbot's body had been found, to ask whether any strangers had been past that day—and to make sure the people were well and had not themselves been attacked. So far they had found nothing, and Mark was keen to finish their task.

The faded and patchy walls of the limewashed cottage showed more clearly now as they came close, and the trees opened out into a wide, trodden yard to show the smallholding. There was a new house; with the chimney gently trickling thin streamers of smoke into the air and leaving the surroundings redolent of its sweet promise of warmth and rest. The windows were close set under the thatch, where the rain could not be blown in to dampen the tapestries behind, and the door was almost in the middle, giving the place a feeling of symmetrical stability. When they reined in at the front there was no sign of the owner, and Mark allowed his horse to skitter restlessly as he peered at the holding. Watching him, Godwen sighed. Mark radiated sulkiness, his black eyebrows fixed in a thick line above the glaring brown eyes, his thin mouth set hard and resolute below the narrow, broken nose. Even his hair, thick and luxuriant as a hedge in spring, seemed to be sprung and taut with his emotion.

"No one here, from the look of it," said Mark, glancing over at him. Godwen grunted. "Knock at the door."

"No need, my loves. I'm here."

Spinning, Godwen saw a short but heavyset man standing behind Mark, who, taken unawares, jerked round in a spasm of fear. Smiling, Godwen kicked his horse forward.

"Afternoon."

"Ah, afternoon to you. What can I do for you?"

He seemed amused by their arrival, watching them from under his bushy brows, the gray hair seeming to fit him like lichen on an old log it was so grizzled and rough-looking. His clothes were almost exclusively leather, from the tunic to the kilt and down to his light boots, and he carried a rusted pike in his hand. Mark seemed to be at a momentary loss for words as he gazed at the man, so it was Godwen who introduced them and explained their visit while the man listened, ducking his head now and again to show he understood.

Cutting the explanation short, Mark snapped, "If you heard nothing, then just say so and we'll be gone. Did you hear anyone? Or see anything?"

Perhaps it was Mark's curt sharpness, but Godwen could almost feel the little man withdraw from them at this. He seemed to almost shrink in front of them, as if he could hide in his coat.

"Oh, no, no, sir. I didn't hear him, I'm sure," he said softly, as if afraid, but Godwen was convinced he could see a little gleam in his narrow, dark eyes.

"Good. That's that, then. Come on, Godwen," said Mark. He whirled his horse around, trotting off as if expecting Godwen to follow like a dog now that he had been given the command.

The woodman watched him go, then turned his gaze to Godwen, where he sat musingly on his horse. "Aren't you going with him?"

Godwen shrugged and gazed at Mark's back as he rode into the trees again, a bland expression on his face. He had no desire to listen to Mark's moaning all the way home. "He'll not need me to help him find his way," he said mildly and turned back to glance at the leathery little man.

His eyes fixed on Godwen's face, the man seemed to consider for a moment before nodding seriously. "I think you're right. He seems to know what he wants. Only trouble is, he's in too much of a hurry."

"Yes. I'm not, though. Can I ask you a couple of things?"

" 'Course!" said the man. "What do you want to know?"

Godwen looked over at the lane, to where it passed through the woods some fifty yards away. "You didn't hear the man as he died, but did you hear or see anything else?"

"Not on that night, no. Nobody came past then."

"Has someone come past since then? A man who could have been a knight on a great horse? He probably had a squire or someone with him on a smaller horse?"

"No, no pair of men, just the one."

"One?"

"Yes, there was a knight came past two days ago, my love. Big man he was. But he was all alone."

"Was he on a war horse?"

"Oh no, no. No, he was on a lovely little gray mare."

imon and Hugh finally arrived home again in the middle of the afternoon, both tired and waspish after their journey, and the bailiff marginally the worse-tempered of the two. He was angry with himself, annoyed, and felt no need to hide it. It came from a feeling of failure, as if he had forgotten or missed a vital hint that could have solved the mystery and led him to the murderer of the abbot. His conversation with the monk, which had left him more confused than ever, had done nothing to improve his temper, and his curtness with his servant was reciprocated in full by the time they returned home.

Both sour and tense, they rode up to the old house in a strained silence, each deep in his own thoughts. Hugh had tried to interrupt the bailiff's contemplation a couple of times, but when his conversation had been rejected he went into a sulk and maintained an aloof taciturnity for the rest of their journey, wondering whether he had taken the right job when he had joined Simon's household.

There was a horse outside the house when they reined in, and Simon felt a thrill of excitement when he recognized it as Black's. He jumped down, threw the reins over to Hugh, and hurried indoors to see what he had to report.

Black was sitting in front of the fire and watching Margaret stirring at a pot as Simon entered. The bailiff walked quickly to his wife and kissed her perfunctorily before eagerly turning to Black and nodding to him as he walked over and sat down on a bench close by. "Any news?" he asked, trying to control his excitement and keep the hope out of his voice.

"Not much, I'm feared," Black said slowly, taking a long pull at the jug of ale Margaret had given him. "We've been all over from Crediton to Half Moon and nobody on the road remembers anyone on a war horse, or anyone in armor. There were several farm horses went by, but none with a man like a knight riding. We did that this morning, and then I sent some of the men down south to ask at some of the bartons down that way while I took the rest up around here. Same thing, so far, though I've yet to hear from a couple of the lads I sent down near the moors. I've been keeping my eyes open for any sign of a man going into the woods by the side of the roads, but there's no signs at all, not as far as I can see. Trouble is, the roads're so messed up since the rains, and we've had so many travellers using them, it's next to impossible to see any tracks at all in the general traffic. They seem to've just disappeared. Have you heard any news from Tanner yet?"

"No. No, nothing. I— Thanks, my love." Simon gratefully took a jug of beer from his wife and took a deep draft as she sat beside him to listen. "I hope we'll hear something soon, but God only knows how long it'll take to check all the roads to the west."

"Aye. Trouble is, with the time and everything, they

may've finished him off at night. They could've made off in the dark. Maybe no one did see them," said the hunter gloomily.

Simon nodded slowly. "I know. And if we find no trace to follow, we might never find out what really happened and who did it."

"What do we do if we hear nothing from Tanner's search?"

"Keep searching. Tell people farther afield. There's not much else we *can* do, is there? If we can't find any trace of them, we'll have to assume they've gone somewhere else and won't attack anyone round here again."

"Aye." And with that monosyllabic response, Margaret felt that Black allowed himself to sink into a brooding melancholy. He seemed downcast by his inability to track the killers and by the thought that there was little more he could do unless Tanner brought fresh news from his search. She was repelled by this depression, it seemed ridiculous to her that he should be so despondent when there was still hope. Simon sat quietly, glaring at the mug in his hand.

After waiting in silence for some minutes she had to try to lessen the strain of the silence. She broke into their meditation with a voice that sounded a little high and unnatural even to her own ears. "Did the monks help?"

Simon nodded slowly and pensively, and Black said, "I heard you'd been over to Clanton Barton again to speak to them. What did they have to say?"

"Not much, really," said Simon with a small frown as he thought again about his conversation with the monk. He quickly told them what he had learned. "At least we know the abbot's name now. He was called Oliver de Penne."

"Oliver de Penne? Never heard of him," said Black, ruminatively shaking his head.

"'No, neither have I. I'm sure he was not from around here, I think he must have been as French as his name suggests."

Black puckered his brow restlessly. "It just seems odd that he should have been killed like that."

Simon's face registered scowling concentration, and then his wife saw his brow clear as he stared past Black's shoulder to the wall behind, musing. Glancing back at John Black again, she saw that the hunter's face showed a mounting exasperation and dejection, as if he was already almost thinking that they had lost, that they would never find the killers, and when she looked back to her husband she could not help a brief flare of pride at the contrast.

Margaret had married Simon not because she had realized that he would become a powerful man in the shire, but because she could see in him the same incisiveness that her father had possessed. As a farmer's daughter, she had been raised as a pragmatist. Whether the decision to be made was to cut the crops now or tomorrow, or to build a new byre or not, her father had instilled in all his children the same common-sense principle: always decide what was needed first. He used to say that it was useless to try to do something if you weren't even sure what it was. Only when the objective was chosen and clear could it be tackled.

It seemed to her now that they were trying to make cob without straw. They had no information, so how could they expect to be able to decide anything? And yet Black had almost given up already; he seemed to have decided that they were defeated. How could he feel like that when they had not even explored some of the possibilities? She rose and returned to her stirring.

"So how much do we really know about this abbot, then Simon?" she asked thoughtfully, her back to the men.

"His name, Oliver de Penne; his position as abbot at Buckland; and the fact that his horse was a gray mare. We know he had money with him."

"And?"

"He had spent time in France—with the pope at Avignon. It appears that he was popular with the last pope, but, if Matthew's right, not with this one. He seems to have been an arrogant man, and prone to fighting, from what David and Matthew both said. Beyond that, not very much."

"And he was scared of being waylaid, from what you saw?"

"Yes. Very."

"Hmm." She carried on stirring thoughtfully. Turning, she saw her husband's gaze resting on her and she smiled before continuing, "He was taken into the woods where no one would hear, and burned at the stake?"

"Yes."

The hunter winced, his eyes screwed into thin slits with his distaste at his thought, as if expecting to be told his idea was nonsensical. "Bailiff, I can't help thinking. . . . well, look, we can't imagine that it was any normal robber did this to the abbot—it wouldn't make sense, would it? No, so we're left with this strange killing, maybe there's some kind of meaning behind it? Now, it strikes me that it's the way they kill heretics in France."

"Yes. Thank God we haven't sunk so low in England. The king won't allow the Inquisition into the country."

"No, but do you think this could be something like that? He was French, from his name."

"It's possible, I suppose." Simon stared bleakly into his drink.

"After all, it's almost like someone's trying to make a show out of the death, if you see what I mean."

The bailiff stared at him. "You're saying he could have been killed to make some sort of a point?"

Shrugging, the hunter said, "Well, I can't see any other reason to kill him like that. Can you?"

"No. No, I can't," said Simon, frowning thoughtfully at his wife's back. He shook his head. This was getting him nowhere—he knew nothing about these things. Could Baldwin help? He was only recently back from France. Then, startled, his eyes focused sharply and he drew a quick breath as his mind considered a new possibility—could Baldwin have been involved somehow? He *was* recently back from France, he had Edgar as a perpetual shadow, he was a knight—could he have had something to do with the abbot's death? Had Baldwin and the abbot known each other before?

It was with a small sigh of relief that he remembered the day he had first seen the monks and then mentioned them to the knight at Furnshill. No, of course it could not have been Baldwin, if so he would surely have expressed some interest in the travellers when Simon spoke of them. As the bailiff recalled, the knight had not shown even a passing curiosity, he had dismissed them and gone straight on to talk about his new estates.

Eyes glazing again, his attention wandered around the room until he focused again on his wife. She was clever, he knew, and keen to understand his work. He could see that, even in the way she had asked about this affair just now when Black had seemed to become so despondent, and her questions had made him start thinking again. If she had not . . . A quick grin suddenly cracked his serious features.

Stirring the pot, Margaret was smiling to herself. It had not taken much, but it had worked—at least Black was thinking again! With a slight feeling of smugness she threw a glance at her husband, and was irritated to see that he was grinning at her with an eyebrow lifted ironically as if he could read her mind. She stared back at him coolly; it was obvious he realized what she had done, but when she turned back to the pot she too was grinning, and had to fight to control a giggle.

"But why should someone have wanted to do that to de Penne?" she heard Black say musingly.

"I don't know. It's not as if he was known down here."

"Same with Brewer. Why would someone kill him?"

"For money, I suppose. And he was hated, Cenred said, by almost all the people in the vill."

"Well, we don't even really know that Brewer *had* any money. It was a rumor, but no one ever saw it."

"So we don't even know that he was wealthy, or at least we don't know he kept money at the farm?"

"No."

Simon raised a hand to his head and rubbed his brow with the back of a fist. "Oh, God. Neither killing makes any sense. Why . . ."

He was cut off by a loud knocking at the door. Margaret stopped her stirring and the two men sat still and silent, all their eyes turning to the tapestry that covered the entrance from the screens. Simon had to contain the urge to leap up and answer it himself in case it was a message from Tanner, and as he sat his eyes were gleaming with hope. As soon as Hugh came in with a young man, slim and dark, who was stained after riding quickly through the puddles in the lane, his face ruddy from the exertion, Simon slumped back in his seat with a grimace of disgust. This was not one of the men from the posse, he would have remembered his face. As the young man entered, he looked from Black to Simon with confusion in his dark eyes until Simon motioned him forward.

"Sir? Bailiff? I've been sent from Sir Baldwin Furnshill. He sends his best wishes and asks if you and your lady could join him this evening at the manor."

Simon shot a glance at his wife and smiled at the unmistakable signs of hope on her face, forgetting his conversation with the hunter. He feigned disinterest, casually glancing in her direction. "I don't know. Margaret? Would you like to go?" he asked, his voice showing his unconcern.

She raised an eyebrow and looked at him with an expression of exasperation on her face. He knew only too well that she wanted to meet the new master of Furnshill, she had told him so; especially now she had heard a little about the strange new knight. She ignored her husband and turned to the messenger with a sigh of patient suffering. "Please tell your master that we will be pleased to join him this evening, but do warn him that the bailiff seems a little confused today. It's probably his age," she said sweetly, and with a slight shake of her head, as if in disgust with her husband, she turned back to the fire and took the pot from the flames.

Simon smiled to himself. He could think of no other man he would prefer to discuss the abbot's death with, especially since Baldwin had seemed so interested in the death of the farmer. Could he help with this killing too?

Later, as they rode together from Sandford to Cadbury, leaving Edith with a maid, Margaret turned and saw Hugh was trailing a short distance behind. Turning to Simon, she gave him a look of wary concern. "Simon, do you really think that the murders can't have been done by the same people? It seems such a strange co-incidence that both deaths should have involved fires."

He grunted noncommittally as he turned his mind back to the mysterious deaths. "The only similarity between the two deaths is in the fact that fire was common to both."

"Surely that's enough of a coincidence, isn't it? When did someone last die from fire?"

"No, that's not what I meant. If both men died in fires at home, then I could understand it. If both were taken on the road and ransomed, then I could happily say, 'Yes, here's a coincidence.' But I can't. One man seemed to die in his bed, one died at a stake. One was definitely robbed, one may—only may—have been."

They fell into a thoughtful silence as they jogged along on their horses. Could there be a small band of trail bastons this far south, Simon wondered, one that had started raiding down south of Crediton, had found the Brewer house and killed him and had then gone on and seized the abbot? And then—in a fit of jealousy at the hostage's wealth, perhaps?—killed him in that senseless manner?

Margaret watched as his hand slowly came up to scratch at his ear, a sure sign of perplexity. His frown would soon disappear, she knew, as a new thought occurred to him, making him lose his glowering concentration as he peered ahead, looking as if he was lost, like an old man confused of his surroundings, until he had worried the thought to death and gone on to the next one. Smiling, she saw the anticipated expression appear and turned her gaze back to the view ahead.

They topped a hill and waited at the top for Hugh, who toiled slowly after them. From here they could see for miles and Simon was happy to rest and stare, forgetting the affair for a moment as he leaned on his saddlebow and breathed in the clean air.

Margaret watched him with a little smile as he sat comfortably on his horse. She was proud of his strength and calmness, and loved him for his gentleness with their daughter, but behind her smile she was worried. She had never seen him as absorbed as he was now with these killings. In the past he had sometimes been forced to get involved with legal matters, when there was a theft in the village, or a land dispute, but generally they had a quiet life together—there were not that many crimes in this part of the world. She was fearful, too, that these killers could strike again, that another person could be killed for no apparent reason. As she thought, though, she suddenly realized that her main fear came from how it would affect him.

She was fully aware that her husband held a position of responsibility, and she was proud that he had managed to achieve it. She would not have held him back from any ambition that drove him, being content to look after their daughter and create the family they both wanted, but she was nervous that this killing could have eaten into him so much. Since the murder he had seemed to become more introverted, quietly mulling over it time and again and withdrawing from her, or so she felt. Would it stop with the capture of the killers? She could not tell. Now all she wanted was an end to the matter so that they could move to their new home and forget it, but she was not sure that he would be able to, not until he had caught the men responsible.

Simon turned as Hugh came near and noticed her staring at him. Grinning quickly, he said, "Come on, then. Let's go and get some food."

Baldwin Furnshill walked slowly with his mastiff along the lane that led to his house. His brother's death had left him with a sizeable kennel to manage, and he now found himself responsible for over twenty dogs as well as the estates.

It was fortunate that he had always liked dogs, he thought. One of the trials of the last few years had been the enforced lack of dogs—not just because of the lost hunting opportunities, although he enjoyed a pursuit as much as the next man, but also because he missed the affection. It was wonderful to see the eyes light up, to see the happiness spread over the black muzzled face at the sudden appearance of the master, and now, while he was still so lonely and keen for a companion, the dogs could at least give him that uncomplicated adoration that required so little in return.

He patted the wiry, fawn coat of the huge mastiff walking beside him. Although he had only been home for a short time, this dog seemed to have attached herself to him already. She had been devoted to his brother, he had been told, and had been inconsolable when he had died, nuzzling at his body where it lay on the ground and whimpering until, at last, she had seemed to realize that he had died, and had sat back to howl her grief to the sky.

But as soon as the new Furnshill arrived she seemed to understand that he was the new master of the house. It seemed to Baldwin that she transferred all of her affection and loyalty to him as soon as she first met him. Perhaps it was because somewhere deep in her canine intelligence she recognized him as the brother of her dead favorite, or maybe he had some similarity to his dead brother in appearance that struck a chord. Whatever the reason, he was grateful for her immediate acceptance of him, as if in some way it demonstrated the legitimacy of his claim to the estates, and he had quickly grown to love her ugly, wrinkled face with the huge, constantly open and dripping mouth and calm brown eyes. In no time he had become used to the fact that wherever he went, within his house or outside, his dog would be never more than a matter of feet away, as if she continually needed to reassure herself that this new master had not disappeared.

From the lane Baldwin could see for over a mile toward the south, so he saw Simon and his small party when they were still a long way off, and he watched them slowly climbing the shallow hill that led to his home with a glowering stare.

Normally he was reserved and cautious with strangers and found it hard to trust people. It took him a long time to develop feelings of friendship for anyone; the life of a warrior was harsh and dangerous, especially when his liege lord was gone, and too much had happened in Baldwin's life for him to be able to take people at face value until he had grown to know them well; and even then he would usually reject a friendly advance.

But with the bailiff he found his natural distrust weakening and the feeling gave him a sensation of wary concern. With a wry grimace, he wondered whether it was the effect of having a stable base, a home at last after so many years of wandering. Was he simply getting soft? Looking for friends, getting too old for the life of a knight? It was possible, he knew, but somehow he doubted it. He felt that it was more due to Simon's obvious honesty and honor. Shrugging, he clenched his jaw in an attitude of determination, the scar blazing vividly on his cheek. No matter! He could not trust the bailiff with his past, not in any detail. How could he? Even a close friend would find it difficult to ignore a background like his. A recent acquaintance like Simon? No—at least, not yet.

He patted the dog on the head and started back toward the house as the party came closer, the mastiff lumbering happily just behind his heel. Then, as if he was determined to enjoy himself and ensure the pleasure of his guests, a vast, welcoming smile spread over his dark features, and he spread his arms wide and bellowed his greeting.

"Welcome!"

A slow smile lightened Simon's features. It was impossible not to be cheerful with a host who was so obviously delighted to see them, and when the bailiff finally dropped from his horse he found his hand being grasped firmly before he could even go to his wife and help her down.

"Welcome, Simon. Welcome, Mrs. Puttock," said Baldwin, smiling broadly and showing his small, square teeth. But the lines of worry on Simon's face did not escape his notice, and the bailiff saw the small beginnings of the frown, swiftly followed by a sharp nod, as if to acknowledge to himself that he had noted the change in the bailiff correctly and filed the knowledge for reference, before the knight turned to Simon's wife.

"My lady, your servant." He bowed low, suiting action to words. Margaret smiled as Simon helped her down and nodded at the knight with a coquettish, mocking expression as she had her first sight of her husband's new friend.

It was plain that this was not a man who had spent his life locally. The erect, proud mien and the clear, glinting dark eyes showed that, and the dark skin pointed to a life spent in regions farther south, where she had been told the sun was hotter. With his square, serious face and curiously powerful gaze, she found him oddly intriguing, and realized why her husband seemed so fascinated with him. There was a niggling thought at the back of her mind, though: he seemed to remind her of someone. It was only after he had appeared to subject her to a careful scrutiny that she realized who.

When she was young there had been a regular annual procession of pilgrims to the church at Crediton to visit the shrine of Saint Boniface, the famous missionary who had brought Christianity to the German peoples. Among them she had once seen a man similar to Baldwin.

He had been a monk, a tall, strong-looking and holy man in a white robe. That he spoke with a strong accent she had first noticed when she had heard him singing. Walking at the head of the column, he had immediately drawn her eyes to him. Interested, and wanting to see what his face looked like, she had followed the line of dirty and threadbare pilgrims for a distance, listening to their songs and chants, until, at last, fascinated by this stranger, she had run ahead to the front of the group so that she could see him more clearly.

At the time, she had felt that this was how Jesus

must have looked. The monk was not like the slender, bookish men she sometimes saw at the church and chapel; he looked like a warrior. He had a massive sword hanging from his waist by his heavy leather belt, and his arms were plainly visible as they held the wooden cross high, the material from the short-sleeved tunic falling back and showing the huge biceps. Those arms were not made so strong by hewing wood or tilling soil; they were created to serve God in war, fighting heretics and nonbelievers. This all came to her as she stared at him walking toward her, his eyes fixed on the distant horizon, walking trance-like, seeming to be almost otherworldly, as if he was dropped from Heaven to raise the masses but would be taken back soon.

Then, as a vague fear of him started to make itself felt, as she began to think about going and leaving the procession to carry on its way, he glanced at her and winked. It was so unexpected that she felt her mouth fall open, and she gaped at him, so obviously astounded that he almost bellowed with laughter, appearing to stop himself with an effort, but then, as he continued on his way, he winked again and the grin stayed on his face, she was sure, until he had quite passed out of sight.

This stern but gentle knight struck her in the same way. His was a similar dark and almost forbidding visage, but today, in his welcome, there was the same preparedness to give himself over to humor and enjoyment that she had noticed about the leader of the pilgrims so many years before. She could see the lines of pain that Simon had described, but they seemed not so pronounced as she had expected from what her husband had said.

She smiled again, graciously accepting the knight's look of frank approval and Simon was pleased to see that his wife was obviously as taken with Baldwin as he was.

"My lady, your husband does you no credit when he describes you. Let's leave him here and go in ourselves." And so saying he took her by the arm and led the way into the house, roaring for his servants to come and take care of their horses.

They all went in, Hugh following with an expression of frowning distrust, to the main hall, where they found the table almost hidden by plates of food. The mastiff wandered over to lie hopefully in front of the fire. It was not quite dark yet, and the room was lit by the sun streaming in through the westernmost windows and the fire, which was surrounded by a wide range of pots. A small lamb was roasting in front on a spit, tended by his sullen and watchful servant Edgar. Before they sat, Baldwin poured them all mugs of mulled ale and insisted on drinking a toast to their new life in Lydford. Even Hugh slowly began to unbend a little in the face of the enthusiastic hospitality of their host.

"It would seem that you are settling in well in your new home, Baldwin," said Simon at last when they were all seated.

Baldwin waved at the food, then patted his dog on the head as she sat beside him, smiling at her briefly. "Yes, it's marvellous to be back, and it does already feel like home."

"Even after travelling so much?"

"Oh, I've seen many other countries and I've stayed in a number, but there's nowhere like the place you were born in, and for me the best country to live in is this."

"So where have you been, sir?" asked Margaret, "and what have you done?"

"I have been all over the known world, lady. I have been through France, Spain, and even to Rome. But you must remember, I have been travelling for many years. I left my home here over twenty-five years ago, and I have been travelling ever since."

"You must have seen many strange sights."

"Oh yes, but nothing as strange as some of the sights you see here in Devonshire. There is little quite as unique as the moors—all through my travels I have been surprised by that. Dartmoor really is astonishing. It has so many different parts—the moors themselves, the forests, the farm land, the quicksands. I went for a ride yesterday and went down through to Moretonhampstead. I had forgotten how beautiful the land is down there."

Simon leaned forward slightly. "But surely in some of the countries you have visited there were more magnificent sights?" he asked innocently, trying to get the knight to speak more about his journeying.

"Oh, I suppose to many there were, but, for me, to be able to stand on the hills above Drewsteignton and look out over the moors with the wind in my hair is worth any number of foreign sights. Margaret, would you like a little more lamb? Or perhaps some rabbit?"

The bailiff sighed inwardly. It was clear that the knight was still keen to avoid any further discussion of his travels, and that he would be happier if he could change the subject.

"So have you heard about the murder, Baldwin?" Margaret said when she had taken more food. Simon looked up quickly.

"Yes, of course. I was there at Blackway with Simon to—"

"But what of the killing of the abbot?"

"Abbot?" asked the knight, looking at Simon questioningly. "Oh, that was why you weren't around, of course, you sent me a message."

"Simon is in charge of the hunt for the men. They took an abbot hostage from the road, he was travelling down to Buckland Abbey with some monks, and they burned him at the stake only a few miles from Copplestone."

"Really? Well, no doubt Simon will catch the men responsible," said Baldwin, turning an expressionless face to the bailiff. Simon was sure he could see a glitter in his eyes for a moment, but then it passed and the knight seemed uninterested. In an obvious attempt at changing the subject he passed a roasted rabbit to the bailiff and said, "So have you any more about the death of Brewer?"

"Yes, I went and spoke to the warrener." Simon sighed; he did not really want to get involved in discussions about the deaths tonight—just for the evening it would be pleasant to be able to relax. "He reckons he saw someone on the night that Brewer died, in the woods over on the other side of the road from his house, but he couldn't say who it was or when he saw him. Oh, and I went to see Ulton's woman. She says he left her early that night, so it seems he could have been back at Brewer's in time."

Baldwin fidgeted, his mouth a thin line, his brows puckered tight as he thought. "Why would Ulton have used her as an excuse for not being there if he knew she would not support him? Does that mean he thought she would lie to protect him?"

'Surely," said Margaret, elegantly dismembering a chicken and sucking her fingers, "surely he would have made sure of her support?" She glanced at the knight.

"Yes. He would, if he had realized that he was going to kill Brewer that night. If he was going to kill the man, he would have made sure his woman would agree to protect him, wouldn't he? What did you think about this Cenred, Simon?"

Swallowing a hunk of meat, the bailiff wiped the grease from his mouth, his knife in his hand. "I thought he seemed honest. He didn't seem to have any secrets, he even admitted that he saw a figure—but did nothing because he was scared."

"Scared?"

"You know, the stories. Old Crockern."

"Oh. Yes, I see. So we're left with this Ulton, anyway. I'll have to think about that. Why do you think he—"

"Baldwin," said Simon patiently, "I'm going to have my work cut out dealing with the death of the abbot. I don't have time to worry about a farmer like Brewer."

"But if he *was* murdered, his killer should be sought," said Baldwin with a small frown. "He may not have been high born, but he still deserves to be avenged."

"Yes, but I am an officer. I must find the killers of the abbot before anything else. The abbot's murderers must take priority."

"I see. Yes, of course," said Baldwin, then airily waved his knife. "Anyway, for now let's forget all about death and murder. Margaret, may I interest you in some lamb?"

Simon felt vaguely pleased; he did not want to have the evening spoiled by talking about the murder. He had no desire to discuss the hunt for the killer, he wanted to enjoy himself, not bring the miserable death of the abbot into the room, and he was relieved that the knight expressed no more interest in the murder.

The knight was obviously in his element while entertaining, and was remarkably well informed about a variety of subjects about which Simon was, at best, only vaguely aware, talking about matters with a depth of knowledge that could only have come from personal experience. He spoke about trade, about ships that carried goods from Venice and Rome as far as Palestine. The cargoes obviously fascinated him, the cloths from Gaza and sweets from the old cities on the coast. It was clear that he knew a great deal about transport and shipping, and he told them about the merchant warships of the Italian cities and how they traded. He told of the great wealth amassed by them, but as quickly as he had begun, he suddenly stopped, a faint, wry smile on his face, as if it was getting too close to his own past, and started to talk about the troubles with the Scots in the north.

Simon was surprised to find that the knight seemed to know a great deal about the troubles with the Scots. Since Robert Bruce's brother, Edward, had crowned himself king of Ireland earlier in the year, the British armies had been subjected to a number of trials, leading finally to the siege of Carrickfergus. At the same time, the Scots had other men harassing the Border counties, even raiding down as far as Yorkshire, killing and looting all the way. Baldwin's deep voice took on a solemn tone as he described the events in the north and his eyes took on a glazed look, as if he could see the hordes running south in his mind's eye as he spoke.

One thing did seem odd to the bailiff during the meal—Simon noticed that Baldwin drank only very sparingly. It made him wrinkle his brow in wonder. The knight's servant often refilled the other mugs on the table, but even as the light faded and the servant tugged a tapestry over the window, Baldwin seemed to drink little but some water and an occasional sip of wine. Simon mentally noted the point. It seemed strange, for everyone drank beer or wine, and moderation was a rare or curious trait, but soon, as he drank more himself, he forgot, and devoted himself to taking advantage of his host's generosity.

When they had all eaten their fill, Baldwin led them over to the fire while his man cleared the remains of their meal from the table.

Being a newer house, the manor had a fireplace by a wall with a chimney, and Margaret found herself looking at it speculatively. It certainly did not seem to smoke as much as hers, where the smoke simply rose to louvres in the roof to escape. Perhaps a chimney would be a good idea for their own house? What did Lydford castle have?

Simon and Hugh carried their bench over to the fireplace and the bailiff sat on it, back to the wall, with his wife beside him. Meanwhile Hugh wandered over to a bench by the wall, stretched out, and was soon snoring, looking like a dog lying out of a draft while sleeping off a meal. After supervising the tidying, Baldwin brought his own low chair over to the hearth and sat nearby, his eyes glittering as he stared at the flames, occasionally glancing up as his man took the dishes away.

He looked strangely noble, Margaret thought dreamily as she watched Baldwin take a sip of his wine. Noble and proud, like a king, lounging with one elbow resting on the arm of the chair as he watched the logs, the other resting in his lap with his wine. She was happy to see that the air of brooding pain that Simon had mentioned after their first meeting at Bickleigh seemed to have gone, to be replaced by an inner calmness. Instinctively she felt sure that it must, in part at least, be due to being home again, to being back in the land that he so obviously loved, in the shire he had been born in, and in the house he knew so well. But she could not help wondering why the man had such an aversion to talking about his time abroad.

She listened and watched the two men while they spoke in low voices, feeling the warmth of the fire seeping into her bones as she considered them both. Simon had the quiet, calm expression she knew so well, the look he wore when he was relaxed and at his ease. He sat with his head a little forward, almost as if he was about to doze, one hand at her head, the other in the air to occasionally emphasize a point.

Their host, too, was obviously at peace. His dark face was still and restful as he stared at the flames with a small smile, nodding now and again to a remark from Simon. But even while sitting quietly, he managed to remind Margaret of a cat. He had the same feline grace, the same apparent readiness, if necessary, to explode into action.

The two men chatted inconsequentially, their faces lit by the fire and the candles. The knight was a good listener and Simon found that he was talking more and more under the gentle prompting of his host, telling of his pride in his new position, of his wish for more children, especially sons, and of his hopes and dreams for the future. Margaret soon started to feel herself nodding gently under the hypnotic effect of the warmth and the two rumbling voices, until at last she felt the weight of her head to be insupportable. Leaning against Simon's shoulder, her breathing grew slower and deeper as she gave in to her exhaustion and began to doze. Simon put an arm round her shoulders, holding her close as he spoke, gazing into the fire. The clearing finished, Baldwin's servant came back in and stood by the door, seemingly relaxed, but to Simon as he glanced at him, he also seemed ready, like a guard on duty. The bailiff shrugged to himself.

"So what will you do now that you are here, Baldwin? Are you going to start looking for a wife immediately?"

The knight nodded gravely, not taking his eyes from the flames. "Yes, if I can I'd like to marry soon. I'm like you, Simon. I want to be able to leave my house and wealth to a son. I have done enough travelling; all it has given me is a desire for rest. I want to finish my days in peace, looking after the people who live on my lands and never having to travel far away again."

"You sound as though your travelling was a bad experience."

"Do I?" He seemed genuinely surprised. "It wasn't really. I certainly don't regret it. No, I had to do something when my brother inherited our father's lands, and it seemed best to leave the area. It was enjoyable, too, at first. Very enjoyable." He smiled reminiscently, but then his cheerfulness faded and his face changed, becoming morose and reflective. "But these things change. When you are a knight without a lord, you are nothing, just a sword arm—and oftentimes you can't even afford to keep your sword." He sounded bitter.

"Your lord died?"

Baldwin shot a quick, suspicious glance at him, but then grinned as if mocking himself for his distrust. "Yes. Yes, he died. We have fought our last war together. But enough of this misery!" He stood, straightening slowly as if his bones were of iron and long rusted from disuse. "I will go to my bed now. I'll see you in the morning, Simon. I hope you sleep well." He crossed the hall and went through to his solar, his man silently watching him go before walking out to his own quarters at the other end of the hall.

The bailiff's eyes followed the tall figure of the knight as he went, then stood and gently eased his wife down to lie on her bench; in case of rats it was better to stay above the rushes covering the floor. Bringing another bench from the table, he set it near her and lay on it, settling comfortably and staring at the fire, waiting for sleep to take him. But as he watched the flames, he could not get rid of a nagging question. Why was Baldwin so anxious to avoid any talk about his past life?

Just as he felt the drowsiness start to wash over him, as he felt his eyes grow heavy under the soporific effect of the flames, another thought came to him. Why had he been so disinterested in the murder of the abbot, an event that had started tongues wagging all over the area, when he was so interested in the death of Brewer? Reproaching himself for getting too suspicious, he rolled over and was soon asleep.

In the morning, Simon awoke to find that the sun was already shafting in from the opened tapestries. Margaret and Hugh must already be up, he was alone in the hall. He rose stiffly and wandered out to the well, bringing up a bucket and emptying it over the back of his head, blowing and shivering under the shock of its coldness but grateful for the immediate sense of wakefulness it gave.

For some reason, he was beginning to find that he felt slower and older when he woke on the morning after a good meal. He was aware that his father had complained of the same problem, but he had not expected the sensation to appear so soon, before he was even thirty years of age. Now, as he stared through narrowed eyes at the view from the house, he found that he felt worse than usual. His belly was turbulent, the acid boiling and readying to attack his throat; his head was heavy, as if full of lead, and he could feel a dull hammering behind his eyes, as if there was a small army of miners excavating his skull. And as for his mouth . . . he smacked his lips a couple of times experimentally and winced. No, better not to think about his mouth.

Slowly, he wandered along the side of the house, to an oak log that sat waiting to be split and cut ready for the fire, and gently lowered himself onto it, so that he could peer down at the lane while he attempted to reorder his thoughts and, in the meantime, take control of his body and stop the mild shaking in his hands.

He was still sitting there and glaring at the view, when Baldwin came out and, smiling, wandered over to sit next to him.

"How are you this morning? It's a beautiful day, isn't it?"

Simon squinted at him. "Yes," he ventured. "It *is* bright, isn't it?"

The knight laughed heartily. "I used to feel like you look when I had drunk too much. I learned to drink in moderation, and that stopped the pain. You should try it!"

"If it is as well with you, I think I'd prefer to try some wine instead. It might help my head to stay on my shoulders," said Simon, and winced when this brought on another bellow of laughter.

They walked back inside. The servants had already put food on the table, and Margaret was sitting and pecking at a full plate. She looked as if she had little appetite and was eating merely to show gratitude for the food provided, rather than from any desire or need to eat. Simon grinned through his hangover. He recognized the look on her face; it meant she would be irritable today—her head was hurting her more than his own hurt him. He winced—how would they feel when Edith gave them her cheerful welcome? She would be bound to be noisy after an evening with her nurse. Margaret sat tentatively absorbed, her face so pale that it seemed almost transparent, and he felt that if there was a candle behind her he would be able to see its flame through her head. Sitting beside her, he found that even with his feeling of fragility, the world began to look better after taking a good measure of wine with some cold cuts of lamb and bread.

They were just finishing their meal when they heard a horse draw close. Baldwin listened expectantly to the murmuring of voices outside. Soon the visitor entered, and Simon almost dropped his bread in his surprise. It was the monk, Matthew.

Even though he was still feeling hungover and in need of a good gallop in the fresh air to clear the fog from his mind, Simon could clearly see the changing emotions chasing each other across the man's face as he came into the room. The monk walked swiftly at first, his eyes firmly on the knight. Simon was almost certain that he could discern accusation in his expression, and anger, but both seemed to be fighting against doubt and confusion. It was almost as if he knew that the knight had done something, but was not quite certain. For some reason he could not fathom, the sight of the monk's expression struck a cold chill, a warning, that seemed to stab at his heart and put him on his guard immediately.

But even as he saw the look, the monk noticed the guests and seemed to slow, almost as if he was regretting entering now he had seen the bailiff. But then, with an almost palpable resolution, he seemed to quicken his steps, and marched across the floor to them, with a look of wary pleasure on his face.

"Sir Baldwin," he said, as if to an equal—which caused Simon to frown in momentary surprise, "A good morning to you. My apologies if I have interrupted your breakfast."

Baldwin rose, with a cheerful smile of welcome on his face, and motioned the monk to a seat. "Please join us, brother. Some food?"

"Thank you, but no," said the monk, and sat opposite Simon. "Bailiff, I am afraid I have some bad news for you."

Simon raised an eyebrow. "Why, what is it?"

"Last night one of your men passed by the Clanton Barton and asked where you were. It seems that your men have had no success in their search for the man who took my abbot hostage, but they have found that there has been another attack, over near Oakhampton, yesterday. He said that some travellers have been killed, although some escaped. Your constable has gone on to the town, and he asks that you join him there. I fear more people have died on the roads, bailiff."

Stifling a curse, Simon let his head fall into his hands and tried to gather his thoughts, but when he spoke his voice was strong and determined. "Did he say where the attack was?"

"Yes, I understand it was close to Ashbury, to the west of Oakhampton."

"And the attack was similar?" Simon looked up and

stared at the monk intently. "Does that mean hostages were taken, or that there have been more killings? More burnings?"

The monk gazed back for a moment, then, as if his eyes had been held by a cord that suddenly snapped, he looked away, and his voice was low and troubled. "The messenger said that the men had been killed—some of them burned in their wagons. Some women have been taken, too."

"Did he say how many people were responsible?"

"No, I am sorry, bailiff. That is all I know, except that the constable asked that you raise a posse as quickly as possible."

Simon led Margaret and Hugh through to collect their horses while Baldwin bellowed orders behind them and fetched two of his own men to send with them, then followed them into the sunlight with the monk at his side.

"Will two be enough?" the knight asked, "I can see if I can get more for you if you need, Simon."

"No, two will be fine. Could you send a man to Black's farm for me? It would save me sending one of my own."

"Yes, of course."

"Good. Tell Black about the trail bastons and ask him to raise a new posse and meet me at Copplestone in four hours. We will ride for Oakhampton as soon as possible."

Mounting his horse, Simon was struck by a sudden thought, and coaxed his horse to walk over to where Matthew stood by the door. The monk seemed to wear an expression of sadness, a look of weary misery, as if he had seen this kind of event too often in his long life and wondered how many more times he would have to witness the departure of the hue and cry in pursuit of outlaws. Speaking low and quietly, so that Margaret would not hear, Simon said, "Matthew, do you know why Tanner, the constable, wanted me to come so quickly? If the attack was over west of Oakhampton, surely the people of the town can cope?"

"Yes, bailiff," said the monk, and his face when he looked up at Simon was troubled, "but he fears that the outlaws are moving toward Crediton. He thinks whoever is responsible may be coming this way."

It was incredible what a difference a horse and money could make, Rodney thought as he left the inn. Over the space of only a few days he had gone from being without money and on a dying horse, to having to make his way on foot with no horse, to now being in a position where he could afford a bed, food, and stabling. His new mare seemed happy and fully recovered from whatever had so terrified her, he had eaten well and slept better, and he only had a few days' travel ahead of him before he could stay with his brother. Life really did seem a great deal better.

Once more on his horse, he slowly rode out of the little village of Inwardleigh and turned his horse's head to the west. The day was bright and clear, the wind had died to a gentle breeze, and even the mare seemed to feel the excitement and joy of their renewed life. It was almost as if there was an empathy between them, as if she could feel his happiness, or perhaps it was because she had suffered too, and she could now feel the same release that safety and comfort had given him.

The road led them up a steep incline at first, taking them up to a plateau which was almost devoid of trees. The sun behind cast their shadow, a joint black streamer before them.

Gradually, he felt his eyes beginning to get heavy as he rode. The lurching of his mount began to cast its narcotic effect, and he felt his eyelids become heavy as he looked ahead at the road dwindling into the distance. It was no good trying to concentrate, his only thoughts were of the comfort of a full belly, his only feelings of the pleasant warmth of the sun at his back and how the lumbering of his beast seemed so soporific.

Every now and again the mare would jolt and cause his eyes to snap open and his head to rise erect with the sudden shock, but then the casual rolling movement would take over again and he would feel his head nodding and falling until his chin was on his chest and his eyes closed, the calming rhythm soothing him with its hypnotic balm.

It had been like this, he recalled, on the ride up to Bannockburn. They had all been tired after their long journeys, all riding half asleep for days, with little to think of or worry about, just the continual rolling movement of the horse underneath as they all planned what to do after the battle that they were about to win. After all, what could the Scots do? They were hardly in any position to harm the massed forces of England, the soldiers who had won over Wales, who had warred against the French, who had beaten the Scots before so conclusively. What could they do?

But win they had. The army of King Edward was exhausted when it arrived on the road from Falkirk to Stirling. Almost twenty thousand strong, it outnumbered the Scots by two to one, and when their enemy began to advance toward them, Rodney could remember his lord's master, the Earl of Gloucester, arriving and calling them forward: "On, men! On!"

A smile rose to his lips at the memory. Ah, but how they had ridden! It was like the sea rushing on, like a landslide, a glorious, inexorable torrent of humanity and horseflesh, pounding the ground to a mire in the magnificent rush to meet the enemy.

But the smile faded and died, even as his friends and the earl had died on the field.

The Scots were ready for them. The charge with the huge war horses foundered on their spears. They hid behind a vast number of holes dug to trip the horses, safe inside the oblong enclosures they had made by surrounding themselves with their shields. There was nothing they could do to get to the jeering northerners, and at last they had to fall back before a charge by the Scottish cavalry.

Even then they might have been able to survive if the cry had not gone up. Someone saw men running toward the Scottish lines and thought they must be reinforcements. The retreat became a rout, the knights and squires trying to escape as quickly as they could, before the Scots could get to them, and that was why they had been caught in the marsh by the Bannock. As they struggled in the thick mud and waters of the river, the Scottish archers had soon realized their opportunity.

Trapped by the ground, there was little the cavalry could do. They tried to escape, watching with horror as their friends fell, trying to see a way clear to avoid the certain death that followed behind, desperately attempting to make their horses clear the misery of the death that threatened, but few succeeded.

Rodney was one of the few. Together with his lord, he had managed to make his way to the other bank of the river, where they had turned to stare at the other side. It was a scene from Hell, with the Scottish foot soldiers darting in and out among the cavalry, stabbing at the horses' bellies to make them rear and lose their riders, hacking and thrusting at the bodies on the ground, grouping around any knight who tried to make a stand and pushing him over with their long weapons, then running up to give the *coup de grâce* when he was on the ground and defenseless.

Rodney had returned to the camp quiet and shocked. So few had survived, so few had managed to get away from that mob.

It was still all so clear, even the red of the blood in the stream as the Scots threw in the decapitated body of Alfred, his young squire, and the way that it slowly wandered down between the banks letting the carmine stain spread. The cries and the laughter, the way that the bloody knives rose and fell, dripping with the blood, the lives, of the men killed.

"Good morning, sir. And where are you going?"

His head snapped up and to his horror he realized that he had ridden straight into the middle of these people without even seeing them. Had he been sleeping? At the least, his eyes must have been shut.

And then he saw the drawn knives and swords, and saw the wide, staring grins as the men measured him, assessing his value as a prize.

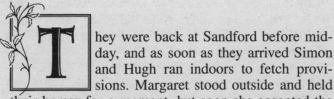

15

They were back at Sandford before mid-day, and as soon as they arrived Simon and Hugh ran indoors to fetch provisions. Margaret stood outside and held their horses for a moment, but soon she accepted the offer of one of Baldwin's men and gratefully threw the reins over to him before following the men inside.

She was weary from the night before and their quick return ride, and her tiredness served to enhance her feelings of concern. It was not only worry for her husband—she knew that he would have the protection of the men in the posse and should be safe. No, it was the fear of what effect the trail bastons would have on the area. She had heard from others how the small bands of outlaws had devastated areas farther north, how they had robbed travellers, how they had killed and raped, attacking anybody who was unwary, whether on the road or at home. Often, when the trail bastons arrived, the rule of the law would fail. The constant attacks and the threat of more to follow forced decent, law-abiding men to stay at home. The murders stopped merchants and farmers from travelling, and others, too poor to be able to pay a ransom, were regularly killed while

wealthier merchants were often captured and held
hostage.

She walked through the door to the hall and sat at
her chair in front of the fire. She could hear the muf-
fled shouts and thumping as her husband and Hugh
grabbed food and water, and then, making her turn
swiftly to the door, she heard a small sob. There at the
door was Edith, her face wrinkled and ancient in her
grief and stained with tears. Margaret quickly rose and
went to her, gathered her up, and carried her to the
chair, gentling her and murmuring softly. Sitting, she
rocked her child, her own eyes watering in sympathy at
her daughter's distress.

"Daddy's going away again, isn't he?"

"Yes, but he'll not be away for long, Edith. There's no
need to worry," said Margaret, blinking against her tears.

"But he might be hurt!" cried Edith. "I don't want him
to go!" She subsided into sobs, and Margaret, suddenly
overcome with a renewed sharp fear, as if her daughter's
terror reminded her of the dangers, could think of nothing to say, feeling smothered by her own dread. What
could she say? That he would be safe, that he would not
be gone for long? Margaret was too aware of the risks to
be able to lie effectively while trapped in her own fear.
They sat together in silence, the girl shaking with her
anxious tears while Margaret stared at the fire.

Soon Simon arrived and stood in the doorway to bid
his wife farewell. He was holding a bag in each hand
and was once more wearing his sword. As he looked
in, he felt almost embarrassed, as if he had interrupted
his wife and daughter in a secret discussion, for he
knew that he was the cause of Edith's weeping, and
there was nothing he could do to cheer her up. He quietly put the bags down and walked over, to stand over

them as they sat, and when his daughter looked up, her eyes huge in their despair, he felt the breath catch in his chest, and knelt and encircled them both with his arms.

"What is it?" he asked gently, looking into Margaret's eyes.

Edith answered, her voice breaking occasionally as she took great gulps of air. "I don't want you to go. I want you to stay!"

"I won't be gone for long, love," he said. "I should be back in a couple of days, that's all."

"But you may get hurt!"

He gave a short laugh and reached one hand up to tousle her hair. "I'll be fine. I'll have lots of men with me to look after me."

She jerked to avoid his hand and hid her head in Margaret's shoulder, weeping softly. He released them reluctantly, confused at his inability to stem the tide of tears, and rested back on his heels, but Margaret looked at him with a smile of understanding as she began rocking her daughter again.

"I think we had better postpone our move to Lydford," he said at last. "At least until this affair has been sorted out. Can you tell the men that we'll have to delay for a week or two?"

She continued stroking and rocking Edith as she looked at him questioningly.

"I don't know how long it'll take us to get these men, so maybe we should wait until they're caught and plan the move then?"

"Alright, Simon." Her voice was calm and low. "Just be careful and catch them quickly. We'll be waiting here. Don't worry about us, just go and catch them and come back as soon as you can." Nodding, he rose, kissed her quickly, and crossed the room to the door.

He picked up his bags and turned to smile at them, then he was gone.

Only when she was sure that her husband had left the house did she begin to weep.

Hugh was already on his horse beside the two Furnshill men, so Simon quickly tied his bags to his saddle and lifted himself up. Mounted, he wheeled his horse and led the way up behind his house to the road to Copplestone.

They rode quickly, the bailiff ignoring Hugh's curses. His mind was on the organization of the posse and what they would have to do when they arrived in Oakhampton, and his face held a fixed frown of concentration as they swept along the lanes. They followed the road along the ridge and were soon dropping into Copplestone, where they met the main group of the posse, some twelve strong, in the town center. Black was not yet there. He had apparently taken it upon himself to ride to all the other men's houses to call them to the posse, and would be coming along later after fetching the last of them.

The men all stayed on their horses while they waited, and the publican of the inn brought them beer, giving the whole affair a holiday atmosphere, as if they were lords at the beginning of a hunt. Simon was concerned at first that some of the men might get drunk, but then he realized that it was probably unlikely. They all seemed to be talking too loudly and laughing, but the beer was slow in going down, and he suddenly understood that they were all nervous and needed the courage that the drink brought, as if they were preparing for a battle. He sat back on his horse and watched them.

They were all firm, stolid men, these yeomen. Although Simon knew only a few by name, he recognized most of them. Almost all were farmers from the area, strong men, well used to the harsh and changeable weather of the moors. Their horses were not the strong war horses of a group of knights, they were all the small local ponies, but they were sturdy and could travel for miles across the moors, feeding themselves by cropping the short grass that lay all around, with no need for extra provisions to be carried.

The men were all nervous and brittle as they waited, as if they all wanted to get the matter over and return to their homes, but it was not merely the nervousness of personal danger. All of the men wanted to help in the capture of the gang, that was obvious. There was a tenseness, a muted excitement in their loud laughter and shouting voices, almost as if they were waiting for a fair to begin so that they could get on with their enjoyment of the day. They were not fearful for their own safety, rather they were keen to get on with the serious matter of catching the outlaws and getting rid of the danger they represented; not just the risk to travellers, but the threat they represented to the whole area.

When trail bastons started in an area, it was common for them to raid outlying homes, raping the women and killing the men. The men of the posse in the square knew what had happened near North Petherton, where several farms had been destroyed by gangs of ruthless killers. In their own pragmatic way they had decided that they would not allow the same madness in their countryside, and they were determined to prevent this gang from surviving.

Black arrived more than an hour after Simon and Hugh, leading a group of six additional men whom he had collected on his way. He nodded gravely to Simon as he came into the village, then rode up to the inn and took a pint of beer, draining it in one long draft. Wiping his mouth with the back of his hand, he urged his horse over to the bailiff.

"Sorry it took so long, but some of the men were in the fields."

"That's fine." Simon looked up at the sky. "It's getting late, though. We'd better be moving if we want to get to Oakhampton."

Black nodded and shouted to the men. Slowly they handed back their mugs and jostled into position, and soon they were all moving off, not in an organized unit like a wolf pack, but a strung-out line of men and horses, a group of individuals bound together by their common need for defense against the threat of the trail bastons. Simon and Black rode in front, not from any need to lead, but simply so that they could set the pace.

They rode along briskly, and had passed the track to Clanton Barton before Simon realized they were there. He turned and looked back at the farm when he became aware, staring hard at the buildings as if he could penetrate the walls and see the monks inside, but there was no sign of them. Had they left already?

"I was thinking," said Black from beside him. "Do you think that this lot could be the ones that killed the abbot? I mean, could the men who killed the abbot have been part of this band? A vanguard out looking for food, and when they saw the abbot they took him for his money?"

Simon turned and stared at the road ahead, his face blank as he thought. "I don't know. I hope so."

They rode on, keeping to a smart pace. They would not be able to reach Oakhampton before night, and Simon was content merely to get as far as possible and find somewhere to camp and finish their journey the following morning. The road led them between thick woods as it curved around the moors, swinging lazily as it took them farther southward. When they had left Bow some three miles behind them the light began to fade and Black started to look for a camp.

At last, as the light was sinking toward darkness, they came to a small stream and Black called the halt. In little time the horses were hobbled and watered, then the men lighted fires and settled down, wrapping themselves in their cloaks or blankets as they sat down to drink and eat before sleeping.

Simon sat a little apart from the rest. He was exhausted after the day. His hangover was gone, thankfully, but his whole body was tense and stiff from his hours in the saddle, and he felt as though he had aged ten years since leaving Furnshill manor that morning. He wrapped himself in his cloak and was soon dozing, propped up against a tree not far from the stream.

Next morning they were all up before dawn and ready to continue before it was light. Grimly, in the chill gray of the early morning, they carried on, making their way along the gentle slopes of the road between the trees.

They had only travelled another two miles from their camp when Simon saw Black frown and stare at the road ahead. He held up his hand for the posse to halt, and as he did, Simon thought he could just hear hoofs up ahead. He felt Black's quick glance at him, then the hunter kicked his horse to amble forward a little. Simon followed, his face frowning as he stared ahead at the next bend in the road, quickly checking his sword hilt as he went, while the men behind went silent and tense, wondering who could be riding so quickly at this time of the morning.

Soon they saw a horse gallop around the bend in the

road, a small piebald horse with a young man on its back. As soon as he saw the posse he reined in and slowed, his expression one of suspicion as his eyes roved over the men standing grimly in front of him.

"Morning," said Black. "You're in a hurry."

"I'm carrying a message," the youth said shortly.

"Who for? Where are you going?"

The youth's eyes held Black's for a moment, then glanced behind him again at the others. "To Crediton."

Simon edged his horse closer. "You need have no fear of us, friend. We're a posse, on our way to Oakhampton to help follow the trail bastons and catch them."

The youth's face radiated relief, the suspicion falling away as if it was dirt wiped away by a cloth. "Thank God! I've been sent to ask you to come, only I hadn't realized you would be this far already—I thought you were outlaws! Quick, you must come back with me, there's been an attack!"

"We heard, that's why we're on our way, we had a messenger last night."

"Last night? But that's when the attack was!"

There was a mumble of anxious voices from the men, but it died when Black turned and glared. Simon leaned forward in his saddle.

"Where? What happened?" he asked urgently.

"Late last night, sir. A group from Cornwall, on their way to Taunton. They were only six miles from Oakhampton when they were set upon and robbed, and many were killed. Two of them managed to get to our farm, a boy and a woman. Our house wasn't far from the attack. They are there still. They said that the robbers were being hunted over to the west of the town, so my father thought I should ride for Crediton and get more help, so I was on my way—"

"Yes, yes, I see," said Simon meditatively, then looked over at Black. "This must be another attack."

"Yes," said the hunter. "So Tanner may not have heard about it yet. We may be the first, the nearest to hand."

"We have to go there and see what we can do!"

Black shrugged and turned back to the boy, who waited with a nervous keenness. "Your farm—is it on the way to Oakhampton from here?"

"Yes, sir."

"Take us there, then."

They rode at a canter, all of them eager now that they seemed to be so close to the criminals, and it was only another hour before they were riding down the muddy track that led to the farm.

At the door, the youth dropped from his horse and ran for the house. Black and Simon told the others to stay outside before following him inside.

The house was an old dwelling, with rough thatch that needed replacing, but inside they found it to be a cheery home, lighted with a warm orange glow from the fire roaring on the hearth. Sitting in front of it were a boy and a young woman.

As they walked in their messenger stood uncertainly by the door, as if nervous of entering, and when Simon looked in he realized why and winced. The young woman could not yet be twenty years old, he could see. She was obviously tall, a strong and slim figure with a firm and elegant body under her robe, but it was her face that caught his attention. She was obviously terrified; it showed in the way that she sat huddled, as though to comfort herself, it showed in the paleness of the face under the thick and long black hair as she turned to stare fearfully at them, in the wide and tear-filled dark eyes, in the trembling of her chin under her tightly pursed lips, and it was so palpable, so clear, that Simon felt the pain himself, and longed to go to her and comfort her.

The boy sat quiet and still, hardly acknowledging them as they entered, but sitting silent in front of the flames, with his straw-colored hair reflecting the glow, and staring at the men with unseeing eyes, as if they were of such little importance that they merited no response. He was beyond fear; he seemed to have lost all sense.

As Simon and Black walked closer, an older couple came in behind them and, while the man caught them by their arms, the woman barged past and went to the two figures.

"Sorry, sorry, but they're . . ." the man said haltingly. Simon gazed at him uncomprehendingly, then glanced back into the room. The older woman was cradling and gently rocking the younger, who clung to her like a frightened child to its mother. "Come outside, please," the man said. "Come outside, we can talk there." Simon and Black exchanged a glance and followed him out.

In the open, the man seemed surprised at the sight of the men on their horses, and appeared to be concerned until Simon's soft voice broke into his thoughts. "Don't worry, friend. We're the posse from Crediton. We're here to help with the trail bastons."

At this the farmer relaxed visibly. "Thanks to God! For a moment I was thinking you could be the same that—"

"What has happened? All we know is what your son told us," Black interrupted.

The old man's eyes misted. "You've seen what they're like, friend. They turned up at my door last night, just like you see them now. We haven't been able to get a word from the boy, he just won't talk at all. Just sits and stares all the time. The girl's his sister, or so it seems. They were riding up to Taunton with their parents and others and camped some two miles yonder." He pointed to the southwest, toward the gray line of the moors. "They had made their camp and were preparing their food when they were attacked."

"Do you know when it was?" asked Simon.

"No. All she will say is that it was after dark. She says that men rode into the camp and killed all the men, and some of the women too. I think that the other women were kept for . . . for . . ."

"You think they were to be molested?" Simon said, feeling his anger grow as he realized what the two indoors must have witnessed.

Black's face grew dark too. "Was she raped as well?" His own wife could not have been many years older, Simon realized.

The old man nodded slowly. "She won't talk to me, but she told my wife." He shrugged and there were tears in his eyes when he glanced at Simon. "When I go into the room she just goes quiet and holds on to my wife. She's so terrified of men, just like when she saw you gentlemen. My wife says she hasn't ever seen anybody so scared."

"Did she describe the men who attacked them?" asked Simon, ignoring the hissed curse from the hunter.

"No. All she would say was that one of them looked like a knight, all in armor, whatever that means. He could have been wearing a hauberk of plate or chain, or dressed in full armor for all I know. The others were just ordinary men."

Black and Simon exchanged a glance, then, slowly, Black nodded grimly.

Turning back to the farmer, Simon said, "Can you

let us have your son to show us where they were attacked? Can he find it?"

"Oh yes. You don't really need his help, it's clear where it happened, but you can have him by all means."

Quickly, Black and Simon swung into their saddles and, when the farmer's son was ready, they made their way back along the track to the road and then south and west toward the moors.

The men were all silent and deep in thought as they went. As he considered the little information that the farmer had been able to give them, Simon found himself shivering, straining under the influence of the greatest passion of rage he had ever felt. It was not just the senseless brutality of the trail bastons, it was seeing the horror-struck girl. Her absolute terror at the sight of him and Black seemed to show the degree of her suffering. He kept returning to the same question: who could do this? Who could inflict such pain on a girl so young; who could shatter the lives of a little boy and his sister; who could produce such misery and live with himself afterward?

It felt as though the breath came in hot rushes, as if he was inhaling flames, and he sat tall and straight in his saddle as he rode, as if his anger had doubled his strength and energy.

The hunter rode beside him with a stolid, hunched mien, riding smoothly and effortlessly, but when Simon glanced over at him he could see that Black was as angry as he himself. He stared ahead, hardly blinking, his dark eyes fixed on the road ahead as he went, and he reminded Simon of a cat, a cat that has just seen a shrew and is slowly stalking it with the intense and total concentration of absolute absorption. But the anger was shown by his quick movements, by the occasional snapping turns of his head as he glared into the woods on either side, as if daring them to hide the men they hunted, and by the sudden, swift, snatching of his hand as he grabbed at his short sword, as if he was caught every now and again by a desire to pull it from its scabbard and *kill.*

Keeping up their fast pace, they soon covered the short distance to the place where the attack had happened, and when they came close the farmer's son slowed and pointed. Up ahead and to the left of the road, they could see smoke rising from among the trees.

"That must be it," he said, pointing and staring in fascination. When Simon looked at him, he could see that the man was trembling—not in fear for himself, but in a calm horror at the thought of the sights that would lie beyond the line of trees surrounding the travellers' camp. Even through his anger, and his desire to avenge the girl and the boy, Simon felt the youth's trepidation.

"You have guided us well, and I thank you for it. Go home now. We will continue and send back word when we know what has happened."

With a grateful glance, the farmer's son nodded, wheeled his horse and made his way back home. Simon and his tracker watched him go, then started off toward the distant smoke, moving slowly and carefully and keeping a wary eye on the trees on either side.

"Bailiff," said Black quietly after a few minutes.

"Hunh?"

"I don't suppose you'd like to send me home too?"

Simon glanced over at the somber man riding alongside him, and for a moment the two gazed at each other with complete understanding, then, as if they had communicated perfectly with a single, penetrating look, they whipped their horses and galloped toward the smoke, like cavalry toward the battle.

16

As they came closer to the smoke the bailiff felt it hard to keep going. Guessing at the sights that would confront them beyond the lines of trees, he wanted to slow so that Black would be the first to see the view, as if that could reduce the shock and the pain. He found that he could hardly keep his eyes on the way ahead. It was as though they wanted to avoid the scene, and he found himself watching the trees on either side, staring at the track, looking up at the sky, *anywhere,* in preference to the camp itself.

Black was riding as though in a trance, hunched and unmoving in his saddle, with one hand gripping his reins and his other lying loose on the saddle in front of him. This would be Simon's first exposure to the ferocity of a trail baston attack, he knew, but not his own. Black had travelled in his youth, before he followed his father into farming and hunting, and had gone as far north as York with merchants, helping them to move their goods from town to town in their unceasing attempt to sell their wares.

Once—God, he could still remember it as if it was yesterday!—they had come across a camp where an attack had taken place. He had only been, what, two and twenty? And he had been exposed to sights that he would not have believed possible before. He had been so shocked that he could not speak for days afterward, and had not slept properly for weeks. Now, as they trotted up the slight rise that led to the campsite, he felt the old anger again, the sheer rage that any man could do such things to his fellows. The last time he had been too young to catch the men responsible, too young to be able to help, and, as a stranger to the area, unwanted in the posse, but he had followed the men as they chased after the gang, purely to assuage his anger by watching the revenge of the local men.

They had not been able to find the gang. The posse had chased after the gang for days, but, at last, they had lost the trail deep in a forest and had been forced to return, the whole group dejected from their failure. That was part of the reason for his depression at losing the killers of the abbot. He, too, had been unavenged for his miserable end. This time Black was committed. They would not escape him; he would hunt them down and destroy them, not only for this attack, but for the abbot and for the poor dead men and women he had seen when he was twenty-two. He looked over at Simon. How would he cope with it, he wondered.

Simon's anger was giving way to fear as they drew closer, fear of the sights hidden by the trees. He had been shocked and horrified to see what had happened to the abbot, but this attack seemed even worse already, after seeing the effect on the young woman and her brother, and he withdrew into himself as they rode, as if he could hide from the sights ahead.

When he glanced behind, Simon realized that he was not alone in his feelings of trepidation. The others, all sturdy men well-used to the sight of dead and injured men and animals, men ready and prepared to kill a wounded beast out of kindness to stop its misery, were riding bunched together in a group, no longer strung out along the road, as if they all felt the need for the mutual support and comfort that only their numbers could bring. They rode with the fixed expressions of men who were fearful, but who would continue with what they knew would be a deeply unpleasant task, as if they knew that only by their dedication could they prevent a repeat of the attack.

Simon turned back to face the road again and set his jaw. If the men could ride with that level of commitment, so could he. He glanced swiftly at Black, who was riding with the same fixed frown on his face, then stared at the road again with a small feeling of desperation. He felt as if he was alone in his feeling of fear, that the others were free of concern and that he alone was scared of what lay ahead.

As they came up to the trees, they slowed to a walking pace. The road led past the camp, and they had to turn off into a small lane to get to it. They meandered down the lane, all feeling their tension and apprehension growing. Simon felt that the men of the posse had a curious mood of estrangement in their unity, as if they were all grateful for the company of their friends, but were all absolutely alone with their thoughts, each standing isolated and apart from the other as he rode, as if they were retreating into themselves for the strength to carry on to the campsite.

The lane curved and wound its way to the camp, but through the occasional gaps in the trees Simon could see the dark and gloomy hills of the moors ahead, so they were heading south. He saw that Black was already trying to make sense of the mess of tracks in the trodden dirt of the lane. He seemed to feel Simon's steady gaze on him and looked up for a minute, but there was no recognition in his eyes, only an angry glittering. He turned back to his quiet investigation.

It was the smell that Simon noticed first—not the bitter, musty tang of an old fire, but fresh smoke from a fire of cured wood, and the smell made him frown and glance at Black again. Surely they weren't still there? The trail bastons would have left by now, wouldn't they? They wouldn't wait and camp at the scene of their latest attack, would they?

The expression on Black's face froze him. The hunter was staring with his face rigid, his jaw locked and clenched, and only his eyes moving. No other muscle worked. It was as if he had been bewitched, as if he was cursed by having all his limbs stilled and rendered immovable. With a feeling of horror, the bailiff realized that the man was stricken with disgust and revulsion, and he felt his own terror return as they rode into the camp.

At first all he could see was the burning wagons. They came into the camp through a small gap in the trees and were suddenly in a little clearing, bordered by a fringe of thin, young trees. Although the grass had long ago been trampled into mud, the first impression that the bailiff had was of a festive and peaceful site, with brightly colored clothes on the people sleeping all round and the green of the trees reflecting off the little pool of water at the other side of the clearing. It was as if they had entered a small oasis of calm, and he felt that if they were to shout all of the people would wake and greet them. But then, as he looked all over the area, he saw that none in the camp would wake again. They were all dead.

Two wagons, parked close together, were smoldering, giving off thin gray smoke that rose and billowed
in the clear air. Two others sat a little farther off, their
contents strewn over the ground in a haphazard tapestry of color. Slowly the sensation of unreality faded
from him and he felt the tears warming his eyes as he
saw that the nearest body was that of a woman, hacked
to death and lying in her own gore. Then he saw that
the next body, that of a man, lay with his arms outstretched as if reaching for her even in death, with a
massive and bloody gash at the back of his head.

He felt as if he was not here, as if he was away from
this scene and looking through another's eyes, as he
surveyed the bodies all over the clearing. It was as if
his brain had become dissociated from his body, as if
in horror of the sight before him, his mind had withdrawn to defend him from the reality of the view.

His eyes smarting, he had to turn away quickly. He
looked up at the wagons again. As he saw the second
of them, he felt the sensation of being elsewhere leave
him, to be replaced by a rage, an anger so deep as to
engulf him completely, a fury that this should have
been done to peaceful travellers here, in this sheltered
glade. It seemed so unjust that this should have been
done, so *wrong*. Then, as he looked closer, his breath
caught in his throat as he saw, hanging from the back
of the smoking, open cart, two blackened arms that
dangled from the smoldering ruins. He sat, as if incapable of movement, his eyes fixed in front of him at
those two sad reminders of what had been a human.

Black dropped lightly from his horse and motioned
to the posse to wait, then he quickly stalked over the
ground, bending now and then at the bodies, gazing intently at the mess on the ground, checking the wagons'

contents, and kneeling occasionally to peer at some traces. Finished, he returned and took his horse's bridle before standing by the bailiff.

"Sir," he said, his voice low and controlled, "there were more than five here. It looks like they came in some hours ago from the tracks, and left some time ago—their marks are a little weathered."

"What happened? Why did they kill all these people?" Simon's voice was muted, almost awed by the immensity of the crime.

"They took all the money, took all the food." Black shrugged. "They had no need for all these." His hand waved, taking in all the bodies in a gesture of seeming indifference.

"Where did they go?"

"South. To the moors. The trail's clear."

"Let's go after them, then." Simon stared at the wagon again.

"Sir? We have to send word first, let the farmer know so that he can call the people over from Oakhampton." Black was frowning as he spoke, trying to break through the cloud of anger that was smothering Simon's thoughts.

"Yes. Yes. Of course. Leave two men here and send one to the farm. The others will come with us."

Quickly the hunter followed his orders, choosing the two oldest men to guard the camp, and the youngest to warn the farm, then he mounted his horse again and, after a quick glance at the bailiff, he kicked his mount into a brisk trot and led the way down past the pool of water and up the incline at the other side, steadily taking them toward the moors.

They went fairly slowly at first as the track took them between the trees. It seemed clear that the men who had violated the camp had not taken many precautions to make their trail hard to follow—it led through the trees where the trunks were thinnest, where the branches hardly made the riders duck, and soon they came to an open moor, where the tracks led straight as an arrow toward the blue-gray hills ahead.

As they went, the feeling of unreality left Simon, to be replaced by a sense of lightheadedness. He could not comprehend the ferocity of the attack: it seemed too vicious, too brutal. It seemed even worse than the attack on the abbot, somehow, the enormity of the crime being increased by the number of the victims, and he felt confused and troubled in the midst of his rage. More than ever, he felt the need for his wife now, for someone who could listen to him as he tried to explain the feelings that crowded his mind with the clamor of confusion. He felt as if his brain must break with the mad array of emotions that battered at him. The anger was still there, burning deep inside him with the flames of his need to avenge the attack, but he also wanted an explanation. He needed to understand *why* this could be done, why men could kill and destroy for no reason. Until he could understand that, he could have no peace, because if there was no reason, then why would God allow it? Surely God in his wisdom would have prevented such barbarity?

Almost without thinking, he spurred his horse to bring him level with Black.

"Black, can you understand *why?*"

The hunter glanced up, his expression one of absorbed concentration, but even as the recognition glimmered in his eyes, he turned to look back at his trail again. "I don't know. I've only seen it once before, that was back long ago when I was up north."

"Well, did you ever find out why they did it?"

"No. I wasn't wanted in the posse because I wasn't a local. Oh, I followed, I wanted to see what the killers looked like, but we never found them. No, I never did find out why."

Simon frowned at the ground. "What could have made them behave like that? All they needed to do was tie up the men and take what they wanted, they were only merchants. They couldn't have put up much of a struggle even if they wanted to."

The hunter shrugged. "I don't know. They were either mad or just didn't want to leave anyone to recognize them later. How can I tell? All I know is I want to get them and stop them before their next attack."

"You think they'll attack again?"

"Aye. They will. While they know they can get away with it they'll carry on."

Simon looked away and up to the horizon in front. "Where do you think they'll be heading?"

"I don't know. It depends whether they know we're following them or not. If they don't, they might swing back toward Crediton or Oakhampton, or keep heading south, to Moretonhampstead, maybe. If they know we're behind, they might keep going south, but they could try to avoid us or even ambush us if they feel strong enough." He paused. "Damn them, the bastards!"

The poison in his voice vaguely shocked Simon, as if even the sights they had left behind them should not have so affected the hunter's usual equanimity. He had not realized how much the camp had horrified the imperturbable man, but now as he looked he could see Black's jaw clenching with a steady rhythm, as if he was chewing at a piece of gristle, and his eyes, normally so calm, were wide and staring with his desire for revenge.

Simon slowed and left the hunter on his own in the lead, dropping back to join the main group of the posse, feeling even more disquieted.

They had been following the trail for over an hour when they came to a road. Black, still quiet in his deep fury, held up one hand to stop the others, then jumped down from his horse and almost ran to the verge, his head swaying from side to side like a dog sniffing for a scent, before he cried out in a pagan yell of cruel delight. Simon spurred his horse and quickly went after him.

"What?"

"They weren't so clever this time! Look!" He pointed down at the grass by the side of the road. There was little here between the road and the moors beyond, apart from the occasional clumps of heather and gorse, adding purple and bright yellow splashes of color. The edge of the road gave onto scrubby gray-green grass and on the verge, Simon could clearly see the marks of hooves, a great number, that had destroyed the grass and turned the verge into thick, black mud. Black looked up at him with a face filled with pitiless pleasure. "I can follow them to Hell now if I need to. There's nowhere else for them to lose their tracks, not here on the moors," he said.

There was a call from behind them, making them both jerk round together. Hugh was pointing up the road to the west, and as they followed his hand they saw a group of six men riding toward them at a steady lope.

Black scrambled over the road and onto his horse, grabbing his sword and unsheathing it, before spurring to ride to the strangers.

"Black, stop!" shouted Simon, staring at them with a small frown. If this was the band, he thought, they would hardly ride so obviously along the king's road. Surely they would have hidden here and ambushed us while we followed them, not come down the road as if they were out for a morning's gallop?

The posse came out of the woods and grouped on the road to wait for the men to get closer, the horses seeming to feel their riders' tenseness, stamping and blowing as they stood.

At last, when the group came closer, Simon felt his heart lift and he spurred his horse with a shout of joy. It was Tanner and his men.

Later, as the darkness crept slowly over them and even Black admitted that they could not continue, they all stopped in the shelter of a great pile of granite and made camp.

They had followed the tracks on an almost direct line south, bypassing several small hamlets as they went, and crossing a number of small streams that, each time they saw them, made them fear that the trail bastons would try to throw them off their track, but each time they found that the trail continued, as if the men they followed were convinced of their invulnerability and safety from attack. It was almost as if they were tempting the posse to chase them, and every now and then Simon felt concerned that this was exactly what they *did* want. Were they just leading the posse on into the moors so that they could turn and fight on their own terms? Were they leading them to an ambush? Somehow it did not seem likely, it seemed more probable that they were so sure of themselves that they had no fear of any group that might chase them.

At last, when the horses had been seen to and the other members of the posse were sitting resting sore legs and bodies in front of their fires and chatting desultorily, their voices making a soothing accompaniment to the spitting and crackling of the burning logs, Black and Tanner joined Hugh and Simon as they crouched in front of their own fire.

Simon lay on one elbow, the better to rest his thighs and backside as the others came up and sat opposite. "So, then, constable. What have you been doing since we split up?"

Tanner's square face was serious and pensive as he recalled his journeys of the previous days. "We started off on the road to Barnstaple, and we stopped anyone we met to ask them about the killer of the abbot, but we had no luck. The trouble is, there're so many roads leading off that one. Whenever we came up to one, we stopped and checked down it a little, but after a half mile, if we couldn't see any sign, we went back and continued on our way. We checked the sides of the roads, but I'm fairly certain no one went off the roads that way. If we were behind them, they must have kept to the roads themselves.

"At the end of the first day we'd got as far as Lapford. We camped outside the village and carried on next day. We checked all the way up as far as Elstone, but we'd seen nothing by the time we got there, so we started back. Some of the men were tired out after all the riding, so I sent them back the way we'd gone, but I thought the trail bastons might've gone across country and we'd missed their tracks, so I took the others with me by some of the smaller lanes, heading south. I was going to go to the Oakhampton road and then back up to Crediton. Well, at the end of the second day we heard about the trail bastons over to the west of Oakhampton, so I thought: might be the same ones that killed the abbot. It seemed from their tracks that they were heading east, toward Crediton, so I sent one of the men back to tell you and came south quickly.

"We've been there since, searching, but some people we saw said they were heading east. Last night we heard there'd been an attack this way, so we came over to see whether we could help."

Simon stirred. "It was lucky you told your man to look for me. I wasn't at home, and he got one of the monks to come and find me."

"Really?" said Tanner, looking surprised. "I didn't tell him it was that urgent, it was just to let you know where we were."

Obviously impatient with the long story, John Black interrupted and quickly ran through the journey up from Crediton and the scene they had seen that morning. "It was awful, Stephen. There was bodies all over the place, and they'd even burned two of them in their wagons."

"Why, though?" said Simon pensively, making the others look at him in surprise. "Why burn the bodies?"

Tanner shrugged. "Often happens, bailiff. They burn to torture, to find out whether there's more money or not, they burn to get rid of evidence. And they burn for fun—they sometimes enjoy it."

"It seems to fit in with the killing of the abbot, anyway," said Black. "And Brewer."

"No, it doesn't," said Simon, morosely hugging his knees as he sat and stared at the flames. The others looked over at him, surprised at his curt denial of their assumption.

Black recovered first. "What do you mean? Of course it does, senseless killing and robbery, and done by men who enjoy burning their hostages. It's exactly the same."

"No, it's not! One man murdered in his house, another taken hostage and burned to death, then travellers attacked on the road? There's nothing similar between them!"

"I agree. Brewer was killed by someone else, even if the abbot was killed by these outlaws." It was Hugh, sitting with his cloak around his shoulders and gazing at the ground in front of him.

"What do you mean, Hugh?" asked Simon quietly, making his servant look up. He had a suspicious frown on his face, as if he doubted that his opinion was being honestly sought, and his eyes flitted over Simon's face as if looking for confirmation that his thoughts were really wanted. At last, seeming happy with Simon's expression of concentration, he continued, talking directly to him and ignoring the others.

"Well, the farmer was dead already, before the fire, you reckoned. The abbot and the travellers, they weren't. They were all killed like they were being tortured. These outlaws kill, but they do it once they have taken everything they can, don't they?"

"But the abbot was still worth money, he was worth a ransom," said Simon musingly. "Why kill him? Why burn him? What were they doing, torturing him to find out which saddlebag his money was in? And surely the outlaws would have killed all the monks together, not just taken the abbot. Like you say, Brewer was killed before the fire started, if he was killed at all. That's why all of the killings seem different to me."

"No, with Brewer they just wanted his money. When they got it, they left. The abbot was taken as a hostage because they wanted what he had in his saddle, but then maybe they were scared off, maybe someone came along when they had burned the abbot and they had to leave in a hurry," said Tanner dismissively.

Simon looked back at Hugh. "Well? What do you think?"

"I think that a small party of these outlaws saw the abbot and took his money. Taking a monk? It must have seemed like an easy target! What doesn't make sense to me is Brewer being killed by the same band. But maybe they found his money, then killed him, and fired the house to hide what they'd done."

"It's possible," agreed Simon grudgingly. "Although they have not been too careful about hiding their traces since then. But the abbot—why kill him like that?"

"Like I said, they were seen by someone and had to get away," said Tanner.

"Had to get away?" said Hugh, his eyebrows rising in disbelief as he turned to the constable. "If it was two men, surely they'd have taken the abbot with them, not just killed him. They can't have been rushed if they had time to burn him to death. And if someone did see them, whoever it was would've raised the hue and cry, wouldn't they? I mean, if *I* saw a body burning in the middle of the woods, I'd've run home quick and got help."

"But maybe they never saw the outlaws or the body burning," said Black, frowning.

Hugh paused to stare at him sullenly, but when he spoke again his voice was high and strained. "And I suppose the abbot was quiet? He was being burned at the stake, and he was quiet? Even if they never saw him they must've heard him."

Black rose with a faintly patronizing smile on his face. "Well, I don't know why they left him either, but I *do* know one thing. The men we're chasing now are the same ones who killed the abbot and probably Brewer as well. Nothing else makes sense. And we're going to catch them tomorrow, so I'm going to get some sleep now."

As Black walked over to his packs, Tanner glanced at the bailiff, who sat, still staring at his servant. It mattered little to Tanner who was responsible for the death of the farmer, his main worry was for the people who could be hurt in the future. Marauding trail bastons could wreak havoc in an area like this, where there were many forests for them to hide in and hundreds of small hamlets for them to attack with relative impunity. During his warfaring days he had seen enough of the companies that devastated the land, robbing, burning and thieving, murdering the peasants and stopping all traffic. His sole desire was to see them caught or killed. The bailiff seemed more concerned about the others, about the abbot and Brewer. Tanner was not; they were past help, in his view. He could understand the bailiff's feelings, though. He was too young to have seen the harm outlaws could bring. Sighing, the constable rose, gave them a good night and left them. There was nothing more for him to do here tonight.

"So, Hugh, you think someone else was responsible for the farmer's death as well, do you?" asked Simon when he had gone.

Hugh nodded, his face bleak. "Yes, I reckon the abbot was killed by this lot, but Brewer wasn't. And you know the bugger about it all? I've got no more idea than you why they did it."

"It doesn't matter, Hugh" said Simon softly but deliberately. "Whoever it was, I will find out. I will find who was responsible and why. Too many have died—it's time to avenge them—all of them."

hey awoke stiff and aching in a clear and bright morning. Simon felt awful. He had hardly slept at all; every time he found himself slipping into sleep, his brain started to tease once more at the question of who was responsible for the murder of the abbot.

He wanted to accept the simple faith of his companions, that the same men had killed Brewer, then de Penne, then had robbed and killed the travellers; but he could not believe it. It seemed too obvious, somehow—too easy,—and, like Hugh, he could not believe that the men who had taken so much from the travellers would have killed the abbot—he was too valuable. And he was confused that only the abbot had been taken. Surely the men who had killed the merchants would have taken *all* of the monks, not just the abbot?

The bailiff stood and rubbed his buttocks and thighs, grimacing at the bustle of the others all around as they quickly packed and started to get their horses ready. He felt cold and damp, tired and miserable. His back and his legs hurt, he had a bruise on one side where a stone had dug into his ribs, and he felt no closer to a definite answer about who was responsible for the killing of the abbot.

He crouched by the fire, trying to absorb some warmth from the ashes, but they were cold and gave him no comfort, so it was with a wry grin that he thought about his warm house, his bed and Margaret's body, thinking, God! What am I doing out here!

"Bailiff!"

Turning, he saw Black striding toward him. The hunter grinned when he came close, seeing Simon's evident ill-humor. "All the men are ready." He paused. "We can leave when you're feeling well enough," he added drily, a grin lifting the corner of his mouth.

"Thank you, Master Black," said Simon insincerely, but he rose and walked with him to the horses. Hugh had saddled both and packed, and now stood at their bridles, scowling his usual welcome as they approached. Taking the reins, Simon mounted slowly, wincing at the aches from the previous day's ride, then they wheeled and followed Black down the slight rise, heading back to their trail.

They rode in single file now, the hunter leading, his eyes constantly flitting from side to side as he checked the trail and made sure that no one had left the group they hunted. Occasionally he would stop, one hand held high to stop the others, as he gazed frowning at the muddy marks on the trail, and every so often he would lean down to read some new sign. But then the hand would wave again and they would all follow.

Simon, Hugh and Tanner were behind him in a small group. The bailiff found the first few miles to be even more miserable than the previous day, the rest during the night had simply tied knots in all his muscles, or so it felt. At first he had thought he was going to have to stop and try to ease the pains, but then, after they had been riding for almost an hour, he found that the exercise loosened him and he could sit more comfortably in his saddle. When they had been riding for two hours he felt almost himself again—apart from a number of new aches in parts of his body he had not known *could* ache.

In the early morning the tracking had been easy, with the sun throwing shadows where the horses had walked, but as the sun crawled up in the sky the job became more slow and difficult as Black tried to read the signs accurately. When they had been travelling for over three hours, Simon grunted to himself and rode up alongside his tracker.

"Black, can't we go any faster?" he growled.

"No, not if we're going to get all of them at the same time."

"Eh? But we can see where they're going, surely we can just keep going and make sure now and then that we haven't lost their trail?"

"We can, but some of them might leave and go off to the side. We need to know we have them all."

Simon stared up ahead with a feeling of exasperation. At this speed they would never catch the men. "Well, if we get the main group, we can—"

"No," said the hunter absentmindedly as he continued his frowning stare at the tracks. "What if a few leave the main group?"

"Well? What if they do? So long as we get the main body of men and—"

"No," said Black, suddenly looking up at him. "We can't take the risk. We might get half or more, but what about the others? If we miss two they could rob a farm and kill the family. I'm not having it. We must get them all."

Simon sighed, nodded, and let him get on with it. He wanted to be able to give chase, not follow slowly like this. He wanted to know that they were catching up with the men who had killed the merchants, to catch them, or, if they would not surrender, kill them. But he curbed his enthusiasm and slowed, allowing Hugh and Tanner to catch up with him, watching Black continue.

It was more than four hours after they had left their camp that they came across a small stream, and Black stopped. Simon quickly rode alongside, Tanner just behind him.

"What is it?"

"Look!" said the taciturn hunter, pointing.

Just in front of them the ground levelled out. There were stones lying around in a rough circle, some on top of each other like a low wall, and in the middle were a number of blackened patches. The three rode forward cautiously and paused at the first. Black leaned down and sniffed, then dropped lightly from his horse—as if he had not been riding for days, thought Simon in disgust—and knelt, sniffing and feeling the ashes while he muttered to himself.

"Well?" said Tanner, obviously as keen as Simon to get on with their hunt.

Black looked up, but now his eyes had lost the introspective look; now they glittered with an unholy glee. "This's where they camped last night. The ashes are still warm." He sank back on his haunches and surveyed the area, but then gave a little start. While the others followed his gaze, he leapt to his feet and ran.

Simon could see what looked like a huddle of rags lying under the wall, and looked at the others uncomprehendingly. Hugh seemed as surprised as Simon, but Tanner cursed and kicked his horse with a face gone dark with anger. The others shrugged and spurred after them.

It was only when they were a few yards away that Simon realized that the pathetic bundle was a partly naked body. With a half sob, half sigh, he saw that it was a young woman.

She could only have been fifteen years old, a slim figure with long dark hair that had been braided but now was roughly tousled and spread over the ground by her head. She was bruised, with large brown and blue discolorations to her skin, and she had weals too. Her feet were uncovered, and her soles were bloody and crusted with scabs. It seemed clear that she must have lived a privileged life, for her hands were unmarked by work when Black gently turned them over. She must have been one of the merchant's daughters.

The group stared in frozen and angry silence at the little figure while the hunter searched for any clues to the people who had committed this crime. He carefully looked through the ripped and torn dress and checked the ground, but there seemed to be nothing to be learned. When he stood again there was a new determination on his face, Simon could see. It looked as though the calm and imperturbable hunter had made his choice: the men he was chasing would not escape him: he would catch them before they could commit any more crimes like this.

Simon watched him as he mounted his horse and organized a man to take the body back. The bailiff was becoming anxious now—how would the men react when they caught the trail bastons? He did not want them all to be slaughtered. But then his eyes were drawn to the body, as if it was calling to him, and he found himself thinking how little older than his own daughter this young girl was and suddenly he realized he did not care how the posse reacted when they found the gang.

They paused at midday near a stream, where they watered and rested the horses while they sat and ate some food. Tanner's men had managed to buy provisions while they had been on the road after the abbot's death, but Simon was aware that his own group's food was being quickly depleted. At this rate they would only be able to stay on the moors for another two days at the most. The men were quiet again. Any joy they had felt from their morning's ride had been dispersed by the sight of that small, sad shape half hidden by the wall, to be replaced by anger and the urgent desire for vengeance. Simon could feel the mood as he sat chewing on some bread and cured meat. They all wanted to find the men responsible, and he knew that they would be difficult to control when they caught up with the band.

He knew he no longer cared how they reacted. He was so disgusted, so sick of the sight of death, that he wanted to kill the men responsible himself. That men could do this in his land had made him furious when it was a matter of a dead abbot and little more, but now, after seeing that poor, destroyed body at the camp, used and then discarded, he felt a rage so deep that it burned white hot within him.

The other men were all sitting around, almost trance-like as they ate. Each seemed to be in his own world; there was little talking, only an occasional hushed murmuring of low voices. For the most part they were quiet and contemplative, as if they were all considering what they would do when they caught the men.

When Black stood, the sudden movement made several heads turn, and then, with a kind of weary calmness they all rose and began to prepare to move off again.

The trail took them slightly east of south now, heading down toward the eastern edge of the moors. The trail was distinct in the green all around. Now and then they would pass in among thick gorse or heather, and Black would ask others to ride at either side in case he missed another trail among the growths, but it still seemed that their quarry was too sure of themselves to bother to hide their traces, and each time the outriders would come back to the main group and the trail.

It was late in the day when they saw the fruits of their pursuit for the first time.

They had just crested another hill, in among a small copse that stood around some old stones like guards around a king, when Black held up his hand again, and Simon heard the breath hiss between his teeth. The bailiff moved up but the hunter ignored him, his eyes fixed intently on the far hill.

Following his gaze, Simon could make out the thin line of the trail as a black smudge against the green of the hill, almost like a crack in the grayish green, and he searched along it, letting the trail pull his eyes upward, toward the horizon. Then his eyes widened as he saw the small group of men and horses straggling up to the top. Ahead of them there was no trail—they must be the ones!

He turned and looked at Black, who shot him the faintest of grins before whirling and cantering back to the rest of the men.

"We've got them! They're just ahead now, maybe a mile or two away. They just went over the top of the next hill."

There was a sensation of suppressed excitement, a flush to the faces of all of the men in the posse as his words sank in, then a confused muttering.

"Shut up" said Tanner, and waited for silence. "John? What do you want us to do?"

"We'll keep tracking them for now. They don't seem to be taking any care. I'll go on ahead with another tracker and we'll keep as close as we can. You all come on behind." He looked up at the sky with a slight wrinkling of his brow, then looked at the sun over to the west. Simon saw that it was low in the sky and looked swollen and red; Damn! It would soon be dark! Black seemed to consider for a moment, then glanced at Simon and Tanner. "It's getting late. They'll be bound to camp soon. I think we'd better follow them until they do, then attack them when they've relaxed and started to eat, as soon as—"

Tanner held up his hand. "It'd be better if we held off until dawn. Have you ever tried to attack a group of armed men at night? *I* have. It's too easy to have everything go wrong, it'll be better to get our sleep and attack when we're all fresh."

"What if they leave in the night? We could lose them and . . ." said Simon, dismayed at the thought of leaving them to their own devices.

"They'll not move overnight, not after leaving these tracks all over the moors. They're obviously not worried about being followed. No, we'll be better off if we get some sleep tonight and attack them with the dawn tomorrow."

Simon looked at Black, perplexed. The hunter's eyes dropped for a moment while he considered, but when they came up again, he nodded. "Yes, he's right. You all follow on slowly, me and Fasten'll go after them now, and when they've bedded down for the night we'll come back and find you. Fasten? Oh, there you are. Come on, let's find them, then." He jerked his horse's head around and rode off, Fasten behind. As the rest watched, the two men split up, Black riding to the left of the trail, Fasten to the right, and cantered easily down from the copse, then up the other side.

Sighing, Simon said, "Come on, then. Let's get on."

It was long after dark when they found a place to rest, a slight bowl in the top of a hill, just out of the wind and away from the direction the trail bastons were taking. There was no wood, not even twigs, to burn this high up, and the men had to huddle in the rough shelter and shiver in the chill of the evening.

Tanner came over as soon as Simon and Hugh had settled after seeing to their horses, and joined them as they crouched under bushes. They shared some meat and bread and drank a little water, all remaining silent in their tension, the action of the following morning lying heavy on their minds.

"Um, Stephen," said Simon after they had all finished their meal. "You've been involved in fights before, how, er . . . how do you think it'll go tomorrow?"

"I don't know," said Tanner reflectively. "I've been in some fights where we've won easily when we shouldn't've, and others where we lost when we should've won. It depends on them, really. The posse is big enough, we should have two men to each one of theirs. But if they're trained in war, they can still win. I don't know."

Simon glanced at the men all around, peering at them as he tried to remember which of them had been in a battle before. To his knowledge at least eight had seen action. Only eight? Out of all the men they only had eight who had seen a battle before? He bit his lip in sudden nervousness. "Did you see how many were there in the band?"

"I didn't really see, no. I counted seven, but there may have been others already over the brow of the hill," said Tanner, as if thinking out loud, but when he caught the expression on Simon's face, he grinned and slapped the bailiff's leg. "Don't worry, bailiff! These men may be used to killing farmers like Brewer, or monks, but I'll wager we'll be a surprise to them! Anyway, we'll find out soon enough when Black comes back."

As he said that, there came the sound of a horse neighing from nearby, and as they scrambled to their feet, drawing their swords, they heard the imperturbable voice of the hunter.

"Fine thing, isn't it, to go and do a job and then be spitted by your own friends when you get back home again! Where's Tanner?"

"Over here, John. I'm with the bailiff," called Tanner, somewhat shamefacedly as he quickly shoved his sword back in its scabbard, looking embarrassed and annoyed with himself that he could have been so easily alarmed. They all sat down again and waited while the hunter saw to his horse before ambling over to them.

"Right, we followed them to their camp. It's a big dip in the top of a hill, about two miles from here, and it looks like they're settled down for the night." He paused as Fasten came up to join them. "I was just telling them about the camp. Anyway, it's in a big dip, and it's almost surrounded by rocks and a rampart. They've lit fires and they're all sitting round and drinking. It looks like they've got beer from somewhere, probably the merchants, I suppose, so I don't think they'll be up early tomorrow. We went around their camp, anyway, walked all round, and they don't seem to have put guards out, so I think we shouldn't have any problems."

"How many are there, John?" asked Tanner.

"We counted nine," said Black. He hesitated, then turned and looked steadily at Simon. "And one looks like a knight, all dressed in mail."

It was still as black as midnight when Simon felt the kick at his ankles, and he grunted and swore as he sat up, blearily rubbing at his eyes, trying to clear them as if the darkness was inside his head. It took him some time to wake fully, even when at home. Now, with the chill deep in his marrow from sleeping outside too often in the cold and damp, he felt miserable, as if he would never be able to get warm again. Once more, with a rueful grin, he thought of his bed at Sandford, which would still be warm and comfortable with Margaret lying in it, like a sanctuary from the wind and rain of the world.

Shaking his head muzzily, he looked up with irritation as the memory of warmth and his wife fled, and looked around the camp, taking stock. Tanner and Black were walking around, kicking into life the huddled figures of still sleeping men. Those already up were seeing to their weapons, cleaning sword blades and sharpening daggers, swinging hammers and clubs in an effort to free up the muscles that had seized overnight or stayed too tense.

It was a weird sight, almost eery, he thought to himself, all these men in the gloom and darkness, half-obscured by the deeper blackness of the rocks behind them as they swung their arms and weapons in strange patterns, the metal of the axe heads sometimes showing as a lighter gray shimmer against the background. It was as if they were in a different world. The men were quiet, hardly saying a word to each other; there was only the occasional hint of activity in the sound of a knife being rubbed against a stone, the wispy gleam of a hammer being whirled, it felt as if he was watching an army of ghosts, and with that thought he gave an involuntary shiver—how many of these men *would* be ghosts later in the day?

Putting the thought out of his mind, he stood quickly and went to help with the horses. As he walked past, a few of the men looked up; some grunted, grinning, but most simply nodded at him. By the time he had found and saddled his own horse most of the men were up and moving. Black and Tanner appeared, talking quietly, coming toward him from out of the gloom, and they stopped when they came close.

"John here thinks we can ride straight into the camp," said Tanner. "It's enough of a natural stockade to keep them in when we enter, and hopefully, if we're quick, we can get in and catch them before they know what's happening."

"Yes, we should be able to. There only seems to be the one entrance, like a gate it is, in the south side."

"So we'll have to ride round their camp?" asked Simon. "Won't they hear us?"

"No," said Black. "The ground is soft all over there, if we go slowly we should be safe."

Simon looked from one to the other. "Should we ride in? Why not leave the horses outside and rush in on foot? There may not be space to ride inside their camp, they may be able to pull us off the horses. Wouldn't it be safer to rush them on foot?"

They looked at each other, then Tanner nodded. "Yes. Alright, but I think we ought to keep some of our men on horses outside, so that they can ride in if things go badly for us." Simon agreed, finished tightening his saddle, and swung up onto the horse.

When Black and Tanner were also mounted they rode to the middle of the camp and Tanner explained what he wanted the men to do. He had brought five men with him, the remains of the original posse hunting the abbot's killer, and Simon and Black had brought seventeen, so all told they were twenty-one now, after losing three at the scene of the travellers' murder and another one to take back the young girl's body.

As they all grouped, Tanner explained his plan. He wanted sixteen men to enter the camp and the remaining five to stay with the horses—if the fight went against them, these men could come in on horseback as a reserve and work as cavalry, knocking the trail bastons to the ground so that they could be bound. They wanted to catch as many as possible, he said. No matter what the posse thought of them, they deserved a trial. His voice was stern and hard as he spoke, as if he too did not care too much for their lives, as if he wanted to be able to kill them all, but he stuck to the plan they had agreed to. He allocated the men to their places while they were all mounted and led them south to the trail. Here Fasten moved up to join him and they led the way along the trail together.

Even in the pitch darkness, Simon could see that the ground was open here. Now and then he could just make out the stunted shape of a tortured tree standing on the skyline, looking like the fossilized skeleton of an ancient creature as it stood on the wind-swept moor, but for the most part there was nothing to see, nothing but the continual sweep of the plains as they rose softly to the hills.

The two men in the lead rode at some distance apart, with the main group following in a bunch. There was no talking now, all the men were wound taut, their nerves on edge as they listened for the slightest sound over the creaking of leather and the metallic tinkle of harness. Occasionally there was a louder noise as someone knocked a weapon against another, swiftly followed by a curse, but apart from this they made no noise as they passed.

They moved down the side of the hill where they had made camp, then followed a brook that wound gently between the hills, the riders keeping their mounts from the water to prevent any noise, making sure their horses kept to the soft earth at the banks. It was ghostly here, with a vague gray glow just beginning to light the horizon to the east. There was no sound to distract the men, no screech of an owl or yap of a fox, just the muted gurgle of the stream and the squeak and jingle of the harnesses.

When they had gone just beyond the curve of a hill, Black turned his horse, leaving Fasten standing still out in front, and cantered back to the main body.

"We're only half a mile from the camp now, it's at the top of that hill. Leave your horses here, we'll go ahead on foot."

Slowly the men dismounted and handed their reins to the men who would hold the horses, then Tanner drew his sword and showed his teeth in a snarl of animal delight. "Come on, then."

lack led them all up the hill, moving slowly and carefully in the faint luminosity of the brightening dawn, his sword a faint gray glimmer against the darker colors around.

Simon felt lightheaded and his chest seemed tight as he toiled slowly behind the hunter. He had a kind of nervous, almost fearful, trepidation at the thought of the fight to come, but step by step he found that it was becoming smothered by his anger and disgust at what these men had done, killing and raping in his shire. He gritted his teeth and carried on. His stomach felt empty, his muscles frozen, and his nerves were all on edge at the thought of fighting, but he slowly became aware of a gleeful expectancy. After all, these men would hardly surrender without a fight, they were trail bastons; they would know that after a trial all they could expect would be the noose. They must fight to the death, expecting no quarter, if they were given the chance. The posse must make sure they had no chance.

They slowly walked on, and then, when they were halfway up the hill, Black held out his hand stiffly in warning and the men all froze into immobility. Simon felt his bowels turn to water as he looked up the hill and saw a figure standing up, high above them, near a tree. If he saw the posse, he could give the alarm—they would lose the chance of surprising the outlaws. The figure seemed to be stationary for a while, then turned and disappeared, and Simon realized with a quick breath of relief that he must have been urinating. The hand slowly drifted away and they moved off again, their tension and excitement growing with every step.

There was a gully here, a steep-sided cleft in the hillside, with a small trickle of water at the bottom, and Black led them up it. The sides appeared almost to be cliffs, tall and gray, looming up on either side, with a slight, lighter grayness above them where the sky hurried toward dawn. They moved slowly and cautiously, trying to avoid the rocks that lay strewn all around as if intentionally placed to catch an unwary blade and give warning, pausing every now and then to listen before continuing.

It was a miserable journey, one that Simon would never forget. They clambered over rocks and mud, trying to keep out of the water, trying to keep their weapons from knocking against the stone of the walls, walking hunched to prevent their being seen, but trying to move quickly so that they could get to the camp before dawn broke and maintain the surprise of their attack. Simon found his mind wandering as though it wanted to avoid thinking about the skirmish ahead, as though it wanted to ignore the danger they were walking into, and by ignoring it make it disappear. He found himself thinking about Lydford and his new role, thinking about his wife and daughter and how they would enjoy the life at the castle deep in the moors.

But then, with a feeling of near relief, he saw the hand come up again and realized that they were almost at the top of the gully. Up ahead he could see the lighter gray of the sky, outlining the top of the hill itself. Simon frowned as he peered ahead. He could see no sign of the trail bastons, no smoke from a fire, no movement. There seemed to be no one near, only the posse itself, and the only sounds he could hear were the heavy breathing of the men behind him and the blood hammering in his ears.

Black moved off softly and disappeared, a darker smudge against the horizon for an instant, then gone. Simon and the men stayed where they were and waited. It seemed like an hour before the hunter came back, but it could only have been a few minutes, and as he stood at the top of the gully he seemed to pause before waving them on.

Simon quickly moved up to the top of the gully and stood beside Black as the others came out. When they were all out and waiting, the hunter led them swiftly up, along a track in the grass, to a mound at the top of the hill which stood slightly proud of the ground all round like a wall. He flattened himself against it and listened, then sidled along, motioning the others to do the same. At last, Simon heard a sound. It was a horse whinnying from the other side of the earthwork, and as he heard it he gripped his sword more tightly as he followed the hunter.

Dawn was a glow in the east now, showing the clouds distinctly and lighting their way as they followed the side of the wall. Apart from the horse there was no sound, nothing apart from their soft footsteps on the grass. There was not even a breeze. His tension mounting, Simon saw the hand signal once more. This time, he was sure, would be the last. They were almost at the entrance now, a darker mark against the gray of the earthen wall. He saw Black turn quickly and glance at the men behind, then he seemed to lean forward and peer through to the camp before motioning urgently. Then he was gone.

Simon took a deep breath, muttered a quick prayer, and darted after him.

When he thought back on the mad scramble of the fight later, it seemed that the next few minutes were a discordant mêlée of disjointed and seemingly disconnected events as the men ran silently into the camp and tried to capture the trail bastons. It was as if the men were all somehow tied individually to their own brief tableaux with their enemies, each small battle with its own participants, each separate and unique, but each linked one to another to create the whole. It seemed to Simon, when he thought about it, that it was like a tapestry. A tapestry composed of a number of individual threads that combined to build the picture, and, like a tapestry, the picture could only be discerned when the whole was viewed together.

But for Simon, as he ran full pelt into the camp, the battle was pure confusion. There seemed to be no sense or coherence in the small struggling groups of men and the only thought in his mind was that they must stop the outlaws and prevent any further attacks.

Just as they came in through the gap in the rampart, he caught a glimpse of Black. He had almost run into a man who was about to wander outside, a young man who was yawning and stretching as he walked, only to stop, dumbfounded, at the sight of the posse rushing in. He seemed too surprised to make a sound. Without pausing in his stride, the hunter thumped him in the belly with a balled fist and he fell with a gasp of pain, his hands clutched to his stomach. Another man was crouching over the embers of the fire, his hands outstretched over the ashes to warm, and Black made for him as he stared at his attacker in stupefaction. But then he seemed to realize his danger and shouted, and all at once the camp seemed to stir. Simon was behind Black, and ran toward the farthest sleeping figure, but as he came close, the man stirred and rose, snatched up a club, and danced lightly away from Simon's first hasty thrust.

Now the camp was full of struggling men. Simon caught a glimpse of a man from the posse going down, but then he felt the club scrape along his jaw in a fast, glancing blow, and he had to dodge back. Crouching, sword making swift movements from side to side pointing at the man's belly, he watched his opponent.

The man's eyes were shifting nervously from Simon's face to the battle behind him. Blinking quickly, his thin, drawn features seemed to radiate confused terror as he licked his lips, but then he pounced, the club swinging up from low to reach toward Simon's face. Moving aside and catching the cudgel on his blade to move it away, the bailiff snarled, "Give up!" as he circled like a wrestler, the heavy sword twitching left to right. "Surrender! You can't win."

From the fleeting glimpses he had of the rest of the battle, it was clear that the posse would have no need of the men on the horses. Already only four outlaws were still fighting, and even as he watched another fell with a scream, clutching at his side where a huge gash had opened his body to show the bones of his ribs. Now there were only three, but as he looked, he realized that one of the three was the man they wanted.

He was a great, square bear of a man, a vast, solid mass of bone and muscle, with a shock of dark hair that fell over his little eyes, black with anger, as he whirled and spun, his sword in one hand, a misericord in the other. He had already wounded Fasten, who lay unmoving on the ground beside him. Black and two other men were surrounding him now, darting in to stab and slash, but even as they moved, he appeared to have slipped away, as if he could perfectly anticipate their every movement, as if he was always slightly quicker than they. If it was not so terrible a sight, it would have been almost humorous, the way that this huge man seemed to be able to dance in and among the other three, but then any amusement disappeared as another of his attackers fell, to crouch on hands and knees, coughing, before falling to his side and shuddering, like a rabbit with a broken back, until at last he lay still, with a dark stain spreading over his chest.

The sight made the bailiff pause for a moment too long, and his opponent took the opportunity to lunge forward, swinging the club down from over his head to strike Simon's skull. Startled, Simon met it on the flat of his blade, but the momentum of the outlaw forced him forward just as the sword was knocked down by his own blow, and as he rushed on, he fell onto the blade.

He seemed surprised, when he looked down, to see the metal jutting from his chest, and when he glanced up at Simon, his eyes seemed to hold only a complete bewilderment, no fear or anger, just a total incomprehension that this could have happened. But then all expression fled and he fell at the bailiff's feet.

Simon stood panting for a moment, staring at the body with a sense of irritation. Why hadn't he surrendered? But even as the thought struck him, he felt the glow of pride at his victory, at winning his first fight to the death. The feeling was soon smothered by noises from behind, and, turning, he saw the knot of men around the big man again. Sword still in his hand, he strode toward the group.

The knight, as Simon assumed he was, was the last to struggle now, and his hoarse voice bellowed his rage at the men who circled him like hounds as he struck and slashed at his assailants, his eyes small black flints of rage as he fought, like the mad eyes of a cornered wild boar.

"Hold! Stop this madness!" Simon shouted as he came close, but, although the man with Black seemed to hesitate, the knight carried on, pushing the hunter and his companion backward, forcing them to give ground as he screamed his fury and battle lust at them. He moved quickly, like a thunder bolt, seeming to always find a slight point of weakness, pressing his advantage, pushing and pushing until the two against him had to fall back, slashing wildly in their attempt to defend themselves.

But then his luck failed him. He thrust hard, knocking aside Black's companion's sword, and stabbed the man deep in his belly, the sword almost disappearing in his body, and as his victim stared uncomprehendingly at the blade in him, Black stepped quickly behind the knight and struck him in the back. Quivering, the knight roared and almost seemed about to spin and strike at Black, but then he tottered and fell to his knees, hands behind him, vainly trying to pull the sword out.

Simon stopped, and as he stared, something caught him at the back of his head and he found himself falling down, not to the ground but into a huge black pit that seemed to open in the grass in front of him, and it was almost with relief that he accepted the cool softness of the darkness as it seemed to sweep up to engulf him.

When he came to again, he found himself lying on his back outside the camp, a rug over him to keep him warm, facing the view to the south. It had become a clear and bright day, with a deep blue sky surrounding the thick, white clouds that meandered slowly across it, and Simon lay and watched them for a while, his mind wandering, losing himself in the pleasure of being alive.

He heard footsteps and turned to see Black and Tanner walking toward him. Trying to sit up to greet them, he found that his muscles seemed to have turned to aspic jelly, and all he could do was slowly topple over. Stunned, he lay there. He heard a laugh, then feet ran to him and gentle hands caught him up and leaned him against the wall of the camp. When he next opened his eyes, he found himself gazing into the faces of a serious Black and a smiling Tanner as they crouched in front of him.

Tanner seemed to be unmarked, but Black had a dirty rag tied over what must have been a long cut in his arm that went all the way from his wrist to his elbow.

"What happened to me? I was going over to see you, Black, when everything went . . ."

"One of the outlaws hit you with a cudgel and knocked you out. He'd been with the horses, over at the back of the camp, and you were in his way when he tried to make a run for it. Don't worry, though, we got him!"

"So, how long have I been . . . ?"

"Not long, bailiff, only a half hour or so. Look, the sun's hardly up yet!" said Tanner, smiling at him.

"Our men, how many are hurt?"

Black answered. "Old Cottey, Fasten, and two others are dead. Three are wounded, but none of them seriously, they only had scratches. I've been marked by that giant from Hell, and you've got a knock on the head. That's all of the damage."

Simon shook his head in sad disbelief. "Four dead? God!"

"Come now, bailiff," said Tanner gently, "we did well, after all we were against a knight, from the look of him, and we're mainly untrained as soldiers. We did well to manage so much for so few lost. And don't forget that the whore's son himself killed two and wounded another. If it wasn't for him we'd've lost few indeed."

"Yes, and any battle will have injured men at the end of it," said Black. "Now, how are *you?* It only looks like a scrape, but it must have been a hard one to make you fall over like that."

Simon cautiously felt his skull. There was a huge lump where his head had caught the force of the club, with the hair matted and gritty with blood and dirt. "I think I'm alright," he said uncertainly. "I just have a headache now."

Tanner peered at the wound and frowned a little. "Yes, it should heal well. It looks clean enough and there's little damage that a good sleep won't cure."

"How many did we catch?" said Simon.

"None got away," said Black. "There were nine, like I thought. Four will swing for their crimes, the rest, well . . ."

"I want to see them," said Simon, struggling to his feet.

"No, no, wait until your head's better," said Tanner, in some alarm at the pale face of the bailiff.

"No, I want to see them *now!* I have to find out what sort of men they are," said Simon firmly as he lurched up and leaned against the wall.

Tanner and Black looked at each other, then the hunter shrugged imperceptibly and stood, giving the bailiff his good arm and helping him over to the entrance.

The prisoners stood in a huddle at the far end of the camp, their arms tied, with two men from the posse standing nearby to guard them, their swords out and ready. Simon allowed himself to be led up to them and stood for a moment, swaying a little with his headache, watching them intently, like a spectator looking at a bear and assessing its fighting ability before the dogs were let loose. In one corner was the figure of the knight, back against the wall as he glared at the posse.

"He won't last long, bailiff," said Black softly.

Walking toward him, Simon was shocked to see the bitter hatred on his face. It was obvious that he could not survive the journey to Oakhampton. A thin trickle of blood ran from the side of his mouth, and as the three men approached they could hear the blood rattling in his throat with his labored breathing.

"Come to gloat? Want to see your victim in his defeat?" The sneering words were harsh, thick with disgust and loathing, and as if the taste of them were poison, he hawked and spat, then coughed, the spasms wracking his body like a vomiting fit. When he looked up at them again, his features seemed as pale and waxen as those of a corpse, making the dark hair seem false, as if it had been painted with tar. The scar was a furious pink flame, but even this seemed to be fading with his spirit, the eyes those of a man in a fever, bright and liquid as they glowered up at his captors.

Squatting nearby, eyes fixed on the knight's face, Simon considered the wounded man and asked, "What is your name?"

Coughing again, the knight spat a thick gobbet of blood to the ground beside him, then stared at it reflectively for a moment. "Why? So you can dishonor my memory?"

"We want to know who was responsible for so many deaths, that is all."

"So many deaths?" The voice was bitter as he looked into Simon's eyes. "I'm a knight! I take what I need, and if any man tries to stop me, I fight."

"You'll even fight merchants? Couldn't you find stronger foes?" asked Simon coldly and the knight looked away. "You're not from here—where do you come from?"

"East, from Hungerford." He coughed, a series of jerky, short motions that made him wince and pause, trying to calm himself and ease his breathing. When he spoke again a fine spray of red mist burst from his mouth, coloring his lips as his life ebbed. "My name is Rodney."

"Why did you join this band? If you were a knight, why become an outlaw?" asked Simon, and thought he caught a fleeting glimpse of sadness in the black eyes.

"I lost my position when my lord died. I was on my way to Cornwall when these men ambushed me, and they gave me a choice: join them or die. I chose life." His lip twisted, as if he recognized the irony of the words given his present position. "I rode into their ambush and would have died—there were too many of them for me to defend myself. I tried, but it was point-less. I did not yield to them, but in the end I gave them my word that I would live with them and they swore to accept me. They allowed me to live, and I agreed to help them. In exchange for my life."

The bailiff nodded. He had heard of penniless war-riors joining wandering bands, searching for new iden-tities and trying to survive by any means. "Why kill, though? Why murder so many?"

The coughing was worse, becoming more tortured as the man's face grew paler and he began to sweat. His voice was labored, as though his throat was parched. "We killed for food and money . . . Those we robbed the other day were wealthy . . . They were only merchants . . . What is there for a knight without a lord? Without land, without money? I had lost every-thing when the outlaws overtook me . . . Why not join them? What else was there for me to do? I could have continued to Cornwall, but there was no guarantee of a living there . . . At least with the outlaws I knew I was accepted . . ."

"But why did you kill the abbot?"

"What abbot?" The words brought on another fit of coughing, and while waiting for it to stop, Simon watched the man with disgust leavened with pity. Pity for the pain of his slow death, but disgust at the con-tempt he showed for any man born to a lower class, and the assumption that mere possession of a sword conferred the right to kill.

When the spasm passed, Simon said, "The abbot you burned—murdered—in the woods. Why did you kill him?"

"*Me?* Kill a man of God!" For a moment there was a look of surprise, quickly replaced by rage. The huge figure heaved upright and glared, so suddenly that the bailiff could not help flinching.

"Me? Kill a holy man!"

"You and your friend took him and burned him to death," Simon continued doubtfully.

"Who dares say that I did? I—"

Even as he opened his mouth to give a furious denial, there came a fresh eruption of blood from his mouth and nose, and his words were drowned as he fell to his side, clutching at his throat in a vain attempt to breathe and thrashing in his desperate search for air and life, his eyes remaining fixed on Simon. There was no fear there, just a total anger, as if at the injustice of the accusation. The bailiff sat and watched, no longer with any feeling, merely with a faint interest in how long it would take the man to die. In his mind he could see the burned corpses still, the blackened arms hanging from the wagons, and the little bundle of rags in the moors, the girl killed so far from her home. He felt that all his sympathy was expended now, spent on the knight's victims.

The end was not long in coming, and when the spirit had left, Simon stood and looked at the body with detached contempt, before glancing up at the other two, and saying, "Get the dead outlaws collected together and have them buried. We'll take our own dead back with us, but these can lie here unshriven."

While Black shouted to the men from the posse and gave his orders, the bailiff stared down at the body. Even after killing so many, the knight had denied harming the abbot. Why? God would know his crimes, and Rodney must have known he was dying—why deny the murder? Was it possible that he told the truth, that he had not killed de Penne?

When he turned and studied the remaining prisoners, his face was set in a frown of consideration. The youngest, a sallow man with pale hair and skinny appearance who looked to be only two or three and twenty years old, stood shuffling his feet uncomfortably under his gaze, and as Black finished issuing his instructions, Simon pointed to him and beckoned. The youth nervously glanced at his companions before cautiously walking over to stand some six feet from the bailiff.

"Hah!" Tanner gave a gasp of amusement. "How did you pick him?" When Simon threw him a quick look of incomprehension, the constable carried on, "He's the man who hit you on the head—the one who was with the horses."

Now that the youth came closer, Simon could see that his thinness was due to undernourishment. His high cheeks stood out prominently in his fleshless face, and his light blue eyes were sunken and looked watery, as if all the color had faded away. His gaze was shifty, looking all round, at Simon's shoes, at his shoulders, over behind him, and only occasionally meeting his gaze before flitting away again in his fear.

"What's your name?" Simon asked, and was surprised at the harshness in his own voice.

"Weaver, sir."

"Where are you from?"

"From Tolpuddle, sir."

Simon looked at Black, who shrugged with an expression of disinterest. He looked back at Weaver.

"How long have you been here, lad?"

He seemed to want to avoid Simon's eyes and stared at his feet. "A month."

"How many have you killed in that time?"

He looked up with a flare of defiance glinting in the

blue of his eyes. "Only one, and that because he would've killed me otherwise!"

"What about the merchants? Do you say you weren't involved in their deaths?"

Weaver stared down at his feet again, as if the brief flame of anger had used all of his energy. "No. I was looking after the horses."

"Do you think that makes it better? You were in the gang that killed them all, weren't you?" He held up his hands in a gesture of disgust. "How many were killed?"

Weaver's glance dropped. He seemed to have lost interest in the conversation. "I don't know. Ten, maybe twelve."

"Where . . ." Simon wiped a tired hand over his eyes. How could this man have helped kill so many? His voice was low and sad when he continued. "Where were you and the band before that?"

"Over near Ashwater." he said sullenly.

Simon looked at the hunter again, but he showed no more interest in Ashwater than he had in Tolpuddle. "When did you leave there?"

"I don't know, maybe a week ago."

"So when did you get to Copplestone?"

"Where?"

"Copplestone. Where you killed the abbot."

"What abbot? I don't know nothing about that!"

"When did you leave Ashwater?"

"Like I said, about a week ago."

"Where is Ashwater?"

All of a sudden Simon became convinced of the man's honesty—he was telling the truth because he knew he would die anyway. He had lost any interest in deception now, he was simply uninterested; all he wanted to do was get back to his friends and find some peace with his own kind before he had to face the rope.

"Over west, north of Launceston," he heard the man say, and heard the breath hiss in Black's teeth as he made to move forward, but Simon squeezed his hand on his arm and the hunter stayed still, glaring at Weaver.

"You're lying, boy. You wouldn't've been able to get to Copplestone in time," Black snarled.

"I don't know about Copplestone." he snapped, then looked at Simon. "I'm going to swing, sir. Why should I lie? I don't care what you think, but I had nothing to do with no abbot."

Simon's mind was reeling. It wasn't these men then? So who *had* killed de Penne? He gathered his thoughts: the monks had said that there had been two men, hadn't they? What if . . .

"When did you meet the . . . the knight?" he asked, his voice faltering.

"Him?" Weaver's voice showed disgust. "Rodney of Hungerford? We only found him a few days ago. We tried to catch him. He rode straight into the middle of us, but he held us off when we attacked; he even killed our leader. He had money but there was little we could do about it. In the end we let him join us, because he could fight."

"Where's his friend?" said Simon, guessing.

"What friend?"

"He was with a man."

"He was alone when we found him."

"Where? Where did you meet him?"

"Oh, I don't know. Down near Oakhampton. He said he was going to Cornwall."

Even Black seemed interested now, and was watching Weaver with keen intensity.

"So did he say where he had come from?"

"Hungerford, like I say. I think it's . . . he said somewhere over east . . ."

"Was he on a war horse?"

"War horse? No." Weaver gave a short laugh. "No, he was on a mare, a small mare."

"A mare?"

"Yes. A gray. He said he'd found it on the way, he said he'd found it saddled and bridled, like its rider had been knocked off."

"Did he say when?"

"Oh, I don't know. Some days ago, maybe two before we found him. He said it had some money in its bags but he wouldn't share it with us."

"Did he say where he found the horse?"

"Oh, I don't know—"

"Think!"

"He might've. I think he said some way east of Oakhampton, but I—"

"And you're sure he said the money was on the horse?"

"Yes." His voice was becoming bored, as if he found the questions tedious now.

"So—" Simon began, but he was cut off by a shrug from the young man, a tiny gesture of indifference.

"I don't care, and I don't see why I need to help you. Whatever he may have done it's nothing to do with me." Simon opened his mouth to speak, but Weaver took a step back, seeming to dare them to question him further. "I don't care. I've told you all I know."

Simon shrugged. Did it really matter? How much could he trust this man anyway? Weaver stared at them both for a moment, then turned and walked back toward his companions, making the hunter's face redden with anger at his impertinence. He seemed about to shout, and would have gone after the outlaw for his rudeness, but Simon said, "No. Don't bother. He's told us enough."

Black stared at him, but then his face calmed and he gazed after the man as he rejoined his group and sat down, glaring defiantly at them. "Yes. Yes, he has, hasn't he? So the knight came from east. He must have come through Exeter, out on the Crediton road, and met the monks on the way."

"But the monks said there were two of them."

"Maybe there were. Maybe they argued and split up. Who knows? Anyway, it's easier now. At least we have the abbot's killer, thanks to God! I suppose he must've killed Brewer on his way through."

"What?" Simon spun to face him.

"Well, he said he was coming from the east, didn't he? He must have killed Brewer, taken his money, then carried on. After he killed the abbot he met up with this rabble and joined them." He tucked his hands in his belt with satisfaction. "Yes, I think today's work has put an end to the killing."

He turned and ambled slowly out of the clearing, and Simon followed, but as they went, Simon heard a quiet whinny and his head snapped round at the sound. "Where are their horses, John?"

"Horses? Oh, over there."

"Let's have a quick look."

They walked over to where the robbers' horses stood hobbled from the previous night. They were a mixture, from small, hardy ponies to some huge draft animals, and Simon stood for a minute looking at them. "Black?"

"Hunh?"

"When you tracked the abbot's killer, you said that

one of the horses was a big horse and was missing a nail on a shoe."

"That's right."

"And the abbot's horse was a gray mare with a scar on the withers."

"Yes."

"Have a look at these, will you? See if one of them is missing a nail. And see if there's a gray mare with a scar on the withers as well." He turned and wandered out again, to lie on the grass looking out over the hills; over the green, grassed and tree-dotted hills toward the sea, and soon he was asleep, dozing in the warm sunlight.

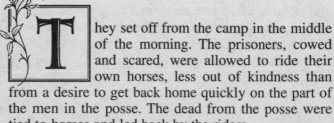

hey set off from the camp in the middle
of the morning. The prisoners, cowed
and scared, were allowed to ride their
own horses, less out of kindness than
from a desire to get back home quickly on the part of
the men in the posse. The dead from the posse were
tied to horses and led back by the riders.

Simon and Hugh went a little way with the others,
but they parted a couple of miles north of the scene of
their battle. There seemed little point in continuing to
Oakhampton with the others and their prisoners, so
Simon decided to cut across the moors and go home by
way of Moretonhampstead and Tedburn.

The others were all eager to get to the town and were
looking forward to being welcomed as the captors of
the trail bastons, but Hugh had seen enough of travelling to last him for several months, and Simon wanted
to get home to see his wife and daughter again. Now
that the band was captured, there seemed little to fear
on the way, so there seemed no need for the bailiff and
his man to have any extra protection.

They parted when they came up to the road that led
back to Moretonhampstead, the huge track that led

right across the moors and down to the coast. Hugh and his master sat and watched as the posse gaily rode off north, waving at their friends until they were out of sight over the next hill, and then they turned and made their way northeast, and back to home.

Simon was deep in thought for the first hour, riding slowly with his chin down on his chest as he allowed his horse to amble, letting Hugh enjoy his riding for the first time since they had left home so many days ago.

It was the first time Hugh had seen him so involved and intense, and as he rode along behind his expression was one of concerned confusion. Hugh had always tried to be a good servant to the Puttocks, who he adored as much as his own family, and although he maintained a melancholic exterior, this was more because of his days when still a youth, when he had lived the rough life of a shepherd up on the hills. A certain dourness was natural among the men who looked after the sheep on the hills around the moors. The loneliness led to introspection, and the attacks from wild and feral animals produced a degree of cynicism, but these did not change the fact that he was thoroughly loyal to his master and his family, and now he was worried by Simon's somber attitude.

Just when Hugh was about to try to break into his thoughts, Simon suddenly looked up, a frown on his face, then turned to his servant. "Hugh, do you remember the conversation we had with Black and Tanner by the fire a couple of nights ago?'

Relieved to be included in his previously private thoughts, Hugh gave him a quick, shy sidelong smile. "What, when we were talking about the abbot and Brewer? When I said the trail bastons hadn't killed the farmer?"

Simon nodded, still frowning. "Yes. Do you still believe that?"

"Well," Hugh considered for a moment, then continued quickly. "Well, no, not now."

"Why?"

"John Black told me that that man, the knight, had joined the rest late. He said he must've passed through Crediton on the way to Oakhampton at about the right time. He wasn't part of the gang then, but he was in the area at the time. He must have done it."

"Hunh! That's what John Black says, is it?"

"Well, it makes sense, doesn't it?"

"What happened to his war horse? And his companion?"

"Maybe his companion had the other horse, I don't know. Maybe his friend stole it. Fact is he had the mare. He must have killed the abbot and stolen it, mustn't he, and it makes sense for him to have been Brewer's murderer too."

"I wonder . . ."

Hugh looked at him. He had reverted to his pensive silence, chin down on his chest as he swayed along, glaring at the road surface under him as if daring it to argue with his thoughts. Taking a deep breath, Hugh coughed and, when this had no impact, said, "Master?"

There was a grunt, but Simon did not look up until they had ridden on for a few yards, and then he peered at his servant with a frown of concentration, almost seeming not to recognize him, so intense were his thoughts. "What?"

"Why did you ask me that?"

"Eh? Oh. Well . . . I was thinking, well, wondering really . . . I still can't believe that he could have killed

Brewer, even if it does look as if he killed the abbot."
His voice trailed off, and he seemed to be contemplating his thoughts again, then, head on one side and without looking at his servant, he started to speak, slowly and concisely. "If the knight *had* captured the abbot and taken him hostage, if it *was* Rodney, it was either a chance meeting and robbery or it was planned and intended—perhaps a revenge attack. If it was revenge for some misdeed, then we'll probably never know what the deed was. Right, but if it was not, then it was a chance attack. What would that mean?"

He was mumbling as he considered, his brow deeply puckered. "The knight and another man found the monks on the road. They took the abbot and carried him off into the woods. They took him a long way, then tied him to a tree, set light to him and watched him die. Why kill him like that? If they had to kill him, why not a knife in the back or a rope round the neck, so that they could get away as quickly as possible? Just because he was killed that way it seems unlikely that it was a chance attack." He shot a keen glance at Hugh. "Does that make sense?"

Hugh thought for a minute, his bottom lip out as he considered the logic with frowning concentration. "Yes," he said slowly, "I think so."

"Fine. Even so, let's carry on. So, assuming that it was mere chance: if they had done all this . . . Let's just think it through. If they did this, if they killed the abbot, then why did they divide? Why did one take all the money and the abbot's mare, the other the war horse? Why? The war horse was worth more—and what happened to the other man's horse? The monks said that both attackers were mounted, so where is the second horse?"

"Maybe the other man took both horses?"

"Why? Why should he? What would be the point? One man with two horses is suspicious, he might raise attention."

"Oh, I don't know! Anyway, John Black must be right, it surely was the same man who killed Brewer."

"What? Him? The knight? Killed Brewer?" His incredulity made his voice rise. "Why, for the money? How would a travelling knight hear about the wealth of a farmer on his way past? Is it really credible? Anyway, let's just sort out the abbot's death first, shall we!

"Right, so I think we have to assume that it was not chance, but that it was an intentional meeting. So the knight and his accomplice saw the monks on the road and attacked. What does that mean? There was no ambush, that seems odd. So maybe the knight happened to come upon them and recognized the abbot—from behind? No, of course not. You don't recognize a man's back on horseback, you only recognize a face. So that means he must have heard about the abbot, have known about him before they came upon the monks, and chased after him, trying to catch him. Perhaps the two of them had been chasing the monks for some time? But even so . . ."

"What, master?"

"Well, why on earth would they split up after the killing? If there were two of them, and they had been chasing the monks for some way, why would they divide immediately afterward? You would think they would stay together—that the immensity of their crime would hold them together."

Hugh was confused now. "So what are you saying? I . . ."

"I just don't believe that he killed the abbot. I can't

believe it! I think that whether he came across the monks on the road by chance or whether he was looking for them, either way he would have kept his war horse. He was a knight, he would not have just left it or given it away! A war horse costs over a hundred pounds!"

"Er . . . well, yes, but . . ."

"So, could his own story have been genuine? Could it be true that he found the horse? Could it be true that he came across it and took it because he had no other?"

"Master, perhaps . . ."

"No," said Simon decisively. "I'm certain the killer of the abbot was someone else. And that means that Master Black's opinion must be wrong. Black thinks that because a murderer went through the area, he must have killed Brewer on the way. I think Rodney didn't kill de Penne. I believed him when he seemed so shocked at the idea of killing a monk, and I think it's equally unlikely he could have killed the farmer—after all, Brewer was very unpopular, surely it's more likely he was killed by someone local, someone who hated him? No, someone *else* must have killed them!" He kicked at his horse and coaxed it into an easy canter, and, sighing, Hugh urged his own horse to keep up.

Without having to follow a trail, and being able to keep to the roads and lanes, they made good time and were in Drewsteignton by midday. They paused to water the horses, then were on their way again, keeping to an easy pace so as not to strain their animals, and were in Crediton at dusk. Hugh expected his master to suggest that they go on immediately, and was surprised when he blandly mentioned his aches and pains and proposed that they should stay the night with the priest at

Crediton church, Peter Clifford. Shrugging, Hugh agreed, but with a suspicion at the back of his mind that his master must have an ulterior motive—he seemed too off-hand about the suggestion.

The priest was delighted to see them. He rushed out to welcome them, arms outstretched, his eyes gleaming with delight. He led them through to his room and, when they were seated by the fire, poured them mulled wine.

"So, my friends, what are you doing so far from home? I heard about the gang killing the abbot, and that you went after them—did you have any joy in your hunt?"

Simon stared at his pewter mug as he spoke. "Yes, Peter, we caught them all, down on the moors. They managed to kill again, though."

"Oh, no!" Clifford's brow wrinkled in his sadness at the news.

Simon leaned forward and fixed a firm stare on his friend. "Peter, do you remember a knight passing through Crediton at about the same time as the monks? Did you hear anything about a stranger? A tall man, very broad, and sitting on a great horse? He might have had a companion with him."

"No. No, I don't think so. Why, who was he?"

"His name was Rodney of Hungerford. We found him with the trail bastons—he seems to have been an impoverished knight. John Black and the others think he might have killed the abbot."

"No, I'm sure I would remember if I had heard anything of him."

"Yes. Ah well, it was worth a try."

"So. This attack, Simon. Did many get hurt?"

"I'm afraid so," said Simon, and went on to describe

the murders, the posse's chase over the moors and the fight with the outlaws. The priest sat attentively, leaning forward with his elbows on his knees and his mug in his hand, nodding his understanding at the tale as it unfolded.

"I see," he said when Simon had finished. "So many poor souls! And all for lust, lust for money and lust for the women. Oh dear God, take them into your care and protect these poor souls." He stared unseeing into the flames. After a pause, he looked up keenly at the bailiff. "But you are not sure that these men were the killers of Brewer and the abbot?"

"Well, now you mention it . . ."

The priest leaned back, a smile on his face. "Come along, now, Simon. You know you'll tell me sooner or later!"

The bailiff laughed shortly, relaxed by the warmth and the wine, before looking across at his friend. "Alright, Peter. I am certain that they *did* kill the merchants, or as certain as I can be, anyway."

"But?"

"I am equally unsure that this knight was involved in the death of the farmer or the abbot. I find it hard to believe that the abbot was killed on a whim—I think it must have been a planned murder. That means I do not believe that it was a robbery—whoever heard of a robber killing his victims like that?"

"So you don't think the robbers may have simply been disturbed? That they panicked and wanted to get away?"

"Peter, really! No, I don't think so. The killer took his time, remember. He tied the abbot to a tree and lit a fire under him. He sat and watched while the man died. If somebody had happened upon the scene, surely it would have been reported? Then again, if they had been seen, surely they would have just stabbed their man. No, it makes no sense for them to have killed the abbot, not in that way, if they were in a hurry."

"I'm confused, then. So why do you think it was done that way?"

"All I can think is that the abbot was killed to work off a grudge of some sort. It's the only thing that makes sense to me. Someone wanted to make a point by the way they killed the man. Perhaps they thought he was a heretic, perhaps they thought he had given false witness against another—I don't know what! But I'm sure it wasn't Rodney."

"So who *do* you think could have done it?"

"I don't know. I really don't know."

They all lapsed into silence and stared into the flames, Clifford with a reflective smile on his face, Simon with a fixed frown as he tried to make sense of the murder, teasing at the facts to pull out the cord of truth, but with little expectation of succeeding. Hugh wore a glare of fierce indifference as he sat with his arms crossed and legs straight out in front. "If only . . ." he mused.

"What?" said Simon sharply.

"If only we knew more about the abbot. Then we might know what reasons there might be for the attack, if it *was* revenge."

Simon put his head to one side, and looked over at Clifford with a studied indifference. He asked, "So, Peter, did you discover anything about the monks while they were here?"

The priest stared at him for a moment, then roared with delighted laughter. "Ah! Ah, my friend. Always so subtle! So that's why you came here, is it? Not just to eat and drink of my best, but to use my mind as well!"

"Possibly," said Simon, grinning back. Hugh sighed and folded his arms, staring at the flames in boredom and letting the conversation flow around him heedlessly, disgruntled at the feeling that his master had taken his thought without any thanks. Then his expression relaxed and he gave himself up to enjoyment of the warmth of the room, ignoring the other two.

"I had not met any of them before, nor did I know of them by name. The abbot came with letters of introduction, and I had no reason to doubt them. They were just travellers on their way to Buckland, I don't think I discovered anything else about them."

"You know the abbot's name? Oliver de Penne?"

"Yes, of course."

"And the others, did you speak to brother Matthew?"

"Matthew," the older man said musingly, staring into the flames. "Matthew. Ah, of course! No, he was the one who had a friend here. It was because of him that the brothers stayed here for so long."

"What? How do you mean?"

"Well, Matthew met a friend in Crediton on their first day here, and he managed to persuade the abbot to wait here for two more days so that he could go and visit his friend at his house. I must say it didn't please the abbot, he was most peevish about it, very upset. It almost seems a little eery now, doesn't it, as if he knew he was in danger?"

Simon leaned forward, tensely gripping the mug in his hand. "Who did he want to meet, Peter?"

Hugh sat up in astonishment as Clifford said, "The new man at Furnshill—what's his name? Oh, of course. Baldwin, that was the man, Sir Baldwin Furnshill."

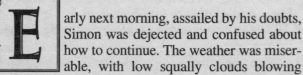

20

Early next morning, assailed by his doubts, Simon was dejected and confused about how to continue. The weather was miserable, with low squally clouds blowing quickly across a blustery sky and the rain falling constantly in a steady flow, driven by the wind from the moors. Hugh and he sat in Peter Clifford's hall in front of the fire and waited for the rain to stop, or at least pause, so that they could finish their journey home.

Simon was torn. He was sure now that somehow Baldwin was involved in the abbot's murder. But what should he do? It was one thing for a bailiff to arrest a sheep-stealer, or to stop a poacher. But to arrest a knight? As the lord's representative, he had the authority, but where was the proof that Baldwin had committed the crime? All Simon had was a series of vague clues, nothing more; not even a reason. He knew that Baldwin had known Matthew, that the brother had delayed the monks on their journey, but that was no reason to arrest him. The abbot had been taken captive by a man who looked like a knight, a man on a great horse; but there were any number of men living around Crediton who could be mistaken for a knight. Just the fact that Baldwin knew Matthew was no proof that he knew the abbot, let alone wanted him dead.

But even as he thought about it, Simon was sure. He knew he was right. Baldwin had arrived from God only knew where, he had travelled widely—he had at least hinted at that, even if he would not say where he had been or why. There must be a reason for the killing in his past, while he was abroad. He must have met Oliver de Penne while he was away and murdered him when he heard that he was in this area—or had he followed the monks here?

Clifford entered and walked over to his chair by the fire, walking quietly in his robe and sitting without saying a word. When Simon glanced up at him, he could see that his friend was troubled. His thin and normally cheerful face was serious and his hands played with the edge of his robe as if trying to distract his mind as he sat.

"Simon," he said slowly, staring into the flames and not meeting Simon's eyes, "I have been thinking about what you said last night about Furnshill. My friend, before you go home, I think you should think carefully about what actions you will take."

"The trouble is, I can't see what the best course is, Peter," Simon said.

"What is the real position now, then? You know that the monk, brother Matthew, knows the knight, don't you? Now, if the knight was going to kill the abbot, the monk would hardly have gone without letting us know that, would he?"

"No, but Matthew may well not have known that Baldwin was going to kill de Penne."

"Hmm. True, I suppose. Really it comes down to what possible reason Baldwin could have had for killing the abbot," said the priest thoughtfully and leaned forward to rest his chin on his hand.

Simon nodded. That was the main thing: to discover a cause for the killing. It seemed to be the result of madness; why else would someone kill in that way? It was as if the killer wanted to make a public statement, as if the murder itself was an execution, a punishment, like the killing of a witch or a heretic. After all, burning at the stake was the way to kill heretics, wasn't it?

"Peter," he said, "could it have been a revenge killing, do you think?"

"What, someone killing the abbot because he had offended them? I don't know, it would have to have been a grave offense, surely?"

"Yes, but think of this. The knight, Rodney, if he was telling the truth, found the horse and the money together, so the killing was not for money. The fact that the money was left shows that. So what other reason could there be? I have put my brain on the rack to think of another reason, but I cannot see one."

The priest pulled the corners of his mouth down in an expression of consideration. "It's possible," he admitted. "But the abbot was a man of God, after all. What possible slight could he have given?"

"He was not always a man of God," said Simon, frowning as he tried to remember what Matthew had said on that day when they had walked in the lane at Clanton Barton. "The brother told me that he was being sent here because of his past, because he offended the pope himself."

Clifford gave a quick laugh, a sharp bark of humor. "If the pope was that offended, the object of his distaste would be more likely to lose either all his positions and rank or his head! I don't think he would be sent to a profitable abbey like Buckland."

"But what if he had been useful to the last pope?

What if he was of use to Pope Clement, and Pope John did not approve? Could he not be sent here to be out of the way?"

"Well . . ." Clifford paused, thinking hard. Pope Clement had died two years before, in thirteen hundred and fourteen. The papacy had remained empty until this year when Pope John had been chosen. He frowned as he thought about it. What if the new pope *did* dislike de Penne for some act during Clement's period of office? De Penne would have been left in place during the interregnum and then removed from his position when the new pontiff took office. Could that be why he was on his way to Buckland now, in thirteen sixteen, because his previous acts had so offended the new pope?

"And Matthew said that there would not be another murder like it, he said that the murderer of the abbot was temporarily mad," Simon recalled. "He must have guessed even then!"

"Surely the monk would have gone to see Furnshill if he thought that, to ask him to confess. It would be his duty, to save his soul."

"He was at the manor on the day I left to follow the outlaws!" said Simon suddenly. "It was he who gave me the message from Tanner about the outlaws!" He paused, frowning as he considered. "And think, if the pope was offended by Oliver de Penne's actions, might not Baldwin have been as well? What if the service de Penne provided to Clement, the service that was so offensive to John, was equally offensive to Baldwin?"

Clifford shook his head. "No. I agree that the timing matches, that it is plausible, but it seems a little too far-fetched. Why should Baldwin's brother die just then, making it necessary for the knight to return home? Surely it would have been easier for Baldwin to kill the abbot on his way through France, or somewhere else, long before he arrived here? No, I find it a little too—"

"But that's the point! What if Baldwin didn't even know that de Penne was here? All he knew was that he was on his way here to take up his new position as the master of Furnshill Manor, and the meeting with the abbot was pure chance? Just like me! I was given my new position, I came home, and found almost immediately that there was a murder! Chance. It could have happened at any time!"

"My friend," said Clifford, smiling indulgently, like a tutor at a child with a new and radical idea. "Don't you think that that is too much of a coincidence? By chance this man's brother dies and he comes home. By chance the abbot is disliked by the new pope. By chance the abbot is sent to Buckland. By chance they meet and the knight kills him. No! There is too much chance, too much coincidence."

Simon nodded, staring gloomily at the fire. "Yes, when you put it like that . . ." he muttered.

"There is one other thing," mused Peter.

"What?" said Simon, not turning his head.

"You are assuming that the killer *was* a knight. What if he was not?"

"But only a knight wears armor!" Simon protested, looking up in despair. He felt as if all of his careful reasoning was being dismantled brick by brick as he listened to the priest. Now, even he himself found it difficult to believe in his own case against the knight.

"Any man may wear armor. What is it if not a shell that can be put on and taken off? Perhaps a man stole the armor from a knight? I don't know, but it is a point you should consider, Simon." Clifford rose. "Now, let me go and fetch some wine for you. You look as though you could use some!"

Simon shook his head and stood. "No. Thank you for the overnight rest, but we must be on our way."

"Very well, if you're sure," said Clifford, looking at him watchfully. "My friend, I hope that God will watch over you on your journey and send you an answer."

"Thank you, old friend," said Simon. Then, with a quick smile, he added, "And I hope he will make things clearer at the same time!"

Hugh and Simon rode slowly out of Crediton on the road to Sandford. Simon's mind was whirling as he tried to concentrate on the murder. No matter how he looked at it, he believed that the knight with the trail bastons, Rodney of Hungerford, could not have been the man who had killed the abbot. Peter Clifford, being the priest, heard quickly about any traveller on the roads because any man journeying in these parts was still a novelty, even if the traffic was increasing now. A knight would surely have been mentioned, especially an impoverished one.

And then there was the problem of the second man. Whoever this could have been, he was not with the knight. Could Rodney have had a companion on the way and left him after the murder at Copplestone? It was possible, certainly, but not very likely. Two men who had committed a crime like that would be bound together by their guilt.

The weather had abated somewhat. The rain was lighter, and the wind had died down, so that drops fell vertically now, instead of being thrown like small exploding stones at their faces by the driving gusts. As they rode out of the town, the sun at last struggled to become free of the clouds, and an uneasy light shone down, as if there had been a truce called between the elements.

Suddenly a thought occurred to Simon as he rode up the steep hill to the north of the town. If there were two men, then they must have had the same grudge against the abbot! He sat up in his saddle as he quickly thought it through. If only one had had a grudge, surely the other would have taken the money even if the first did not? If only one had had reason to kill de Penne, the other would have taken the money—especially if they were shortly to split up. "So what does that mean?" he wondered aloud. "That both had the *same* reason to kill the man?"

"Sorry?" Hugh was, as always, a little behind and he was concerned because his master was so deep in thought as he rode. He saw Simon wave an impatient, dismissive hand as if annoyed at the interruption of his thoughts and so, offended, he reset his features into their normal taciturn mold.

"So," Simon mused, "there were two men. Both had the same desire for revenge against the abbot. One was a knight, or at least in armor. The other was dressed as a man of war—an esquire, perhaps? They had a reason to kill de Penne, a reason that made them want to kill him in a dishonorable way, like a heretic. But they did not steal from him. Why? Knights take spoil from their enemies when they are victors. Was it an affair of honor? A woman?" He shrugged.

He knew that in war women were often taken by knights as part of the spoil. If the knight had lost his woman, perhaps he and a friend had decided to avenge her by killing her rapist? It was possible. He shot a glance back at Hugh.

"Hugh?"

Hugh glared back.

"Hugh," Simon asked hesitantly, "if someone was to rape Margaret, and I decided to kill the man, would you help me to get him?'

His servant stared in frank astonishment. "Of course I would!" he said hotly.

"Hmm." Simon returned to his solitary glare at the road and said no more.

They ambled slowly down the other side of the hill and by the side of the Creedy stream as it meandered along the bottom of the valley that led to Sandford, Simon silent all the way as he continued his contemplation. Hugh was quiet too, not sure how to break his master out of his reverie, but worried at his obvious distraction.

Hugh rode less stiffly now. The previous evening had been an absolute delight to his tired and worn body. The warmth and hot food and drink had worked a magical cure on his misery from too many days in the saddle and too many nights sleeping rough by the road and on the moors, especially the last one when they had not even been able to light a fire—and he felt calm and relaxed at the thought of being at home again and being able to sleep on his own palliasse.

But he was not happy at the way that Simon kept worrying at this murder like a cat with a mouse. Certainly Hugh had been upset by the killing, but his master was taking it too deeply, he thought, and that could not be good for him. He tried to speak occasionally as they went, padding slowly on the road, talking about Margaret and Edith, and how glad they would be to see them again, but he only got angry grunts in response, so in the end he gave up and followed in disgruntled silence.

At last, as they started up the hill that led to Sandford, he felt his spirits rise and could not help the smile that slowly spread across his face at the thought of the fire in the hall, and he was about to try to speak to Simon again when he saw his master pause at the road into the village.

Simon sat stationary on his horse, staring north up the road that led to Furnshill. "I'll know soon. I'll figure it all out soon," he murmured, then jerked the reins and trotted to the lane that led home.

Why should Baldwin have killed the abbot? That was the question that kept nagging at his tired mind—for, try as he might, he could see no other explanation for de Penne's death. It had to be his friend. At last, as they cleared the village and wound along the track that took them out to the house, he set his shoulders with a new determination. He knew who was responsible for one death, but any confrontation could wait. There remained another to solve.

"First let's see if we can find out what happened to Brewer."

It made his heart lurch to see his wife again. She stood at the door as he and Hugh rode up the lane to the house, a slim and elegant figure, with her braided hair hanging over each shoulder, smiling at the sight of them.

He had stayed away longer at other times, when he had had to travel to see the de Courtenay family in Bristol or Taunton, but for some reason this time it had seemed even longer than before, and he found himself almost holding his horse back for the last few yards, as if drawing out the enjoyment of their reunion.

Springing from his horse, he strode to her and stood gravely holding her hands, staring into her eyes. Margaret was amazed to see how the last few days had changed him. He had suddenly developed lines of

shock and worry where before there had been none, a
series of slashes on his forehead and at either side of
his mouth, and her face showed her concern as she
gazed back at him.

"My love, you—" he began, but before he could finish there was a sudden flurry at the door, and there
stood Roger Ulton, standing as if exhausted, one hand
on the jamb, the other up on the lintel as he peered out
at the bailiff. Simon looked at his wife with resignation. "I suppose it'll wait," he sighed.

"So where did you go when you left Emma's house?"

They were back in front of Simon's fire. Hugh was
still seeing to their horses, Margaret helping him, having handed her husband a fresh pot of mulled cider and
two drinking cups. Now, sitting on the benches before
the flames, Simon and Roger Ulton were drinking.

The bailiff thought that the young man seemed
scared. He sat on the edge of his seat, leaning forward,
the cup gripped in both hands as if fearful of dropping
it. His eyes rarely met Simon's. For the most part he
stared down into his drink.

"I went for a walk. It was a nice evening, and if I'd
gone home they would have known something was
wrong. I didn't want them asking me questions about
me and Emma."

"Yes, so where did you go?"

"All over. I walked past the village and up toward
the hills, but then I got cold. I kept going. I suppose I
was thinking about just keeping on walking, maybe
going to Exeter or somewhere, but I couldn't. I'm no
freeman. If I'd gone, I'd just've been caught and
brought back."

"When did you come back?"

"I don't know, but it must've been after ten. I came back from the north and walked down the street—that late there seemed no real point in avoiding the village, everyone would be asleep long before."

"Ah. It *was* you, wasn't it, who helped Brewer to his house?"

"Yes." The pale face glanced up at Simon's, but on seeing the stern features concentrating so hard on him, he looked away again. "Yes, I did. Brewer was just being thrown out when I came past, and the innkeeper, Stephen, asked me to take him with me. He'd been fighting again."

"Who?"

"Brewer. He often used to fight."

"Do you know who he had been fighting with on that night?" asked Simon, leaning forward in his eagerness.

"No, you'd have to find out from Stephen. He'd know."

The bailiff leaned back a little, frowning at the youth. "Why didn't you tell us all this before? Why did you lie to us?"

"I didn't want everyone to know about me and Emma. I didn't want to break off with her. But then I heard from . . ." His voice trailed off.

"Who? What did you hear? Who from?"

His eyes rose and at last he found the courage to hold Simon's gaze. "From Stephen at the inn. He told me he knew I was lying, that the Carter boys had seen me there, had seen me going up to Brewer's house with him. They were following us. They must have killed him, and they're trying to put the blame on me. It's their word against mine, Stephen said. He told me I'd better leave—run away."

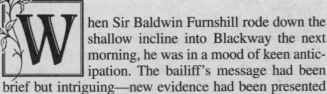

hen Sir Baldwin Furnshill rode down the shallow incline into Blackway the next morning, he was in a mood of keen anticipation. The bailiff's message had been brief but intriguing—new evidence had been presented and, in the light of Baldwin's earlier interest, would he like to come and help? The knight had set off immediately, and found Simon and Hugh sitting outside the inn on one of the benches. His friend seemed tired, his face showing how much strain he had been under in recent days, and Baldwin was surprised that the bailiff's welcome appeared muted, his eyes seeming to flicker over Edgar and him as they arrived. There was no answering smile to the knight's cheery greeting. Beside Simon was Hugh, his face drawn into its customary scowl.

"So, bailiff," said Baldwin. Somehow he felt the need to use Simon's title. "How are you? I understand that you've caught the killers of the merchants?"

"Yes," said Simon, looking up at him. The black moustache and neat beard framed the knight's small, square teeth as he grinned down at him. Then he kicked his feet free of the stirrups and dropped to the ground.

"Landlord!" Baldwin stood, arms akimbo, waiting for the innkeeper.

"We have some questions for this man," said Simon while they waited, and quickly told of his conversation with Ulton the day before. Then his eyes met the knight's with a sudden intensity. "I am determined to find out what really happened, Baldwin. I will not leave the death of even a poor villein unavenged when I go to Lydford. I think he was murdered, and I mean to find out who was responsible. When I have, I'll get the abbot's killer too. Will you help me?" His tone seemed almost to imply a challenge to the knight.

Baldwin met his gaze coolly. "Of course. It's my duty to my lord to help his bailiff—and Brewer was my villein. But I heard the outlaws had killed the abbot? That was the tale in Crediton."

"Possibly," said Simon shortly, but just then they heard a step approach and, turning, saw the landlord, his eyes flitting nervously from the bailiff to the knight under their suspicious gaze.

"Yes?" he said. "What do you want of me?"

"Edgar, go and serve yourself," said Baldwin. "And fetch me an ale!" he added in a bellow as Edgar disappeared inside. Glancing at the bailiff, he sat beside Simon on the bench before fixing a grim stare on the unfortunate innkeeper, and Stephen suddenly knew he was in great trouble. He could feel the tension: these men were judging him, and, at the thought, his hands dropped from his belt, as if suddenly nerveless, to dangle by his side.

Simon drew a deep breath and let it out in a quiet sigh. The depression and doubt were lying on him heavily. Could Baldwin be involved in the murder of the abbot? Everything seemed to point to him, and when he threw a quick glance at the knight, he saw Baldwin was tense as well, as if he knew the suspicions Simon held. What if . . . He squared his shoulders and sat upright on the bench, and when he looked over at the knight again, there was a calm, appraising expression on his face. They stared at each other for a moment, then Baldwin suddenly grinned, as if the cares of the world had fallen from his shoulders, and Simon felt his own features creak into a wan grimace in return.

When he turned to face the innkeeper it was with a renewed vigor. With that glance and brief smile the knight had seemed to be trying to demonstrate his understanding, to show that no matter what happened he would not blame Simon.

In any event, Simon felt, now was not the time to speculate about the abbot's death, that could wait. As he had said, Brewer's death had been first, and the investigation deserved his concentration. Putting all thoughts of de Penne's murder aside, Simon glared at the innkeeper for a minute in silence.

"Stephen," he began softly, "we want to ask you about the night that Brewer died. This time we want you to tell the truth."

"Oh, but sir, I'm sure I never—"

"Shut up." It was Baldwin who spoke this time, his voice flat and dismissive, tainted with revulsion, as if the man disgusted him.

"You lied to us last time we were here," Simon continued.

"But I'm sure I—"

"You told us you didn't see who helped Brewer. Who was it?"

There was no mistaking the fear now, Baldwin thought. The innkeeper had appeared to go quite cold, his face clammy and almost yellow, even in the bright late-morning sun.

"I said, it was dark and—"

"It was Ulton, wasn't it?"

After the question had been asked there was a long silence and pause, as if the whole village was waiting for the man's response. He stared at Simon as if transfixed, his eyes wide and staring, with small gobbets of sweat breaking out on his head.

"Well?" asked Simon.

"Yes." His voice came as a low mutter. "Yes, it was."

"Why did you lie to us before?"

"I didn't lie! I told you it was dark, that I couldn't hardly see. Anyway, Roger was helping me by taking Brewer away. Why should I make you think it was him killed the old man? The old bastard could have made a saint want to kill him, and you were bound to hear what his temper was like. Why should I make you think it was Roger?"

"So you say you don't think Ulton killed Brewer?"

"No, of course not!"

Simon glanced over to Baldwin briefly, and saw him nod with conviction. There was no doubting the sincerity in Stephen's voice. Looking back at the publican, the bailiff asked, "Were there any strangers here around then? Did you see a wandering knight here in the days before Brewer's death?"

The publican's eyes dropped to his feet as he thought back, but when he looked up again he gave a single emphatic shake of his head. "No."

"So who else was here that night?"

"Who else? Oh . . . there was Simon Barrow, Edric, John, the Carters—"

"What? The Carter boys were here that night?" said Baldwin, leaning forward and frowning at the man.

"Why, yes . . ." Clearly terrified, the landlord gazed back, wondering what he might have said wrong.

"Did they say anything to Brewer?"

"Well . . ."

"Was it the Carters Brewer'd been arguing with that night?"

"Yes."

"What about?"

"Brewer was in a foul mood." Now he had started, the words fell from the stout character as if he had kept them dammed and now the sluice was opened he could not halt the flow. "He said the boys were wasters, no better than beggars. He said that he could buy them up three times over—them, their farm, their parents . . . everything! And still have money over. Edward tried to calm him down, but he was mad. It was the drink always did it to him, I think. He tried to punch Edward, and Alfred got in the way, and Brewer hit him. That was when I got him out—I didn't want any fighting in my hall. I took him out and there was Roger, he said he'd take the mad bugger home. He couldn't kill, he's no murderer—he's a kindly sort, not a killer."

"Yet you told him to leave the area? You told him to run?" asked Simon, leaning forward and resting his elbows on his knees.

Stephen stared back fearfully. "I . . . like I said, it can't have been Roger . . . but the Carters, they've been saying he was there, that they were going to tell you they saw him. I thought you'd think it was him if he didn't go away. It was for the best, sir, it just seemed unfair to think . . ."

Baldwin leaned forward as well, his elbows on his knees as he stared hard at the man. "And what time did the two Carter boys leave the inn that night?"

"The Carter lads?" The thought seemed to strike horror into his voice. "The Carter boys? But they—"

"Answer the question!" rasped Baldwin.

"Not long after, I suppose." His voice was low once more, as if he was scared that he might say too much if he raised his voice. "Not long."

They left the horses at the inn and wandered down the lane toward the Carter house. Hugh had been sent to fetch John Black, so there were only the three of them when Simon rapped hard on the door.

Baldwin seemed to understand something was wrong, but left Simon scowling down in pensive gloom, as if he knew what the bailiff suspected. When Simon caught his eye, he thought he saw an expression of near relief, as if the knight was glad to have been discovered. It made the bailiff feel even worse, and it was with a growing anger that he waited for the door to open. It creaked open a short way to show a tired young woman, dressed in a dark tunic with an apron. She looked as if she had been cooking, and from her hands came the scent of fresh-baked bread to tantalize them. Smiling, Simon asked, "Are Alfred and Edward here?"

Her eyes seemed confused as they peered up at him. She could only have been a little over five feet tall and she seemed smaller as she stood diffidently wiping her hands on the apron. A couple of strands of light brown hair strayed from under her wimple, and one curl was twitching with the breeze just under her eye. Her eyes still on his face, she caught at the hair and pushed it back. "Yes," she said. "My brothers are here. Why?"

"Could you ask them to come to the door, please?"

She seemed reluctant, but then Edward appeared and

smilingly asked the three to enter, and join them indoors, pushing his sister aside as he opened the door wide.

Simon and Baldwin followed him through into a wide and noisesome room. The farmhouse contained all the human and animal members of the farm during bad weather. Some semblance of refinement had been attempted by fencing off one side, so that the animals and humans were separated, but it did not help much. In the family area there was a large fire, roaring in its clay hearth with the smoke rising to the rafters and slowly leaking out to the open air through the louvres. There was only one sign of modernization in the room—a platform had been built on stilts, with a narrow ladder leading up to it. Obviously this was a separate solar for the family, away from the stench of the farmyard below.

With the animal smells and smoke the atmosphere was disgusting. The ordure from the beasts assailed the nostrils, the bitter tang of the smoke caught in the throat, and the atmosphere was altogether brutal, attacking the senses with vicious sharpness. The light from the thin windows was pale, and shafted down to illuminate small pools of dirt on the floor, struggling on the way to fight past the thick smoke.

Coughing, Baldwin beckoned to Edward and Alfred and went back to the clean air at the front of the house. It was with relief that he managed to pass out through the front door again.

Once in the open air, Simon said, "About the night that Brewer died. We want to ask you some more questions. You both said that you were looking after your flocks."

Edward seemed to catch his breath, freezing in an instant to become as still as a statue, his face fixed into a mask of fear. His brother was not affected. His thin features gazed back at the bailiff with what seemed to be a sneer fixed to his lips.

"So?" he asked. "Is there something wrong?"

At first Simon gazed at him in simple dislike—the man clearly cared nothing for the death of Brewer, although that was hardly surprising in view of the farmer's unpopularity. But then all the anxieties of the last few days, the tiredness, the horrors, the pain and fear, suddenly caught hold of him and focused in an unreasoning rage against Carter.

In his arrogance, this little man seemed almost to be taunting the bailiff over his inability to find the killer of Brewer. It felt as if he knew too of Simon's suspicions about Baldwin, as if his patronizing smile ridiculed Simon's efforts, and the fury blazed white-hot in response; it insulted not just him, but all the others as well—it demeaned the old farmer, the abbot, the merchants, the poor, broken, solitary girl on the moor, even those in the posse and the trail bastons who had died. The bailiff had seen more death and destruction in the last few days than ever before, and the brutality, the senseless butchery, that he had been forced to witness had left its mark. A blind loathing gripped him, almost choking him with its intensity.

With a snarl, he reached forward and grabbed the young man by the throat of his smock, twisting the cloth as he pulled it toward him, yanking the man off-balance as he dragged him forward.

His action caught even Baldwin by surprise. All of a sudden the knight found himself gazing at his friend with a new-found respect. Simon, he could see, had hauled the boy three feet against his will with one arm, and the knight found himself trying to control a smile as he lifted his finger to scratch at his ear. This bailiff could be a right bastard to have a fight with, he thought to himself.

And now Simon was speaking to the Carter boy through gritted teeth, his voice low and venomous, eyes bulging. "We know you lied to us. I am in no mood for games! What did you do after you left the inn? Did you go straight to Brewer's house? Kill him as soon as Ulton had gone? What happened?"

"We did nothing!" The boy was averting his face; they were so close their noses almost touched. "We came home!"

"Why did you lie to us?"

His voice was almost a whine now, wheedling to persuade the bailiff. "We didn't think it mattered. If we'd told you our father might have found out, and he'd have thrashed us for not looking after the sheep when we were supposed to."

"What time did you get home that night?"

"We told you. We told you it was about eleven."

"You're lying!" Simon bawled the words into the now fearful face. "You're lying. You left the inn a little after Brewer. You left the inn just after the innkeeper threw him out, just after Ulton took him by the arm and helped him to his house, didn't you? You followed them because you were so angry at his attitude at the inn, because you hated him, because he had money, because he hit out at you. You hated him, didn't you?"

"No, no I—"

"You watched while Ulton put him in, didn't you? You went in after him, didn't you? You killed him, and set fire to the place so no one'd think it'd been a murder, didn't you? *Didn't you?*" Bawling, he stared into the fixed, terrified face.

"Simon, Simon," murmured Baldwin, touching the stiff

arm that held the petrified villein. "Calm yourself, Simon. Too much choler can be bad for the health. Now," this to the shaking boy, now released as Simon turned away in disgust, who stood feebly stroking the side of his neck above the smock with a trembling hand where the cloth had burned the skin red. Shrugging, the knight grinned as he decided that a slight bluff could be risked. His voice reasonable, he said, "Alfred, we only want the truth. Nothing more. Did you know that Cenred saw you that night?"

The boy's eyes were huge in his sudden horror and he shouted, "No!" Mouth hanging open, he stared at the knight, his gaze fixed with an awful intensity. "No! He can't have!"

"Oh, I know you ducked back into the trees quickly, didn't you, eh? But yes, he saw you. So I really think you'd better tell us the truth."

At last Edward seemed to shake himself. He glanced at his brother with an expression of withering—what, scorn? Pity? Baldwin could not be sure, but there was something there that implied almost disgust with his younger brother. He began talking quietly, as though he was repeating the tale for himself, reminding himself rather than telling it to his audience. As he started, Baldwin noticed Hugh and John Black walking up toward them, and quickly motioned to them to wait, so as not to interrupt.

"Yes, we followed them back. It's true." His voice had an empty quality, and Baldwin thought it was as if he was absolutely exhausted. "Alfred was mad at him for hitting him. It wasn't a bad thump, not as bad as our father would have given us for not seeing to the sheep, but then Alfred never really did get hit like that, did you? Not being the little one." He looked up at Baldwin. "We didn't do it, though. He was already dead when we got there. Roger must have killed him."

Staring at him, Baldwin was sure he was telling the truth. He seemed to have conviction in the way he stood there, his eyes fixed rigidly on Baldwin's face, his body stolid in the way that his legs were set a little apart, almost as if planted and rooted in the earth. Baldwin could see that he was not pleading or asking for belief, it was as if he knew that he would be trusted if he told the truth, and now he was doing so for that reason.

"Yes, we went up there and waited in the trees until Roger went away. We saw him scuttle out of the door and run down the hill. And that was when we went up. I didn't want to go, but Alfred wanted to hit him back. He wasn't happy that Brewer had hit him in the inn and got away with it. I went to the door and knocked, but as I did Alfred heard someone coming, so I ducked down and he ran away, over to the other side of the road. It was Cenred, but he walked past like he'd seen nothing. So I knocked again when he'd gone. Alfred came up, but there was no answer."

"What then?" said Baldwin, shooting a quick glance over at Simon. The bailiff stood, head bowed, listening intently but quietly, as if ashamed of his previous reaction.

"Alfred walked in. The door wasn't locked. I followed. Brewer was lying on the floor, near his mattress. The fire was low, and we couldn't see much, but Alfred went over and kicked him, and Brewer did nothing. It scared us, we understood something must be wrong. I lit a candle from the fire, and then we could see. Brewer was stabbed—four, five times in the chest."

"Yes, so what then?"

"We started to get out, but then Alfred wanted to see if it was true about the money. He wanted to see if Brewer really did have the money to buy us out, so he wanted to look." Edward could not prevent the sneer from appearing on his face as he stared at the knight. "I let him. I'd had enough, I told him. I left him to look while I put Brewer back onto the bed—I don't know, it seemed more respectful to leave him there. Well, Alfred found Brewer's purse and a wooden chest, and he took them. Then, when we were going to leave, he said, 'If it's known he's been murdered, we'll be the obvious ones to think of.' People would hear about the argument, the fight. They'd be bound to think it was us that killed him. So we thought we'd better hide the killing. It wasn't as if it would hurt anyone else, after all. Brewer wasn't going to care. And if it was never known there'd been a murder, there'd be no need for anyone to think we'd done something. So we set fire to some hay and left it burning."

Of course, Simon thought—all that ash on the ground, it was from a hay store in the house. "And then you went home? You left the place burning and went home?"

"Yes. But then, when you seemed to realize that Brewer *had* been killed, we knew we had to do something. We thought if Roger heard we'd seen him helping Brewer home from the inn, he'd run away. You'd have to know it was him then. Whatever he said when you caught him, you'd know he'd done it."

Baldwin nodded contemplatively, then spun to face Alfred. "What was in the box?"

"Nothing! Only a few pennies, and the same in his purse."

"Bring them!" Then, to Edgar, he said, "You wait here. Take the purse and chest when he comes back, and keep them here. You'd better keep the Carters here as well. Is that alright, Simon?"

"Yes. For now, I think, we need to have another talk with Roger Ulton."

22

T he dilapidated house stood as if forlorn as the four men walked up to it. Baldwin thought it looked like a ruin, like a destroyed castle after the besieging force has left, with the broken dark wood of the roof beams standing out like the burned and blackened remains of an attack from Greek fire. The picture was so clear in his mind, recalling so many past battles, that he involuntarily shuddered. Even the way that the corner of the far wall had fallen seemed to remind him of the way that a corner tower could fall after mining or catapult attack, and he half expected to see bodies on the ground as they came closer.

Simon and he left Hugh and Black behind as they walked up to the door and knocked. When it opened Roger Ulton himself stood before them.

"Bailiff, I—" He stopped as he saw the knight and then caught a glimpse of the other men behind, pausing with his mouth open in despair.

"We know all about it, Roger," said Baldwin gently. "The only thing is, we don't know why. What did he say to you to make you kill him?"

Wordlessly Roger went back in and they followed

him inside. The pale and skinny man seemed to fall back as they walked in, as if he could fade away in the darkness of the house, his waxy features disappearing in the gloom. The hall had a fire glowing gently in the hearth, with three benches nearby, and Ulton fell on one, staring up at them.

"I don't know," he said, his eyes wide in his fear, but also, Baldwin felt, in a genuine disbelief. "I had been with Emma, and she told me she didn't want me anymore. I walked around until it was time for me to go home, so that my parents wouldn't guess—I was hoping to talk her round later. But when I walked past the inn, Stephen almost threw Brewer at me. I couldn't refuse to help him.

"But he kept going on and on about money and things. He kept telling me that I was useless, as bad as the Carters, not as good as his own son, who's a merchant. He kept telling me I had hopeless parents—they couldn't even keep their house up. He told me the best I could do with women was Emma, when anyone else would get someone better. He kept going on and on, even after I'd put him inside the door. I turned to leave when he said that he could buy Emma if he wanted: he could buy houses like my parents', he said he could buy anything. I just had to shut him up. I . . . I don't really know what happened. One minute he was sneering at me, next he was on the floor . . ."

"What did you do then?" asked Baldwin gently.

"I shut the door and ran home. It was only when I got here I realized I had my knife in my hand."

They left the house and Roger walked with them to join Hugh and Black.

"Baldwin, if you could take him and the Carters to the jail, I'll see you at your house later.'

The knight's surprise showed in the way that his eyes gazed fixedly at him. "Yes, yes . . . of course . . . if that's what you—"

"Yes. I must go home first. I should be at your house in about three hours."

Baldwin stared after him with dismay as the bailiff walked to Hugh and led him away, back to the inn, where they had left the horses. Then the knight turned, grinned at Black with an embarrassed shrug, and led the way back to the Carters' house. Black followed, his hand on their prisoner's arm, ready to take him on to the jail in Crediton where he must wait for his trial.

"I have no idea what to do. I am sure, but I don't know whether it's right to arrest him."

Margaret stared at her husband with exasperation puckering her forehead. Since he had arrived with Hugh he had been wandering around like a bear ready for baiting, restlessly pacing the room with a thunderous but anxious frown on his face. Now, as she sat watching him, he slapped one fist into the other palm and started circling the room again.

Taking a deep breath, she said, "Would you like to explain a little more?" She sat calmly upright with her hands clasped in her lap, her eyes following him. He had never been like this before. He seemed distraught, confused and unsure of what to do for the best. Something had happened, she knew that much, but he appeared too upset to be able to explain.

At last, unwillingly drawn to her like a dog called to heel from the scent, he walked over and plumped down on the trestle near her.

"Good, now try to explain what the problem is."

His eyes flitted over the room as he tried to find the words he needed before they finally settled on her, and it seemed to her that when they met her firm and steady gaze a little of the restless worry left him, as if her calm posture passed to him a little of her peace.

"We had to arrest Roger Ulton this morning. When we checked it seemed clear that he had killed Brewer. Others saw him take the man from the inn, take him to the door of the house. Then he ran away. The next people at the house found Brewer dead."

"Good, so that's all settled, then."

"Oh, yes. Yes, that's settled. The trouble is, I've been thinking about the abbot, wondering what could have happened to him. Everybody thought that Brewer and the abbot's deaths could be linked because they both died in flames, or, at least, both had fire involved in their deaths. But if Ulton killed Brewer, there was no reason—and probably no way he could have got there—to kill the abbot.

"Black and Tanner thought that Rodney, the knight with the trail bastons, had killed the abbot on his way through. But if he had, where had his accomplice gone? And why did he do it? I can see no reason why he should have. But what he *did* say was that he had found the horse and the money on the road. If he had, it means that the killing was done by someone who did not want the money—that it was no robbery."

"Yes, I can see that. But why kill him, then?"

"Because it was revenge. I don't know why, but it was in return for some insult or dishonor—or it was a punishment. If you think about it, that would make sense. Rodney finds a horse; he has no companion— his story is true. So who could have killed the abbot?

It would have to be someone who had been abroad, because the abbot had never been in England before, according to the monks. It had to be someone who had travelled widely. It had to be someone who had a squire, someone who was close to him, someone who had been with him abroad."

"Why? Why does it have to be a close squire, someone who had been with him abroad? Couldn't it have been someone that he had hired since getting back?"

"Yes, it's possible, but how could a man rely on a recent hireling to keep his mouth shut? It's possible, but is it credible? On the other hand, if it was a man he had been with for many years, if it was a man he had known and trusted—possibly someone who had suffered from the same insult—wouldn't that make more sense?"

"And you think you know who, don't you?" she said, her hands clasped tightly now, her eyes fearful.

"Who else can it be?" he confirmed, his eyes desperate.

hen they finally clattered up the drive to the manor it seemed as though the house was deserted. There was nobody at the front, and although they went through to the stable yard they could see no one. Even the hostlers were away, so they made their way round to the front and, while Hugh waited with the animals, with a face still black from what he considered to be a wild-goose chase, Simon pounded on the door.

After a few minutes there was the sound of heavy feet stomping down the passageway inside and the door was opened. It was Edgar, Baldwin's servant.

"Yes? Oh, it's you, bailiff."

"Yes, where is your master?"

Edgar's face had an arrogant and supercilious air, as if he was not concerned by Simon's interest in his master, but was vaguely amused by his presence. "Sir Baldwin is out riding. He should be back in an hour or so."

"Fine. I'll wait for him inside, then," said Simon, pushing the door a little wider, but then he stopped as a thought struck him. "Er, we'll just see to our horses first."

He turned and took the reins of his mount from Hugh, leading it round the house to the stables at the side. The yard was still empty, so he led the horse to the open door and tied it up, before taking the saddle off and rubbing the horse down. Hugh followed and, still silent in mute reproach, began to see to his own horse.

When he had finished, Simon walked to the stable door and looked out. There was still no one in the yard. He crouched down and examined the floor of the stable. It was packed earth, strewn with straw. Then he stood up and started to kick the straw aside, bending every now and again to look carefully underneath it. He covered the whole floor in this way, finally standing with an expression of frowning disgust, his hands on his hips, surveying the stable, before going out into the yard.

To Hugh he seemed to have gone mad. He finished rubbing down his horse and saw that it had hay and water before running out after his master, his face full of concern at this new evidence of his eccentricity.

He found Simon standing and leaning against the wall of the house, a sad smile on his face as he stood staring at the view. Hugh walked over to him cautiously and hesitantly.

"Master?" he enquired softly. "Master? Are you well? Would you like to come inside and rest in front of the fire?" He had heard of similar maladies before, now he thought about it, from his mother. She had said that often shepherds who spent too much time alone up on the hills in the cold and wet could get confused in their thoughts. Usually the next stage would be one of shivering, before a fever took over and ran its course. Maybe this was the aftereffect of their days on the moors? He nervously held out a hand to touch his master's arm.

"What?" Simon snapped and turned at the interruption to his thoughts, fixing Hugh with an acerbic eye. "What are you talking about? What is it?"

"I thought . . . Are you alright?"

"Yes." The word came out as a sigh. "Yes, I'm alright. Look!"

Hugh's face turned slowly in the direction of his finger, but his eyes stayed glued to his master's face. He risked a quick glance. Simon was pointing at the ground. Hugh looked back. Simon seemed to be saddened by the mud, he was staring at it with an expression of resigned misery.

Confused, Hugh looked back at the dirt, staring, wondering what this meant. All he could see was the mess of a stable yard, thick with dirt and straw, and here and there the prints of the hostlers and their charges. Simon seemed to be pointing at a patch lying in the protection of the stable wall, where the rain of the last two days had not dropped, but it was close to the entrance to the stables themselves. He stared at the prints of feet and hoofs. He frowned and peered, leaning as he looked, at one hoofprint, a deep print, the print of a big horse, a print that showed itself to be missing a nail.

"I suppose we're lucky that it was here. The rain didn't get to it, so close to the wall, or it would be impossible to read. But I think it proves that I was right and—"

"What is it? What are you doing?" They both whirled round to see Edgar standing a short distance away, glaring at them.

"Come here, Edgar," said Simon quietly—but for all the apparent calmness, Hugh could hear the bitterness in his voice. "We've found something interesting."

"What?" the servant said suspiciously as he walked closer. Simon pointed down with his left hand. Edgar seemed to find his eyes drawn irresistibly down, following the finger, but when he looked up, confused, he found himself staring at Simon's sword point. He stared in astonishment at the blade held in Simon's hand, then glared at the bailiff.

"What is this?" he said, his voice registering angry incredulity.

"*That* is the print of a large horse, a large horse missing a nail on one shoe. It's the same as the prints we found by the dead body of the abbot of Buckland," said Simon softly.

"No. No, it can't be!" Edgar said, looking from one to the other as if in complete bewilderment. Then he seemed to sway weakly, toppling to his left, and raising his hand to his face as if about to swoon.

"Bugger! Quickly, Hugh!" said Simon, but as he spoke, the man seemed to explode into action. Shooting upright, Edgar leaned away from Simon's sword, which had followed him as he staggered, knocked it aside, and sprang forward and caught Simon by the throat, forcing him to the ground, the bailiff's eyes wide in his surprise and shock at the sudden attack as he fell with the servant on top of him.

Hugh sighed, watching them roll in the mud and dirt of the yard. He reached for his purse and untied it, hefted it in his hand for a minute, then brought it down on the back of Edgar's head with a solid and satisfying thud. Edgar slumped to lie comatose on top of the bailiff, and it was only with difficulty that Simon could roll him off, crawling out from underneath the suddenly collapsed body.

"I . . . er, maybe you should tie his hands, Hugh,"

he said, wincing as he staggered slowly upright with one hand to his throat. Hugh nodded dourly and went into the stables. There were some leather thongs hanging on a hook, one of which he brought out, and he soon had the unconscious Edgar trussed like a chicken. They picked him up and dragged him round to the front of the house, through the door, and into the hall, where they dropped him in front of the fire.

It was over half an hour before he came to, wincing painfully as he shook his head slowly to clear it and glaring at the two men sitting nearby.

"I think you should explain why you killed the abbot," said Simon, leaning forward and contemplating the man with his chin on his hand.

"I didn't kill him, I—"

"We know you did. The hoofprint proves that. We know that the monk Matthew knew Baldwin, and that he asked the others to wait while he came here to visit your master. We know that when the monks left Crediton you and your master followed them and caught up with them beyond Copplestone. You took the abbot into the woods and killed him. Then, when he was dead, you went north to the road and came home. All I want to know is *why?*"

Edgar seemed to waver for a moment, then his jaw set into an expression of determination. He struggled, wriggling until he was sitting upright, then glared at the two on the bench.

"We know you did it, but why?" Simon repeated. "Why kill him in that way? Had he offended your master? Was it a woman?"

The servant still stared, but at Simon's question he seemed to start. When he began to talk it was in a slow, contemplative voice, almost as if he was reciting slowly from memory.

"It . . . it was a woman. She was my wife. De Penne caught her and raped her, and I swore vengeance. I had tried to catch him in France, but when we got here I saw Matthew in the town and he said who he was travelling with. Matthew knew nothing about it. When they left, I followed with a friend and caught up with them outside Copplestone. I captured the abbot and . . . I killed him."

Simon leaned forward, a frown of disbelief on his face. "You tell me you killed him like that for a woman? Your wife? You were married while you were in service to a knight? While you were travelling all over the world?"

"Yes. My master gave his permission."

"And your master was not present at the killing?"

"No."

"But the print, that was from his horse."

"Yes, I took his horse."

"And his armor?"

"I . . . I have armor."

Simon looked at him without a word for a moment, then said, "So you are saying that he had nothing to do with the matter? So who was with you? Who was your friend?"

"I will not give him away." It was said angrily, as if the question was an insult, as if the suggestion that he could betray a friend was inconceivable, was contemptible.

The bailiff stared at him musingly, his chin still resting on his hand. His eyes never left the face and eyes of the man on the floor in front of him, gazing intently at him as he considered, until Edgar dropped his angry gaze and glared at his lap.

"No," he said at last. "I don't believe you. I think Baldwin must have been involved and you're protecting him."

"It was as I have said! *I* did it. Sir Baldwin was not there."

"We shall see." Simon rose and walked over to the door. "Stay here with him, Hugh. I need to think."

He walked out, went to the front door and stood outside to wait.

It was very difficult. Simon had only recently made the acquaintance of Baldwin, but he felt as though they had been friends for years. He liked the knight's calm and steady gaze, the way that the man seemed to throw himself into whatever he was doing, as if he was determined to enjoy every day to the full, like a young man who has recently discovered new pleasures. And now he had to accuse this man, his friend, of a hideous murder. Almost before he was able to get to know him he must denounce him.

He felt a bleak depression stealing over him as he considered what he must do. And how would the man react? Would he reach for his sword? He was a knight, after all. He may well decide to deny his guilt in trial of combat with his accuser, and Simon was uncomfortably aware that it would require a great deal of heavenly assistance to overcome such a strong opponent. He walked round the house to the log where he had sat only a few mornings before while he nursed his hangover. It seemed so long ago now, so long since he had enjoyed the evening with this man, since his wife had laughed at every sally made by the grave but witty, educated knight.

Slowly he eased himself onto it and stared out over the grounds in front.

Baldwin arrived almost an hour later, dirty and soaked from his ride. As he came up the track, he waved and roared a greeting to Simon, who still sat on his log. He returned the wave, smiling briefly at his friend's obvious pleasure in seeing him, then ambled round to the stable yard as the knight came up to it.

"Simon, so you're back then. You were quick. I wasn't expecting you yet," Baldwin shouted as he dropped from the saddle and reached forward to shake Simon's hand. "Have you brought your wife? Is Margaret here?"

"No, Baldwin. I thought it best not to bring her. Not today," said Simon, his face haggard. He tried to smile as he shook hands with the knight, but although the mouth obeyed his brain's command, his eyes could not lose their look of hunted fear.

"You look very serious. Is there something the matter?" said Baldwin, pausing as he led his horse to the stable. Simon shook his head dumbly, and, shrugging, the knight continued. Simon felt his eyes drawn down, and he stared in misery. There could be no doubt. There on the ground in front of him was the proof. He put his thumbs into his belt and followed the knight, who was taking the saddle off his horse and patting its neck.

"What is it, Simon? Can I help?" said Baldwin, the sympathy showing in his grave eyes and making Simon feel even worse.

"The abbot," he said flatly, making the knight pause in his patting.

"Yes?"

"Why did you murder him?"

Baldwin's eyes glittered, a spark of anger lighting his features, but as quickly as it had flared it died, and he sighed. "How did you find out?" He sounded almost uninterested as if he did not really care but thought the question should be asked for form's sake.

"I didn't, really," sighed Simon. "I felt it couldn't be the trail bastons, but I didn't really know it was you until I saw your horse's hoofprints."

The knight looked down in surprise.

"You're missing a nail in one of the hind hoofs. We saw that at the murder scene. It was the only thing we had to follow."

Baldwin patted the horse's neck again absentmindedly. "Well, we'd better go indoors and talk about it," he said, and slowly led the way into the house.

As he entered the hall and saw Edgar sitting on the floor in front of a grim-faced Hugh, who was sitting with his sword drawn and pointing at him, Baldwin turned in anger. "Why do you hold my man like this?" he grated. "Is it not enough that I—"

"Sir Baldwin! Sir Baldwin, I have already admitted it," said Edgar, quickly interrupting. When Simon looked at him, he thought that the man seemed almost to be pleading. He sat there with an expression of desperate yearning, as if he was anxious that he should be permitted to confess, as if the knight should not take away this chance of . . . what? Confession? Absolution? Simon turned back to the knight as he slowly made his way to his servant.

"You have admitted it? You?" Baldwin said softly. He walked to Edgar's side, then crouched by him, his hand on the man's shoulder. "Will that help us? We have nothing to fear, Edgar. If die I must, *I* will die happy at last. But I will not let you die for something I was responsible for." He looked at Simon. "I can guarantee this man's obedience. You have no need to leave him tied up like an animal."

Simon heard Hugh's cry of "Master!," but he kept his eyes on Baldwin. He gazed back, not with anger, but a kind of indifferent sadness and pain, as if this was the last thing he wanted, to have brought his servant to this pass and put the bailiff, his friend, to this trouble. Simon could not discern any remorse, any guilt. It was as though he was fully aware of what he had done, but that he felt it was nothing—of no importance. With a curt gesture, Simon acquiesced, and Baldwin took his own dagger and released his man.

"Go and fetch wine. There is no need for us to suffer thirst while I confess," he said, parting Edgar on his shoulder. He walked unhurriedly to the bench. Seated, he motioned to Simon, who slowly walked over and sat opposite, next to Hugh.

The knight sighed, the firelight throwing occasional flashes of orange and red on his face and making his eyes glitter. He studied Simon carefully, a small smile on his face even as his brow wrinkled, as if he was wondering how to tell his tale.

"I killed him because he was a heretic and evil, and because he caused hundreds of my loyal companions to die."

24

"I suppose I have to begin with why I left the country and what happened to me. Otherwise it will all make no sense to you; it won't explain why I had to kill de Penne.

"It all seems so long ago now, but I suppose that's how things happen," he said, staring at Hugh and Simon with a weary calmness now that he had begun. "I told you that I left my home when I was young, did I not? Well, you are too young, I suppose, to remember, but then, when I left, the whole of the world was in a ferment. The kingdom of Jerusalem was falling to the Saracens, Tripoli had fallen a year or so before, and King Hugh sent to the kings of Europe for aid, for men and money to defend the cities that remained, few as they were.

"I decided to help if I could. After all, I had little to keep me here. Under the law of primogeniture I was an embarrassment to my brother, who was the elder of us. He inherited the lands from our father when he died, so there was little to keep me here. I decided to do as so many had before and go to Outremer to see if I could make my own inheritance. The news was just coming

in of a new Saracen army that was being sent to take
Acre, the last great city in the Holy Land, and it
seemed a good time to go there. I joined a small ship
and went to join the defenders. I managed to gain a
place on a Venetian ship and arrived in early April, in
twelve hundred and ninety-one.

"The whole city was under siege from the Saracens.
They had huge weapons—nearly a hundred catapults!
It was obvious that they meant to take the city, and they
had the men to be able to do it." He stared into the fire
for a moment, then carried on. "There must have been
a hundred thousand men against the city. And what did
we have? Barely fifteen thousand knights and men-at-
arms, all told.

"They began their assault in early April. I was serv-
ing under Otto de Grandison, the Swiss, who was there
with a small number of Englishmen when it began. At
first they merely battered at the walls—my God! It was
awful to see those great stones coming at us—and then
they started throwing in clay pots, filled with Greek
fire. As soon as the pot broke, when it hit the ground or
a building, it burst into flames and it was almost impossible to put out the fire."

Edgar came back in, carrying a jug of wine and
some tankards, and he set the jug by the fire and
poured them all wine, listening to his master as he
worked.

"Thank you, Edgar. Well, for the first few days I
thought we could hold out. We still had the port, and
the Saracens had no ships, so we could still get sup-
plies in and evacuate the wounded. I thought we
should be safe. After all, I was young. I had never seen
city walls like those of Acre. They were huge, a pair of
double walls with ten towers in the outer one, spread-

ing to the north and east of the city. South and west was the sea, so all the Saracens could do was try to destroy the walls to be able to get into the city." He sighed. "But I did not know how much damage could be done by them.

"We suffered from the catapult bombardment, from the rocks and the fires, from the arrows and the constant attacks of the enemy. It seemed as though there was nothing we could do to keep them away, but then, after I had been there for about a month, King Hugh of Cyprus arrived with his soldiers, and it seemed that we might win—but it was too late even then.

"Less than two weeks after he arrived, the towers started to crack and fall. We did not know it then, but the Saracens had mined deep under the walls, balking the tunnels with timbers soaked in oil. Then they fired the tunnel. As the wood burned, the tunnels collapsed, pulling down the walls and towers above. I have seen it since, but at the time it was a shock, it was as if the ground under us was rejecting our claim to defend the Holy Land as the towers fell.

"And then they attacked. They came against all parts of the wall; there was nothing we could do, we did not have enough men to defend the whole area, and they managed to capture the middle tower—it was called the Accursed Tower, and it was well named." He fell silent, but soon continued.

"The hordes worked their way along the top of the walls, and when they managed to get to the middle they opened the gates and the rest flooded in. We had to fight in the streets, hacking and stabbing as best we could in the narrow alleys, struggling to contain them, but it was futile. If we held them off in one street, they would work behind us in another and come at us from behind. We had to give in.

"De Grandison took some Venetian galleys and the English climbed aboard. Everyone who could was leaving now, but I was delayed. I saw Edgar was hit by an arrow as I ran for the docks, and I stopped to help him. He would have died for certain otherwise, so I tried to carry him to the ships, but we were too late. With Edgar suffering so much in his pain, we couldn't hurry, and by the time we got to the port the ships had already gone. In the end we just managed to get to the Temple, to the fortress of the Templars, before they bolted the door.

"It was madness in there. The place was filled with people. Everyone who could not get to the ships had flocked there, and it was full of women and children, the wives and children of the men who had died on the walls and in the streets. There were not enough men to protect it from the hordes, though, there were only some two hundred Knights Templar. The Muslims ran through the streets, killing all the men, catching all the women for slaves, killing any who were too old or top young. They stole everything, destroying all the churches and temples as they went. God! It was awful to hear the cries of the people as we sat inside, but what else could we do?

"The Templar in charge was Peter de Severy, God bless him! I owe him my life. He had some boats and ships at his disposal, and he sent some of the wounded away. I was one, Edgar another. I had managed to break my leg when I stumbled over stones while I helped in the defense, and I could help no longer. Edgar's wound was bad too, so we left together. It was only a few days later that the Temple fell, and all inside were killed by the Saracens.

"Edgar and I were taken to Cyprus, where we were looked after by the Templars and nursed back to health. We were lucky—many others died. I was still young, but I had no cause to fight for and no land to keep me, and Edgar was without a knight to serve. It seemed to us that we were part of a divine plan, we had been given a new reason for existence. We were able to speak to the knights and observe their ways, and we were so grateful, and so impressed with them that we decided to join them. I had nothing to come back to England for—I had no home, not since my brother had taken the estates—so I think it was from a feeling of loyalty and a sense of God's will that I joined the knights. They had helped me and shown me kindness, and I wanted to repay the debt."

"You were a Templar!" said Simon, sitting bolt upright and staring at him with horror.

"I was honored to become a Templar," said Baldwin calmly. "Do not believe the stories. Do not think we were blasphemers or heretics. How could we be? My companions had fought and died for the Holy Land, to win back Jerusalem and Bethlehem. Would they have done that if they were heretics? Would they have accepted death rather than renounce Christ? Have you heard of Safed? No? When the castle at Safed was taken by the Saracens, two hundred templars were captured and offered life if they would renounce their faith. Two hundred, and *all* chose to die. They were killed, one at a time, in front of the others. Not one agreed to denounce his faith, not one! Can you really believe that such men were heretics?

"No. I was proud to become a Templar, to be accepted as a warrior for God. My only regret is"—his voice dropped a little as he stared at Simon—"that I was still alive when the Order was destroyed."

Simon and Hugh stared at him as he spoke. Simon could remember clearly the stories about the Templars, the dreadful knights who had betrayed the whole of Christendom with their revolting crimes, and yet . . . It seemed that this man, for whom he had respect, revered them. How could that be, unless he was badly misled by them? Could he be guilty of the same crimes?

Baldwin continued, a little defensively now as he read the expression on Simon's face. "We were warrior monks, you understand? We took the same vows as monks—of poverty, chastity and obedience. We were the oldest order of knights, far older than the Teutonic Knights, and older even than the Hospitallers. We were created after the First Crusade to defend the pilgrims travelling to the Holy Land, and we were in every battle from then until the fall of Acre—that's two hundred years."

"So why were you all—" Hugh started, sarcastically.

"Shut up, Hugh, let him finish," Simon snapped.

"Well, maybe you will understand when I have finished," the knight continued. "I joined the Order. I was sent back to France to learn how to fight and to be shown how best to serve the Order, and I lived there, in Paris, for several years." He looked over at his servant as he spoke, and there was a softening in his eyes. "Edgar was with me. I had saved his life, and when I joined the Order he asked to join me there. He had no knightly training, no training in how to use a sword, but he could work with me, so he became my esquire.

"It was good to feel a part of the army of Christ, to have forsworn the earthly pleasures and to be able to live a life dedicated to the honor of God and Christ. It was all I really wanted.

"But one day—it was Wednesday the fourth of October in the year thirteen hundred and seven. I remember it so well!—I was sent to the coast to deliver a message to a vessel sailing for Crete. I do not know what was in the message, but it was urgent, apparently. The new Grand Master, Jacques de Molay, had asked that it be sent quickly and, because he too was English, he asked me to take it. That is why Edgar and I were out of Paris when it happened.

"On Friday the thirteenth the Temple in Paris and all other temples in France were raided by men sent by the French king. God! That date will live forever as the blackest in history—only the death of Christ himself could be more deplorable!" His eyes gleamed with an almost maniacal rage as he shouted the words, but he calmed himself with an effort and fell back, tired by the burst of energy it had taken.

"We were on our way back when we were warned about what was happening in Paris. It seemed impossible, *incredible,* that the Order should be arrested. But it was." His voice was flat now, dead; as if his life had ended with the destruction of the Temple he had served for so long. He shuddered once, in a great convulsion that made him spill some of the wine in his mug, but then he smiled sadly, staring again at the flames.

"Edgar refused to let me go and find out. He insisted that I stay outside the city while he went inside to discover what was happening. We parted in a wood outside Paris, and arranged to meet again two days later. Well, we met as we had agreed, and he confirmed what we had been told. The Temple was accused of crimes so revolting that the king himself was forced to take matters into his own hands. He did so, with great enthusiasm!

"He ordered that all Templars should immediately

be arrested, even the Grand Master, Jacques de Molay. Poor Jacques! They were all taken and put in irons. There were not enough prisons for the Poor Soldiers of Christ, so most of them were chained within the Templar buildings all over France. Held in their own Temples!

"Edgar and I travelled around the country, and by chance we came across friends, in the woods south of Lyons. That would have been in thirteen hundred and ten. By then, of course, we had already heard about the confessions. Did you know how the men were questioned? No? Be thankful you will never have to answer to the Inquisition! And they accused *us* of being evil!

"We were with the men outside Lyons when we heard about the pope's council at Vienne in the following year." He gave a quick laugh, like a mirthless bark. "You should have seen him! He held his great council to denounce us. Us, the Templars! We who only lived to serve him and God, he wanted to denounce *us*. The others there, the archbishops, the bishops and the cardinals, all wanted to hear our defense. You see, when the men in the prisons had been asked whether they would defend the Order, any who said they would were killed, burned at the stake by the archbishop of Sens, damn him! Over fifty men in a morning, just because they said they would stand up and defend the Temple. So, when the pope asked for other Templars to defend the Order, I think he thought there were none who would come forward. But the other men of God at Vienne, the bishops and archbishops, guaranteed safe passage to any who would come and defend the Order, so I and six others thought, well, why not? And we went!

"I thought he was going to pass out when we walked

up the steps to the chamber! Clement sat there on his throne, and when we walked in wearing our Templar tunics, he went bright red and, if his throne's arms were not so high, I think he would have fallen out!

"The clergy were grateful for us, I think, because they honestly wanted to know what our evidence was, and they listened to us carefully. But when we said that there were more of us near Lyons, nearly two thousand of us, the pope seemed to have a fit of the vapors! He ran from the chamber, and we were told a little later that we were to be arrested. I think it was because his palace was close to Lyons, and he feared for his life with almost two thousand Templars so close to his home. Anyway, the other clerics all clamored for our release because they had promised us safe passage, and we were set free in a short while. We left Vienne by night, unobserved, and returned to our friends.

"After that it seemed clear that there was nowhere safe for us. It was obvious that the pope was willing to see the Order destroyed, so there seemed no point in continuing. Many of us left and returned to our homelands, and many joined the other Orders. Some joined the Teutonic Knights, some went to the Hospitallers, and many joined the monks. Some of us, though, wanted to know what had happened, and we determined to find out, and if it was possible, we wanted our revenge." He sipped from his mug. "It took two years, but at last we found out the truth."

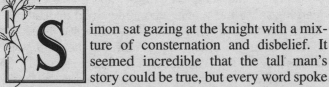

25

Simon sat gazing at the knight with a mixture of consternation and disbelief. It seemed incredible that the tall man's story could be true, but every word spoke of his conviction. Baldwin sat relaxed, his eyes roving slowly from Simon to Hugh, and moving on to the fire, occasionally resting on Edgar. He seemed to have passed beyond worry, as if he knew his tale would not be believed, as if he knew he was to die and cared little for the fact. He seemed to have given up, as if he had dreamed of rest and peace down here in the quiet of Devon, but had found only a new struggle to cope with.

His eyes were half-lidded now, making him look tired, as if weary from the strain of recollection, but Simon could still see the glitter in them. At first he had thought it was the gleam of anger at being discovered, but now he felt sure it was directed not at him but at Oliver de Penne, the man he had killed, as if killing him had not been enough to wipe away the depth of the crime he had committed against Baldwin and his friends.

Hugh shifted uneasily in his seat as the knight continued.

"It was obvious we could not stay in France. The French king and the pope seemed to be dedicated to the destruction of the Temple, and to the death or removal of all Knights Templar. The punishments were varied, but any man who had confessed under torture and then retracted his admission was to be burned at the stake.

"The Order was fortunate in having one man who could defend it, Peter de Bologna, a man who had been Preceptor of the Temple in Rome, and a man of great learning as well as a man who understood the Church. With his knowledge he could fight the case using the Church's laws. When he examined the witnesses against the Order, it soon became clear that there was no concrete proof of anything. The witnesses referred to hearsay, or were proved to be liars, and de Bologna took full advantage of our enemies' confusion.

"Now, at about this time, the old archbishop of Sens died, and a new man had to be found. The new archbishop was a friend of the French king, Philip de Marigny. As soon as he took office he moved quickly. He confirmed sentences on the individual Templars in prison—even while their trials were continuing. In one morning he had fifty-four Knights taken out to the stakes and burned."

Baldwin's head dropped, as if in prayer, and Simon felt a chilly stab of pain as he saw the tears falling down the knight's face. Baldwin put a hand up to his brow, holding his head for a minute in silence. The only sound in the room was the fizz and crackle of the burning logs on the fire, and Simon's eyes were drawn to them as he thought about the deaths of those men.

The knight sat up, wiping his face. "My apologies, but I had friends among that group," he said, his eyes on the floor. "Peter de Bologna was taken by this same archbishop and sentenced to life in prison. He was not allowed to continue his defense of the Order. But Peter was a shrewd and resourceful man. He managed to escape from his bonds in his jail, and made off, living rough in the countryside until he managed to make his way to Spain. I met him there.

"Peter was ever a stalwart figure, as I remembered him. When I found him in Spain he was soldiering again, but not with one of the Orders. I had gone there because I had the idea of joining the Knights Hospitaller. The Spanish were never convinced of the guilt of the Templars, as, indeed, our own king, Edward, was not. The Spanish had always fought alongside the Templars in their struggle to keep the Moorish hordes at bay, and they knew that the Templars were an honorable Order, so it seemed a good place for me to go to. I thought I could join another Order and find peace.

"But Peter de Bologna wanted none of that. You see, during his trial, he had been able to see some papers while he was trying to defend our Order. He could not join another Order afterward—he was too bitter. He remained as a soldier of fortune, fighting for what he believed, fighting to protect Christendom.

"I should explain, for you probably don't know how the Templars were organized, but as the Pope is Christ's vicar on earth, and therefore has power over all men, even kings, so the Knights Templar were answerable only to the Pope, because they were the most holy of all Orders, being created to protect pilgrims. What Peter saw during his defense of the Order was a paper that gave the names of all of the men who had given false witness against us. One of the commissioners was helpful and allowed Peter to see more when he asked, I think because he wanted to see the Order have a fair trial, and some of them showed that there was a conspiracy against us.

"At first, Peter could not believe what he saw, because it seemed too awful. The papers showed that the French king and the pope were in league to destroy the Order, but not because of the crimes alleged. No. For one reason only—*they wanted our money!* That was all!" He was sitting forward now, his despair at the futility of the destruction of his Order plain on his face as he stared unblinking at Simon, as if trying to transfer his feelings of betrayal and anguish in that single, penetrating and concentrated gaze.

Simon found his own feelings stirring in sympathy and he had to struggle to control his own composure. Now, at last, he could understand the dreadful scars of pain and loss he had noticed when he had first met this man.

"The king wanted our money because he owed the Order for several debts, and he wanted to be able to forget them. We had loaned him money for his daughter's dowry when he had arranged her marriage to Edward of England. We had loaned him money for his wars. We had helped him in many ways, and he wanted to be able to take all that we had and not repay the debts. He decided to destroy the Temple so that he could take everything, everything we had. The pope was in his power, because he lived in Avignon, not in Rome, and he wanted to have our money too. Not for the Church, but for himself." He gave another short, sharp laugh. "And it worked! We never considered that the pope could betray us so badly, and we believed, in our innocence, that the French king was grateful for the help we had always given him. We never realized that because we had helped him he would decide to destroy us!" He subsided and glared into the fire again, his eyes full of the hurt of the betrayal.

"When Peter saw that, he swore never again to serve king or pope. From then he chose to serve God in his own way, and he did, fighting the Moors in Spain until his death a year ago. But before he died, he told me what he knew.

"The French king had a helper called Guillaume de Nogaret. He was the devil himself, an evil man. He was bright and intelligent; he had been brought up by the Church after the death of his parents, and yet he seemed to hate it. It was he who decided that the way to destroy the Templars was to accuse us of heresy, and he went about it with vigor. He organized false confessions for money. Wherever there was a Templar who had been ejected from the Order, de Nogaret would search him out and bribe him to give false witness against the Order.

"One man helped him more than any other. He arranged for false confessions of murder, of heresy and of idolatry, and then made sure that they were published. He spread tales of the evil-doings of the Order.

"The same man arranged for confessions from among the Templars' servants, admissions of idol worship and of new members being forced to spit on the cross—"

Simon interjected with heat. "But how can you say this? Are you telling me that all these accusations were false, all these crimes were invented? There were many, even I know that. Surely you cannot expect me to believe that they were all untrue?"

The knight looked at him with a small, sad smile. "But, my friend," he said, "can the reverse be true?

Think! All men who joined the Order were knights in their own right. All joined because they were holy, because they were committed, because they wanted to become members of an Order that demanded of them that they take the vows of a monk, that demanded them to be honorable and godly, demanded their obedience and demanded their poverty. If you were to go to join an Order like that, would you then spit on the Holy Cross on your first day? Of course not! If you had decided to dedicate your life to Christ, if you had decided to give everything you had, if you had decided to fight whenever you were told in the Holy Land, would you as a first step defile the very symbol of God's power? Could you believe that a monk would do that? Why should you expect a Templar to? It is not possible." His sad eyes stared at Simon for a minute or two, until Simon was forced to nod. Put like that, it did seem improbable.

"So, this man invented these things. He was not motivated by honor, he wanted money and power. And he won them. Oh yes, he won them!

"We did not know his name or anything about him, he was too well guarded. All we knew was that he had been a Templar, a knight who had been recruited but who was evil. A twisted, vicious, greedy man who should never have been able to join our ranks. But how could we find his name? How could we discover his identity? Peter never did, but I managed to.

"In thirteen hundred and fourteen, we who remained found out that there was to be a show of penitence for our Order. You must realize that even now, even knowing about this man who had betrayed us all, it seemed that something must have been wrong with the Order, for the very reason you gave just now—how could so many crimes have been invented? And why?

"In that year, only two years ago, the Grand Master, Jacques de Molay, and three others were to confess their sins in front of the whole of Paris, before Notre Dame cathedral. When I and some friends heard of this, we drew straws to choose a witness. I was chosen."

He fell silent again, his head dropping almost on to his chest in his sadness at the remembered pain, and when he continued his voice was low, as if he was recollecting the deep injustices done to him and his companions from far in his past, not events from only two years before. He had withdrawn again, seeming to sink in upon himself, as if he was not in the same room as the others and was talking to himself, like an old man recalling ancient memories and forgetting the existence of his audience.

"I went to Paris. I stood in front of the platform until they all arrived, draped in chains like common thieves. They all denied the accusations, and a little later Jacques de Molay and the others were all burned at the stake in front of the cathedral. A huge crowd went to see them die, but I did not. I *could* not! Jacques—dear, strong, honest Jacques! How could I go and see him destroyed by the flames? How could I?" He turned to Simon, his face full of grief, his eyes searching his face as if hunting desperately for his support. "When the soldiers went back the next morning to clear up the ashes, they could find no bones. The people of Paris had collected them all and taken them. After all that had happened they knew that the accusations were false. They believed the bones were holy relics. Even small finger bones." His eyes stayed fixed on Simon as his hand went to his throat and pulled at a string. A small leather pouch was attached to the cord, and Baldwin looked at it for a moment, then nodded at the bailiff before dropping it back down the front of his tunic.

"I had to tell my friends what had happened, and then we went our own ways, to tell of the end of the Order and to keep the memory alive of Jacques de Molay and his final martyrdom. But I had to find out who had betrayed us." His mouth twitched in a sardonic grin. "And it was the pope himself who told me who it was!"

Simon started, his eyes wide in astonishment. "The *pope* told you? How . . ."

Laughing quietly, as if to himself, Baldwin took the jug and refilled his mug. Still smiling, he gazed at Simon. "No, he didn't mean to! It happened this way. After the farce of the Notre Dame confessions, I decided to find out who was responsible, as I said. At first it seemed impossible, but Edgar and I travelled widely and talked to many who had been members of the Order, and gradually some threads seemed to come together to point to a few men. But each who I saw seemed to have suffered for his admissions. Each seemed not to have benefited from the fall of the Temple. None was wealthy, in fact, most were monks—and not senior, just unknown men who were dedicated to God and their new lives. Many, in fact, were as bitter as I about the way that the Order's high ideals had been perverted. But with many of them, one name kept appearing. One man seemed to have spoken to many while they suffered in their dungeons. He was another prisoner, but he seemed to have been moved to any number of jails and, wherever he went, men admitted to crimes that they denied to me.

"I kept my own counsel, but continued on my hunt.

He was in Paris, he was in Normandy, he was in the south, he even appeared in Rome! Why, I wondered, would a man who was a suspected heretic be moved around so much? Wherever he had appeared he was in chains with the others, but no one ever saw him being tortured. Where he went, the other prisoners heard about the tortures being inflicted upon their brothers, they were told of the dreadful pains being suffered and made to fear their own ending. They were told what would happen if they did not confess, and this man, this Templar knight"—he spat the words out in his disgust— "This poor suffering knight told them what to say, told them how to ensure that they were saved from the fires.

"Then I heard from a man in Rome about him, about how he had told the men there that even the Grand Master had confessed, that he had admitted to the sins of the Order. It seemed odd to me at the time, but I could not see why for several months. Then I realized.

"At the time he had been in Rome, the Grand Master had not confessed to anything. It was too early. At last I began to suspect this man and to wonder whether he could have been installed in all of these prisons as an agent of the king and the pope, to persuade the Templars to confess and thus avoid their punishments. It was only later that I realized that I was right, and it took me another six months to prove it.

"It was after the death of a friend near Chartres that I saw the final proof. I went there to pray for him as soon as I heard that he had died, and was there for the burial. Another friend in the same abbey heard that I had arrived and insisted that I stay with him. His abbot had heard of my past and showed me a great deal of sympathy, listening to my story and allowing me to stay with him for some weeks. By then I was exhausted in body and spirit, deeply wounded by the trials of my search and almost ready to give up after a year of continual travelling, but the abbot showed me a papal bull which had been issued some time before which soon renewed my energy.

"It was a statement about the men whom the pope wanted to deal with personally. The pope had chosen some men for special treatment; they were to be punished by the pope himself, their treatment to be decided by no other man. There were several names there, including the Grand Master, some preceptors and others—I cannot remember them all—but one stood out for me. It was the name that I had heard all over Europe during my travels: Oliver de Penne. He was an ordinary brother in the Order, a man of no consequence, not a great leader like Jacques de Molay, just one of the warrior monks. He had been chosen with the others, the greatest men in the Templar brotherhood, for special treatment. Why could that be? A monk? Singled out for personal attention by the pope? Now I was *sure* I had the right man.

"Of course, I wanted to be certain, so I tried to find what had become of him. It took me weeks of travelling, weeks of speaking to the few who survived, talking to men whom I had hardly heard of before, and I suffered any number of setbacks. Some of the men would not talk to me; twice I was denounced and had to fly; once I had to fight. But at last I had my information. At last I discovered his punishment, his penance for his Templar crimes. His punishment was severe: he had been elevated to archbishop in southern France: the Pope's punishment was promotion, and not that alone, for the king rewarded him as well, with lands and money. Now I was absolutely without doubt. All the evidence pointed to him.

"But when I tried to come close to him—this would be a little over a year ago—it became obvious that it would be impossible. He never left his palace, and the building itself was guarded so well as to make an attack on him inconceivable. Edgar and I waited for weeks, but it seemed clear that we could do nothing. And all the time I was getting more and more ill, with weakness in my body and mind from the constant searching and living out of doors. In the end I decided to come home to England and forget my revenge, mainly thanks to Edgar, who said that if we stayed any longer I must die. He was right, it was time to forget and try to find a new life, return to England and forget my past.

"It seemed as if God had forsaken me. All I had wanted was to avenge the destruction of His Order, but he had even put this villain out of my reach. I was tired from travelling, my mind was damaged from all that had befallen us on our way, and as we came home I fell into a fever that almost killed me. Edgar managed to help me back to health, but then we were told that my brother had died and that I could return here, to Furnshill, and take up the manor. We resolved to come here and forget revenge, to live quietly and in peace. And I confess that I began to wonder whether God really was interested. We decided to relinquish any opportunity of repaying de Penne for the crimes against our Order and our friends. We chose retirement to the satisfaction that our souls craved.

"But we had only been here a few days when Edgar met brother Matthew in Crediton. Matthew had been a Templar too. He never suffered the torture; he was in Spain, fighting the Moors, when the Temple was destroyed. When he learned the fate of the Order he renounced his calling and joined the monks. When Edgar saw him he invited him to visit us here.

"Matthew asked his abbot to delay their departure until he had visited me—he explained that I had been a Templar and that he would like to stay with me for a night. Matthew knew that de Penne had been a Templar and thought he would understand his wish to visit us, so he was surprised at the abbot's response. It made the abbot furious! He ranted at Matthew, angry and peevish, but Matthew thought he was just overreacting, he thought that his abbot simply wanted to forget and was annoyed to be reminded of his past. Matthew was ever a kindly man. He knew that his abbot had fallen from grace in the Church when Pope John took the throne and I think he thought it was because the new pope had found out about his past in the Order. *I* think that Pope John saw how de Penne had managed to become elevated and disliked it. He chose to send de Penne as far away as he could, and Buckland is almost as far as it would be possible to send a man from Avignon.

"So my old friend Matthew came to visit, and while we spoke he mentioned who his abbot was." The knight's face became pensive as he recollected. "I was amazed. It could only be by divine interference that de Penne had been sent *here,* surely—sent here to me? I believe that, in any case. Why would God have put him in my way if I was not to be his agent of justice? Ah, I was taken with a madness of desire. I felt filled with the Holy Spirit; I was thrilled that God had selected me for his will!

"Matthew stayed with us that night, and I must have seemed excited to him. I was careful not to tell him what de Penne was, for I knew that Matthew would not want to see blood spilled. He would want to let him escape and go to Buckland. But I think I had drunk too much that night in my delight for I cannot truly remember much of the evening, and I think he was worried, for, as you know, I do not drink to excess usually. On the morrow, I sent Edgar to town with the monk, to protect him on the road, but I also told Edgar to stay in the town and watch, and to come back to tell me when the monks were about to leave.

"I could not rest. I could not sleep. My revenge was so near, so close, that it seemed to burn in my soul with a holy light." He turned and gazed into the flames again, a small smile playing around his lips.

"But then, when Edgar came to me and told me that they were on the move, I was struck with indecision. I could not convince myself that this really was the man. How could I be sure? I tried to recall all that I had heard, to make sure in my own mind that he was the one, that he deserved death, but how could I be certain? I dithered for a day, but then I decided to take him and question him. After all, surely it was too much of a coincidence that he should come here and his presence be made known to me? It *had* to be God's will!

"I rode off in the late morning. I could remember the roads to Oakhampton, and Edgar was sure that this was the way they had taken, so I followed alone. Edgar saw that I had gone and decided to follow me to try to stop me. When he saw that he could not, he came with me. I could not stop him, he had lost as many friends as me to the stakes and the flames.

"We came upon them, as you know, just outside Copplestone. We took him from the monks and led him into the trees. We had no desire to hurt the others, but we scared them enough, I think, to stop them from wanting to follow us. But Matthew recognized who we were, I think, even though I wore a tunic with no signs. I think he recognized my voice. Well, we took de

Penne deep into the woods and tied him to a tree and I wondered what to do with him. It seemed wrong to just kill him. God in his wisdom chose to make me feel sorrow for him, as if taunting me with my own weakness. So many had died already, what would one more death achieve? I sat and looked at him and as I watched him I realized I could do nothing.

"But I had to be sure that he was the man. I had to know whether he truly was the agent of the destruction of the Temple."

Baldwin wiped a hand over his brow as if trying to wipe away the memory. "I asked him about the Templars. I thought he would not admit if I asked him directly about his part, he seemed too fearful and nervous, altogether too callow to confess to any wrongdoing, so I accused him of being a Templar and therefore a heretic." He laughed. "He thought I would kill him for that! He confessed everything to show how he was without guilt: how he had conspired with de Nogaret to find evidence against the Order, how he had conspired to invent crimes that he knew were false, how he had gone to prisons and persuaded the Templars to admit their guilt. As proof, he told me that he had found favor with the pope! He had been given his archbishopric as a reward! And he expected me to free him for his crimes!

"It all came forth, all of his guilt and all of his misdeeds, his perjury and his lies. I knew enough to know that what he said was true. I had spoken to the men he had betrayed, and what he told me showed his guilt. It made me mad. My sympathy and my compassion left me.

"I walked to him, taking off my helm so that he could see my face, and I spoke to him. I told him who I really was. He stared at me. He did not seem able to believe it at first, he kept shaking his head with his mouth wide open as if he could not believe his own ears. And then, then, I told him that I was going to kill him in the same way that he had caused the others to die."

He shuddered, once, as if in a sudden pain. "He stared at me. His mouth was open, his head still moving from side to side, and then he started to plead, to beg me to have mercy. Mercy! When had *he* shown mercy? He had killed for money, for his own prestige and wealth. He had forgotten all of his vows, disregarded his friends and ruined a noble and honorable Order. Mercy? From *me?* He could not bear the thought of the same death he had brought on so many others. I only hope that even now his soul is burning for what he did to the others.

"There is little more to say. We could have left him there to starve, but he might have been saved. We could have simply stabbed him, but then there would have been no point to his death. The only way that seemed right somehow was the same death he had given to our companions—the heretic's pyre. Then there would be a reason for his death. Edgar agreed when I suggested that it would be better to leave him as a symbol, to show that he was a man of dishonor, to show his guilt. How better? At least then there would be an indication, a sign. We collected the wood and twigs and lighted the fire while he shouted and screamed at us. I think he had lost his mind by the time we lit it; he seemed to be incapable of understanding when we spoke to him. I sat in front of him and watched as he died. As his body burned. There was no pleasure, my friend, believe me. It was like performing the last rites for a criminal—in a way I suppose it was. But the smell, the stench, was revolting, so when he was dead we left the body burning and returned here."

"You were very careful to obscure your tracks," Simon observed quietly.

Baldwin looked up in frank surprise. "No. No, we just rode north until we came to a road, then followed it back toward Crediton until we could turn off home. I was not thinking about my own protection, after all, I may have killed him but I felt no guilt—he deserved it! And it was God's will that he should come here, that he should be made known to me. It was God who took his life away, not I. We made no effort to cover ourselves.

"I daresay you will find this tale unbelievable—I daresay I would if our positions were reversed—but I swear on my oath that this is all the truth. I decided to kill him for what he had done to the Templars and, when I could take my revenge, I took it. It was God himself who permitted it by putting him in my path. I am sure that he was guilty and that God used me to give him the justice he deserved."

Simon stared at him, trying to make sense of the knight's astonishing story. Baldwin was sitting now, avoiding the bailiff's eyes and gazing into the fire again. He did not seem embarrassed; rather he looked relaxed, almost elated, as if the confession had taken a huge weight from his back so that he could face his future with peace at last. How long, Simon wondered, how long had he kept this story to himself? How long had he been searching for this man? How long had he been trying to find out all the details so that he could find out who was responsible and why? He said that de Molay died in thirteen fourteen, so for some two years he had searched, sifting the information, finding new people to corroborate or add to the tale, until he found de Penne at last. And what then? As soon as he found the man he had to give up, return to his home, and admit to himself that he had failed.

How would I feel if I had gone through all that and then, just as I had given up all hope of revenge, found that my quarry had followed me, like a lamb walking into a wolf's lair? Would I believe it was God's will too?

His stare hardened and he took another sip at his drink. "What about the monk? What about Matthew? How much did he know?"

"Matthew?" Baldwin turned, faint surprise showing on his face. "He knew nothing. Not until we took his abbot and he heard my voice—I think he realized then who we were. When he found out what we had done to de Penne he came here as soon as he could. He couldn't come immediately, but he arrived while you were here. As soon as you had gone he demanded to know why we had done that . . . that thing to his abbot."

"That was why he was so sure that the murder could not be repeated. That was why he said it was a temporary madness. He knew it must be *you!*" said Simon reflectively. Looking up sharply, he said, "And you told him? You confessed?"

"Oh, yes. Yes, I told him. He did not forgive me, how could he? But I think he understood."

"He has not told anyone?"

"No, he is a good man, and I told him first that I would only tell him on his oath of silence." He drained his cup with a determined gesture and stood. "So, my friend, I am ready. I yield to you. Do with me as you see fit."

26

One week later, Simon rode over to see his friend Peter Clifford for one last visit before he went to take up his new position at Lydford.

"Come in, come in and sit down, old friend," said the priest when he entered, handing his cloak to the servant at the door. When he was seated and had a full tankard of wine in his hand, the priest sat back with a contemplative smile and surveyed him.

The last time they had met, on Simon's return from the hunt for the trail bastons, Simon had seemed older. There had been new lines of worry and anxiety on his face and brow, deep impressions like scars. But now the priest was pleased to see that peace had returned to his features, making him seem younger once more. It was as if he had tested himself in a severe trial and found himself satisfied with the result. The memories of the horrors he had seen would never leave him, Clifford felt, but he already seemed to have been able to put them into perspective.

The priest nodded to himself. He was happy that his young friend was more than capable of the new job he had been given. He was not like so many officials,

Investigate the Hottest New Mysteries!

Sign up for the FREE HarperCollins monthly mystery newsletter,

The Scene of the Crime,

and get to know your favorite authors, win free books, and be the first to learn about the best new mysteries going on sale.

To register, simply go to www.HarperCollins.com, visit our mystery channel page, and at the bottom of the page, enter your email address where it states "Sign up for our mystery newsletter." Then you can tap into monthly Hot Reads, check out our award nominees, sneak a peek at upcoming titles, and discover the best whodunits each and every month.

Get to know the magnificent mystery authors of HarperCollins and sign up today!